LORI HOLMES

Daughter of Ninmah

Book Two of The Ancestors Saga

First edition

ISBN: 9798372682993

This book was professionally typeset on Reedsy.
Find out more at reedsy.com

Contents

Acknowledgement

A huge thank you to the team at *Writing.co.uk Literary Consultancy,* for all their hard work and endless advice on editing this manuscript and helping me shape this book into what it is today.

Another big thank you goes to the team at *Damonza.com* for their incredible design skills in creating the wonderful book covers for *The Ancestors Saga.*

Dedication

*To my mom, Vicki, from whom I inherited my love of reading
and whose throwaway comment, 'what could people have
become if we had only followed a spiritual path rather than a
technological one', struck a chord. The seed was sown and the
Ancestors Saga was born.*

Daughter of Ninmah

Book Two of The Ancestors Saga

Love or loyalty? Destiny hangs upon a single choice...

Living deep within the mysterious southern forests, the spiritual Ninkuraaja people are being hunted to the brink of extinction by bloodthirsty raiders known only as Woves.

Nobody knows better than a Ninkuraa that a Wove deserves only death.

But when a twist of fate places the life of an injured Wove into young Nyriaana's hands, she is horrified to discover that the destiny of this most hated enemy is irrevocably tied to hers.

As their burgeoning relationship threatens to tear her whole life apart, Nyriaana comes to realise that she must face a terrible choice: sacrifice the Wove or betray the lives of her own dying people.

Will Nyriaana find the strength she needs to save her tribe? Or will her love for the Wove ultimately doom them all?

The Ancestors Saga

Exciting and compelling, *The Ancestors Saga* takes you on an epic journey 40,000 years into our own dark and forgotten past. As the world teeters on the brink of another glacial winter, homo sapiens are not the only human species to walk the Earth.

When the destiny of the entire human race hangs in the balance, the prize for survivors will be Earth itself.

The Ancestors Saga is a fantasy fiction series, combining mythology, folklore, metaphysical elements and adventure, to retell a lost chapter in the evolution of humankind.

1

Prologue

Children.

The lithe form of a maamit swung high overhead through the trees, far out of Nyriaana's reach. She giggled as he leaped deliberately into the path of one of his fellows. Bound to him as she currently was, Nyri could feel his mischievous energy and fuelled it with her own. With a piercing squeal, the two furry creatures rolled into a ball, wrestling playfully.

"Hey!" the child next to her protested. He had been bonded with the maamit hers had just sabotaged. The troop of long-limbed climbers reflected the troop of small, leaf-clad children scrambling after them on the forest floor. All watched hungrily as the maamits bounded closer to the sweet, sticky fruits that grew high in the canopy. The fruit was beyond the reach of even the most skilful Ninkuraaja fingers, but not the paws of the nimble maamits.

The forest was warm, interspersed with shafts of golden light tinged green. The smell of the rich earth, swirled together with tree sap, enticed Nyri's senses. The air was alive with the busy chitter of the maamit troop and cries of delight as the fruit dropped into the children's waiting hands. It wasn't long before both troops were sticky, dirty and deliciously well fed.

Fruit consumed, the maamits began to slink away in search of a secure place to sleep. Nyri, however, felt about as sleepy as any child stuffed with sugary fruit. An idea struck as a trailing maamit passed low overhead. A quick intent from her, and the creature obediently swung down, landing on top of the nearest boy's unsuspecting head. Yaanth cried out in shock, stumbled backwards over a tree root, and fell with a splash into a pool of water. The maamit bounded away amid peals of laughter.

Battle lines were swiftly drawn. Nyri wasn't fast enough and in an instant found herself sprawled beside her victim. Water cascaded everywhere, but she barely noticed its iciness as she pulled free and splashed away, squealing delightedly.

Ninmah's golden spirit passed unnoticed through the Day Sky and set in a haze of running, ducking, hiding, and jumping. Leftover fruit smeared faces and retreating backs as juice dripped from their wild, matted hair. They would be scolded for wasting precious food, but no such thoughts crossed their carefree minds. This was just too much fun.

Finally, Nyri had to stop to catch her breath. It plumed before her in a thick mist. Dusk was falling fast, drawing the chill behind it. Ninmah retreated lower behind the frilled fingers of the trees, the sky now a cool mix of blues and golds. It was late in the Blessing, almost time for the Fall, and Ninsiku, Ninmah's greedy mate, was keen to extend his icy grasp. Already his slitted silver eye was peeking amidst the gathering darkness. A sliver of apprehension snaked through Nyri's hitherto untroubled thoughts. They should not have strayed so far from the safety of the tribe. Juaan would be worried.

She pictured him pacing back and forth inside their dwelling. He would be angry with her; she had promised to be back long before nightfall. She couldn't guess now why she had made such a promise. She didn't want to be cooped up yet. She was having too much fun with the other children.

The demon Woves had not returned to prey on their tribe for a long time now. Many of the Elders believed they might never come back, that they had perished in the terrible Furies further north. It was a growing hope, and the children were now let to play beyond the watch of the protective adults. They had begun to relax, if only a little.

Not Juaan.

"Nyriaana!" His voice sliced through the cold air. Nyri's head sank into her shoulders. *Uh oh.* It was worse than she had imagined. He had gone beyond pacing and had come to seek her out.

Deep indigo eyes glanced sheepishly in the direction of the tribe. Juaan was marching towards her, weaving between the thick trees. The forest was dark behind him, but his tall form cut in and out of the golden light cast by the *girru* moss, spores glowing forth from the trees themselves. "Nyriaana, you come here right now!"

A nervous giggle broke the disbelieving silence that had fallen over the group. A girl's voice breathed in Nyri's ear. "You're not going to let *him* order you around like that, are you?" Kyaati whispered. "He's not your mama."

Nyri gasped. Pain chased away the last of her high spirits, and emptiness followed swiftly in its wake. No, Juaan was not her mama. Her mama was dead. The Woves had killed her. Her father, too. Nyri barely remembered them, but the need for her mother's warmth and comfort, her love, was never far away, always lurking beneath the surface. Kyaati's words broke that surface and everything gushed forth in a fierce tide. Anger flowed strongest, and it had focus. Juaan was embarrassing her in front of her friends.

She felt the weight of the others' eyes upon her as they anticipated her reaction. Lifting her chin, Nyri straightened to her full eight-Blessings-old height and readied for battle. He had no right to order her. He was not her mama; he wasn't her papa. He was *nobody*.

Juaan was drawing close. Close enough for her to see the tense set of his shoulders and rigidity of his stride. She did her best to keep a hold of her resolve and not cower before him.

It was hard. He was old. Thirteen Furies old, and he towered over her. He was taller than all of them, even though some of the other boys were of the same age. His rich, reddish-gold skin was several shades darker than theirs, too. Smooth, brown hair flowed wildly around his face, but it could not hide the fact that his brow was devoid of the tattoo that marked all Ninkuraaja from birth. His eyes were a startling green.

"*Monster*," Kyaati hissed.

Nyri had the sudden urge to turn and smack Kyaati in the mouth, but she could only direct her anger in so many ways at once, and Juaan was still the target. This was entirely *his* fault. She was sure Kyaati caught the dangerous undercurrent in her mood because the older girl drifted away without another word.

Juaan came toe to toe with her, and she bent her head back to meet his gaze.

"You promised me you'd be home before dark." His annoyance lashed against her tender senses. "What are you still doing out here?"

Juaan's frustration was met with anger. "Just who do you think you're talking to, Forbidden filth?" This time it was a boy's voice that spoke, and it brimmed with loathing. "Why should she keep promises to you? She is Ninkuraaja, a Daughter of Ninmah. You..." a bitter laugh, "what? We don't even know what *you* are." Daajir was the eldest of the boys here, and his hatred for Juaan was no less than that of the rest of the tribe. Out of the corner of her eye, Nyri saw Daajir's fists clench. He was itching for a fight.

Juaan turned his head slowly from Nyri, keeping his eyes upon her until the last moment before fixing them on Daajir. The silent threat was obvious. The smaller boy was unnerved, but daringly held his ground. "You can't do anything to me, you a-abomination," he stumbled over the big word. "I'll—"

Whatever Daajir was about to do, no one had the chance to find out. One moment he was on the ground, next he was dangling in the air, the woven leaf-leather covering his chest clutched firmly in Juaan's powerful grip. Juaan held the smaller boy at eye-level before him. He lifted an eyebrow. "You'll what?"

Nyri thought Daajir would explode like an over-ripe seedpod. His face burned. His eyes bulged. Too furious to form words, a strangled cry emerged from between his teeth.

Tension vibrated in the air. The entire group was holding its breath. Yaanth and a few of the other boys took a step forward. Nyri's heart squeezed. She didn't want them to fight. Daajir had been looking for his chance to provoke Juaan for as long as Nyri could remember.

She had to do something before everything went badly wrong. This was *her* argument anyway.

"Juaan, put him *down*. I don't wanna go home yet!" She shifted their attention back to her. "You can't make me!"

To her relief, he did as she asked and lowered Daajir to the ground. He added just enough of a nudge to topple the angry boy onto his backside.

Daajir scrambled to his feet. He made to fly at Juaan, but when the larger boy readied himself for this, he changed his mind. Instead, he settled for a dreadful threat. "I'll kill you for this! You do not belong, *Forbidden*. One day, I *will* kill you!"

Amidst the shocked gasps, an icy hand slipped around Nyri's heart and tightened. Juaan took a step forward and Daajir backed off.

"Nyri," Juaan growled. "We're going home right *now*."

"No!" Nyri burst out. She was tired, hungry, and very disturbed by what she had just witnessed. She had been so happy only a moment ago. *It was all* his *fault*. He had had no right to come after her. "I'm not going! Leave me alone! You're not my mama!" All the tension inside her broke, and Nyri suddenly felt like bawling her heart out. She bit her bottom lip, too proud to let herself go. "You don't belong here!" She lashed out. "Leave! Go away! You're no one!"

Juaan stiffened as if struck. His rich skin paled. Nyri sucked a sharp breath, shocked by her own cruelty. She had gone too far; she knew it. Her anger drained away, and she shrank down. Juaan looked like someone had stabbed him through the heart. The pain in his face was almost more than she could bear.

Unconsciously, she reached a hand towards him, but he pulled away from her touch. It was her turn to be stabbed. Her eyes stung. She opened her mouth, trying to think of something to say to make it better, but no sound came out.

"You heard her," Daajir drawled. "She does not want you anymore. You have no place here. Leave."

Juaan's wounded expression vanished beneath a mask. Now Nyri could sense nothing from him. Not one flutter of emotion. His eyes were green stones.

He found his voice first. "Have it your way," he said. "Stay out here and freeze. I don't care. Woves take you." Wrapping his long arms deeper into his ill-fitted coverings, he strode away and did not look back.

"Well done, Nyriaana," Daajir said after a moment's silence. "You shouldn't mix with *that*. I don't know why the Elders won't cast him out. He's no Ninkuraa. By the Will of Ninmah, he shouldn't even be alive."

Nyri was barely aware of his harsh words. Her bottom lip trembled dangerously.

Calls came floating through the trees. The other children sloped away, back to their waiting parents. No voice called for Nyri, and soon she was left all alone.

Alone.

Tears slipped down her flushed cheeks as the extent of her stupidity hit home. Juaan's departing form had already

7

disappeared into the dark. This did not surprise Nyri. Juaan could move fast.

Sniffling, she shuffled off toward their home, avoiding the thickest growth by treading in the slight track he had made. The deepening chill pinched at her skin, and her tears gathered in strength. Her thin coverings were damp from her play. Nyri tucked her hands into her armpits, whimpering. She wanted to call out and make Juaan come back for her, but she feared his rejection.

The undergrowth became more manageable as her home came into sight. The grove of massive *eshaara* trees buzzed with night-time activity. *Girru* moss glowed from inside their bulbous forms, golden spores spilling into the dark. The great trunks and branches twisted together in various forms against the deepening sky. Her forefathers had trained the trees to grow in such a manner long ago, creating protective dwellings that lasted for many lifetimes.

This forest was where her People had lived for generations. The Ninkuraaja were made for trees and the trees were made for them. Nyri sometimes wondered what lay beyond the forest, but she could never imagine being brave enough to leave her home... or Juaan. Instead, she satisfied herself with listening to the stories he told her before sleep and wondered at the fantastical People in them. Tales of others like the Ninkuraaja, but not like them. The Thals of the North. The wily and clever Cro clans from the West, whom she had never even glimpsed. Nyri was fascinated by them all.

Juaan forbade her from sharing these tales. The Elders would punish her, he said. They did not like to hear. It was blasf- blasphemous. That was it. His own mother had taught

Juaan these stories from her travels outside the forests. Nyri couldn't imagine such a thing, a Ninkuraa beyond the trees. She felt cheated not having met Rebaa. She had died when Nyri was very young. Nyri had of course tried to wheedle more answers from him, but any mention of his mother would send Juaan into a dark mood she found difficult to free him of, and so she had given up.

No one had ever seen Juaan's father. The Elders did not speak of it. The story among the children was that Rebaa had left to join another tribe away to the north before returning with the baby Juaan. Daajir had done his best to frighten her; spinning stories that Juaan's father had been a monster. He claimed to know this because his own papa had told him so, smug that he was now old enough to know such things. Nyri did not believe him. She was not a baby, and Daajir was just mean. Juaan's father could not have been a monster. How silly.

She was curious, of course, and had been relentless in her pestering until Juaan had revealed that his father had been part of a Cro clan.

Whoever he had been, Nyri guessed Juaan's father had died, and that's why Rebaa had returned, surviving only until Juaan was eight Furies old before she, too, had joined with the Great Spirit. Nyri's own mother had taken the orphaned Juaan into her family when no one else would. Nyri had idolised him, believing nothing could threaten her own happy world until the Woves came and slaughtered her family, leaving her and Juaan with only each other. From that day on, Juaan had become Nyri's everything.

Pain cut through her. She wondered if he would ever again let her hold his hand or tell her stories while she fell asleep.

She wondered if she could even survive without him. The rest of the tribe would look after her, yes, but it would not be the same—

"Ow!" Nyri cried out as a boar charged past her legs, knocking her to the ground in its haste. "You! Be more—" But her scolding cut off at the sight of the hunted eyes sweeping back at her. Waves of fear buffeted across her senses as the animal continued his flight.

Nyri frowned, confused. There were no wolves in the area to threaten him, but the boar was running as though his very life depended on it. He crashed away through the undergrowth as fast as he had come, leaving Nyri alone in silence. It was only now that she noticed everything had grown unnaturally still. Her breath was the only sound.

Then she felt it. The Great Spirit quivered and the hairs on the back of Nyri's neck lifted in response. Flocks of birds bursting into flight through the canopy above shattered the silence, screeching in alarm. Nyri jolted and took a hesitant step backwards, trying to keep her attention on everything at once. Her heart thudded in response to the shift in the forest's energy.

Thwack!

Nyri cried out as a long, unnaturally straight branch had seared past her ear and embedded itself, quivering in the nearest tree.

"OOOOOAAAAHHHHGGGG! OOOOAAAAHHH-HGGGG!"

The shriek shattered through the trees; long, drawn out, piercing. It shivered into nothingness before repeating. The sound sank into Nyri's very bones. The darkest nightmare of her young life. She could not gate the cry of denial that emerged from between her own teeth.

The forest burst apart. A score of huge, man-shaped beasts with skulls for heads cleaved into view through the trees, baying like forest wolves on the hunt. Branches burning with the light of Ninmah threw their gruesome faces into terrifying relief; the bony, animalistic features white against the blackness behind.

The real monsters had returned.

Run! A part of Nyri's mind that still functioned shrieked. *Run! Mama told you to run and never look back.*

The sense of malice and murderous intent gaining on her from behind was as the hot breath of a predator on her exposed neck. The pounding of her heart deafened all else.

Nyri fled through the trees. Gasping from the effort and using every shred of will she possessed, she darted towards her unsuspecting tribe. She did not think of leading the beasts elsewhere. She thought only of reaching the safety of home. Her throat was so dry she could barely raise the alert. "Woves!" she cried ahead. "Woves!"

She could see them now, her people. Some were standing at the foot of their dwellings, still scolding their errant children. They looked up, alarmed by her cry. For a moment they stood rooted, disbelief and denial contorting their faces before the panic cascaded and Nyri's cry was taken up. *Woves. Woves.*

The Elders appeared as Nyri flew into the midst of her home, drawing the monsters in her wake.

"Into the trees! Get into the trees!" For all their might on the ground, the Woves were not masters of the trees. In the highest branches, the Ninkuraaja would be safe.

Bloodthirsty howls drowned out the screams as the beasts

came crashing through on Nyri's heels. She was still too far from the nearest *eshaara* tree.

Only one thought kept her on her tiring feet and stopped her from collapsing to the ground in helpless terror amidst the chaos.

Juaan.

She had to find him. Everyone else was scrambling into the branches. Capture was not an option. Juaan might not have heard the warning.

Nyri gasped as a terrible light flared to life all around her, glowing violently in the dark. It seared her eyes, blinding her. She stumbled, holding her hands reflexively before her face. As her sight adjusted, she realised the light was formed of hot bodiless tongues. They licked at the base of the trees. Ravenously, they climbed higher and higher, devouring everything in their path. New screams of terror and pain ripped the air.

The Elders had always taught Nyri that the Woves were demons. Now she truly believed it. Her people were trapped in their trees, helpless to escape the hungry onslaught of the glowing spirits the Woves had unleashed. The light unveiled their enemies in all their terrifying glory. Dead and rotten eyes rolled blindly in the bony sockets of their flayed, skull-like heads.

The scorching tongues licked higher into the trees. Nyri screamed in denial as she watched members of her tribe, her family, throw themselves into the air, falling into the waiting arms of their demonic assailants below. The beasts lifted away the women and children while savagely putting the men to death.

Maddened with fear, Nyri did not know where to turn as

she battled her way through the screaming mass. The air turned thick and black, sticking in her throat. Disoriented, she stumbled on.

"To the river!" someone cried. "Get to the river!"

Nyri sensed a sudden intent, and a hand grabbed her shoulder.

"Nyriaana!" the man who had caught her shouted. She did not recognise him in her panicked state. "Come with me! This way!"

Nyri clung to that one clear thought in her mind. "Juaan! I have to find Juaan!" She could not lose him to the Woves, too.

The man dragged her along with him. "He'd have fled by now! We have to go!"

"No!" Nyri fought back. "He wouldn't go without me!" She knew that truth to the core of her being.

"Leave the Forbidden filth! Daajir informed us of his attack. His life is—"

Something sliced the air and hit the man full in the chest. With a heavy grunt, he toppled to the ground; the air leaving his body in a long gasp. He lay motionless, eyes unseeing beneath half open lids. Blood oozed from around the long, straight branch protruding from his body. Nyri stared. The presence of life that had been beside her just an instant ago was gone. The figure on the ground was now a terrifying shell of emptiness. She could not contain the blood-curdling screech that tore from her.

She stumbled back, turned, and scraped her knees in her haste to escape. No thought or purpose guided this new flight, only the blind urge to run, run and put as much distance between her and death as possible. Hot tongues licked from all around. She barely noticed their sting as they tasted her skin.

Nyri did not know how far she had gone before something knocked her backwards off her feet. It felt as though she had run face first into a thick branch. Pain seared through her mouth as she struck it at full pace and rebounded, her head snapping back. She tasted the bitter tang of blood just as the ground slammed the breath from her lungs.

The world stopped. It hung there, breathless, detached.

Am I dead?

A hulking form loomed into view, and sensation returned in a rush; the pain, the fear, the stench of destruction. It hadn't been a branch. She had run straight into its waiting, outstretched arm. Nyri scrambled backwards on her hands and feet to escape the dark figure which stood twice as tall as any Ninkuraaja.

The half-skinned skull resembling that of a bear sat upon the massive shoulders. Four eyes glared down at Nyri. Two were lidless and glazed with death, the other two dark and living, peering out from sockets in the centre of the skull. A tangle of flaming, wiry hair framed everything, flaring in the light of the burning spirits. The blackness of the monster's soul flowed over her like tar.

One thick arm, bristling with snapped bones and sharpened horn, reached down towards her. "You do nicely." The voice rumbled from an unseen throat. "Where Scarred One?"

Nyri did not hear it. She screamed before she could think. "Juaan! Help me! Juaan!" And then she did think, and her mouth snapped shut. *What have I done?* She did not want him to come. She did not want to see Juaan as an empty shell upon the ground. All strength left her as the image flooded her mind. He could not win this fight.

A crooked, human-like hand at the end of the bony arm caught her by the woven green cloth at her chest and lifted her from the earth. She could smell the rotting flesh of the skins dangling from the beast's body.

Strength returned in a blaze through her veins. The hatred she felt for this demon burned at her. She wanted to hurt it, any part she could reach. Wild, Nyri kicked, clawed and bit like an animal at bay. She was only half aware that she was screaming with rage. The monster's grunts of pain were satisfying, as was the bloody mess her teeth had turned its horridly pale hand into. Satisfying, that was, until it swung her out at arm's length and held her there like a leaf on a branch.

Nyri hung from the fist, struggling, until her rage burned out. She whimpered and cried as she pulled fruitlessly at the thick fingers, smearing blood. All enjoyment had melted from the dark eyes at the centre of the skull. They were pools of death. Nyri saw them flick towards a burning tree.

Her blood ran cold. "No. Please," she whispered, even though she knew in her heart that no amount of pleading would sway the creature. It would throw her into the ravening spirits and enjoy watching them devour her. "No! Please!"

"Nooo!" A furious howl split the air. There was a clash of heavy bodies, and the demon holding her aloft bellowed in furious surprise as it stumbled to the side. Nyri's weight overbalanced it, forcing it to let go of her to break its fall. Nyri tasted earth again. The tang of smoke and blood mingled with leaf mould on her tongue, but the foul concoction had nothing to do with the roil in her stomach.

He was here.

She watched as Juaan untangled his long legs from her assailant's and leapt to his feet. "Leave her alone!" he screamed down at the stunned demon and aimed a hard kick at its side for good measure. He held a long, thick spear in his hand. His face was unrecognisable as he raised it above his fallen enemy, point down; murder in his eyes.

"Juaan!" Nyri cried. "Juaan!"

The sound of her voice pulled him around, and a trickle of reason returned to his features. He forgot their enemy and rushed to where she had fallen. Then Nyri was off the ground again. Juaan had grabbed her hand and was dragging her in the wake of his long, swift strides. Nyri's terror for him warred with relief. She was no longer alone. He would get them out of this.

Nyri tried her best to keep up, running as hard as she could, but Juaan's legs were too big. She was already choking on blood, smoke, and pain. It wasn't long before she stumbled and fell. Juaan pulled at her arm. "Come on! Get up!" he urged. "You've got to run!"

"I-I can't," she choked, sobbing. "Juaan, I c-can't."

Through streaming eyes, she saw Juaan whip his head this way and that. It was as if he was looking for something, but then just as quickly concluded it was not there. He scooped Nyri up in his arms and stumbled on through the billows of smoke and darkness.

Nyri wrapped her arms around his neck and hung on, closing her eyes against the red glow of destruction that raged all around her. She did not want to see. She did not want to feel the sting of heat against her cheeks or smell the suffocating smoke. She buried her face in Juaan's jolting shoulder and inhaled his familiar scent, mixed now with the bite of sweat.

Juaan struggled on, avoiding the worst of the flames and the screams. He was running with purpose, but to where, Nyri could not guess. Eventually, though, even Juaan's strength had to run out, and he collapsed to the earth, choking and gasping as he lowered Nyri gently with him. "Close enough," he rasped.

Nyri did not ask what he meant. She clung to him, shaking and sobbing. Juaan leaned them against the base of a tree. He put his arms around her and rocked them back and forth, trying, she thought, to be comforting.

It was quieter here, the stillness unnatural after the chaos and the bloodshed they had left behind in the *eshaara* grove.

"Don't be afraid, Nyri, Nyri, Nyriaana," he half sang but, for the first time, the familiar rhyme did nothing to comfort her. Nyri did not think she would ever know peace again. Their home was gone. She could feel it dying around her as the Woves slaughtered her people. She pressed her hands to her ears, whimpering nonsense words to block out the distant screaming.

"What's going to happen to us?" She forced the question through chattering teeth.

"Shhh," he whispered. "You'll be safe. I promise to make you safe. Have I ever broken a promise to you?"

Nyri shook her head, but her heart remained a stone in her chest. Those demons were out there. They were searching. They were coming. They could not escape. That monster had terrified her. Thick grey smoke wrapped them in a cloying veil, wrapping them in their own little pocket of desperate anticipation. It would not hide them for long.

Nyri sniffed. "Why did you do it?"

"What?"

"Come back for me?"

Juaan stiffened. "Why in Ninmah's name wouldn't I come back for you?"

"I hurt you. I was cruel."

He sighed. "It doesn't matter. You are my Nyri and I will protect you to the end."

Nyri sobbed, great wracking hitches of breath. This was all her fault. *Why* had she wandered so far from home? She had led their enemies straight to her tribe. It was all her fault!

The sharp snap of a twig and a shout made them both flinch. Juaan clutched his spear before them. Nyri was clinging to him so tightly she was sure her nails were stinging his skin.

"Please, let's go. I want to go." Her skin was prickling with the nearness of the devils. *"Please."*

"Shhh," Juaan hissed, then spoke in a breath. "We have to wait here."

"Why?" She pulled on him, feeling them draw closer. "Let's go! I wanna go! Please! *Please!*" Nyri was practically crawling out of her skin, but she may as well have been trying to move a mountain.

A strange noise made her pause in her efforts. It was like the sound of an animal bellowing a furious challenge. Wha—

Juaan's stiff shoulders fell. Nyri could have sworn she felt relief radiate from him. It was as though the sound had been something he had been waiting for. She had no time to think, for he was shaking her urgently. "Nyri, listen! *Listen!*

When I tell you, you must run that way." He pointed with the spear into the smoke. "Run as fast as you can. As *fast* as you can!"

"Why? No! I wanna stay with you!"

Juaan's face closed, emptying of any emotion. She tried to cling to him, but he pried her hands from around his clothing with frighteningly little effort. He caught her face between his long hands. Green burned into indigo. "Run."

"Where?" a muffled voice mocked from the gloom. Nyri moaned. Juaan was on his feet in an instant, spear raised. She grabbed onto his free hand and was dragged up with him. He was careful to keep her shielded between himself and the tree behind, but this did nothing to protect her from the sight of ten hulking shadows emerging from the murk to form a loose semi-circle around them. Their pale, lipless faces grinned in the darkness. Nyri huddled against Juaan's legs, her grip hard on his hand. She refused to acknowledge the tremble she felt there.

"Brave, boy." It was the bear-skulled demon that lead the others. Nyri's knees weakened at the sight of the demon as it drawled haltingly. It was as if it did not quite know how to speak the words. The creature stepped closer, idly swinging a stout branch tipped with the fleshy knee bone of an elk before it. "You think you challenge me and walk way? Foolish. Should killed me. Few get chance." The two living eyes at the centre of the skull flicked over Juaan, then widened in shock as the two dead orbs rolled wildly upon either side. "You?"

The demon then caught sight of the spear in Juaan's hand and recoiled further before recovering itself. It growled something Nyri could not hear. Juaan's only answer was to tighten his grip on the weapon.

"You not these People." The monster grunted. "Let me take girl. Come willingly and I let you live."

"Never!" Juaan spat. "I'm not one of you, either! I will not let you take her."

Their tormentor huffed. One of the others spoke rapidly. This one's face was that of a skinned elk. The sharpened antlers flared from either side of the bloody head. At least, Nyri *thought* it spoke. The noises it made sounded like words, but they formed no pictures of understanding in her mind. The leader snapped back at the other demon, making the same sounds before returning its attention to Juaan. "Stubborn boy. Seen it before, always the same ending. Move. You not know how use weapon." The figure took a menacing step forward. "I not ask again."

Nyri willed him to run. Willed him to run with all her heart, but Juaan only set his feet and raised his chin, levelling his spear. Nyri felt like she would die right there. Juaan was finished, and she did not know what fate awaited her.

The standoff broke as the earth vibrated. The sound of hoofbeats drummed on the dead air, getting closer. A single grey stag barrelled from the gloom. Nyri could hear its breath; feel its frenzied energy, the urge from its rider to run ever faster.

As if in slow motion, Nyri watched as the stag and rider bore down upon them. The rider was one of her tribesmen, and he charged the demons surrounding Nyri and Juaan without breaking stride. Curses flared as the unprepared Woves leaped aside, the speed of the attack shocking them for a few vital moments. In those eternal heartbeats of time, the great, grey creature was alongside the two children. The rider was reaching down. Juaan's hand ripped from hers. A grunt of effort and suddenly Nyri was in the air.

Too late, she realised what was happening. Too late to cling to her life. Another pair of hands was tearing her away, lifting her onto the stag's hot, heaving back. The icy wind whipped Nyri's face as she was borne into the night.

"Goodbye..."

She thought she heard the whisper as her heart shattered into a million pieces. Juaan slipped behind, further with every mighty stride.

"No!" Nyri screamed and writhed. "No! Don't leave him! They'll kill him! Take me back!" She was half mad.

Strong arms steadied her. "I can't, child. He cannot come with us. He knew that, but he had to save you first." The man sounded as though he was weeping, too. Nyri did not care.

"Go back! Go back! Please!"

"I can't," the man repeated over the beating of hooves. "Your friend is already dead."

And in her own heart of hearts, Nyri knew this to be true. The centre of her world was gone, and now everything else was collapsing inward. This new world of tears, darkness, and pain turned black, and she knew no more.

* * *

2

Nightmare

even years later...

"No!" Nyriaana screamed, waking herself from a fitful sleep. The smoky world resolved into the clear, familiar shapes of home, and the beating of hooves morphed to the heavy thudding of her own heart.

It was still dark. The hush of pre-dawn hung thick upon the air. Nyri drew comfort from the living walls cradling her in their embrace and let the silver shivering of leaves outside soothe the rush of blood in her ears. She flexed her hands to rid them of the panic-induced tingle. She was safe, and the monsters of her dreams were far away.

For the moment, at least.

Nyri lay back, stirring the moss and leaves of her resting place. Breathing in the earthy scents of her home, she centred herself, stilling her soul.

In a well worn routine, Nyri blocked the dream from her mind. She should not dwell. No amount of grieving would bring those loved and lost back to the living. They walked now in the company of the Great Spirit, riding the wind, flowing in the waters, never to look back or return. It was a hard lesson her people had learned well; they who lived in death's constant company.

But Nyriaana could not forget. She would never forget.

Keeping her eyes closed, she stretched her senses beyond her body, feeling for the ever-present flow of the Great Spirit of KI and her place within his world. Nyri could feel Him in the slow, stately presence of the trees, the silent sentinels of life that supported them all. He was there in the quick intent of the birds. A snake concentrating on being invisible as it lurked outside of a nest. Nyri felt the individual spirits of the people; all that remained of her once vibrant tribe. So few and yet their energy shimmered with vital thought and hope as they woke to the rising of Ninmah, the great Golden Mother. Indeed, as Her warm veil crept slowly into the sky, chasing the darkness before Her, the troubles that stalked their lives seemed very far away.

Nyri sensed the summoning before she heard it.

"Nyriaana!"

Kyaati's presence was an insistent nag on the ground outside the giant tree. Nyri threw an arm over her eyes and groaned. She would have liked to have been left alone with her thoughts for a little longer, but Ninmah was awakening and there were duties to attend to.

I'm coming. Nyri extended the intent. She pictured Kyaati's arms folding, her toes scraping impatiently at the dark earth.

Rising in one smooth movement, Nyri emerged from the thick nest of moss, feathers and leaves that filled the cradle of branches that was her bower. She shivered in the cool air. It was early Fall, but the morning was as chill as if it were already passing into Ninsiku's Fury. She tried to ignore the sense of apprehension this evoked. It was always cold now. Reaching for her leaf-leather coverings, she donned them gratefully, grabbing a woven Gathering basket as she went.

"Ninmah's greetings." She flashed a smile to Kyaati as she swung down from her tree. Dawn mist swirled in the semi-light as she landed. Nyri was expecting the lash of Kyaati's tongue, barbed with irritation, but her friend said nothing. She just eyed Nyri's agility with thinly veiled envy.

"Ninmah's greetings," she replied in a clipped tone. Her hands smoothed over her rounded belly; nearly full with child. The skin around Kyaati's pale lavender eyes was tight, the smooth, honey skin of her forehead creased beneath her silvery-white hair. "We'd better hurry or we'll be late for the Gathering."

Nyri's heart dropped like a stone. The Gathering. She wasn't in the mood for a Gathering. As always in the wake of one of her nightmares, she just wanted to be alone or, better yet, to be with Baarias, burying herself in his teachings. She did not wish to spend the morning wandering the failing groves, struggling to find what little food there was while looking into the faces of barely fed children learning at their heels. It was too stark a reminder of what they faced.

Nyriaana masked these feelings from Kyaati, however. It would not do for her mother-to-be companion to guess her thoughts. If Kyaati detected her reluctance, she chose not to show it. Deep down, Nyri knew she was most likely feeling the same. Probably worse.

They walked in companionable silence as the light of Ninmah grew stronger. The cool mist that shrouded the *eshaara* grove began to lift and the great, red-gold trees became more clearly defined. As she listened to the music of the river flowing away in the forest beyond, she made her customary blessing to Ninmah for the gift of this sanctuary. Without it, her people would not be here to worship the Golden Mother's beauty.

The horrors of her dream broke through her control and danced before Nyri's eyes. Maybe it would be easier to bear if they were just that. Dreams. Not genuine memories of a burned life.

That night, seven long Furies ago, the Woves had not just taken lives, but everything her People's existence depended upon. They had razed the trees to the ground. Shelter, food sources, everything. Gone.

A single *eshaara* tree, germinated by the spirit of a passing Kamaali, took years of energy and patience to grow to maturity. Her People could not simply make new homes when driven from the old. They had been turned into the very nomads they despised; defenceless and starving. Worse still, the demon Woves had somehow shifted the Balance of the world. The power of the beloved Ninmah was diminishing.

As Her warming touch withdrew, Nyri's tribe was left increasingly at the mercy of Ninsiku's dark and icy grip and the evil of his creations. Strange beasts, driven down from the north, had picked off the weak. Every Fury following the massacre had threatened to be their last, the frozen days and crushingly long nights filled with starvation and despair.

The survivors of the attack diminished to a mere handful of souls throughout those unspeakable days. And even they would surely have perished along with their brethren had they not stumbled across this abandoned *eshaara* grove.

The trees had been strangers, seeded by the unknown Kamaali of another tribe, but the empty dwellings, twisted into the mighty boughs, had offered protection and shelter at last. Nyri did not know what had become of the tribe that had once lived here. They had not encountered others of their Ninkuraaja kind for many cycles, but her people had not questioned their good fortune. Ninmah had smiled upon them, and they quickly settled into their new home. During the seasons that followed, they had attempted to rebuild their lives.

Walking through the now familiar trees, Nyri and Kyaati passed by members of the tribe who could not join the Gathering, those too old or too infirm to carry out the duty. Nyri caught sight of an ancient woman sitting at the base of a great, gnarled *eshaara*. Several well-worn tools surrounded her, along with a pile of aacha leaves. She was making garments. Close at her side, the roots of the tree formed a large bowl, filled to the brim with preserving t*yraa* sap.

Nyri watched the withered, red-gold hands, trembling from the effects of use and old age yet steeped in the skill of both, select a large, deep green leaf and dip it into the waiting sap. The old woman left it to soak and pulled another leaf from a second pile. This one had already been treated and left to dry in a pool of light, its perfection now preserved and strengthened by the miracle sap. An extremely tough material made ready for crafting.

Nyri touched the smooth, leathery sleeve draping over her arm. The same old tribeswoman had taught her how to fashion it. Slipping her fingers beneath the green coverings, Nyri felt the soft warmth of the cotton pods attached to the inside. She had hoped that this addition would offer protection from the increasingly bitter cold. Nyri smiled sadly. It seemed nothing in her tribe's power, none of their ancient skill or knowledge, could protect them from that.

Kyaati must have sensed the shift in Nyri's mood, for she paused and followed her gaze. "What is she still doing here?" she asked in mild surprise. "Shouldn't she be at the Gathering?"

Nyri shrugged and walked over to where the tribeswoman sat, lifting her palms open and skyward, a greeting symbolising trust and welcome and hope for the same. The ancient one raised her own palms, sticky with sap. Opening her hands, opening her soul. "Nyriaana."

"Sefaan." Nyri bowed her head in profound respect to the once great Kamaali guide of her people. Nyri did not care what the Elders whispered about her weakened mind. In Nyri's eyes, Sefaan would always be the greatest of them all.

She was always a little over-awed by the sheer power of Sefaan's presence. The energy infused within the old body glowed against Nyri's senses. A Seeress of the Great Spirit, KI, Himself. His voice for their tribe. Such a one was born only once in every generation. Upon Sefaan's forehead, standing above the twisting mark of Ninmah borne by all Ninkuraaja, was the symbol of KI. An honour reserved for the Kamaali alone.

A large *enu* nut dangled from a twisted thong about Sefaan's throat. Nyri eyed the seed worriedly. An *eshaara* nut only fell upon the birth of a Kamaali. This seed had fallen and been tied around Sefaan's neck even as she had drawn her first breaths. It would remain next to her skin, infusing itself with her energy, until the day she became one with the Great Spirit. When that day came, it would be planted, a new *eshaara* ready to be shaped by Sefaan's successor.

The time for planting was overdue. The *enu* tied about Sefaan's neck was showing signs of sprouting; it had already waited too long. But no successor had appeared to guide it to adulthood. The Elders were growing increasingly anxious. Every female birth was anticipated with a desperate hope, and each time those hopes were dashed when the nut of an *eshaara* failed to fall. No child had been marked for Sefaan to guide in her wisdom.

Most believed now that Sefaan was the Last, giving rise to the murmurings that the End of Days was upon them, signalled by the weakening of Ninmah and the growing strength of Ninsiku's children. If that were true, then Sefaan was the one fabled to save them all. Sound of mind or not.

Sefaan raised an eyebrow. "You have no need for new garments, child. The ones on your back are barely two seasons."

"No, Sefaan," Nyri forced a smile. "The Gathering is about to leave. I need something else." She hid the folded basket she already possessed behind her as she bent to lift a newly made one from Sefaan's pile of completed articles. "This."

The old Kamaali smiled. "Take it. May it serve you well." She went back to her work.

Nyri hesitated. Like Baarias, Sefaan possessed an energy that had the power to calm those around her. Nyri wanted to cling to that comfort for as long as possible. "Would you like to walk with us to the Blessing?"

In truth, the Kamaali should already be there. The Blessing couldn't very well go ahead without her. Nyri glanced into the rippling canopy, assessing the angle of the light now falling through the leaves. Ninmah was creeping higher. "Aardn will get anxious if you are not there."

A wicked twinkle flickered to life in Sefaan's eyes. She slid another leaf into the *tyraa* sap in what Nyri judged to be a deliberately protracted motion. "There is a Gathering today?" She said in mock surprise. "Oh, my."

Nyri shifted in the face of Sefaan's casual disregard. *She* certainly would not want to provoke the senior Elder's wrath. Sefaan, on the other hand, seemed to revel in poking the hornets' nest. Then again, she was *still* the Kamaali. The Elders could not outwardly show her disrespect.

"Tell Aardn I will be there when I am ready. Look well at her reaction. I want you to describe it to me later."

Laughter bubbled from Nyri's throat. Shaking her head, she reached into a pouch folded into her garments and pulled out a small gift; a beautiful, bright red feather. Nyri knew Sefaan would never take the gift without giving something in return; hence her pretence at needing a new basket. Sefaan could work the feather into one of her finer creations. Perhaps for one of the Elders. They favoured red as a symbol of their position.

"You always bring me the most glorious materials, Nyri." Sefaan admired the silken gift. Nyri's heart swelled at the sight of the ancient one's simple pleasure. She had collected it days ago. As soon as she had seen Sefaan working and feared for her fate, Nyri had known where this prize belonged. The Last Kamaali deserved everything beautiful before…

Sefaan's attention shifted abruptly from the feather to Nyri's face. "Your thoughts are heavy this day, Nyriaana.

What troubles you?"

"Nothing," she said, then, knowing she could not hide anything from Sefaan, she told part of the truth. "I have simply been dwelling on the past, when I know I should not."

"Ah," the Kamaali's depthless eyes were sympathetic. "Such thoughts would crack the hardest of hearts." She tilted her face towards the trees twisting above, light and shadow playing across her crinkled features. "Strengthen yours, Nyriaana. You have endured much suffering in your short life, but I fear we have not yet seen the last of our trials. Not since the Great Fury has the Almighty KI trembled as He does now. Ninsiku is not finished with us yet. In fact... I believe he is only just getting started."

As if in answer, the wind shivered through the leaves. Its icy breath brushed the back of Nyri's exposed neck. Stifling a shudder, she followed Sefaan's gaze. She knew all too well what the old Kamaali meant. She studied the strong trees twisting protectively overhead, picking out the increasingly obvious signs of disease and decay. Several of the mighty *eshaaras* already stood dead and empty, their skeletons whistling eerily in the breeze, their Kamaali spirits shrivelled and spent.

The End of Days...

Nyri gritted her teeth. It terrified her to think of the prayers and offerings Ninsiku's Wove children were making to lend the Cold One such strength. The snows should not reach this far south. Not even frost should touch these lands. Ninmah had always protected them with her warmth and light; now her strength was diminished. Even healthy homes stood stark and empty; no families sheltered within their growing walls. In the absence of joy and laughter, the wind whispered too loudly.

"Ah," Sefaan clapped her hands, startling Nyri's attention back to the present. She had that strange look on her face and Nyri knew what was coming. "Don't mind me, Nyriaana. You will prevail. I keep telling you-"

"Yes, Ariyaana is coming. Who *is* Ariyaana?" Nyri knew she would not get any further. She never did.

"I do not know!" Sefaan laughed. "The Great Spirit does not say. But you will know her when you see her and she will lead the way."

Nyri sighed. Sometimes she worried the Elders were right and Sefaan's wits were starting to fray.

Sefaan grunted and Nyri's cheeks grew hot, mortified that the Kamaali might have picked up on her thoughts, but Sefaan was no longer paying attention. The Kamaali glanced briefly at Kyaati before refocusing on the red feather. "I know what I'll do with this." She turned the feather in her wrinkled hands as the light hit it and intensified its colour. "You had better be gone, child, and I had best be going, too. I think I've antagonised Aardn long enough."

The old one struggled to her feet, over-used bones creaking as she peered into the trees behind her, and Nyri felt the power of her will extend. Moments later a large, brown doe trotted from the undergrowth and came to stand at the Kamaali's side. Sefaan rubbed the beautiful creature's neck and its large, liquid eyes gazed back in adoration. "Time is of the essence. We need that Gathering. It is the last before the Fury finds us."

"That's what I keep trying to say," Kyaati chimed.

"I'm *coming!*" Nyri answered. She turned to leave as Sefaan called after her.

"And do not think I missed the basket you already had hidden behind your back! I'm old, not blind. Now you'll have to work twice as hard. See if you can find some of those soft fruits, if there are any. You know the ones I like. They're kind on my gums."

Sefaan's merry laugh died away behind them as Nyri moved off with Kyaati into the trees.

"Poor old woman," Kyaati lamented once they were out of sight. Nyri felt the shift in her friend's mood and could not help but notice that her hands were restless on her belly once again. Nyri guessed what was on her mind and grew uncomfortable. She could hardly comfort herself, much less anyone else.

"What if it is true, Nyri?" Kyaati burst out. "What if the worst is yet to come and the End of Days are upon us? What am I bringing my child in to?" She gripped Nyri's arm, searching for assurances Nyri could not give. "What if I end up like Sefaan? Childless and alone with my mad ramblings. If there's something wrong with my baby and I lose it, just like…" she choked off.

"Kyaati!" a scolding voice broke in. Nyri had been so distracted; she had not detected Daajir's approach. This was an achievement. He exuded his energy like a storm before him. "Stop this. You will not lose your baby. I am certain of it."

"*Certain?*" Kyaati spat at him, hot tears springing to her eyes. "What could make you so *certain* when such outcomes elude even the Last Kamaali? Who are *you*, Daajir?"

"Sefaan is not what she once was." Daajir brushed aside her words. "You are carrying the future hope for our tribe,

Kyaati, perhaps the next Kamaali *herself*! We do not know that Sefaan is the Last. Ninmah will *not* let us perish. We are her beloved children. You have to be strong now and keep faith that we will prevail."

Nyriaana's irritation peaked at his insensitivity. Kyaati stared him down. "Ninmah? *Ninmah* will protect my baby? I ask you, Daajir, where has Ninmah ever been for me? For us?" Her voice rose. "*Nowhere*. Look around you. She is abandoning us!"

Daajir blinked, mentally agape in the face of her blasphemy. He recovered and began puffing himself up, indignant.

"Let's go," Nyri said hurriedly before Daajir could deliver a sermon against Kyaati's heresy. "The End of Days will be here that much faster if we don't eat through the Fury."

Kyaati huffed and stalked on. Daajir blew out a breath. "Thank you," he muttered. "I thought she was going to snap my neck. She's bad enough when she's not pregnant."

Nyri glared at him, letting him feel her annoyance. "I don't blame her. You know what she's been through, Dar. You could at least try to be a little more sensitive."

His pale red-gold face tensed. "We do not have time for such weakness. We must prove our worthiness to Ninmah. We must bring Her back to strength!"

"Kyaati is anything but weak! How can you even suggest such a thing? If I had been through half of what she has—"

"I know, I know." Daajir cut her off, grudgingly. "I just… wish I could do something more to reassure her."

Nyri's anger drained away. They all had to find some means of coping. Daajir's unassailable faith in Ninmah and the destiny of their people was his. Out of the corner of her

33

eye, Nyri observed Daajir as he walked alongside. A bully as a child, Nyri had nevertheless been forced closer to him as they had endured their harsh adolescence together.

She supposed their tenuous friendship had grown out of necessity. Daajir, Kyaati and Yaanth were the only children besides herself to have survived the massacre seven Furies ago. A couple of Blessing's older than Nyri, Kyaati and Yaanth had been completely inseparable. Much like she and... Juaan had always been. There had been no room for others within their little world. This meant that Nyri and Daajir had been given no choice other than to sort out their differences.

Nyri knew if things had turned out differently, she and Daajir would have probably gone on keeping one another at arm's length. He still wasn't the easiest person to get along with, and it had taken him a good while to forgive her for her previous choice of companion. Nyri was quick to halt that particular thought in its tracks. Even after all these seasons, it still hurt too much.

Daajir's dark purple eyes were watching the soft ground as it passed beneath his feet. Black hair, bound in a tail down his back, swayed in time with his gait. His spare frame, as with all in their tribe, bore testament to the times they faced. A life on the edge. His proud features had grown hard over the seasons since they were children. All too soon, the boyishness had left his face. His chin was chiselled and sharp, skin lined before its time. His haughty eyes bore the callouses of hardship. The joy had been stolen from them.

Nyri clenched her fists, digging her nails into her palms. As they neared their destination, a crushing wave of help-lessness overcame her. She wanted someone to protect her from it all, to make it right and bring the joy back to their lives. Of course, this was a foolish desire and she should know better. Such cosy illusions of safety had been torn away with her childhood. In many ways, Nyri had never really woken from her dream. It continued all around.

A living nightmare.

3

Gathering

The trees thinned as Nyri and her friends broke at last into a small clearing. A tall rock reared from the grass in the centre, a bone of the earth, as old and as constant as the world itself, pointing upward in worship towards the heavens. Smaller rocks were scattered about it. This place had become a sacred focal point for the tribe, an opening onto Ninmah Herself.

Nyri couldn't help but smile when she saw Sefaan was already present at the standing stone. The doe was grazing peacefully nearby, still puffing slightly. Beside the Kamaali stood Aardn. Next to the Kamaali's serene presence, the Elder appeared disgruntled, thin lips pressed together and large, dark eyes disapproving. Black hair, streaked heavily with grey, framed the severe lines of her unforgiving face.

Nyri and her friends were the last to arrive. The rest had already collected in the clearing, even those who would traditionally not be away from the relative safety of the *eshaara* trees, the Elders, Kyaati in her current condition, and the youngest of the children.

The children. All five of them. Five small, half-formed beings carrying all the hope of the future. The base mark of Ninmah stood between their brows. A simple line of purple colour. Only when they reached maturity would two twisting lines be added around it; the Mark of Passage into adulthood. If they were to earn a position of honour or skill within the tribe, the mark of Ninmah would be further embellished to symbolise their particular achievement.

Nyri wondered how many would survive long enough to even receive their Mark of Passage. Their faces were pallid, their eyes unnaturally large in their half-starved features. And the Fury had still yet to begin.

Nyri closed her eyes; she could not let them detect the weakness she was feeling. She was not a child anymore. She brushed her forehead where her own marks were inscribed, identifying her as an adult of her tribe, a protector and a guide. Nyri tightened her control, lest her turbulent emotions leak through to the youngsters. She had to be strong, as Daajir said, even though every fibre of her being wanted to run, screaming through the trees, searching for... she did not know what.

One small boy drew her attention. He was sitting upon the ground, resting between the paws of a great smoke-grey forest wolf. Omaal had been born blind with the addition of a half developed leg, but Nyri's heavy heart lifted as she watched the wolf swipe at the boy's face with his tongue. The boy squealed, making gagging noises as he playfully pushed the wolf's muzzle away. The great animal's tongue lolled in wolfish amusement.

As a People, they all had the gift to bond with the Children of the Great Spirit and to each other. It was how the

Ninkuraaja survived but, even among the tribe, Omaal and Batai's connection went above and beyond the ordinary.

A bond forged out of tragedy. Nyri remembered that fateful Fury when the boy had been born. They had barely welcomed Omaal into the world when his grandfather, Chaard, had disappeared in early snows. Omaal's parents, already mourning the prospects of their crippled newborn, had set out with half of the tribe to search for him. Along the way, they had reached out to the local wolf pack, hoping their keen senses would help track down the missing tribesman. They had found the old man; locked in the jaws of a strange and terrifying feline creature bearing teeth as long as a forearm.

It was too late for Chaard, but the wolves had attacked the cat, driving this new predator from their hunting grounds. The resulting fight had led to the death of a she-wolf before the cat finally fled. A she-wolf with one surviving pup. Omaal's parents, in return for the wolves' aid, had taken the struggling pup and cared for it.

What they hadn't counted on was the friendship that would grow between the wolf pup and their newly born son. Batai had become Omaal's eyes, his way around, his constant companion. His blessing.

"Sons and Daughters of Ninmah. My People." Nyri's musings shattered as Aardn's commanding voice rang out. Ninmah was now peering over the edge of the clearing, Her light touching the waving grass. It was time to begin. The Elder raised her arms, and the feathers bound into her greying hair swayed in the slight breeze. The symbol of the Elder stood boldly upon her forehead, the Mark of Passage crowned with an inverted half circle in honour of Ninmah.

"Let us greet this golden day and look upon Ninmah's beauty with hope and thanks." Her eyes, hard pools of experience, met each one of their own. "Our most revered Kamaali will help us seek the Blessing of the Great Spirit as we pray for Ninmah to smile upon us with a bountiful harvest."

Everyone grew still in silent anticipation. Aardn bowed and moved back as Sefaan came forward. Gone was the eccentric old woman. Sefaan stood straight and proud, defying her great age. The power she radiated knew not the count of time. "This is a day of Gathering." Her voice, cracked though it was with age, rang out as she spoke the traditional words. "The Great Spirit, KI, provides all beneath the loving gaze of Ninmah. One cannot exist without the other. We must come together as we have done since the dawn of time and join our strength to the Great Spirit. Only through Him can we know the true Purpose." She raised her trembling hands.

The tribe gathered in a close circle around the standing stone. Many reached out to touch their neighbours, a hand on a shoulder, Joined mates linked fingers. Others, like Nyri, simply stood with their hands to the sides of their bodies, palms open and souls receptive.

Emptying her mind of any conscious thought, Nyri let go of her worries and focused solely on the energy flowing within, much as she had when she had first woken. Only now, led by Sefaan, the experience was that much more profound. Burning at the centre of all, the Kamaali guided their spirits to join with KI, binding them together as one.

They needed this, this reaffirmation of their bonds to each other and to the world around them. Any creatures in the area readily picked up on the ritual and were drawn in.

The clearing was alive as Ninmah rose to a point above the standing stone and shone brightly from above, filling the clearing with Her warmth and light.

In her mind's eye, Nyri saw the power that was the Great Spirit of KI. He always appeared to her as a strong, golden presence, flowing in great Rivers that crisscrossed the earth beneath their feet, forever feeding and influencing everything in his path. Their forest grew over one such vein of guiding energy. Tendrils of light rose up from the ground, extensions of KI Himself, existing within and guiding the souls of all his living things, his own Sons and Daughters of the earth. Guardians of his crucial Balance. So much of his wisdom was a mystery to Nyri's People, the Children of Ninmah, so many secrets that danced just beyond understanding, vast and incomprehensible.

To even begin to comprehend, one had to learn to connect with the Great Spirit's Children. Only through them could Nyri's People hope to gain an understanding of the world upon which they had been created. As one they stretched out now, touching and joining with the tendrils of light surrounding them, and KI grew all the brighter.

Nyri drew a breath, the cool air vibrating in her lungs. The beauty of this act never ceased to take her breath away. For these few precious moments, she was a part of everything. She could see everything. Feel the pressures of the air, the changes in the wind, the insects in the earth, the birds in the sky guided by the Great Spirit's Rivers, and the vital connection between all that was the Great Spirit Himself. It was a most sacred experience. Nyri envied the Sons and Daughters of KI, the creatures of the earth. They were born knowing their purpose, their wisdom ingrained into their souls from the moment they were born. They never questioned. They knew.

Reluctantly, Nyri came back to herself, revitalised and ready to begin the challenges of the day. The tendrils of light around her resolved back into the trees and creatures of the forest. A maamit troop had come to sit in the surrounding branches. They chattered expectantly, ready for action.

Batai gave a soft whine, yellow eyes fixed hungrily on the agile creatures above. Nyri laughed. *No,* she gave the sense of her words to the wolf through her basic connection with him. *Leave them. You can go hunting later.* The wolf huffed and lowered his head between his paws next to Omaal. The boy scratched his ears sympathetically. The yellow eyes of the hunter remained in the trees, however.

"Go now," Aardn bade. "Ninmah's blessings be with you."

Blessings. They would need them. All the rich trees that their forefathers had worked to create now only bore enough to keep half the tribe's number fed. At least the maamit troop that had joined them would be of help. They could reach where even the most skilful climbers could not.

The tribe separated into groups, spreading out to cover as much ground as possible. Splitting up was dangerous but necessary. The groves that the previous occupants of their home had planted covered a great area. A single morsel could mean the difference between survival and starvation.

Daajir, Kyaati and Nyri formed their own group. A few of the children followed. Most were orphans, eager to attach themselves to the closest adults. As the youngest group, Nyri supposed she and her friends were the most appealing company to the infants. Omaal followed his companions, hanging on tight to Batai's thick fur. His parents were on sentry duty. Omaal had been allowed to join the Gathering to learn with the other children, provided he stayed close to Batai.

Kyaati seemed pleased by the extra company. Her fine features relaxed and softened. Nyri was indifferent; she wasn't a natural with children, but as long as she had Kyaati and Daajir with her, she supposed she wouldn't have to interact with them too much on her own.

If the young ones thought they were in for an easy time with Nyri's group, however, they hadn't counted on Daajir. They had not travelled far into the forest when he pulled them to the side.

"Now, you all listen to me." He turned the full force of his will upon their tender senses, and their heads shrank into their shoulders.

Nyri and Kyaati frowned in warning. The children could feel Daajir's admonishment, but only an adult's finer senses could detect his enjoyment at this ability to intimidate. He had never fully grown out of that fault. Bullying habits died hard.

"We are heading for the grove closest to the Pits, so stay close," he instructed. "The ground is treacherous and could swallow you up if you do not do exactly as we say. I do not want to have to explain to the Elders that you fell to your deaths because you strayed where you were not supposed to.

"You know what happens to children who do not listen, don't you…?" He let the words hang, and the little ones drew closer together in fearful anticipation. "The Woves drag them from their trees at night and devour them in the dark. No one ever sees them again." The sense of menace increased. Batai growled low in his throat, hackles rising, and some of the children whimpered.

Kyaati's eyes widened in horror. She crouched awkwardly before them. "He doesn't mean it. Don't be scared. No one is going to take you away…"

Nyri's forehead creased. She understood Daajir's concern, even if she did not agree with his method of scaring the children half to death. The Pits, as they were called, were a cluster of deep holes carved into the earth by mysterious forces. Lying east of her tribe's home, the Elders had decided to use them as a defence against Wove raids and ordered them to be carefully covered with sticks and leaf matter. If one did not know they were there… if the fall did not kill the unfortunate victim, then starvation surely would. The sides of the Pits were sheer rock, eroded and underscored by countless rainy seasons. No one could escape unless they had aid from above.

The bodies of at least a few unfortunate Woves might very well be lying at the bottom of those Pits. Nyri did not know and could not say that she cared. No one ever bothered to check them.

Daajir smacked his hands together. "Get going!"

Relieved to be released, the children ran on ahead, though with noticeably more caution. Omaal clung to Batai's fur, viewing the world through the wolf's keen eyes as he touched him. The blind boy probably had better senses than the rest of them in this present moment, Nyri mused, certainly a better sense of smell.

"You *snake*," Kyaati glared at Daajir as she heaved herself back to her feet. "What in Ninmah's name do you get out of terrifying children? If you ever try to intimidate my child like that, I'll have a Thal rip your arms right from your puny body."

"A healthy fear of consequence never hurt anybody," Daajir returned. "They need to be kept safe." He sighed then, dropping the hardened facade. "Do not judge me for what you see as undue harshness, Kya. I act the way I do because I care and I will care about your child, too. Know that I will do anything to keep our People safe. *That* is what I get out of it.

"Anyway, how many Thals do you know? I'm not certain those hulking beasts even mastered the art of speech. All they understand is how to beat each other over the head with rocks."

Kyaati opened her mouth, but Nyri cut in before their bickering escalated into a more serious fight. "As interesting as this debate is, I really think we should get moving. This tribe isn't getting any more fed and the children are getting away." She turned her head to indicate the now child-free area and raised an eyebrow. "Shouldn't we be watching them? I don't particularly want to be explaining to the Elders that we lost our most precious members, either."

"Oh, very well!" Daajir snapped as he turned and stalked on, chagrined.

The day grew unusually warm as they wandered through the groves. As they harvested, Nyri and her friends taught the children how to extract the best, most succulent roots from the ground, how to identify edible fungi, and warned them away from anything harmful. They helped them climb trees to collect fruit and nuts. The young ones were eager and quick in their lessons. Digging became a game as they tumbled around in the earth.

Their carefree presence was uplifting and distracting. Nyri was happy now that the children had accompanied them. Together they scoured their chosen area of the forest, reaping the best the trees and plants had to offer. By and by, Nyriaana and Kyaati began to sing, voices joining in praise to Ninmah. The sound of singing was rare in these uncertain days, and it lifted their spirits to new heights.

Ninmah passed higher overhead and soon all were removing their outer layers, letting their skin breathe as they caught the welcome rays stealing through the protective canopy. The soft undergrowth wore a pretty pattern of light and shadow.

"Nyriaana?" a tentative voice asked.

Nyri looked up from where she had been busy pulling some fleshy roots from the ground. Little Naaya, the only female child and daughter of their youngest Elder, Oraan, was staring at her expectantly. "How do we make the trees grow?"

"Er," Nyri glanced around for help but Daajir was halfway up a tree and Kyaati was busy catching the fruit he was dropping. She was on her own. Turning back to the little girl, Nyri tried to think of how to explain this ancient knowledge in terms she would understand. Naaya's pinched little face stared, waiting patiently. Both of her hands were bent and twisted. Nyri bit her lip, fighting down another wave of hopelessness. Poor child.

She was saved by the drone of tiny wings. A bee buzzed lazily through the air, and her frown became a smile. The Great Spirit was with her. "Come," Nyri pointed to the little creature going about its service. "Let's follow her and see what she does." Naaya's eyes lit up, and she followed eagerly after Nyri as they kept the bee in sight. They didn't have to go far before the insect lighted upon a late flower and set to work. Nyri crouched down.

"Watch her," she said. "She's gathering nectar to make honey. The bee is getting what she needs to survive from the flower."

"I like honey!" Naaya whispered. "Papa got stung last time he tried to get me some." She giggled at the memory.

"Honey is nice," Nyri agreed. She turned her attention back to the miracle going on before them. "So we know what the bee gets from the flower, but what does the flower get from the bee?"

Naaya appeared perplexed by this, so Nyri enlightened her. With a finger, she pointed carefully at the bee's fuzzy body and the yellow grains that clung there. "The pollen is sticking to her. Watch what happens when she moves to the next flower." Sure enough, the obliging little insect took off and buzzed to the neighbouring plant.

"She's putting the pollen onto the other flower!"

"Yes. And now the plant can form seeds to make the next generation. The plant and the insect work together to ensure the other's survival."

Naaya's face was alive with wonder.

"And what do the plants do to attract the bees?" Nyri questioned.

The little girl frowned. "They… have pretty colours…" she ventured. Nyri waited. "And they smell nice!"

"Very good! That's a start. Plants are extremely clever. Perhaps the most ingenious of all of KI's creations. They have learned how to attract everything they need to them and overcome the greatest of obstacles, sometimes in very incredible ways indeed."

Naaya nodded. "But how do we get the plants to grow how we want?" she asked, not making the connection.

"Ah," Nyri said. "Our forefathers were also very clever and close to the Great Spirit. They learned the wisdom of this partnership between the insects and the flowers and used it for their own. They assumed the role of the insect and, over time, the trees and plants adapted to grow in ways and forms to attract *us*."

"Oooh." The little girl clapped her deformed hands as best she could. "They were very clever, weren't they?"

Nyri laughed at her delight. "Yes, they were. But trees and plants take time to adapt and grow. Our ancestors had to use our own special Gifts to speed things along. Here," Nyri took the child's arm, led her to the nearest sapling and crouched down next to it. "Put your hand on this young tree. Now, tell me what you feel."

"The Great Spirit. He's inside, coming up from the ground."

"Yes." She was perceptive, this little one. "And the Great Spirit is part of you. You know this, you can feel it. A part of him exists within the souls of all of our people. Ninmah herself made us with his essence and gifted us with higher thought, giving us the ability to harness this energy and use it well. Concentrate Naaya. Add your soul, your piece of KI, to the energy within the tree. Extend it through your fingertips. Speed it up, tell him to go faster."

The little girl's face screwed up in intense concentration as she did as Nyri asked.

The sapling extended about as much as a gnat's wing, but that did not dishearten Naaya. Face covered in sweat from the effort, she jumped up and down in excitement over what she had done.

"Thank you, Nyri!" she squealed, and then ran off to tell her friends of the exciting new things she had learned. Nyri watched after her, smiling.

"You tell blind stories, Nyriaana." The amusement in the tone softened the criticism. Nyri looked up to see Kyaati leaning against a tree, watching her with a smile. "Despite your claims, I believe you are a natural with children."

Nyri blushed. She had not known she was being observed.

"Hey! Look there!"

Nyri started at Daajir's sudden exclamation. He was pointing into the canopy. She followed his direction and spied a bunch of honey fruits bigger than any she had seen since they were children.

"Ninmah be blessed," Kyaati said, looking hungrily into the heights. She smirked at Daajir. "Bring me a few of those and it might go a small way to restoring some of this faith you keep insisting I have."

A slow smile crept over Daajir's face. An electric vibe travelled between them and Nyri matched his expression. Time to do something else they had not done since they were children.

Neither of them gave any outward signal, but in the same instant, they turned and bolted toward the tempting fruit, hooting and calling challenges all the way. Daajir reached the base of the tree first and climbed nimbly into the air. Nyri pushed herself to catch him up.

She would *not* be beaten. She had never lost to Daajir, and she wasn't about to start now. She threw herself recklessly into the tree, swinging herself into the tangle of branches.

Her strong fingers and toes sought the best holds while she mapped the tree in her mind, searching for the quickest path to the fruit. The cheers and laughter from the children below spurred her on.

"You're out of practice, Nyri!" Daajir shouted down, already halfway to the fruit. Determination tempered Nyri's indignation. Let him enjoy his lead while he could. She could see the path that would carry her to victory. It was risky. She had no doubt Daajir had seen it and had just as quickly decided against such a dare. But Nyri knew she could do it. Her agility was far superior to Daajir's.

Balancing carefully on a broader limb, she crouched and then jumped as high as she could, grabbing the branches above and pulling herself up, twisting and turning with reckless abandon, often catching a branch only at the very last moment. She knew if her timing was off by the merest fraction, she would tumble to the ground beckoning far below.

Her timing was never out, and soon she was even with Daajir, revelling in his consternation.

"Careful, Nyriaana!" Kyaati admonished from below, her concern thick in the air. "It's not life and death, you know!"

Huh. Maybe not in the way Kyaati was thinking. Nyri, however, could never live with Daajir's smugness if he won. With a last burst of effort, she pulled herself ahead and grabbed the first of the golden fruits.

She grinned in triumph at Daajir as he caught up. "Out of practice? Not a chance."

Disgruntled, he pulled himself up beside her. He hated losing as much as she did. They were both too proud for their own good.

"Well, now it's decided that Nyriaana is still the greatest climber that ever lived," Kyaati called. "How about throwing some of that fruit down here?"

The children had gathered around her and were waiting eagerly. Omaal, knowing he could not play the pending game, wandered off a little way and distracted himself with a young maamit sitting in the low branches. With his charge occupied, Batai curled up at the base of a tree and closed his eyes.

"Catch!" Daajir pulled a second fruit from the tree and tossed it into the air. Squealing, the children ran about, snatching up the falling fruit in their arms. Daajir laughed along with them. Nyri's heart swelled at the sight of his carefree face. She had almost forgotten what Daajir's smile looked like. It contented her to see her friend and cousin behaving how he used to when they were children. He constantly acted as if their People's survival and way of life rested squarely upon his shoulders alone. Such priggish self-righteousness made it hard for Nyri to be around him much of the time.

The game lasted until all the fruit was collected and safely stored. Nyri climbed back to the earth with Daajir, breathless and happy. They saw the bulging baskets, and their smiles widened. Nyri was hard pressed to imagine a more pleasant sight.

Daajir turned his gaze towards Ninmah, shielding his eyes against the rays breaking through the rippling canopy as he judged their angle. "We should be getting back now."

There were a few groans of protest from the children, but Nyri could tell they did not really mean it. The Gathering had worn them out.

Making sure no fruit had been missed; Nyri hoisted her two heavy baskets onto her shoulders. Daajir plucked Kyaati's from her hands and carried it off before she could argue. Her mouth opened and closed in silent protest. Nyri hid a smile as the children skipped ahead, eager for home.

She followed slowly in their wake. She was feeling so unusually happy and content out here in the groves. She had not expected to find such solace on the Gathering, and she found herself wanting to prolong the feeling for as long as she could.

Daajir would never agree to let her stay out here alone so far from the tribe, but perhaps she could slip his notice. Nyri glanced ahead. Daajir and Kyaati were conversing animatedly. She suppressed another smile and dropped behind further still. Within moments, her companions were lost in the trees; they had not noticed her absence.

Daajir would be furious when he discovered she had strayed alone, but Nyri quieted her guilt at causing him stress with the promise that she would not be long. The forest was peaceful. She could not detect the barest shiver of a disturbance. A few moments of freedom would do no harm.

Strolling now with no particular destination in mind, Nyri allowed herself to bask in the glory of her surroundings. The forest pulsed all around, alive and vibrant. A fallen tree, bathed in a pool of Ninmah's light, beckoned her. She sat gratefully, removing the two heavy baskets from her aching shoulders. Placing her palms against the tree's soft, mossy covering, she tilted her head back and closed her eyes.

For a stolen moment, she thought of nothing but the warmth on her face; the breeze brushing her cheeks and the moss under her fingertips. The trees sang amongst themselves, creating a soft backdrop to a bird's sweet music somewhere far above.

What bird?

Nyri's eyes jolted open as her fingers curled in agony. She had remembered his voice so clearly in that moment that it startled her, and she looked around in hope before she could prevent it. She screwed her eyes tight shut, berating herself for such foolishness. *Did you really expect to see him standing there?* But the sound of that song had torn back the seasons until Nyri was almost a child again, sitting high in a tree, playing a game with her best friend. A time of happiness and almost innocence.

And as quickly as that, her moment of happiness fled.

She wrapped her arms against her chest in an attempt to protect herself from the onslaught of sorrow and yearning. *Shut up!* She thought at the bird and his suddenly annoying song. It was a relief when he flew away, taking his haunting music with him. Nyri sighed, balling her fists in frustration. She wondered if she would ever get over this loss. The ghost of his presence never seemed to leave her, ready to strike at the slightest provocation. *I wish I could have saved you... It was my fault.*

It was time to go back. She really was being foolish staying out alone like this. Straying from home was the reason her life had fallen apart in the first place. She reached down to pluck the food-stuffed baskets from the ground.

A low whine caused her to pause. Nyri lifted her head to see Batai ghosting through the trees. The wolf was alone. The sight made her heart flutter. Daajir and Kyaati must have already made it home and returned Omaal to his parents, freeing the wolf to go hunting. She had been gone longer than she thought. Daajir would be *furious*.

But even as she scolded herself for losing her sense of time, Nyri paused, a frown cutting between her brows. Daajir and Kyaati's energies were still on the edge of her outer awareness. They were nowhere near home yet. Her frown deepened. Batai was not focused on hunting or finding his pack. As the wolf drew closer, sniffing the ground, waves of distress came rolling from him. His frantic energy was like a slap to the face.

He had lost Omaal.

Nyri was on her feet before she was conscious of moving. Hot and cold all at once, she struggled to remember the last time she had seen the boy. With a sharp gasp, she realised she had not laid eyes on him since she and Daajir had been in the tree throwing fruit. Amid all the high spirits and laughter, Nyri had not given the child a second thought. Now he was gone.

If anything had happened to the boy, she would never forgive herself.

Batai's whines of distress became more acute. Reaching out with her own senses, Nyri moved to Batai's side. "Where is he, Batai? Find him, quick—!"

Her words cut off as the quiet of the forest was shattered by the bloodcurdling scream of a child.

It was already too late.

4

Predator

"Daajir! Kyaati!" Nyri screamed, throwing her distress to the air for anyone to hear. She knew she should wait. It was stupid to run into danger alone, but there was no time. Nyri abandoned her baskets to the undergrowth and ran. The child's scream had come from the east. From the Pits. If the child had fallen, then he was surely dead.

Frantically, Nyri searched the energies ahead. No, she could feel him. The boy was still alive, but he was in mortal danger. His panic jabbed like thorns against Nyri's senses.

"I'm coming, Omaal!" She threw the promise out in both voice and soul. "Hang on!"

She pushed herself to move faster, but as she did so, something else grazed across her hypersensitive awareness. A sinister presence lurking just on the edge… Nyri concentrated harder. Her heart, already elevated with terror for the boy, thudded wildly in panic as she understood.

No!

She would never be fast enough. Nyri was made for

climbing, not running. This flight was a fruitless effort. Even if the child could be spared from the Pits, something altogether more deadly would take him, regardless of her presence. Attracted by the child's cries of distress, Nyri could feel the single-minded focus of a predator zeroing in on its prey.

A blur of dark fur streaked past her, reminding Nyri that she was not alone. Sprinting through the trees, she ignored the growing burn in her lungs until at last she saw him. Only Omaal's head and arms protruded from the edge of a Pit. His small hands scrambled desperately at anything he could reach, trying to save himself from the maw beckoning below.

"Help me! Somebody!" Omaal sobbed. "Help!"

Nyri was close.

Closer still was the cat.

There she lurked, shoulders rocking, readying for the spring. A monstrous predator. Never had Nyri seen such a Child of the Great Spirit with her own eyes, only shivered at the tales. *Grishnaa*, they had named it. Her stride faltered at the sight. Thick set and armed with razor claws. Two long, blade-like teeth curved down past her white chin. It was surely the same beast that had killed Omaal's own grandfather.

"Omaal!" she cried.

Too late. With a snarl, the cat burst forth; ripping claws seeking the child in her sights. They slashed out, cutting into the boy's shoulders, and Omaal's cry split the air.

"Batai!" Nyri screamed.

Snarling furiously, the wolf barrelled into the cat just a second too late. With no apparent thought for his own safety and with Omaal's screams of shock and panic spurring him on, Batai attacked the monster head on, a beast half again his own size and bulk. His bone-crushing fangs were bared and agape. The hairs on Nyri's arms rose at the sight of his grisly expression.

The force of Batai's charge knocked the unprepared feline off her feet and into the air, away from the stricken child. Without thinking, Nyri raced to the edge of the Pit behind the wolf, catching hold of Omaal's arms just as the boy toppled back into the space below. He squealed as her effort to drag him up pulled on his slashed and bloodied shoulders. Nyri lifted him away from the edge as Batai faced down their quarry.

The wolf's body blow had taken the cat unawares, but with surprising agility, she had twisted and landed firmly on her paws. Now she crouched, spitting and assessing. Her eyes flickered to Nyri, then back to Batai. Easy prey and only one forest wolf to challenge her. With no pack to support Batai, she judged the confrontation to be in her favour. She coiled, ready to fight for her prize.

Desperate, Nyri tried to reach out to her, but the cat was too focused. She had no room or care for Nyri in her thoughts or soul. She did not know or understand. The Great Spirit within drove her to do what he had created her for, to weed out the weak and the sickly. She would fight to the death to survive.

The standoff broke with a vicious snarl, and the cat struck out at Batai with her forepaws, slashing and ripping. The wolf's thick fur offered only a little protection to those hooked claws. Nyri paled at the sight of the long fangs reaching down past the cat's snarling lips. If she got a hold on Batai with those, it would be over.

Nyri could not help him. She quickly assessed Omaal. His shoulders were bleeding, the muscles and sinew exposed to the air.

Curling over the injured boy, Nyri offered what little protection she could while they waited for their fate to be decided. Climbing into a tree with Omaal as a burden was out of the question. And if she ran, the feline would give chase. Batai would not be able to stop her. Nyri's only option was to hold her ground and pray.

Batai dodged the cat's slashing claws with difficulty. She was lightening quick. The wolf had to get the cat in his teeth to have any hope of winning the fight. Disregarding the danger, Batai lunged forward, forcing close quarters, bearing the cat to the ground, biting, snapping, snarling, seeking the death hold. Fur flew into the air. Over and over, the two deadly predators rolled, ripping and clawing at each other. Pulling Omaal tight, Nyri closed her eyes against the savagery. She did not want to watch. She held the screaming, bleeding child as still as possible.

A sickening crack cut off a mewling screech. Then silence. Shaking from head to foot, Nyri did not dare raise her head. Death or survival awaited.

She flinched and bit back a cry as something caught at her arm. A soft growl quieted her. Batai. Nyri forced her eyes open. The wolf was lying on his brisket at their sides, his muzzle slashed and stained. Nyri could feel the warm wetness of blood on her arm where he had nudged it. Numbly, she shifted the arm out of his way and the wolf snuffled at the distressed boy on the ground.

"Batai." Omaal flung his arms around the wolf's neck and cried himself out into the matted fur.

Nyri made the mistake of glancing past their saviour and flinched as she met sightless yellow eyes staring straight back at her from across the forest floor. The cat's neck was crushed and broken. She tore her gaze away, but her flesh crawled at the proximity of death. She wanted to leave.

"Nyri! *Nyriaana!*"

Nyri started at the sound of Daajir's frantic voice. He came sprinting through the trees, his face covered in sweat. She did not know how far he had needed to run to answer her call of distress. "What *happened?*"

Nyri staggered to her feet. Her muscles felt weak and cramped. As she struggled to gather herself, only one thought stood out in her mind. Omaal. He needed help. She could not let the shock of what had happened take hold. She had a duty. "Dar, we have to get Omaal back to Baarias, quickly! Help me with him."

"What's wrong with him?" Daajir shot forward, assessing the boy's condition. He caught sight of the open gashes. "Ninmah's mercy! You little fool! What did you think you were doing? You could have been killed!"

Nyri grabbed Daajir's arm. "Daajir, stop! He did not know. Batai got here in time."

"Do not make excuses for him!" Daajir's temper flared like wildfire as he shook her hand away. He rounded on Omaal again. "He is one of the strongest. His parents were carefully selected. He's too precious to us and to our survival to be lost in one act of carelessness."

Omaal's cries intensified. A low rumble of warning was emitting from Batai's throat.

"Daajir!"

"And where were *you?*" He now unleashed the full force

of his anger upon her. "I turned around, and you were gone. You're just as bad as the child! We could have lost both of you! Did you even stop to think about what that would do to our People? Has it escaped your attention that our entire race is dying out!"

His words struck Nyri and hung brutally on the air.

"Of course it hasn't," she said in an expressionless tone. "I have to face that truth every day, just like you, Daajir. During my every waking moment, I face it." She pointed at Omaal. "And you take your frustrations out on him? A boy who should not even be away from the protection of the *eshaara* grove but has been forced too far too soon through no fault of his own." Nyri turned her back on Daajir without waiting for a response. She was in no mood to fight. "I'm taking Omaal to Baarias, he needs his wounds treating."

"Nyri, I'm..." Her words had doused his anger, but the damage was done.

"I have to go." She cut him off. "If I don't get him to Baarias, these wounds will fester." Nyri could not bring herself to even look at him. She had suffered enough of his temper tantrums during their lives together. This was one too many.

"I will see you back home first," Daajir muttered gruffly.

Sighing, Nyri stooped to lift the wounded boy under the armpits. "Come on, Omaal. Let me get you some help."

Though he must have been in pain, Batai pictured what was needed. He got to his feet and then stooped, offering Nyri his broad back. Grateful, she helped little Omaal climb into place behind his shoulders. Daajir walked along behind them as they set off. Nyri ignored him.

"You need some attention, too, young wolf," she spoke as they travelled, scratching his ears. "Thank you for saving our lives." She translated her human feeling of gratitude to him in a way he would understand. He swiped her arm with his tongue, showing he understood.

Omaal whimpered at every motion.

"Shh, shh," Nyri soothed him awkwardly. "We'll get you to Baarias. You're safe now. You are safe."

The words were as much for her own benefit as they were for Omaal. She tried to stop her hands from shaking and failed. She was struggling against the shock, starting badly at every little sound. They had just felt the hot breath of death across their necks. Much as Nyri hated him right now, Daajir was right. They had come close to losing two members of their tribe today. A loss her people could ill-afford.

Never had a *grishnaa* come so close to their home. Nyri tightened her hold on Batai, seeking strength she did not feel and could not help but ask herself what tomorrow would bring.

She lifted her eyes towards a break in the rippling canopy, desperate for reassurance. Ninmah gave none. She simply turned Her face behind a veil and left Nyri in shadow.

5

Healer

When the *eshaara* trees of home finally reached out to surround them like a protective cocoon, Daajir came up alongside Nyri, and tried to get her attention. "Nyriaana."

She wasn't ready to forgive him and turned her shoulder. "Just... find Omaal's parents, Daajir. We're safe now, you can go."

It surprised her when he heeded her dismissal and moved away from her side. But, despite his repentant demeanour, Nyri knew he would report her behaviour to his precious Elders before he attempted to find Umaa or Imaani. She snorted.

Baarias' dwelling was at the very centre of the *eshaara* grove. He had chosen the tree specifically for its location and for the network of chambers that made up its trunk. Unusually for a Ninkuraaja dwelling, most of the chambers could be accessed at ground level. As the tribe's master *akaab*, this feature was essential for Baarias. He could not expect the badly injured or sick to climb very far for treatment.

"My teacher," Nyri called over Omaal's whimpering as she walked inside the tree. "I need you!"

"Not for long, I suspect," a soft voice spoke behind her. "My dear Nyriaana."

Nyri let out the breath she hadn't realised she had been holding. Baarias' assured presence had always possessed the power to steady her through anything. Just the sound of his gentle tone made it easier for Nyri to focus her mind and close out all else.

"Omaal was attacked." All business now, she pulled the boy from his wolf's back and laid him on his side upon a waiting bower of cotton moss. Omaal flinched and cried as the motion disturbed his wounds. "A *grishnaa* cat like the one who killed Chaard. Its claws wounded him before Batai could get there."

"Let me see," Baarias came forward, carrying his healer's staff, the herbs he used in his work swaying from the tip. Silver-white hair fell past his brow as his forehead creased, disrupting the Marks of the master *akaab,* the tribal healer, second only in respect behind the Elders and Sefaan herself.

Baarias' features were careworn; the lines of countless sorrows made him appear older than he was. His pale lilac eyes, however, were intense as he took in his patient's injuries. The prominent scar that slashed across his ageing jawline tightened as his lips pressed together, and he tutted. "Five deep gashes across the shoulders. You're a lucky boy, Omaal."

"Batai s-saved me," the boy hiccoughed.

"Of course he did," Baarias soothed. "He's a brave one. Just like you."

The boy gave him a weak smile, sightlessly staring towards

the sound of Baarias' voice. Baarias sighed and touched Nyri's arm, focusing his thoughts upon her. *Yet another sad victim of our folly.*

Our *folly?* The only folly had been her own in not watching the boy.

Just like Sefaan, Baarias was given to making these cryptic comments. If the two did not antagonise one another so much, Nyri might believe that they collaborated behind her back to cause her as much frustration as possible.

Baarias' only answer was a shake of his head. "Never mind. Come, my *akaabi,* let's get to work." He paused, taking in Nyri's pale face. "Unless you need to rest? You are not hurt, are you?"

"No." She shook her head. "Let me stay, Baarias. Please. I'm not hurt." If Baarias sent her to rest, she would only dwell on what had just happened.

Baarias scrutinised her face for one moment longer, then turned to the wounded boy and stood, waiting silently for Nyri to join him. Relieved and grateful for his acceptance, Nyri surmised she was old enough now for Baarias to respect her choices. She moved to stand beside Omaal's head. The boy's eyes were glazed with pain, and his breath came in quick gasps.

"It's all right, young one." Baarias soothed. "We'll get you put right. Nyri, ease his discomfort while I examine the injury."

Obediently, Nyri crouched and placed her hands against the boy's temples. She watched as her teacher chose a few select herbs from the bunches hanging from his staff and crushed them into a collecting bowl formed of one half of a *haala* nutshell. Drawing water from a clinging *aquilem* vine,

Baarias made a paste and smeared the sticky substance onto the boy's wounds to purify the area. Omaal flinched and cried as the mixture stung his exposed flesh.

Breathing deep, Nyri followed the precise steps that Baarias had taught her, focusing first on her own body and closing out any external distractions. Concentrating, she stretched her energy inward, becoming acutely aware of her own heartbeat, the flow of blood in her veins, the zing of messages being sent to her brain from every part of her body, the perfect balance of Ninmah's creation.

As soon as she was completely attuned, Nyri carried her awareness down to her fingers where they touched Omaal's head. She could feel the warmth of his skin, slick with sweat, and the pulse of his blood next to hers. She gathered her life's energy in her fingertips and pushed outward until it merged with the boy's. They became one.

Pain lashed against Nyri's senses. With a practised effort, she blocked it out and focused solely on what she needed to do, shifting her attention to the injuries. Omaal's nerve receptors were like blue fire in Nyri's mind's eye, thrumming their fierce warning. *Stop.* She formed a cocoon around them, blocking the impulses, soothing them like a balm. Omaal sighed with relief. His breathing became more even. His body uncoiled. Good. Nyri moved to the next task.

Baarias' work would be easier if the boy was completely still. *Sleep.* She pushed the word and the essence behind it into his mind, visualising him recumbent, out of pain and dreaming of warmer days playing with Batai. The words were pure habit, helping Nyri to form the image of what she needed to achieve. Using her connection to the boy, she sent his body the sense of deep exhaustion. It wasn't difficult. He was almost there on his own. His body bent to her will, and Omaal fell into peaceful oblivion. His breathing deepened.

"Well done." Nyri heard Baarias mutter from a great distance. "My turn. Watch carefully."

She knew better than to open her eyes. That was not what her teacher had meant. Nyri's awareness was extended further still as Baarias linked his life force to theirs. She felt his power gather in the boy's wounded shoulders. The healer encouraged more blood to flow to the area, willing it to condense and form clots, knitting the rent tissues together, sealing the wounds. He used his energy to speed up the body's natural processes. When Baarias was finished, Omaal would only have five faint scars to show for his ordeal.

Nyri watched with pride and admiration as her mentor worked. His skill and precision never ceased to amaze her. She only hoped that one day she could be half as talented. The task was complete before she knew it.

Nyri withdrew her awareness and blinked her eyes open. The dim light of the healing chamber now seemed over-bright. She focused on the twisting reddish walls and the drying herbs hanging from them as her eyes adjusted.

There came a low whine from the corner of the dwelling. She'd almost forgotten about Batai. The wolf looked in worse shape than she remembered now that she knew Omaal was safe. Nyri went over to where the bloodied Son of the Great Spirit lay and put a hand in his warm fur. "Baarias, we need to tend to Batai now."

Baarias laid a hand on her shoulder. *You don't need me. You have all the skills and knowledge you need to heal Batai yourself. You have learned your lessons well, my* akaabi. *It's almost time for me to complete this.* He brushed the half finished *akaab*

65

mark on Nyri's forehead. *Ninmah herself would be proud.*

Nyri beamed up at him and touched his hand in thanks as he left the chamber. Another step taken.

Batai gave a long-suffering sigh as Baarias disappeared, eyeing Nyri warily as she squatted in beside him.

"Hey," she said, mildly insulted by the look in the wolf's eye. "We can't all have the master *akaab*. I've got to practice, you know. Now, hold still or I might attach things to the wrong place."

Wall-eyed, Batai licked his lips anxiously. Nyri smiled to herself as the wolf lay flat out and did as she asked.

Working slowly but carefully, Nyri focused her entire attention on the task, directing energy from the Great Spirit. Baarias made it look so easy, so effortless. She had to remember every blood vessel and how to seal the skin in precisely the right way. The level of attention and knowledge that was required was staggering. It had taken long seasons of careful teaching before Baarias had even let her near her first wound. Nyri had chafed at his restrictions, but now she had a healthy respect of the need for such patience. Sweat dripped from her brow. The task required no small amount of power.

Concentrating, she knitted the torn tissues back together, bit by bit, layer by layer, mindful to not miss any stage that would cause further problems later on.

At long last, Nyri was finished, and the wolf leapt impatiently to his feet. He was hungry. He shook out his ragged fur, sniffed at the still sleeping Omaal to assure himself of the boy's well-being, then ran out into the lengthening shadows, off to find the rest of the pack and whatever scraps he could scrounge from the day's hunt.

Nyri rose and stretched, wincing as the blood jabbed like thorns inside her numbed legs. She was exhausted, but was still not quite ready to seek her own space. She settled beside Omaal, watching the boy sleep as she fought to keep her own eyes open. His parents should be here soon, Daajir would bring them.

"Nyri?"

Nyri glanced up at the sound of Kyaati's voice. Her friend had been hovering in the entranceway but moved quickly inside at Nyri's bleary acknowledgement. Kyaati appeared as worn as Nyri felt as she lowered herself heavily to the ground, studying Nyri's face.

"You look like you've been dragged through a tree backwards." Kyaati attempted to smooth Nyri's tangled hair and remove some of the dirt that Nyri hadn't even known was smeared upon her skin.

She caught Kyaati's hand, stilling it and drawing it away from her face. She had let no one fuss over her in such a way since… Nyri halted the thought in its tracks and smiled gently at her friend, softening the rejection. Kyaati had always tried to treat her like the little sister she had never had. This touched Nyri, even if she could never accept it. It would hurt too much to let anyone else get so close.

"Where did you go?" Kyaati asked, taking her hand back. "We turned around to talk to you, but you had disappeared. Dar nearly had a fit. Then we heard you scream. Daajir sent us all running for the tribe. Then he went back for you himself. You scared me, Nyriaana. What in Ninmah's name were you thinking, wandering off alone like that? What happened?" She made it clear she would not move until she had answers.

Nyri sighed. She did not want to relive her brush with death, but she knew better than to resist. Her friend would only stress further if she wasn't forthcoming.

"Omaal nearly fell into a Pit. There was a *grishnaa* cat. She wounded Omaal but Batai fought her off and saved us. She's dead now." Nyri suppressed a shudder and her sorrow at the loss of life. Sometimes KI could be a hard master.

Kyaati put her hands over her belly in a protective motion. "A *grishnaa?*" she whispered, horrified. "Here? So close to the tribe?"

"She's dead now," Nyri repeated dully.

Kyaati nodded as her hands continued to rub. "I saw Daajir briefly," she said, looking for a topic of distraction, which was fine by Nyri. "He seemed upset…"

Nyri grimaced. That was putting it mildly. She considered covering the truth to save trouble, but Kyaati would know if she lied. "When Dar found us, he got… *upset* with Omaal and then with me for defending him. He was furious. He was scaring Omaal with his temper." Nyri picked up Kyaati's wrist and replayed the scene for her. She didn't have the energy to explain with words.

A feeble voice interrupted them. "Am I in t-trouble?"

Omaal's eyes blinked open. He was still sleepy, but Nyri could feel a growing undercurrent of anxiety. "Daajir was mad at me. I was only playing. And t-then, and then…"

Kyaati reached out to brush his cheek. "Shhh. No, little one, no one is mad at you. You be a good boy now and rest. We'll watch over you until your mama and papa get here."

The boy clutched at her hand and drifted again. They waited until he fell back to sleep before Kyaati grabbed Nyri by the wrist. *Wait until I get my hands on him!*

Nyri sighed. She didn't want any more fighting. *Save your breath. Daajir is Daajir. It's too late for him to change. He takes our situation hard.* As if that wasn't true for all of them. Nyri changed the subject. She was focusing overmuch on what had passed. Her hands were shaking again, so she clenched her fists. She could not let herself succumb to the shock. *And anyway, I don't think he'd mind you getting your hands on him.*

Nyri thought back to before the attack and the appreciative look in Daajir's eyes as he and Kyaati had walked together. Kyaati was very beautiful. The lavender shade of her large eyes was the envy of all tribeswomen. Her hair was a shocking waterfall of a now rare silver, offsetting her red-gold skin.

Not that any of that mattered. Kyaati's most seductive feature in attracting a mate was her strength. The essence of the Great Spirit flowed true within her soul. She also bore no defects. It couldn't have escaped Daajir's notice that Kyaati was now unJoined. Nyri's certainty hardened. *In fact, I think he'd like it rather a lot if you got your hands on him.*

Nyri received the mental equivalent of a pinch.

"Ow!"

Don't even think it. After I lost Yaanth, I swore I would never take another mate. No matter what happens. Kyaati stroked her swollen belly, a look of eternal sadness and loss shadowing her face.

Maybe this hadn't been the best subject to have started after all. Nyri, however, frowned. *Even if the Elders decide it's a suitable match? How could you refuse? You are strong, Kya. Ninmah blessed you with a powerful Gift, as She did Daajir. They would have Joined you to him before if you hadn't gone off with Yaanth and had Sefaan Join you in secret. Now that Yaanth is... gone, it might be a match they feel they cannot afford to pass up.*

Kyaati stiffened, and Nyri felt her anxiety spike. *My father would never do that to me.*

Kyaati's father, Nyri's own father's brother, was an Elder. Pelaan loved his daughter dearly, but Nyri doubted Kyaati's wishes in this matter would sway him from a powerful match to ensure the survival of their people. He had been furious when Kyaati had gone behind his back and Joined with Yaanth, whom he had seen as far beneath her potential. Kyaati was his only surviving child and his only chance to pass on his progeny to future generations. Nyri believed Pelaan would do anything to achieve that goal. Even Join his daughter against her wishes.

Nyri prayed nothing went wrong with Kyaati's pregnancy. If she bore a healthy living child, then maybe she would be freed of this obligation. Maybe.

Kyaati's next thought startled her. *And what if the Elders decide you should be Joined?*

Nyri's thoughts scattered. *What?*

Oh, come, Nyriaana! You think I am strong? I am only half of what you are. You're possibly the strongest female in the tribe besides Sefaan, with an aptitude for healing, too. Ninmah has indeed favoured you. Did you honestly think Baarias chose you as his akaabi *just because he felt sorry for you? Do not be so naïve. You were the only one with the potential to learn his work.*

Nyri did not answer. She stared ahead, a dreadful anxiety quickening in her stomach with Kyaati's every word.

And don't tell me it has also escaped your notice that you have now reached childbearing age. Kyaati continued. *It has not escaped others' attention, believe me. Daajir has never yet been Joined. The strongest male. Isn't that strange? They are waiting for one worthy enough.* You *are certainly more than worthy.*

But, but... we barely made it as friends, Nyri argued. *How could we possibly be Joined?*

Kyaati snorted. *I don't think that would be taken into consideration.*

What about Raanya, Nyri thought desperately, clutching at anything she could think of. *She is unJoined and older than I.*

Raanya is not meant for Daajir. She is not that strong. You have been spared so far because Baarias took you under his wing and you needed to learn his art without distraction. But his teaching of you is nearly complete. It may well be time for you to fulfil your ultimate obligation to our people—securing our future, if you can.

Nyri blanched. This was one worry that had never crossed her unsuspecting mind. The *grishnaa* now seemed a small threat by comparison. Why had she never considered this possibility? And who was there other than Daajir? He was certainly the best choice for strong children. She had known him her entire life, but she could not imagine being Joined to him as his mate.

Nyri shuddered. They might have moved beyond mere kin and become friends, but there were still parts of his soul that turned hers to ice and those parts of him were growing in dominance the more desperate their situation became. His reaction to Omaal was just one example. Sometimes Nyri felt she did not know him at all. Times when he seemed to be more fanatical than all the Elders put together. No. She could not bear the thought of being Joined to him in mind and soul.

What can we do?

I don't know, Kyaati thought sadly. *All I know is that we have enough to concern ourselves with at the moment.* She touched Omaal's forehead and shivered as an icy wind blew in from outside. *I have to concentrate on bringing this child into the world safely. My last connection to Yaanth. That is all there is for me.*

A fresh wave of fear for her friend nearly overwhelmed Nyri in that moment. There were times she could not comprehend how Kyaati was still standing. The words she had spoken to Daajir that morning were true. If their places were reversed, Nyri was not sure she would be. Too many babies and children had been Cast to the river. Their bodies given back to the Great Spirit before they even drew their first breath.

Kyaati had already Cast three.

* * *

6

Blessing

Baarias returned to his tree bearing the herbs he had gathered. Kyaati was just slipping out into the evening light. The young woman pressed a finger to her lips as she passed him and pointed back into the chamber beyond. Nyri had fallen into a doze next to the healed child. Baarias squeezed Kyaati's hand in acknowledgment.

His charge was exhausted from her ordeal. He winced at the sight of the position she had fallen into. It looked painfully awkward, and she would suffer for it later. The healer in him longed to wake her and send her back to her own tree where she would be more comfortable, but as her guardian and teacher, he knew she was not ready to be left alone. Her mind needed time to recover.

Keeping his tread soft, Baarias stooped down next to her and brushed a strand of dark hair away from her face. He resisted touching her cheek as his heart contracted. *So like Rebaa...*

"Omaal!"

The sound of Umaa's frantic voice startled Baarias, and

73

he took a hasty step back. Shaken from her doze, Nyri's dark indigo eyes flew open. Upon seeing Omaal's mother rushing into the tree, she rose to her feet. Her bowed head and flushed cheeks told Baarias all he needed to know: she blamed herself for the danger the child had been in. He pressed his lips together, promising himself he would speak with her later.

Imaani joined his mate at their son's side. Baarias took in their strikingly similar faces and resisted the urge to cast his eyes to Ninmah. Half brother and sister. But what did that small issue matter to the Elders when the strength of Imaani's and Umaa's Gift was so evenly matched?

He hid his feelings behind a serene smile as Umaa rushed to her son, hands fluttering over him as she asked: "Will he live?"

"Of course he will live, Umaa," Baarias assured. "He's just scratched and in shock but Nyriaana and I fixed him up like new. He's resting now." He emphasised Nyri's involvement in Omaal's recovery, hoping it would ease her misplaced feeling of guilt. Disappointment thudded through him when the praise had no effect, and her eyes remained downcast.

"Thank you," Umaa whispered to them both.

"Mama." Omaal blinked his blind eyes open.

"I'm here," Umaa comforted as Imaani leaned forward to better see his son.

"What were you doing so far from Batai?" Imaani scolded.

Omaal sniffed. "I was following a maamit. Batai was asleep, and I got bored. I didn't know I had gone so far," Omaal moaned. "I could see so high into the trees. I-I did not see the ground!"

Imaani's exasperation filled the tree. "What have I told

you about getting so lost in another creature's senses that you forget your own, foolish boy?"

A tear leaked from Omaal's sightless eyes. "I'm sorry, papa," he whimpered as Umaa hugged him tight, shushing comfortingly.

"I think a valuable lesson has been learned today." Baarias stepped in. He could understand Imaani's frustration with his son's actions, knowing how they had almost cost Omaal his life, but the boy did not need any further trauma if he was to recover. "Scold him no more, Imaani, he is just a boy. Take him home, let him rest. Come to me if anything changes."

Umaa rose to her feet and Imaani moved in to scoop his son from the nest of moss and leaves.

"Thank you, master *akaab*." Umaa's eyes were filled with tears as she came to stand before him and held up her hands. Baarias raised his own, meeting her gesture fingertip to fingertip, bowing his head so that she could rest her forehead against his in thanks. His heart lifted as her gratitude flowed through him. But as Umaa stepped away to follow the rest of her family outside, Baarias' smile dropped. He had helped so many in his life as a healer, but it would never be enough, never enough to heal his soul.

Dusk had fallen in the forest beyond, and it was getting harder to see inside. Nyri was moving about the walls, brushing the *girru* moss into life. It glowed beneath her slender fingers, seeking more of her warmth and attention. Its soft light filled the inside of the tree, the released spores dancing through the air.

Baarias knelt on the ground and began sorting the herbs he had gathered into bundles. Finishing with the moss,

Nyri came to kneel at his side. She did not speak. Only the sound of the dried herbs brushing together broke the stillness. Baarias observed her out of the corner of his eye. Her movements were as deft as ever, but her energy was far from peaceful. Anxiety hummed around her like a swarm of restless bees.

"What's troubling you, Nyriaana?"

Her hands twisted sharply around the herbs she was bundling. Irritation zinged on the air. It was clear that she had not wanted him to pry. He was so surprised by her reaction that he forgot to scold her for ruining his herbs. But as quickly as her anger had arisen, she let it out on a breath. Now she was... embarrassed.

Baarias was puzzled. What did she have to be embarrassed about? She had saved Omaal from certain death. "Are you sure you aren't hurt?" he prompted carefully, not wishing to rouse her strained temper again. "Maybe you should go home now and rest a while. You have been through a lot. A *grishnaa—*"

"No, Baarias." She cut him off with a shake of her head. "There were times I thought Omaal and I..."

He watched as she visibly shuddered. His hands twitched, wanting to reach out to her in comfort. His heart thudded as the thought struck that it had not only been Omaal who had escaped with his life today. He could have lost her—

"But that's not what troubles me!" Her voice broke into his thoughts. "It's..." She hesitated for a moment, then the words flowed out in a sudden rush. "Kyaati just made me face a reality I never considered before, but now she's spoken of it, I cannot think of anything else."

"What reality could be more disturbing than a *grishnaa*

76

attack?" His voice bubbled with an incredulous laugh.

"That I may have to be Joined soon!" Her dark eyes were wide with horror. "Joined and expected to bear children."

"Ah." Her words hit him in the gut. Anguish tore through him. Covering his tension, Baarias fussed over arranging his bundled herbs while gathering his thoughts. He had hoped they would not have to face this for many seasons to come. He studied his charge surreptitiously under his lashes.

How she had grown, and he had not even realised it. Before him sat a young woman, beautiful and capable. His heart swelled with bittersweet pride. No wonder Aardn had queried him about her readiness, wanting to know when her training as a healer would be complete. "Time has caught up with us indeed."

"So it's true then?" He heard her breath catch in her throat.

Baarias rubbed at his face, feeling the long scar at his jaw pull slightly. He wished he could have denied reality for her and staved off the tears that were springing to her eyes, but that would mean lying, and that was something he would never do.

"Yes, I'm afraid it is true. The Elders will soon wish to see you Joined. Rest assured that I," his voice hardened, "do not."

"You don't?" The vehemence in his tone surprised her.

"No, I do not." He would not wish such a fate on his worst enemy, much less upon the girl he regarded as no less than his own daughter. "I have tried to protect you from this for as long as it has been in my power. Right from when you were that lost little girl I swept up onto a stag all those years ago. Your strength and potential shone out even then, and when I looked down into your broken little face, I knew I could not allow the Elders to use you in their misguided plans. I'm ashamed to say, I have played out your teaching for far longer than I should. You were ready to ascend long before now. For that I ask your forgiveness."

He saw her sit back in surprise at these words. *Oh, Nyriaana,* he thought, *how little you think of yourself.* He felt a pang of guilt knowing that, in holding her back, he might bear some responsibility for her doubt in herself.

Her face, however, was already soft with forgiveness. "And now?" she asked.

"I will try to keep you at my side for as long as I am able, if that is what you wish?"

He had failed to protect Rebaa when she had needed him the most. His sister's wasted face, frozen in death, would haunt him for the rest of his life. He would *not* fail Nyriaana, too. He did not care if the Elders did to him what they had done to Sefaan; diminishing the tribe's respect for him until they doubted every word for the ramblings of a madman.

If she was Joined, then she would face only death and misery, same as Kyaati. Dead baby followed by dead baby. Her tender heart would fail. Baarias closed his eyes so that she could not see the anguish in them. He realised his own hands had now crushed the herbs he still held.

"I know you will do everything you can for me." Her gentle voice broke through his turmoil. "You always have. But even you cannot challenge the Elders' will. It will be done."

Over my dead body.

She stared at him in open desperation. "Baarias, I am not ready for this."

Baarias banished his own agony with an effort and placed a steadying hand on her shoulder. She needed his strength now. "I know. We are seldom ready for what fate throws into our path, Nyriaana. All we can do is to be strong, weather the consequences, and hope that whatever power is out there sends us a miracle."

"Or Ariyaana." Nyri laughed humourlessly, but did not elaborate on what she meant. "I do not believe in miracles."

"Maybe not, but try to remember, as your beloved mother once said, the future isn't certain and we can only do what is within our power in the present moment. It is a waste of energy to worry about things that may not be."

At that moment, the summoning horn sounded from outside. Baarias pulled himself reluctantly to his feet. "We'd better get to the auscult. Time to see what the Gathering has brought in." He offered Nyri his hand. She took it and he helped her to her feet. Together, they walked out into the evening light, following the others as they all made their way to the clearing where the Elders were waiting by the standing stone. Ninmah hung low behind them.

The tribe was placing its earlier harvest next to where the Elders stood, before moving to sit upon the scattered tree roots and stones forming the meeting circle.

Baarias felt a wave of guilt roll out from beside him.

"What's wrong?" Baarias asked, glancing down at Nyri. She was staring at the piles of food, chewing her lip. She had never been very good at hiding her emotions.

"I-I had two gathering baskets," she muttered. "I-I must have dropped them when I heard Omaal scream. They were full of forage."

Baarias patted her shoulder. "You did what you had to. Take Daajir and go back for them at first light. I'm sure most of what you gathered will still be there."

She squeezed his hand.

Everyone sat murmuring amongst themselves as they waited for the Elders to begin the evening's proceedings. The tribe came to this place at the end of every Gathering as Ninmah diminished but before Ninsiku rose in the heavens to look down on them with his ever blinking silver eye. It was a time for stories to be told, wisdom to be shared, or important announcements to be made. The Elders looked pleased with the results of the earlier labours.

"That is the best sight I have seen in a long time," Kyaati said as she appeared at their sides. She was looking to the centre where the Elders were combing through the food, judging how best it should be divided and stored for leaner times. It did not appear that anyone would go hungry for a while. The coming Fury looked just that much more bearable.

"Where is Daajir?" Nyri asked.

"He volunteered for sentry duty tonight." Kyaati answered. "He's keeping watch near the Pits."

Baarias was secretly glad of the boy's absence. He knew Aardn had plans for him. Plans that revolved around his Nyriaana. His heart burned at the very thought.

A radiant presence glowed against his senses, and Baarias lifted his gaze in time to see Sefaan approaching. The Kamaali's energy was light, happy, but Baarias stiffened at the sight of her.

"Kyaati," Sefaan spoke, ignoring both he and Nyriaana as she lowered herself gingerly into a sitting position. It did not escape his notice that she had positioned herself on the opposite side of Nyriaana. As far away from him as she could get and still be a part of the group.

The Kamaali winced as her bones protested.

80

"I can give you something to help with that," Baarias murmured before he could stop himself. The last thing he wanted was to draw Sefaan's attention to him, but he couldn't bear to see anyone in discomfort, knowing he could help.

Her response was exactly as he expected. "If I wanted your help, young man, I would ask for it." Her voice was caustic. "As much good as it would do me—"

"Sefaan," Baarias warned, his own voice cooling in response to her bite. "I do not wish to hear it. Let the spirits rest." Why couldn't she leave it be? He could torture himself enough without her continued reminder of a mistake he could not change. He could not bring Rebaa back. No matter how much he might want to.

The thought of his ill-fated sister made his stomach turn, and he twisted his shoulders so he could hide from Sefaan's accusing stare.

"What's going on?" Nyri's confusion filled the air. She had never understood the hard feelings that existed between the Kamaali and himself, and Baarias did not have the heart to tell her. She would turn her back on him if ever she found out the truth, and that was something he could not bear. "Sefaan, why won't you let Baarias help you?"

"It is none of your concern, child." Sefaan told her in a firm tone. "As your teacher said, let the spirits rest. His own inner demons are punishment enough. It wasn't either of you I came to see, anyway."

Nyri flushed at Sefaan's blunt dismissal, and Baarias felt her questioning gaze come to rest upon his back, searching for answers. For once, he did not enlighten her.

"I've made these." Sefaan's energy was light once again as

she addressed Kyaati. "For the baby. I thought you might like them." Out of the corner of his eye, Baarias watched as she handed a curious Kyaati a leaf-wrapped bundle. "Take it, take it."

Baarias watched as the girl unwrapped miniature items of clothing, including coverings for the baby and the warmest blanket that Sefaan could weave. At the very centre was a small toy made of leaves wrapped in the shape of a hare. A red feather draped from one of its long ears. Nyriaana's bright presence glowed at the sight of it.

Kyaati's eyes were sparkling with unshed tears. She hugged the gifts to her chest. "Thank you, most sacred Kamaali," she whispered in a hushed tone. "I'm sure she will love them." For the first time, Kyaati did not speak of her baby with fear or anxiety. She was simply happy.

Baarias pressed his lips together, probing the energies around Kyaati's pregnant belly. He could not sense that anything was amiss yet. Only time would tell if this babe was meant to survive. He hoped with all his heart that it would, for Kyaati's sake.

"She?" Nyriaana raised an eyebrow. Kyaati nodded, and Nyri's smile broadened until it split her face in two. Baarias read the hope upon their faces; the same hope that would bloom through the entire tribe upon learning this secret. The promise of a female child could mean the next Kamaali had come at last, staving off the End of Days for another generation. All eyes would search the *eshaara* trees, eagerly awaiting the falling of a seed. Sefaan glowed. She placed a hand on Kyaati's head in solemn benediction.

"May KI give you strength and keep you both safe."

Kyaati beamed as she bowed her head respectfully beneath

Sefaan's touch. Baarias had not seen her so happy and carefree in a long time.

Aardn signalled for silence. The auscult was about to begin.

* * *

7

Auscult

"Great People!" Aardn's voice broke over the soft buzz of chatter as Nyri looked up. "We have been blessed by Ninmah with a plentiful Gathering. We will not know hunger this night, nor for many nights to come. It fills my heart with gladness to see renewed hope in your eyes." She glanced at Kyaati for a moment. "Together we will share in this good fortune as we did in the days of old. We have suffered much hardship, we few, but we have endured. By holding true to our ways, we will live until the Blessed times come again and those that seek to unbalance Ninmah and bring the accursed Ninsiku to power have perished into dust." She gazed around at their faces with pride. "Our youngest members have not yet heard the story of our beginnings, but I believe now they are old enough to hear and understand."

Nyri watched as all the children present leaned forward in eager anticipation. Omaal was not among their number, she noted. He must still be resting. He would not be happy about missing out.

"We are the people of the forest," Aardn began. "Our ancestors taught us we were born of the trees. It began when Ninmah, the Most Sacred, came down from the sky in a ball of light in the company of Her heavenly brethren. They each looked upon the world and decided they needed a People to serve them. None of these Sky Gods could agree upon a single form, however, and so to accomplish their task, Ninmah and Her kin went their separate ways, each with an idea of what their People should be.

"Ninmah was by far the greatest and the wisest, a healer and a lover of all things beautiful. She travelled into the forests and imagined beings who would learn from this world's many secrets. A People who could watch over its beauty, gathering wisdom until they were worthy to follow in Her name. Taking the red-gold bark of the *eshaara* tree, Ninmah fashioned a being in Her image and breathed life into it. Thus, the very first of the Ninkuraaja was born.

"Ninmah was pleased with the form She had created, but as yet the being had no Soul, no Sight. Such a Gift would be needed if Her new people were to fulfil the ultimate destiny She had foreseen. Using secrets known only to Her, Ninmah drew on the life energy of the earth itself and infused that first Ninkuraa with the power of KI, the Great Spirit, Gifting her with a powerful awareness of Him. She became the First Kamaali of our people. Ninmah named her Ninsaar."

"Ninmah taught Ninsaar how to harness her Gift and how to become one with the Children of the Great Spirit, the wolf, the great bear, the horse, each of his offspring, great and small, for all were significant to his Balance. The Sons and Daughters of the Great Spirit were to be our guides. Through them, Ninmah hoped we would gain the wisdom and knowledge needed to fulfil Her plan and to watch over this paradise in peace, protecting its vital Balance and enhancing its beauty.

"Once the teaching of the First Kamaali was complete, Ninmah returned to the trees to make more of Her Ninku-raaja and the new Kamaali taught them how to use their gifts as Ninmah had taught her. Though none were so powerful as she, many new Gifts did the First Kamaali find among the people. Some had inherited Ninmah's great skill of healing, others in growing plants, some had a stronger affinity with the Children of the Great Spirit.

"When the Kamaali was finished, Ninmah knew She had indeed created a People greater than any of Her siblings. A People who would one day follow her into the heavens, a wise and powerful race. Ninmah looked to our future with such hope and pride that she defied the agreement made between her brethren at the beginning of the Creation and bestowed upon us the sacred gift of children; a gift given with the solemn vow that we would never share it with the Peoples of Her brethren.

"For a time, Ninmah dwelt among us, teaching us the sacred lores. Through Her wisdom, we grew more powerful and heard the will of the Great Spirit ever more clearly. Our forefathers were able to communicate thoughts over great distance, encourage plants to grow far beyond their natural speed. Our tribes met often to exchange learning and to Join their strongest members. The Peoples of Ninmah's kin dared not come near our forests. It was an age of blessing and our People grew close to achieving Her plan and Ninmah was pleased."

The children's eyes were wide in imagining such a time.

The adults looked on with sad longing carved upon their faces. Nyri could feel the dark turn of fortune looming in the tale.

Aardn sighed. "Alas, it was not to be. Ninsiku, the Joined one of the sacred Ninmah, became jealous of his mate's creation. The Children he brought into the world were no more than shadows of our race, fierce and greedy. As with the rest of Ninmah's kin, Ninsiku's creations were born Blind and Soulless, savage flesh eaters and ground-dwellers like the Thals with no knowledge of KI's Spirit."

"What's a Thal?" Nyri heard a nearby youngster ask.

"A beast from the Fury wastes." His parent whispered back. "Hairy, thick set, pale. An unintelligent creature in a twisted Ninkuraaja form." The child shuddered.

"The Great Spirit rejected such abominations," Aardn went on. "They went against the Balance. Knowing not the secret of how to gift his own children with our Sight, Ninsiku instead gave his demon sons and daughters another power. The power to dominate and destroy anything in their path. Their hearts were black and without mercy. Thus it was that the Woves came into being."

The children and even a few adults shuddered. Nyri felt the wind more keenly about her as she shifted upon her rock. Just the word Wove was enough to send a chill down her spine, evoking images of horror and death.

"It was then that Ninsiku himself came for our people, bent on destruction. He knew us to be the greatest challenge to his own children. The world grew cold, marking the beginning of the Great Fury that lasted for generations. Enraged by the betrayal, Ninmah fought against Her Joined one.

"Their battle shook the foundations of the world. Earth-shakes tore the land, and burning mountains rose from the rock, spewing destruction into the air. Ninmah saw that if She did not leave and take the battle to the heavens, it would turn the beautiful world She had grown to love to ash. Ninmah knew Her mate would not stop until he had achieved his goal of destroying Her beloved Ninkuraaja.

"With a mighty effort, She threw down Ninsiku and dragged him with Her back into the skies. There She imprisoned him in the dark, binding him in such a way that he could never return. With his departure, the Great Fury receded and our world warmed once more, though it would never again be the same. Few of us survived the freeze, and there was great sorrow. But through the power of those that endured, our people saved the *eshaara* trees and preserved our way of life. Through Ninmah's love and wisdom, our People defied Ninsiku and survived his plan to destroy us."

"Yes!" a little one hissed in proud exaltation.

The corners of Aardn's mouth turned up for a moment before she continued. "Sadly, his power was so great, Ninmah realised that even imprisoned within his heavenly cage, Her Joined one could still do harm to our people. And so with a great sorrow, Ninmah decided She must remain in the heavens to guard against Her mate's sinister reach and hold him in careful balance, never returning to the People She had so loved.

"It is from the heavens that they continue to watch over us. Ninmah burns in the Day Sky, the Golden Mother, giving our world life, warmth and hope. Ninsiku watches in the night from his dark prison, his silver eye slowly blinking.

Their power has always rocked back and forth. Night and day, Fury and Blessing. A battle doomed to continue to the end of time until one finally defeats the other."

Aardn paused. "It was our First Kamaali who foretold that should Ninsiku ever gain dominance over his Ninmah, the Great Fury would return and when that happened, we would no longer be strong enough to survive it. Our way of life would wither for good and our people would perish. She named it the End of Days."

A cold wind blew as though it, too, felt the significance of this foretelling. Nyri thought back to her earlier anxieties and the increasing ailments seen within their forest home.

The Elder continued her story. "But over the generations, Ninmah and Ninsiku's power remained equal, and the world flourished. Our people recovered from the Great Fury and strove to regain our former greatness."

Aardn drew a breath. "This final part of the story brings us to the main purpose of tonight's auscult. Ninmah taught us the value of making each generation stronger than the last. She permitted only the most powerful to bear the children of the future. Following the Great Fury, our forefathers continued this sacred teaching as Ninmah had ordained, hoping that one day, She would deem us worthy enough to join with her as equals."

"And are we?" little Naaya breathed, sitting in her mother's lap. "Are we worthy yet, great Elder?"

Aardn sighed. "No."

Naaya's face crumpled. "Why not?"

"The Woves came, child. Unable to defeat Ninmah in the heavens, Ninsiku sent his demon children to hunt us on his behalf. They found their way to our lands many Furies ago, travelling from their scorching birthplace in the south. At first they ignored us and our people waited, watching this strange new race carefully from the safety of our forests. It did not take long for us to realise that they were the dark children of the unholy Ninsiku.

"Curses spread among our tribes, killing many and tainting more. Shortly after, the balance in the skies shifted. Our People weakened, and we heard the voice of KI, the Great Spirit, less clearly, regressing from Ninmah's vision of what we could be. As we diminished, the Woves' dark power increased and the grasp of Ninsiku strengthened, finally tipping the balance against Ninmah. His Furies once again grew longer and colder. Frosts touched our forests for the first time since the time of the Great Fury. Our trees and plants sickened and died. It became harder and harder to feed and shelter ourselves. We declined once more, encountering other tribes less and less. The Wove curses increased and our children were born misshapen."

Out of the corner of her eye, Nyri saw Baarias give a despondent shake of his head. On her other side, she could feel Sefaan staring him down. If she could guarantee the motion would not draw everyone else's attention to her, Nyri would have got up and moved from between them.

"It did not take long for Ninsiku's spawn to smell our weakness, and the beasts attacked, no longer ignoring us as they had. They had worked their dark magic. They have mercilessly driven us from our homes, dragged our children into the night to feast upon, kidnapped and pillaged; pushing us further to the brink."

Baarias' gaze was distant. Nyri could see that he was in another time. She touched his hand in comfort. He had seen more Wove raids than she could imagine.

"They have brought terrifying predators from the north to stalk our steps even when they cannot," Aardn continued. "They are mindless in their destruction. It is because of them that many of our skills and strongest members have been lost. Some say the End of Days is indeed upon us, as was foretold. Who knows when we will be attacked again."

A collective wave of unease swept over the audience. Leaf-leather rustled as everyone shifted, glancing furtively into the lengthening shadows as if a Wove may well stalk from the under-brush at any moment. The children huddled closer to the adults.

"But do we lie down and go quietly from the world? No!" Aardn raised her hands. "We will go on. We are the Ninkuraaja, beloved of Ninmah, servants of the Great Spirit of KI. We will continue as our forefathers taught us and grow strong once again. I seal this promise with an announcement. Step forward, Khaad and Raanya."

Nyri stiffened as the brother and sister moved from the shadows and came to Aardn's side. Khaad held Raanya's one good hand nervously. Her other arm was withered and useless. Her thin hair had been woven with the traditional red leaves of the blood tree. Nyri knew what was about to happen and her throat closed with renewed anxiety. Kyaati had been right. Raanya would not go to Daajir. She was to be bound to her brother.

Khaad had already lost his first mate and no other tribeswoman of childbearing age was unJoined besides Raanya, Kyaati and Nyri herself. Of course, Kyaati was currently out of the question and, if her friend's words were to be believed, the Elders had other plans for Nyri. Raanya and her brother would now be Joined, tied in both mind and Soul, the closest bond any Ninkuraa could form to another. Their devotion would be total. Ninmah had guided them so. The bond had to be strong if they were to bring children into the world.

A wave of consternation shook Nyri from her thoughts, and she was in time to see Baarias drop his face into his hands. The depth of emotion she felt rolling from him shocked Nyri. He was struggling to control himself and remain seated. On her other side, Sefaan was still watching him.

"You both possess the skills worthy of our ancestors. By the wisdom of the Elders, you are to be Joined in our most sacred tradition of *ankidaa*." Aardn searched the crowd and with one last withering glare at Baarias, Sefaan rose from where she sat and moved into the circle. Her face was grim as the pair knelt before her. Sefaan placed a hand on both of their heads, preparing to seal the Joining.

"You will bear children that will ensure the survival of our—"

"Sefaan! Stop!" Baarias shot to his feet. Shocked, Nyri tried to pull on him to get him to sit back down, but he shook her off.

"What is the meaning of this?" Aardn demanded.

Baarias stared her down. "You are wrong in this, Aardn. You and the other Elders." He indicated the three figures standing in Aardn's shadow.

Nyri heard several hushed gasps, her own among them. Eyes darted between the usually softly spoken Baarias and the formidable Aardn. The tension in the air crackled. No one challenged the Elders' wisdom. Their unquestionable experience and knowledge was the reason they were chosen to lead.

Aardn raised a warning eyebrow at Baarias, but he forged ahead recklessly.

"Look at them!" He pointed at the couple standing uncomfortably at Aardn's side. Nyri felt for them. This was going to be ugly. "Brother and sister? And their father was their mother's sister-son. We are *wrong*. Open your eyes. *Look* at us, look at our children. The deformities and the stillbirths are increasing-"

"Enough!" Aardn snapped. "I have entertained your concerns once before, Baarias, and you are mistaken! Are you so arrogant as to proclaim yourself wiser than Ninmah? It was she who made us who we are. The only true Human. We must preserve our strength. It is our sacred Gift!"

"At the cost of our *children?*" Baarias clenched his fists. Nyri had never seen him so close to the edge. It was unsettling; Baarias' steadfast nature had always been the one thing she could depend on. "In the time of Ninmah, we were many! We no longer have that luxury, Aardn. The Great Fury took that from us. We must abandon this folly! I am a healer. You are foolish to close your eyes to my knowledge as you have closed your eyes to the Last Kamaali *herself*! This misfortune is not because of the supposed power of the Woves! It is of our own creation in following of misguided teachings of a deity who has *abandoned* us!"

The blood drained from Nyri's face. The blasphemy spouting from her own teacher's mouth was unthinkable. It frightened her to hear him speak of Ninmah so.

"Too long have we been isolated. We must try to find other tribes, other *Peoples* if we must. It is our only hope. If you continue down this path you have set, you are dooming us all. We bring the End of Days upon ourselves!"

The shocked silence that came in the wake of Baarias' words rippled with an undercurrent of outrage. Reach out to other Peoples? The Soulless, sub-Human creations of Ninmah's brethren and willingly commit the Forbidden? Nyri stared at her teacher, questioning his sanity for the first time in her life.

"Enough!" Kyaati's father, Pelaan, joined the fray. His anger lashed at Baarias and Nyri flinched, close as she was to his target. "We will not tolerate such defiance! Have you lost your mind, Master *Akaab*? Ninmah herself forbade such defilement of her own creation. I should cast you out for your blasphemy against the Sacred."

"No!" someone cried and was quickly quieted. Nyri stared at Pelaan with wide, frightened eyes. Baarias was out of line, but the Elder could not mean that. Unconsciously, she clutched a handful of Baarias' clothing; a childish gesture, but she did not care. To be cast out was the death penalty. In the harsh world beyond the protection of the tribe, a lone Ninkuraa could not hope to survive for long.

The colour drained from Baarias' hitherto flushed face. His fists fell limp at his sides. He took a step back from the Elder who was making threats upon his very life. Nobody moved. The breeze whispered loudly through the trees.

Nyri got to her feet; fighting the sick feeling taking hold in the pit of her stomach. She glared at Sefaan's expression of vindication as she tightened her grip on Baarias and pulled. She had to get him out of the Elders' sight before they made good on their threat.

"Come on," Nyri urged, tugging harder. She dragged her

mentor out of the auscult circle and away, terribly conscious of everyone's eyes on their backs.

Baarias said nothing as he let Nyri tow him back through the *eshaara* trees. The shock was wearing off, and her own anger with him mounted as they neared his dwelling. The one person in this world she had allowed herself to gravitate to as a protective figure, and here he was endangering himself with heresy against Ninmah Herself.

"What was *that*?" she demanded as soon as they were inside his home. "What in Ninmah's name were you thinking, Baarias?"

He blew out a ragged breath, putting his hands into the small of his back and stretching. Nyri felt his fury draining away as quickly as it had come. "All the right things," he said. "I could not stand by any longer when I possess a knowledge of the truth. Sefaan is right, I've been a coward and I can no longer hide, not when you might be the next one they inflict with this mania of theirs."

"Mania? Baarias, I don't know what Sefaan is up to or what her quarrel with you is but, you are mistaken. Don't risk getting yourself cast out over me by antagonising the Elders. What do you think that would do to me? I need you!"

He laughed humourlessly and shook his head. "What would you have me do? I am not mistaken. You will be made to have children and they will be born sick and die. That is the reason I cannot bear to see you Joined. It will destroy you and I cannot let that happen."

"You cannot *know* that, Baarias," Nyri argued. "You said yourself that the future is not certain. And if my children are born cursed, it will be the fault of the Woves, not you."

"How wrong you are, my dear Nyriaana," he said sadly. "You can never know how wrong. The Elders see our impending doom, and it frightens them. They will do anything to regain our former strengths. They see us as the only true People, blessed by Ninmah, set above the likes of the Thals and the others, whom they convince us are nothing more than Soulless beasts camouflaged in our form. They focus all our hate and blame for our misfortunes on these raiders, these *Woves*, as we call them—"

"And they are right to do so!" Nyri burst out. "Baarias, please, stop this. The Elders do not have to focus anything. We *know* who has done all of this to us! Aardn is right. They have terrorised us, driven us from our homes and murdered our people. They have taken *everything* from us. They are monsters. Evil spirits. How can you stand there and say that they are not to blame while accusing the sacred teachings of Ninmah *Herself*? The evidence is right before your eyes."

"Is it?" He raised an eyebrow. "Despite what the Elders would have you believe, the Woves are made of the same flesh and blood that we are, same as the Thals and the rest, same as the Children of the Great Spirit. Do you believe anyone of such mortal bindings could empower Ninsiku and unbalance Ninmah?" He stared at her. "Think, Nyriaana, you are an intelligent woman."

"We have no idea what they are." Nyri thought of the visage that tormented her nightmares, the demonic face that had considered throwing her into the burning spirits of its own conjuring. Nyri could not accept that creature had been a living being. "They are evil," she said with conviction. "They are *not* of the same flesh and blood."

"Oh, but they are," Baarias said. "Of *that* I am certain." His words rang with an unassailable finality.

Nyri threw up her hands. "Well, if that is so, how else has this happened? How else has Ninsiku grown so powerful that he can once again extend his Fury and banish Ninmah's Blessing?"

"I do not have all the answers, Nyri. There are powers in this world that we can never know. I agree the Woves are a brutal race who should be feared and mistrusted." He rubbed once at his scarred jaw. "I learned that the hard way, as have the rest of us, but they are a long way from being evil spirits. They are not responsible for the changes in the world, and they are certainly not the ones who are diminishing our people in the worst imaginable way. For that, we only have ourselves to blame."

Nyri closed her eyes and turned away. "Please, Baarias."

"Do not hide your face, Nyriaana. Listen to me. I do not say it lightly, I know how much distress my words are causing, but I have delivered too many dead or deformed babies in my life to not see it. As a healer, I have a deeper understanding of how life works. Can you look at boys like Omaal, blind and crippled, and not see that something is terribly wrong. No Wove, bitter Fury or predator can do this to us. Our own Elders are responsible. They have cut us off from the rest of the world because of misguided teachings and now they are reaping the misery of their actions."

Nyri shook her head. "No, Baarias. If I allow myself to believe that, I will go mad. The Elders are right to keep us away from outsiders. Ninmah Herself forbade it. I do not question the wisdom of the one who gave us life, and I do not know how you can. The Woves are the only evil I see here. It is *they* who have done this. They are demons, every single one of them."

Nyri felt his irritation spike. "Truly, Nyriaana? I would have thought you of all people could see past petty differences. Remember, Juaan—?"

Nyri stiffened. "Baarias," she warned. He of all people should know better. She felt the pain Juaan's name always inflicted stab like thorns inside her chest.

"Well, don't you?" He ignored her warning. He seemed to enjoy pulling the tail of the *grishnaa* tonight.

Nyri rounded on him. "Yes, I remember! Ninmah only knows how much I remember!"

"Good. That's something I suppose." Baarias turned away.

"What?" Nyri demanded. "What is that supposed to mean?"

He waved a hand. "Never mind."

Nyri pinched the bridge of her nose to ward off the headache that was taking hold. "Why are you doing this to me?"

"To make you see your folly."

"And what folly is that?" Nyri whispered.

"That everything we have been taught is wrong and unless everyone wakes up to that fact, our people are finished!"

Nyri took a step back, tears of shock welling in her eyes. She turned her face abruptly away and stared at the ground, determined to hold back the hot tears. She shook her head slowly back and forth, denying him.

Baarias relented, but his voice was heavy when he spoke. "You are not the first to close your eyes and hide behind your hate. Sadly, I know your eyes will be opened. I just hope you do not have to see and be a part of as much loss as I before they are. I hope you can make a difference one day. That is my wish."

Nyri drew a shuddering breath and then released it in a long sigh. She would not argue anymore. For the first time since that morning, she just wanted to be alone. Baarias had poked open old wounds, and she was bleeding. He had frightened her deeply with his heresy and shaken her faith in him. She needed space for a while to sort out her feelings before she could face him again. She turned to leave, keeping her eyes downcast.

"I am truly sorry for scaring you, Nyriaana. Please know that I have not lost my mind. I only seek to protect you."

Nyri grimaced and left him, walking out into the night. The forest was black and grey around her, silent but for a soft breeze twisting through the leaves. Nobody was in sight. The disastrous auscult was over, it seemed. She wondered idly if the Joining had been completed.

Nyri reached her tree and scrambled up into her home. She was too exhausted to even think, and she welcomed that. Throwing herself into her bower of leaves and cotton moss, she stared into space, glad that this day was finally over.

Nyri did not remember falling asleep. The only thing that she could recall in later days was the desperate warning that woke her as it came screaming through the trees.

"Woves!"

8

Trapped

Nyri was on her feet before her eyes were even fully open, every nerve alive and pulsing. Her heart was in her throat, mouth bone dry as she leaped from her tree and swung to the ground. There was movement all around as the entire tribe gathered together. Nyri could taste the panic in the air. They stared around, peering into the shadows, testing the forest's energies, reaching out to each other for support. Nyri clung to the belief that this could be a false alarm, the wild imagination of a young lookout, an idea of a poor joke.

Like hunted rabbits, they all flinched and almost bolted as the sentry threw himself from the trees into their midst. He was breathless and trembling from fear and exhaustion.

"Woves!" Javaan panted. The terror glazing his eyes confirmed that this was no deception. No hope that it was just a bad dream. Reality stood before them unchanging, stark and terrifying. Families pulled each other closer, some wailed in despair, knowing lives were going to be lost.

The Elders were quick to take charge, silencing the noise.

Pelaan grabbed Javaan by the arm, holding him up. "Where?"

"Heading from the east," the sentry gasped. "They're coming this way."

"Did they see you?"

"No," Javaan said. "They are searching but do not know of our presence yet. We need to move from here, deeper into the forest before they discover us. Daajir is keeping watch on them from a distance."

Nyri's heart thumped hard as she listened. Kyaati grabbed her hand, her palm slick with sweat. Nyri felt her friend's energy zing against her own, escalating it twofold. Baarias appeared and shifted closer to both of them in a protective motion, his face grim. Nyri was grateful for his presence. What had passed between them following the auscult ceased to matter. She wanted him with her. The air was vibrating. Just the word *Wove* was enough to send them all flying like deer before the wolf.

"Everyone!" Aardn raised her voice to bring control and focus. "Listen! *Listen!* Our enemies are upon us at last. We knew this day would come. My fellow Elders and I will lead you to safety. We will retreat to the thickest parts of the forest, leaving our home until the threat has passed. If they do not find us here, they may leave it standing. Gather your possessions; carry as much food as you can. Make it as if we were never here. Go! Hurry!"

The harvest from the Gathering was still inside the auscult circle at the centre of the clearing. Nyri followed as they all descended upon it, picking up everything that they could carry and concealing the rest in the thick undergrowth. They then rushed in the direction of their homes.

Separating from her companions, Nyri bounded into the

branches of her tree and threw her few possessions into a gathering basket. Her hands were shaking so badly she could barely function.

Images of past destruction and bloodshed flashed through her mind, overwhelming everything until all she could see before her eyes were flames and death. It took all of her courage not to collapse to the floor in a helpless heap of terror.

Nyri forced the memories back and glanced around the young tree that had been her beautiful home for the last few cycles of her life. She wondered if she would ever see it again or whether it would be murdered and burned to ash before this night was finished.

Sudden fury burned away her terror. Just one more thing the Woves would take from her. Nyri touched the living wall in a brief farewell, grieving its sleepy presence, as yet unaware of the coming danger, and clambered back to the ground.

The tribe waited until all were present and then fled into the darkness without looking back. The Elders led the flight. Branches and leaves whipped at Nyri's face. It was pitch dark. She counted it a blessing that Ninsiku's half-open eye was veiled behind the clouds. He would not see them unsheltered and vulnerable. She followed her tribe using her higher senses, latching on to the panicked energies flitting through the dark ahead and to the side of her.

Nyri was so focused on running, she nearly smashed straight into Kyaati, standing bent double in her path.

"Kya," she breathed. Kyaati was gasping, clutching at her side, face contorted with pain and exhaustion. Nyri gripped her arm, letting some of her strength pour into her friend.

She should not be running, but what choice was there. "Kya, we need to go! Come! Come with me!" Nyri grabbed her hand and struggled on into the night, dragging her heavily pregnant companion in her wake.

To Nyri's increasing dismay, she realised they were falling further and further behind. The presences up ahead were almost beyond her senses now. Where were they going? Nyri struggled on, forcing Kyaati along. She needed to catch up and get them both to safety.

"Nyri." Kyaati's voice was so weak it was barely recognisable. She gripped Nyri's hand. "I c-can't go on any further."

Nyri's throat constricted. It was far too close a reminder of that night long ago when she herself had been dragged through the trees. It was happening again. Tears started in her eyes as Kyaati sank to the ground.

Nyri stared into the darkness in open desperation. They were now completely alone, the distant noises fading into nothingness. It was as if the very world was holding its breath around them. She started when a bird flapped from the trees. The tribe had left them behind. In the panic, their presence had not been missed. Nyri wondered if the Elders would dare come back for them with the Woves this close. Such a move would risk the entire tribe.

Nyri opened and closed her fists in a motion of stress. What could she do? They were exposed, alone, and would be found by their enemies if she did not think of something. Her teeth chattered, but not from the cooling night. She was trembling from head to foot with fear.

Kyaati's hand flexed in hers.

Kyaati. Knowing her friend needed her now gave Nyri the strength she needed to push the growing panic aside enough to think. She looked to the trees.

"Come on," she heaved Kyaati to her feet. "We're going to climb. We will sit in the branches until the danger has passed. It's our best chance."

"I don't know if I can." All Kyaati wanted was to stay on her knees.

"Yes, you *can* and you *will!*" Nyri snapped, losing patience in her desperation. "Let me rephrase. It's not our best chance, it's our only chance and I'm not leaving you on the ground, it's too dangerous. Think of your baby, Kyaati. Ninmah help me, you are going to climb!"

To her surprise, Nyri thought she sensed a faint smile. "Yes, exulted Elder."

"That's better. Now come." Nyri found a tree with multiple branches thick enough to make it an easy climb. It was no *eshaara,* but it would have to do. Nyri pushed Kyaati towards it and her friend heaved herself up at a painfully slow pace.

Nyri danced with the urge to throw herself into the branches and climb right to the top. It was wrong to be on the ground when safety beckoned above. Every shadow seemed to morph into the skull of a Wove before her darting eyes, every snap of a twig or shift in the undergrowth became the movement of an enemy waiting to pounce.

At last, Kyaati got to a reasonable height and Nyri started up after her, supporting and guiding. They were three quarters of the way to the top when Kyaati could go no further. Wedging themselves into the crooks of the branches, they settled themselves in to wait. At this height, they would be invisible unless anyone looked too closely. Their clothing and skin were the perfect camouflage.

"Where do you think Dar is?" Kyaati asked once she had regained her breath. She shifted in discomfort. Nyri's heart went out to her. *She* was uncomfortable, sitting crouched on her branch; she could only imagine how Kyaati was feeling.

"Hopefully keeping himself out of harm's way and not trying to prove himself," she answered.

They fell into an uneasy silence, isolated in the night. The bark of the tree was rough against Nyri's cheek and hands as she leaned against the trunk. Time passed, and the temperature dropped. The air pinched at any exposed skin. Her hands and feet grew numb. Focusing inwards, Nyri raised her body temperature to counteract the effects. This took energy. She could not keep it up for long.

They waited. Anxiety crawled over Nyri's skin. She had no way of knowing what was happening outside of their worried little world. She imagined her tribe captured and killed by the Woves; leaving her and Kyaati alone in the world.

No, she denied her spiralling imagination. The tribe was safe. She would feel it if something had happened. She would know. Had the Woves moved on? There was no way she could know that.

It seemed like the entire night was passing as one thought after another skittered through Nyri's mind. A stiffening breeze unveiled Ninsiku's roving eye. Silver light and black shadow chased each other silently through the undergrowth. The leaves stirred around them, lulling. A night bird hooted.

Nyri's head was just beginning to nod forward when a presence rattled against her senses. She was alert in an instant, straining to see into the darkness below as her throat tightened.

They were no longer alone.

"W-what's happening?" Kyaati whispered through chattering teeth, unaware of the closing danger. "I c-can't stay up here much l-longer—"

"Shhh!" Nyri hissed. "Something is coming."

Kyaati's body stiffened as she felt it, too. Her hand clutched at Nyri's. For a few endless moments, all that could be heard was the sound of the restless trees rustling around them and the occasional chatter of a wakeful bird. Then it came, the soft, rhythmic brushing of undergrowth getting louder and louder.

A large figure burst from the trees nearby. Nyri flinched at the sight of the Wove. A vision from her darkest nightmare made solid. A *grishnaa* skull took the place of a head, the bloody pelt hanging in grisly rags scalped from the bone. One eye socket was empty, the other housed a milky, lidless eyeball. The gaping fangs curved down towards the beast's man-shaped shoulders, where grisly furs hung about the tall frame. The embodiment of death and misery. Bile rose in Nyri's throat.

Nyri always forgot just how big they were. Hatred mingled with her fear. Her mind flashed again to the moment she had dangled from the fist of one of this demon's kind, fighting for her life, all the while knowing the flaming-haired monster would throw her into the burning beast and feel no remorse. A small child.

Unblinking, she and Kyaati watched the demon from their lofty hiding place. Any sound from them and it would be over. Kyaati's hand tightened painfully on Nyri's as the Wove came to stand right beneath their feet.

What are we going to do? Kyaati thought at her. She was

close to panic. *He'll see us and eat us!*

Be still, Nyri urged. The creature stood beneath their tree, eyes scanning the darkness. It was tall and lean beneath the concealing furs, but in the dimness, Nyri could make out little else with her eyes.

Leave! She wished with all her heart that she possessed the power her people once had. She would have stopped the demon's heart and watched it choke. Instead, all she could do was sit, perched in a tree thinking pathetically, *leave, please leave us alone.* She dared not extend her will and kept her Gift bound, lest the demon pick up on their presence with its dark power.

Why wouldn't it *go?* It was just *standing* there. Then Nyri understood. It was waiting. One by one, more of the skull-headed devils emerged from the darkness. There were ten of the beasts. They seemed wary of the forest, turning often to watch their backs, weapons held ready against any threat. If she weren't so terrified, Nyri would have found such a scene amusing. What could be more of a threat than they?

The rest of the Woves joined the leader beneath the branches of the tree in which Nyri and Kyaati hid. Some were even bigger than the first. Nyri studied their weapons with revulsion. A few carried long staffs tipped either end with curving stag's antlers, the crowns honed into deadly points, others bore stout sticks with heavy rocks bound to the end and spears armed with sharpened flint. Knives fashioned from grishnaa teeth were tucked into the furs of their waists. Every one of them a bringer of death.

Kyaati was shaking so hard Nyri feared her friend would give them away. All it would take was for one of them to look up. Nyri bit back a cry when several of them sank to the ground and squatted before their leader, muttering among themselves.

Nyri was still staring balefully down at them when it happened.

The sound of splintering wood cracked through the silence.

"*Nyri!*"

She was powerless to prevent it as the branch supporting Kyaati gave way under her weight. The startled Woves leaped to their feet, their lifeless faces turning upwards to fix on Nyri and her stricken friend as the branch broke away.

"Nyri!" Kyaati screamed as she tumbled away into empty air.

"No! *Kyaati!*"

Nyri tried to hang on to her, but it was no use. Kyaati's hand tore from hers. She could only watch, horrified, as Kyaati fell, striking another branch on the way down and then hit the ground with a sickening thud. Her cries of fear and pain choked off. She lay motionless in a crumpled pile.

"No!" Without a thought, Nyri threw herself down the tree after her friend. The twigs and branches tore at her skin and coverings, but she barely noticed. The Woves were recovering from their shock. The leader approached Kyaati, one hand outstretched. It clutched its grishnaa knife in the other.

Furious, Nyri leaped the remaining distance to the ground, ignoring the painful jolt through her feet as she landed squarely in front of her fallen friend. She grabbed the nearest object she could find, the broken branch lying at her feet. Nyri could barely lift it, but she struggled to brandish it in front of her, nonetheless.

Unperturbed, the Wove continued to approach.

"Get away!" Nyri screeched up at the lifeless eye of the skull. She swung her weapon back and forth, the tip of it scraping the ground pathetically. "Leave her alone! Get away from us!"

The rest of the Woves standing away in the darkness laughed, the sound grating out between bared jaw bones. They were amused. Nyri could see herself in their eyes. A tattered Ninkuraa woman heaving a stick twice her size in an attempt to frighten them. A mouse before the *grishnaa*. She bared her teeth.

The lead Wove continued to approach.

"Get away!" Nyri hissed. It towered above her, drawing close enough for her to smell the rotting stench of a corpse. She took an involuntary step back. The laughter in the shadows grew louder. To her surprise, the approaching Wove turned and snapped at them. Nyri could not understand its words, but the meaning was clear. The rest quieted instantly.

The demon's small show of compassion, however, held little weight with her. So what if it did not want its followers to laugh while it did who knew what to them? Nyri stared at the blade in its hand. The tip was cruel and stained with layer upon layer of dried blood. Helpless tears fell down her cheeks as the demon took another long stride towards her.

"I'm sorry, Kyaati," she whispered.

Caught up in her defeat, she did not sense the approach. A large grey form flew past her ear, coming to her rescue for the second time in a day. Only this time it was followed by another and another. The air was suddenly filled with snarls and the snapping of teeth. Then the voices came, shouting and angry.

"Leave them! Leave us alone! Monsters!"

For an endless moment, the wolves and the Woves stared each other down. The Woves were woefully outnumbered. Both sides knew it, and with a howl of challenge that raised the night itself, the wolf pack charged as one.

The greatest of hearts would have quailed at such a sight. Ancient instinct consumed the fierce will of the Woves. They turned and ran before the pack, many dropping their weapons in their haste to escape. But it was too late. The fleet wolves fell among them, bearing several to the ground, ripping at exposed flesh.

Nyri collapsed to her knees, all strength leaving her. The need to protect Kyaati had been the only thing holding her up. The world blurred in a bloody mess of fur and flesh. Dazed, Nyri found her eyes being drawn to a strange thing. The lead Wove was still standing close to where she knelt, strangely unmoving and untouched amid all the chaos. Its blank face stared at her. The moment stretched before the demon turned and disappeared into the darkness, swift as a deer. The rest of the demons who had avoided the lupine jaws had already fled, running for their lives between the trees. A few wolves followed, snapping at heels, driving their message home.

A cheer of victory was the last thing Nyri heard before the shock and exhaustion caught up with her, and a wave of darkness sent her crashing to the ground.

9

Tragedy

"Nyri? Nyri! Can you hear me?" Someone was tapping her cheek. Nyri wished they would stop. It was irritating. "Brave child, wake up! Baarias needs you."

Baarias. His name was like a douse of cold water. Nyri wrenched her eyes open. She sat up quickly, and the world swam before her eyes. She was on the forest floor, a woven cotton-moss drape covering her body.

"Wha—" she rubbed her forehead, fighting against the disorientation.

"Easy, child." Sefaan was beside her. "The Woves are gone. You're safe."

Woves. That dreaded word brought everything flooding back in gut-twisting detail. One grisly image stood out high above the rest. The sight of Kyaati lying crumpled at the base of the tree, broken and silent. Nyri was glad that she was still on the ground.

Her eyes darted around the immediate area. Where was Kyaati? All she could see was Sefaan and, beyond the

Kamaali, the blood-soaked ground where the slaughter had taken place. One wolf had been lost to a lucky spear. The remaining pack stood mourning their fallen with soft whines. Nyri closed her eyes, breathing deep as her stomach heaved. Nausea crawled up her throat.

"Nyri," Sefaan insisted. "Baarias needs you. It's—"

"Kyaati," she finished.

Nyri pulled herself to her bruised feet. She did not stop to listen to Sefaan's warning of what she might find. Nyri pulled from the Kamaali's weak grip and stumbled away. She could feel Baarias' presence a way into the trees.

The crowd was the first thing Nyri saw. The entire tribe was there, and the collective sense of fear and despair was overwhelming. She fought her way through them with difficulty. By the time she neared the centre, Nyri had reached her limit. She could hear Kyaati now, crying out in pain. The sound fuelled her anger and irritation. Her tribe's despondent emotions threatened to crush her, and she exploded like a wildcat on its prey.

"All right! Baarias needs to concentrate and you are not helping. Leave! Go home!" She could not bear to feel what they were feeling.

Their eyes widened at the ferocity of her will, but they heeded her words and retreated. Nyri spied a couple of Elders eyeing her reproachfully, but could not find it in herself to feel any remorse or embarrassment for her actions. That would come later.

Baarias appeared at her side, reaching with a bloody hand to touch her arm.

"How—?"

"She's no longer in danger," he said. "Aside from severe

bruising, she had a head injury, which I've stabilised, and a broken arm."

Relief sluiced through Nyriaana. Kyaati was going to live. A miracle after such a fall. "Thank Ninmah," she breathed. Guilt and embarrassment at how she had overreacted in front of the entire tribe swamped her. She would have to apologise.

Baarias took her shoulder in a steadying grip, his face grave. "But Nyri," he continued. "The baby is coming."

Nyri stiffened. "No! It can't be, Baarias! It's too soon!"

"Shhh!" he hissed. "Kyaati was fairly close to her time. There might still be a chance. I need you to be strong, Nyri. I know you're exhausted. I know you have already gone through too much this day, this night, but I have to ask more of you. We need to deliver this baby safely for Kyaati's sake."

Nyri straightened her aching body under his gaze. Baarias did not have to tell her what would become of Kyaati if they failed. They could not fail. Gathering strength she did not think she had, she turned with Baarias to the task at hand.

Kyaati was lying upon a hastily gathered bed of cotton-moss in a sheltered thicket, heaving in the throes of labour. Sweat was pouring down her reddened face, mixing with the blood of her head injury. One of her arms was crooked. Nyri swallowed back bitter tears. Why had Ninmah allowed this to happen? Kyaati did not deserve this fate. Her father, Pelaan, was at her head, whispering rapid words of encouragement and support, but his eyes were wild.

Baarias sensed Nyri's struggle and squeezed her arm. *Can you do this?*

She balled her fists. *Yes.*

Nyri felt his pride in her before his thoughts turned back to

Kyaati with a single-minded focus. Nothing would distract him now. He moved to kneel beside Nyri's friend, placing his hands on her belly, assessing the situation. Nyri dropped onto her heels beside him. Her teacher was the only calm force present, which made it even more frightening when his hands tightened into tense fists.

Nyri, he thought, grabbing her shoulder so that only she could hear. *The baby is facing the wrong way. I need to turn her if she and Kyaati are going to live. I have given her extracts to ease the pain, but she will need more than herbs for this. I need you to help her while I try to deliver the baby safely.* His words were quick and to the point. *Ease her pain. Now.*

Nyri moved to Kyaati's side and took her hand. Kyaati gripped her fingers so hard she thought her bones would crack. Her friend's glazed eyes rolled in her head. "Nyri," she gasped, "what's happening?" She was barely lucid. Her face contorted as another contraction convulsed through her. Although the night was cold, the air inside this sheltered place was hot and heavy. It stank of sweat and blood. The leaves above them hung unmoving, even they seemed to feel the gravity of the situation.

"Shhh," Nyri tried to soothe, "everything will be alright, we'll get through this, Kyaati. J-just do everything Baarias says and your baby will be here soon." Her voice cracked. She was trying to focus, to do her duty, but she could not find her centre. She could not extend her power. Kyaati screamed as agony racked her. Pelaan's tenuous composure broke apart. Nyri squeezed her eyes shut as she began to drown. Her friend was going to die. Torn from the inside out.

"Nyriaana!" Baarias' voice cracked the thick air. It cut

through the waters of despair closing over Nyri's head. She sucked in a breath and then another. She *had* to do this. She reached out to the surrounding forest, drawing on its power. *Great Spirit, lend me strength!*

Placing her free hand on Kyaati's heaving side at a point halfway down her back, Nyri focused and extended her life's energy inward. Kyaati's body became hers. Nyri found the column of bone that was Kyaati's spine and all the vital connections contained within. She fought the backlash of sensation leaking through the connection and numbed the searing messages, stopping them from reaching their target.

Kyaati sank into her bed of leaves, panting in relief. The grip on Nyri's right hand loosened. Grabbing a handful of leaves from Kyaati's bed, she wiped at her friend's sticky brow. Pelaan was frozen, watching Baarias work. Nyri shied away from the silence she heard coming from Baarias' direction, lest it break her concentration. The air should be filled with the lusty sounds of a baby's cry by now.

"Nyri," she heard Baarias whisper. Careful to keep her connection with Kyaati, Nyri moved around to her teacher. He placed a hand, sticky with blood and fluid, on her spare wrist. *Can you feel anything?*

Nyri floundered for a second, unsure of what he meant. Then she understood. She reached out, searching for the baby's signature presence only to come up against... a void. Nyri shook her head in violent denial. No, that could not be. No, no, no.

Do something, Baarias! She pleaded, tears spilling from her eyes. She hoped Kyaati could not see; she hoped she was so drugged on Baarias' remedies and exhaustion that she could not sense that her baby was lifeless.

The head crowned.

"Kyaati. Push hard," Baarias commanded, no hint of a waver in his voice. If they could not save the infant, he still had a duty to save the mother. Exhausted as she was, Kyaati gasped and strained, giving her all to deliver her precious child.

At last she was out. Naked, she did not gasp or fight for her life. She did not cry at the harshness of this unknown world. She lay blue and limp, dwarfed by Baarias' steady hands. Her tiny mouth hung open. One arm was wasted, and both feet were deformed lumps of flesh.

Baarias! Nyri was desperate.

"Dry her," he urged. Together they rubbed the baby down with the leaves from Kyaati's bed. "We have to get her life force moving."

"What's happening?" Kyaati had regained enough sense to understand that something was wrong. "Where's my baby?"

"Sit with them," Baarias commanded. "I'll do what I can here."

Nyri froze. She did not want to go to her friend. She did not want to look into Kyaati's eyes knowing what she did. A sudden urge to run overcame her. But that cowardly way out was not an option.

She moved to Kyaati's side as her teacher commanded. She did not speak, she simply clutched at Kyaati's hand as her father gripped her friend's shoulders with white knuckles, holding her flat to the ground where she could not see. His frightened gaze flickered to Nyri as they both watched Baarias turn the baby and slap her tiny back. Nyri could feel Pelaan's hope for his family's continued existence fading with every fruitless moment. If this infant could not be revived, his powerful bloodline came another step closer to oblivion.

"Nyri," Kyaati's glazed eyes fixed on her, beseeching. "Where is my baby?"

Nyri opened her mouth and choked on the air. She could only stare helplessly at her friend, blinded by tears. There was still no sense of life in Baarias' hands. It seemed like forever and no time before he admitted defeat and bowed his head.

It was over.

"I... I'm so sorry, Kyaati." It was the first time Nyri had heard his voice waver. Defeat was etched into his every line as Baarias handed Kyaati the little body. "She's gone."

"No," Kyaati whispered. Her bewildered eyes flicked from Baarias to the baby and back, over and over, as if waiting for reality to change. Her shaking fingers brushed repeatedly at the damp, downy brow. Then it hit, and her body shook as the cries ripped from her chest. "*No! No!*"

Pelaan was on his feet. He flew at Baarias and grabbed him by the shoulders. Nyri was on her feet, too, frightened by the Elder's loss of control as he shook her teacher. "Do something! You are an *akaab* healer!" Kyaati's despairing wails punctuated every angry word. "Save the child! What good are you if you cannot save one child?"

Baarias did not protest against this treatment or move to defend himself. He waited until Pelaan let go of him. "One man cannot change nature, Pelaan. I do not have the power, no matter how much you or anyone else may wish it. Nobody does. I am so sorry for your loss."

Pelaan's anger burned out in the face of Baarias' calm. His knees buckled like a broken tree in the wind. Nyri choked on his grief, drowning as she was in her own. Kyaati's despair could not be comprehended. Nyri heard a gasp and glanced into the trees. She saw Daajir's form standing away in the darkness. His face was stone as he took in the awful scene. Nyri knew what was going through his mind. The loss of this young life was not just a blow to Pelaan's family.

It was a death knell to the tribe itself.

10

Flight

Nyri felt Baarias at her side; she was so dazed that she could not move and he had to pull her with him back into the trees, leaving Kyaati and her father to grieve their dead.

"Baarias," Nyri could hardly speak. He looked as weary and as defeated as she had ever seen him. The horror bubbled from her throat like infection from a wound. "That can't be it? Why... What was...? We can't—" Nyri tore at her hair. "It's not fair!" Her grief turned to burning rage in its need for an outlet. In her mind's eye, she saw the lifeless child in her mother's distraught arms. Overlaying this image were blank skull faces, waiting in the dark. "It's not fair! It should never have happened! *It's all their fault!*"

"Whose fault?" Baarias asked wearily. He knew what she meant, but he was going to make her say it.

"The demons! If it wasn't for them, this would never have happened! Those foul beasts! Those foul, bloodthirsty, murdering *beasts*! Haven't they taken enough from us? I hate them, Baarias! I-I—," her rage struck her dumb. There were no words to articulate what she was feeling. She would surely explode with the emotion. Nyri seized a stick and swung it at a tree, wishing it was a Wove. The stick shattered satisfyingly on impact.

Baarias, as usual, was unmoved. His calm was maddening. Where was his rage from earlier? Nyri would have welcomed it now. "So eager to hate and cast blame, Nyriaana?"

For the first time, she wanted to strike him. She wished she hadn't wasted that stick on the tree. "Don't start defending the monsters again, Baarias," she seethed. "I do not know how you can stand there now and deny that they are the cause for every wrong that has befallen us."

"The baby's chest was malformed. She could not breathe."

He may as well have punched her in the gut. "W-what?"

"The baby could not breathe, Nyriaana," Baarias repeated. Had he always looked this old? "All that I have told you is true. I would not lie. Our condition is getting worse. Kyaati's baby would never have survived, Wove attack or not."

Nyri swayed on her feet. Robbed of her fury and outlet, she sank to her haunches, head in her hands, trying to absorb what she was hearing. The baby had never had a chance.

"I'm s-sorry, Baarias," she whispered. She did not know what else to say.

Baarias touched her shoulder. He stepped away, pulling herbs from the pouches hanging on his staff and mixing them in the *haala* shell that always dangled from his garments, ready for use.

In the end, all Nyri could think of was Kyaati. Whoever was to blame, her child was dead and nobody could bring her back. A sob escaped her lips. She dug her fingernails into her scalp, biting back a shriek of despair.

Baarias passed her by, heading back to where Kyaati and her father remained. Daajir was now with them. Numb, Nyri rose and trailed her teacher. She leaned against a tree, watching as Baarias administered his remedy, urging Kyaati and her father to take it. Nyri could not look at the motionless bundle still clutched protectively in Kyaati's arms. She fixed her eyes instead on an object lying forgotten on the ground next to the tragic scene.

It was a mistake.

Nyri's already splintered heart shattered at the sight of the toy hare. She knocked aside the calming remedy Baarias was now offering to her and gave in to the call of the night and the escape it promised. Nyri did not hear Daajir shout. She just ran. Ran from that terrible place. Ran from death. Most of all, she ran from the sight of the abandoned gift with its red feather and the baby who would never play with it.

Nyri did not know where she was going. The frigid air stabbed her lungs as she fled. Her tears froze on her face. She ran until her legs burned. She did not care. She wanted the pain. She welcomed it. These were sensations she could handle. Sensations she could comprehend. The forest blurred by, on and on.

In the end, her body betrayed her will. Nyri stumbled and collapsed against a tree, gasping and trembling. Alone in the darkness, she let herself go. Every stone and fallen branch within her reach went flying, smashing into tree trunks and shattering against rocks. Nyri screamed her pain and confusion to the night.

She stopped only when her bleeding fingers clawed at the empty earth in futile search. There was nothing left to throw. Raw, Nyri sank to the ground. The darkness settled around, cloaking her. She closed her eyes.

She remained that way for a long time. She did not know how far she had run or where she had come to rest, but Nyri did not care. The forest went on, unminding of her presence in its midst, like her fury had never been. How symbolic. Leaves whispered and creatures passed until the sweat grew cold on her body and she shivered against the night.

Opening swollen eyes, Nyri looked around. The trees were grey sentinels in the darkness, whispering to each other in their own peculiar way. A night bird ghosted overhead.

The silence was oppressing, all-encompassing. Nyri got up and wandered swiftly on. She did not want to think. She could not let the pain catch her.

She had never been this far away from the rest of the tribe after dark before. The idle thought crossed her mind, not really caring if it was heeded or not. She stared unseeing at the ground as it passed beneath her feet. The cold hurt her toes. She should really take to the trees where she would be safer, but she could not muster the will to climb.

Disturbances in the earth drew her attention. Scuff marks here, large footprints and a snapped branch there. Over-laying all were impressions of paw prints. The Woves must have come this way in their flight from the pack.

That thought sent a chill through Nyri's body, shaking her a little from her daze. Woves. She wondered how far the wolves had driven them. For all she knew, they could still be here, lurking in the darkness, just waiting for a foolish victim such as her to cross their path.

A sense of self-preservation, if nothing else, resurfaced beneath her numb shell. Every shadow now hid a sinister secret. A sudden movement in the trees made her flinch. Like a spooked animal, Nyri stumbled into a run but, in her senseless flight, she had got herself lost. She did not know what she was running into. Panic set in, and she ran faster.

Nyri bit back a yelp as she tripped on something soft, falling hard into the leaf mould. The scent of earth and decay filled her nostrils. Coughing, Nyri pulled herself up and came face to face with the staring eyes of a cat. She hadn't even sensed its presence. Crying out, she reflexively grabbed a rock from the ground and scrambled backwards, trying to put as much distance between herself and the predator as possible. A futile effort. She knew it was already too late, and she was as good as dead.

But the cat did not move. Nyri halted her hasty retreat, confused. As her blind panic subsided and instinct gave way to rational thought, she realised why she had not sensed its presence. The cat was dead. It was just a shell of fur and sinew lying stiff and unmoving on the ground. Nyri recognised it as the same creature that had attacked Omaal that very morning, a lifetime ago now, it seemed. She turned away from the grisly sight, made even more unnerving in the dark.

She knew where she was now. Her flight had brought her all the way to the Pits. She was lucky not to have fallen prey to one of the hungry maws. Nyri shuddered at her own foolishness. Ninmah must have been watching over her. She had to get a hold of herself before Ninmah washed Her hands of such a foolhardy Daughter. She breathed through her nose, once, twice…

"Hhugghh."

Nyri stifled a yelp as the moan sounded from the darkness. Raising her rock, she spun to face the noise. The hand that held the makeshift weapon trembled. *That* had not been an animal. Leaves rustled. Whipping her head around, she tried to keep her eyes on everything at once, searching for the owner of the disembodied moan.

Then the presence she had missed until now brushed across her senses. Not an animal. Not Ninkuraaja. The energy was different, off, muted. A Wove. Her breathing quickened. She wished with all her might that she was back at home, safe within her tree.

Snap. Crack!

Nyri twisted. The sound of movement was coming from the Pits. Only now did she notice that the sticks and branches covering the nearest hole were broken and tumbled inward, mere strides away.

Nyri burned with the need to take flight, but an inexplicable compulsion drew her forward. Before she knew it, she was peering over the edge, rock at the ready. She blinked as her eyes adjusted to the deeper blackness below. A shadow was lying right at the bottom of the Pit. A demon Wove captured in the trap. The empty eye socket of the *grishnaa* shaped skull stared balefully up at her.

Nyri flinched and jumped back as the dark figure stirred, then stilled. It was unconscious. It was a miracle the demon creature had survived the fall. She wasn't about to wait around for it to wake up. She backed away, intent on retreating into the night, leaving this monster to its fate. It deserved nothing but death. She should never have left her People.

She had taken but a step when the voice snared her. Soft, barely there, it whispered.

"Nyri, Nyri, Nyriaana."

The rock slipped from her numb fingers and tumbled to the ground.

Juaan.

11

Empty Shell

"Nyri!" her mother's voice broke into her sleeping world. She mumbled a protest. She was cosy and warm. She did not want to get up just yet. "Nyri!" A hand nudged at her. "Come on, sleepy cub."

"Mama."

"Come on, wake up, there's someone I want you to meet."

"Mmmpphh."

A soft laugh. Hands lifted her. She was being carried. Her mother made her way unerringly down their tree, despite her burden. Nyri tightened her arms around her mother's warm neck. She kept her eyes closed, clinging to the sleepy cocoon.

"Nooo," she protested as she was plopped into a sitting position upon the ground. She blinked her eyes against Ninmah's light and the green, green trees.

"Nyri," her mother's soft voice whispered. "I want you to meet Juaan."

Nyri stiffened. Someone was looking at her. She met eyes as green as the trees themselves. Strange eyes. She turned her face away, hiding from this stranger. She did not like being looked at.

Tottering to her feet, she moved to hide behind the protection of her mother's legs. She spotted her father standing not far away. His arms were crossed. He was not happy. Nyri frowned back.

"Nyri, Juaan lost his mama last night. He is going to be a part of our family now. We have got to look after him because no one else will."

Nyri heard her father snort. She was confused. This strange boy was joining their family? But her papa was not happy. She did not move.

"Nyri?" her mother questioned. "Nyri." She gave her a nudge with her heel. "Nyriaana!"

"Nyri, Nyri, Nyriaana."

Nyri giggled suddenly. The strange boy had spoken, turning her mother's call for her attention into a silly rhyme. She dared to peer from behind her mother's legs. He was still standing not far away, watching her warily. Some of her shyness left her and she crawled further out from behind her shelter.

He was very tall. His skin was dark beneath deep brown hair. Strange boy. She looked closer and saw with a shock that he was sad; his eyes were red. He had been crying! Nyri's heart twisted. She didn't want him to be sad. He needed something. Someone to hold him. Being held always made her feel better. Taking to her feet, she tottered the rest of the way to the boy who was now part of her family. She threw her arms around his legs as far as they would go and clung to him. What had her mama called him?

"Hello, Juaan. Don' cry. I be your friend. Make it better?"

The boy took a shaky breath. He was crying again. Nyri held him tighter. Maybe she was doing this wrong. But then she got the sense that the boy was feeling better, if only a little. She did not let go of her hold on him.

"Hello, Nyri, Nyri, Nyriaana."

* * *

Daylight touched Nyri's eyelids, stirring her unwillingly from her troubled sleep. She opened her eyes and stared up at the familiar boughs twisting above. She did not move. Exhaustion pulled on her every limb. One image after another chased through her mind as she tried to rationalise her thoughts.

Everything from the night before was an unreal blur of darkness and despair. Everything except the voice. A voice that had cut through death itself, speaking the rhyme that had comforted her, amused her and distracted her as a child. A secret between two friends spoken from the unconscious mouth of her enemy.

Nyri squeezed her eyes shut again. As soon as she had recovered from her shock, she had fled, terrified to hear or feel anything more that might make that cruel illusion a reality. She had not stopped until she had reached her home and climbed into her tree, throwing herself into the protective cocoon of her bower, shaking and crying until exhaustion overtook her.

Nyri could not believe now that it had been anything more than a trick of her senses. In the clean, cold light of day, the deception was that much easier to throw off. That was not Juaan lying at the bottom of the pit. That was not Juaan, skull-faced and wrapped in black furs, carrying a deadly weapon against them. That was *not* Juaan, her beloved Juaan, become the thing of her nightmares.

All she had heard was the desperate imagining of an overwrought mind seeking an impossible comfort. Juaan was dead. He had given his life to save hers. That twisted thing dying out there in the forest, if she hadn't indeed imagined the whole thing, was something else entirely. Nyri refused to believe anything else.

If Juaan had been alive all of this time, he would have come back to her. No matter how much her lesser self yearned for the illusion to be real, Nyri would not go back to look on this creature and taunt her heart. She would not.

She was proud when she almost believed herself.

Nyri rolled over. Ninmah had risen. She was just wondering at the phase of the day when true reality came crashing down upon her. *Kyaati.* Nyri balled up as the pain and the horror of the night's events found her at last. The emotions were as raw as they had been when she had stood over Kyaati and her baby. She had not let herself face it. She had not worked through it. She had fled. Now it was all the worse because, besides the pain, another emotion was growing in strength. Guilt. She had abandoned Kyaati. She had left her tribe-sister in the middle of the forest while she screamed over her lost baby. Such a crime should never be forgiven.

Nyri staggered to her feet. She had to find her. She would do or be anything Kyaati needed now.

Still dressed in her tattered clothing from the night before, bruised, scratched and bloodstained, Nyri climbed stiffly down her tree. The night's running had taken its toll. Hard physical activity was not a wise choice when food was in short supply and her people always did their best to avoid overexerting themselves where possible. Nyri stepped gingerly to the ground.

Hardly anyone was around. Even so, the energy hanging

over the *eshaara* grove weighed upon Nyri like a death shroud. She shuddered and hurried on as fast as her aching body would permit.

She guessed Baarias would have brought Kyaati back to his own home to keep her under his eye. Nyri was afraid to reach out for fear of what she would feel. She made the short distance and ducked through the entranceway of Baarias' dwelling. She found him sitting in the nearest chamber, staring into space.

"Baarias."

He looked up at the sound of his name. Relief flooded his grey features at the sight of her. It struck Nyri that the last time he had seen her, she had been running heedlessly into the night on the heels of the men who had come to destroy them. He didn't look like he had slept for the entire night. Her guilt found new depths.

Baarias got up and took her by the shoulders. "Are you all right?"

She could not have been further from it and certainly must not look it, but she nodded. "I'm sorry, Baarias, I just…"

He caught her in his arms and Nyri felt his breath shudder against her. "I was so afraid last night," he whispered. "When I realised you were no longer with us, I tried to come back. I fought with the Elders but they would not let me, they would not risk… If Daajir had not thought of the wolves, I-I don't know what would have happened. I am sorry we took so long to return. Maybe… if we had just come sooner…"

Nyri pulled away as Baarias dashed the tears from his cheeks. She knew what he meant. "It was not your fault, Baarias," she murmured. "I am sorry, too. I should not have run. I… I just…" Nyri choked on her own tears.

Baarias shook his head, quieting her. "There's no need to explain. I can't tell you the amount of times I have wanted to react in exactly the same way."

"I bet you never gave into the urge, though," she said, shamefaced.

He offered a haunted smile. "Once. And I was much older than you are now."

Nyri sighed. His words eased her slightly.

"But never in the wake of a Wove raid." He frowned. Now that he was assured of her safety, his annoyance was stirring. "They could have been anywhere, Nyri. I was out of my mind, thinking you might be captured. You are so lucky you didn't stumble into a trap."

Trap. Nyri averted her eyes at the word. No, it was not she who had fallen into the trap. "Don't worry, Baarias. There was no sign of them. The wolves must have chased them far from the forest." Nyri could not bring herself to tell him of what she had seen. Best to forget it. The Wove, if real, would be dead soon enough. "They're gone."

He closed his eyes in silent thanks, calmed, and patted her shoulder.

"How is she?" Nyri blurted.

Baarias' shoulders slumped. "I don't know, Nyriaana. Honestly, I do not know. She hasn't spoken a word since last night. I'm keeping her here for now. She will not eat. It is like she has given up."

It was as she had feared. "What can we do, Baarias?"

"Nothing. When she lost the others, she still had Yaanth. Now she has no baby and no mate. I have no cure for a broken heart. That is up to her."

"Can I see her?"

His mouth lifted slightly. "Of course. You are her friend, the sister of her heart, who knows; maybe you can reach her where her father and I have failed."

Nyri could not return his smile. Some sister she had turned out to be. Drawing upon a resolve she did not feel, Nyri moved through to the next chamber. Spores from the *girru* moss floated in the air, casting a soft, golden light that warmed the browns and greens of the surrounding shelter. Kyaati was lying in a moss-filled bower. She was alone. She did not look up as Nyri approached, though she must have both heard and sensed her.

"Kyaati?" Nyri ventured. No answer. Nyri moved over until she was crouching by her friend's side. Kyaati's eyes were closed. At first Nyri thought she was sleeping, but the rhythm of her breathing and the flavour of her energy told Nyri that this wasn't so. "Kyaati. I'm here. I am so sorry I ran last night... I..." she trailed off.

Silence.

"Can you ever forgive me?"

Nothing. Kyaati's skin looked waxy. Her eyes were sunken and shadowed. Nyri shook her arm, needing to be reassured that some spark of spirit still existed within her feisty friend, but she could feel nothing from her. All that met her senses was a chilling emptiness. Kyaati may as well not have been there. A living shell. Whatever Baarias had told her, Nyri had not been prepared for this. "Kyaati, *please!*"

Not even the flicker of an eyelid graced her plea. Nyri rushed from the chamber. "Baarias!" She grabbed his arm. "What's happened to her? She won't even look at me." She had hoped to see at least some sign of life, withdrawn but awake, able to heed words. Not this.

132

"Shhh. I know." Baarias attempted to calm her, but she could feel his keen disappointment. "We have not been able to get the smallest response from her since we brought her here. If even you can't—"

"But why?"

"I cannot say. The workings of the mind and heart are a mystery even to me. I can only guess that she has been so traumatised by grief that this is the only way her spirit can protect itself."

"And there is nothing at all that we can do?" Nyri was desperate.

"I have examined her. There is nothing physically wrong with her. There is nothing to fix. All we can do is watch and wait and hope that she comes back to us. But, Nyri," he took her shoulders, "please prepare yourself; losing this child has been a severe blow. She may not want to come back."

Nyri shook her head. "She can't leave us! We need her." Nyri needed her. "We need everyone."

Baarias shrugged. "Sometimes it is not about what we want, but what is best for the person we care about. I for one would not blame Kyaati for running into the arms of the Great Spirit where she can be with her loved ones and know peace. What would she be returning to except further pain and death? Our situation will not change. The Elders *will* not change."

Nyri was still shaking her head. *She* could not take any more grief. She would not add Kyaati to her list of loved and lost. She straightened her shoulders. "I will *not* let her go, Baarias. There could be so much more left for her to live for. You might have given up, but *I* say we are not finished yet!"

133

She turned her back before she could have her resolve shaken by the pitying expression on Baarias' face and marched back to where Kyaati lay. Settling in beside her friend, she picked up her hand, gripping it in her own. "I will not let you give up," she vowed.

No response. Nyri laid her head on the bower beside Kyaati, feeling the springy moss tickle her cheek. A silent tear escaped, and she almost choked on the words. "I wish I could change what happened last night. I am so sorry I made you climb that tree. I am so sorry you lost your baby. And… I understand if you don't want to face anything for a while, but you cannot leave us. I am here for you. We are all here. Your father needs you. Try to think of Yaanth. Think of your children. None of them would want you to just give up." Nyri stroked the beautiful silvery hair back from her friend's paled brow.

The words dried up, so Nyri simply sat, holding Kyaati's hand. The horrors of the previous night would not lie quiet. She kept seeing the lifeless bundle in Kyaati's arms and the abandoned hare lying on the ground. Nyri chased these images away, only to find herself standing once more on the edge of the Pit, looking down on the demonic figure trapped there. She did not know which image was worse at that present moment.

Nyri, Nyri, Nyriaana. His voice echoed through her mind, over and over.

Squeezing her eyes shut, Nyri murmured old tribal songs to drown it out. If Baarias were to hear her, he would assume she sang for Kyaati, which was partially true. Kyaati had always enjoyed listening to her sing. Nyri could not imagine why.

The light was fading when hunger finally drove her from her vigil. Nyri rose from Kyaati's side after giving her promise to return. Baarias was in the next chamber. He was sleeping at last, wrapped tightly in an *aacha* wool blanket for warmth. Nyri touched his brow as she passed, but did not wake him.

The chill in the air hit as she stepped from the majestic tree. The golden spirit of Ninmah was waning in the west, scattering her tiring rays through the branches of the trees. Nyri shivered and hunched her shoulders against the cold. Her people had returned from wherever they had been but were already sheltering in their dwellings, so Nyri walked through the lengthening shadows alone.

"Nyriaana!"

Almost alone.

The voice was sharp. She turned to see Daajir stalking towards her. It was easy to tell that he was not happy with her in the least. Nyri scowled. She was not in the mood for what was coming. There had been a time when his temper had frightened her. No longer. "Don't start," she warned. "I have enough to think about."

"Do you? Where in Ninmah's name did you get to last night? Did you learn nothing from the *grishnaa* attack? That's twice now that you've put yourself in needless danger—"

"Oh back off, Daajir." She kept walking. The hardening ground leached the warmth from her feet, but she ignored the discomfort. "I'm safe. I'm back. I did not find any trouble. I just… needed to be alone." She dared not tell him about the Wove in the Pit, either.

Nyri felt his ire spike at her attitude. "How were you to

135

know that you wouldn't find trouble while you were 'alone'? How were *we* to know? Were it not for the need to look after Kyaati and get her home safely, I'd have come after you and dragged you back by your hair."

Nyri's temper flared. She had never taken kindly to being treated like a child, even when she had been a child. Her brewing tirade was cut short, however, when she tasted the guilt he was trying so hard to hide. Nyri bristled. She was not going to suffer it like she had with Omaal the day before. She stared Daajir down. "You really feel that? Well, you can stop taking this out on me, right *now*. Stop blaming everyone for what you feel are your own shortcomings! It is not your fault that you weren't there to protect her, Dar. It would not have changed a thing."

That smacked him on the nose. "I—"

Nyri raised an eyebrow at him, daring him to contradict her. She watched as he worked through his conflicting emotions. In the end, he simply ground his teeth together. "I don't know what to do. She won't respond."

"I know." Nyri lowered her eyes. They should not be fighting like this. They should concentrate on making their friend well again.

"She stayed upright long enough for us to Cast the child to the river," Daajir said. "Then she just collapsed and hasn't moved or spoken since."

Nyri felt another stab in her gut. She had missed the Casting. She nodded in acknowledgment. "I have been by her side since Ninmah reached her zenith. There is no change. I'm going back as soon as I have eaten."

"Ha!" Daajir barked, catching Nyri off guard. This time, however, his bitterness was not directed at her. "Good luck with that! No one has told you? We carried away what we could last night, but we could not carry it all. The sentries reported the Woves split up. While most of the pack came searching for us, the rest remained and took all that we could not take with us. We did not have time to hide the food from the Gathering properly and they also raided the tree stores."

The news stole the air from Nyri's lungs. She choked as she glared up at Daajir. "They took our food?"

"What do you think? They wouldn't care if they left us for dead. It's what Ninsiku made them for. If they can't capture or kill us for the feast, then why not starve us while taking everything for themselves?"

Nyri straightened with an effort and walked on. She hoped the Wove out there in the forest rotted in the Pits of Ninsiku's damnation. She would not shed any tears over him. She would go back and dance on his grave as soon as she was sure he was dead and no more poison could pass from his lips.

They reached the nearest tree used for storing food. With Daajir following, Nyri climbed into the branches, quieting the stinging thorns that guarded against raiding with an absent thought; raiding from birds and maamits at least. The entrance to the store was set high into the bulbous trunk of the *eshaara* tree, creating a deep, cool chamber within. She felt sick when she saw the nearly empty space. All of their hard work to lay provisions for the long Fury—all for nothing. Yesterday's fruitful gathering had never even made it this far. Many of the baskets and hanging nets were gone. Cut free and carried away by the enemy.

Entering the tree behind her, Daajir peered into one depleted basket; his lips were white with anger. "The Elders

137

are assessing the situation. Rations may have to be cut to one piece of food per day."

"No! Daajir, that will never be enough! The weakest members of the tribe won't survive on such rations." Hot tears started in Nyri's eyes.

Daajir's were dry and hard as stone. He had done his grieving. Now it was time to do what had to be done. "There is no other way!" he said. "If we do not, the provisions will fail by mid-Fury. Even rationed, there is only enough for—" He cut himself off and turned his back. His shoulders were stiff beneath the leaf-leather and his fists clenched tight.

Nyri stood silent for a moment. She had no words. Giving Daajir space, she allowed herself to choose just one small fruit from a half empty basket. She may as well get used to the bite of hunger. It was a long time until the Blooming. How many of them would live to see it?

The pulp was tasteless in her mouth as she ate. Daajir regained his composure and stared into the deepening night. "They'll be back. They know we're here now. They will be back."

A chill pierced Nyri's heart. When she and Kyaati had fallen so conveniently into their enemies' laps, they had destroyed any plan the Elders had put into place. Their enemies knew the tribe was here now. Daajir was right. They would be back.

Daajir shifted. "Half of the Elders say we should leave this place and flee. Aardn has overruled them for now. Where do we run to with the Fury so fast approaching? There is nowhere else for us to go. Without shelter or provisions, we will die." He paused, weighing his words. "Our only option is to defend ourselves. We need to fight back. It served us well enough last night."

For a long time Nyri stared into the darkening sky, feeling it reflect the hopelessness within her soul. She fought against it, but it was like trying to push back the night itself.

"What are you thinking?" Daajir asked finally.

"That I want to run into the forest again and never stop this time."

He glowered at her.

"What can we do, Dar? We got lucky. We caught them by surprise last night. Their weapons are powerful, and they are bigger and stronger than we are. How can we ever defend ourselves against them? Such a course would spell our doom as surely as anything else. We can't expect the wolves to protect us. Would we sacrifice the lives of the Great Spirit's Children for ours? The Woves will be ready for them next time. They'll bring more weapons to kill them."

"I'm taking care of it. You just focus on taking care of Kyaati."

He disappeared back down the tree before Nyri could ask what he could mean by that. She sighed. She would not interfere; let him indulge in whatever helped to distract him from this. Nyri needed to return to her own distraction before she was crushed beneath the weight of it all.

She climbed back down to earth, wincing now at the touch of the ground on the soles of her feet. Her breath plumed in the air. She needed to find shelter fast.

Hurrying back to the warmer walls of Baarias' dwelling, she was grateful to find he had set more of the *girru* moss glowing. Nyri found her teacher kneeling beside Kyaati. He had her head propped on one arm while dripping water into her mouth with his free hand. Her eyes were still closed, but the water was going down. Baarias looked up as Nyri came to stand beside him. He took her hand. *Still no response, but she is swallowing liquids. That's a blessing. She would soon perish without water. I can feed her honey. If we have any left...* He trailed off.

I'll watch over her tonight, Baarias. Nyri thought. *You need to get some rest.* He still looked exhausted.

You don't look much better.

I'm younger, tired old man. Nyri smiled half-heartedly.

Baarias laughed and gave way to her. "Ninmah watch over you this night, Nyriaana," he said as he moved out to his private chamber. "I should sleep better knowing you're safe in my home and not out running with Woves."

Nyri's nerves thrilled. "Go," she said, hiding her eyes from his, lest he read something there. She settled down beside Kyaati as he left, cocooning herself in the leaves and moss, and tried to get warm. It allowed her the illusion of safety as the temperature plummeted. She wondered if the Wove in the Pit could survive without shelter. Nyri felt a shiver of concern before she quashed it. *It's not Juaan, you fool! That's your enemy out there. Be glad that it'll most likely freeze to death. One less beast to come after you.*

Nyri turned her attention to Kyaati when her rebellious heart refused to quieten. She brushed her fingers through her friend's hair. "It's a cold night, Kyaati," she murmured. She did not focus on the negativities of that. She had to make Kyaati feel like there was something to live for. After her talk with Daajir, she was hard pressed to think of anything. If she was honest with herself, it would be a relief just to close her own mind to the world, lie down, and accept the inevitable.

"It's going to be a beautiful morning," she said instead. "Can you imagine it? Clear skies, no clouds to interrupt the dawning of Ninmah. You always loved those mornings. It'd be wonderful to share it together." No response. Nyri watched her friend's steady breathing for a few more moments and gave up. "I'll be right here if you need me, Kyaati."

Nyri's eyes were heavy. She hadn't been awake for long, but the recent events still dragged at her, sapping her energy. She laid her head down, keeping the image of the morning forefront in her mind so that it might hide all else as she slept.

* * *

12

A Line Drawn

Daajir paced through the trees. The path he trod had become a well-worn route. His mind took him to where he needed to go without the need for conscious thought.

His fingers flexed into claw-like appendages as the previous night's events ran through his mind, stinging and ripping as they went. Kyaati, her baby. If only he had been quicker. If only he had tested his plans sooner, he could have protected her from those beasts. He had been weak, and that had cost his people dearly. Cost *him*.

His hopes for the future lay shrivelled at his feet. He had planned, once Kyaati's baby had been born, to approach the Elders and ask for their approval of the match. He would have been Joined to her at last — as he should have been from the start. It had been that weak fool Yaanth who had first taken her from him all those seasons ago. A match that should never have been. Aardn was right. Sefaan had much to answer for. Because of her misguided actions, Kyaati had lost three precious lives. But the last, the last was on him.

Daajir kicked savagely at the ground as he recalled Kyaati's lifeless eyes as she lay in Baarias' tree. The object of his desire. Ruined. If Kyaati had been robbed from him a second time, that left one other possibility. He wasn't blind to the intents of the Elders. He knew their secret hope.

Nyriaana.

Daajir snorted through his nose. That maddening slip of a girl. Reluctantly, he turned the possibility over in his mind. She was certainly strong in Ninmah's Gift. Stronger than Kyaati, perhaps. *Hmmm.* Despite all her flaws, it was tempting. He would have to wait, of course. Baarias seemed to be in no hurry to name her a full *akaab,* but he could not put it off forever. The thought of the children they could produce filled his mind. Perhaps he would even have the honour of fathering the next Kamaali, replacing the dangerous fool, Sefaan at last. The thought banished his gloom for a few glorious moments.

Then he thought of Nyriaana herself, and the glow retreated. Even for a Kamaali offspring, the thought of sullying himself with the Forbidden-lover turned him cold. The way she had *fawned* over that thing as a child. Daajir's stomach roiled. He regretted that the satisfaction of finishing that abomination had not fallen to him. Yet another thing the Woves had robbed him of.

He grumbled to himself. Maybe it was no matter. Nyri had been nothing more than a misguided baby, and in the passing seasons since the abomination's murder, he had found it in his heart to forgive her, if only a little. Nevertheless, she had still grown into a foolish girl. Her actions over the past days had proven that much. He flexed his fingers in vexation.

Suppose she had been killed by the *grishnaa* or taken by

the Woves? He would have had to live with yet another life on his conscience.

Perhaps if he was Joined with Nyriaana, he could curb her more flighty tendencies. He could see to it she grew up at last and took her duties to her people seriously.

As he had failed to do.

Daajir came to a halt when the dank smell of the hollow filled his nostrils. He had reached his destination without even realising it. He looked around. The overhanging trees shrouded the place in shadow, never quite letting the black soil at their roots dry up. Puddles gathered here and there. The scent of rotting leaf mould hung over everything in a shroud.

Breathing through his mouth, Daajir started into the hollow, making his way to a fallen, half-rotted trunk. The earth squelched between his toes as he pushed the log back.

The hissing snake reared up to greet him. Its irritation lashed against Daajir's senses and before he could think, the serpent struck, catching him upon the arm with its venomous fangs.

"Ah!" Daajir fell back a step as the burning began in his wrist. The snake coiled, awaiting his next move as it watched him with lidless eyes. Daajir growled as he studied the puncture wounds. Another visit to Baarias. But that would have to wait. He could hold off the venom's effects long enough to do what he needed. Extending his will, he slowed the blood flow in his arm, containing the deadly substance before it could reach his vital innards. If it got there, death would be instant.

He glared at the snake. "I have no time for your games today." The snake spat, hissing low in its throat. Daajir bared his teeth. "Fight me if you wish, but I have run out of patience. You *will* serve me."

Until now, he had given the snake a choice to do as he asked. It was Ninmah's lore that the Children of the Great Spirit should be respected, but such restrictions were becoming a hindrance. He grabbed hold of the snake's mind with all of his power.

It resisted, fighting against Daajir's hold. And Daajir fought back. Each time it tried to wrench its mind free, Daajir caused it pain, jabbing at its nerves as it writhed and twisted before him in the dirt.

Fury turned to fear as the creature realised there was no escape. Daajir felt its terror saturate his tongue and... he liked it. A heady sense of power flooded through him as the snake accepted it must bend to his will or die.

Its struggles ceased, and it lay exhausted in the dirt, head bowed, ready to do whatever he wanted. A slow grin slid over Daajir's face as he drew out a haala nutshell half. He extended it towards the snake's lowered head.

Bite. He commanded.

Obediently, the snake opened its mouth and bit down on the shell, allowing Daajir to push it up into his fangs and draw the venom from its sacks.

"Good." Daajir sent the thought. "Remember this next time we meet. You serve me now." The snake did not meet his eyes as he dropped the log back over it.

Daajir swirled the deadly contents of the shell before him. Potent. But too fast acting for his liking. He did not want things to happen too fast. Quick was a mercy, and their enemies did not deserve mercy.

Fortunately, Daajir believed he had found the answer. A

carnivorous *vaash* plant grew close to where he stood. Its downward pointing thorns, each one twice as long as his finger, dripped a purple poison into the slimy reservoir that it had formed around its stem. The perfect trap for unsuspecting rodents to fall into and dissolve slowly into the plant's digestive juices.

The action of the *vaash* plant's poison was slow. Best of all, there was no cure for it. Carefully, Daajir plucked a thorn from the plant's stem and dipped its deadly tip into the snake venom. In theory, he had created the perfect concoction. Slow acting, painful and incurable.

But that was all it was. Theory. His courage had failed short of testing this invention. That cowardice had cost him Kyaati. Daajir looked at the dripping thorn in his hand. Its tip was razor sharp. Sharp enough to pierce the skin of its intended victims. It would suffice in delivering the poison. He had everything he needed. It was time to test it—

A rustle of leaves brought his head up. A deer was browsing through the undergrowth. It returned his regard calmly for a few moments before continuing on its way.

Daajir gritted his teeth, his courage wavering. To control a Child of the Great Spirit against its will was a serious trespass. To *kill* a Child of the Great Spirit...

Daajir shuddered, almost turning away until the memory of Kyaati's despairing face stiffened his spine. What was one life when he would save so many more?

Gripping the thorn between his fingers, Daajir started after the deer in his sights...

* * *

13

Secrets

Ninmah had dawned bright over the canopy as Sefaan emerged from her tree. The basket of materials she carried in her hands was hard against her stiff fingers. The sky above the gently waving leaves of the trees was shot with a rainbow of colours. She drew a rattling breath of the crisp air as the ground bit at her toes, exacerbating the ache in her joints.

Sefaan sighed. Discomfort was becoming her constant companion. *Too old, too old...* It would be a relief when Ninmah finally allowed her to join with the Great Spirit. But, tired as she was, she knew there were vital tasks ahead. The Great Spirit still needed her, and so here she remained.

Sefaan spied Aardn walking through the trees at a distance. Dislike curled through her stomach. Vital tasks to be done, and yet the Elder had done all that she could to make Sefaan's role in guiding her people almost impossible. She had severely underestimated the wily determination of Aardn.

Aardn's words from long ago rose in Sefaan's mind. *Mark my words, you have brought a curse down upon us this day. I*

147

will never forget it. Nor had she forgiven.

Her hatred for what Sefaan had forced the tribe to accept that day had forever tainted her respect for the authority of the Kamaali. She had been determined that such a heresy would never be accepted again. Sefaan knew that if Aardn could exclude her fully from any participation in the tribe's function, she would do it.

Sefaan raised her chin. She had done what the Great Spirit commanded. That was her duty as Kamaali. To do otherwise would be to go against Ninmah's will. Aardn was too blinded to see it.

A movement caught Sefaan's eye, and she turned her head to see young Nyriaana emerging from the healer's tree. The girl's brow was creased with concern, and her stride lacked its usual energy.

"Nyriaana," she called. The girl paused at the sound of her name and then came towards her. Her troubled expression did not lift in greeting, but she relieved Sefaan of the basket she carried without hesitation, helping her to place it on the ground. She would make a fine healer one day.

"How is Kyaati?" Sefaan asked. She already knew the answer, but it was obvious that Nyriaana was too distracted to speak and she wanted the girl to talk.

"There's no change," she answered. "She's just… lifeless."

Hmmm. Sefaan dropped her gaze. *This is not how it is supposed to happen. That girl* cannot *die.* Sefaan had not yet divined the reason for Kyaati's great necessity in the Great Spirit's plan, but she knew in her bones that the girl needed to live. She only hoped that Baarias would be up to the task ahead.

Sefaan's brow creased at the thought of the healer. Baarias

was the most important of all. The Great Spirit swirled around him. Everything depended upon a choice he would soon make, and it remained to be seen if he had the courage to make the right one. He had failed so many times in the past. It had been pleasing to see him stand up to the Elders at long last, but was it enough?

"Sefaan?"

"Hmmm?" She realised the girl was still standing before her.

"I was going to find some honey." Nyriaana spoke. "She can only take liquid."

"Ah." Yes, Kyaati needed food. Baarias knew what he was doing in this regard, at least. Sefaan reached around behind her for the *haala* nut containing her breakfast. The curving brown sides were sticky with the cloudy yellow substance, spilling from a hole in the top. "Here." She pushed it into Nyri's hands. "I was keeping it because I know what it's like to only be able to take liquids." She flashed her weakening teeth at Nyriaana.

"Sefaan," the girl protested, trying to push the large shell back at her. "I can find some more. You might need this."

"Kyaati needs it more, child. You take it for her. We need her. She is vital. Believe me."

Nyriaana nodded. Sefaan knew she did not divine the true meaning of her words. The girl was only thinking of her friend's importance to herself.

"I'll get Daajir to find me more," Sefaan soothed Nyriaana's conscience in taking the honey. "That boy needs something healthy to focus on. I don't like the path he is following. I feel a great sadness is approaching, and he is at the centre of it..."

149

The Great Spirit had shivered last night. A balance had been tipped, and not for the better.

Nyriaana shifted her gaze over Sefaan's shoulder, uncharacteristically disinterested. The crease between her brows had not loosened since Sefaan had first laid eyes on her. The Great Spirit danced. *Look...* the energy seemed to whisper. *Look now...*

Sefaan had been a Kamaali too long to ignore such a tug. She caught hold of Nyriaana's hand and extended her will. The girl's shock rippled as she hastily tried to throw a guard up around her thoughts.

"Ah... Daajir is not the only one keeping secrets, it seems," Sefaan muttered. She closed her eyes, concentrating. Behind Nyriaana's defences, Sefaan could feel the great conflict raging inside her. "Your heart and your head are very much at war over it."

Nyriaana stiffened under her touch as Sefaan's words hit their target.

"What are you hiding, young one?"

Nyriaana's thoughts raced against Sefaan's mind. So great was the girl's anguish that they could no longer be contained.

Nyri, Nyri, Nyriaana. A voice called.

Juaan. The girl's own voice answered.

Then there were more images. They flashed behind Sefaan's closed lids. Images of a fur cloaked, skull-faced horror lying at the bottom of a Pit. No sooner had the image formed in Sefaan's mind than the picture morphed and the nightmarish figure became a boy, lying broken, freezing and starving to death at the bottom of a deep Pit. Dying alone. Agony swirled around the image.

Nyriaana...

No, the girl's voice again. *You're dead. You can't be there. It's not you.*

Nyriaana...

"No!" Nyriaana tried to pull away, horrified by her betraying thoughts. "Please, Sefaan, don't! I must be alone in this and my decision is made."

The Great Spirit spiked at this declaration, despairing.

"No!" It was Sefaan's turn to deny the girl as panic shot through her. "Time is running out. Fast!" More. She needed to know more. Sefaan tightened her hold on Nyriaana's hand. The Great Spirit swirled about them and Sefaan gasped. She had got it wrong. Perhaps she was losing her grip after all. *This* was the choice upon which the future depended. "Decide soon or it will be too late. Act, child!" Her voice was sharp in her own ears, and Nyriaana flinched as she released her hand. "I was wrong. It wasn't Baarias. Not him. It is *you*." The girl was always so close to the healer, it had made it easy to mistake the direction of the Great Spirit. "The choice *you* make could change everything. The future is fast arriving. It sits in your hands, waiting."

"How? Why?" Nyriaana asked, bewildered.

"I cannot tell you because you will not confide in me. The secret you hold is too great." Sefaan turned away. She needed to think, to focus. "I will say this: do not become the coward your teacher has always been. Be brave like your mother and follow your heart, Nyriaana. I know it will never lead you astray."

* * *

151

14

The Choice

The future is fast arriving. It sits in your hands... waiting. Sefaan's words became an inescapable torment as Nyri made her way back to Baarias' tree. How could the future be sitting in her hands? The only secret she kept was the whereabouts of an enemy. That meant nothing. And yet... her traitorous heart kept running out into the forest, back to fret over that cursed Pit.

Nyri, Nyri, Nyriaana.

Nyri tightened her control; pulling her heart away from the edge. There was no way she would go back out there. Even if she wanted to, it was too dangerous. Baarias was right, their enemies could be anywhere. The sentries had not yet discovered the whereabouts of the Woves or confirmed that they had left the territory. They could be out in the woods right now, searching for their fallen companion, hunting for her people. She shivered.

Baarias thankfully did not comment on her distracted state as they spent the day treating those that had suffered injuries in their flight from the Woves. Perhaps he was simply as distracted as she, worrying over Kyaati.

"Ah!" Daajir flinched as Nyri applied a poultice to the puncture wounds on his arm under Baarias' supervision.

"Be careful, Nyri," Baarias admonished as she continued to attend to the wounds, her mind only half on the task. He sighed. "Why in Ninmah did you wait so long to bring this to my attention, Daajir? Any longer and I wouldn't have been able to do anything for you."

Daajir's arm shifted in Nyri's grip as he shrugged in sullen response. Nyri looked up from her work to study his face. His features were drawn, his eyes haunted. He grimaced at her when he saw her scrutinising him and turned his face away without a word. She scowled back and tightened the poultice around his arm with unnecessary force. What did she care about how he had got bitten by a snake? She had enough worries to occupy her mind.

"Ow!" His protest was worth Baarias' scolding.

As darkness fell for the second time since the Wove attack, Nyri remained by Kyaati's side. Curled deep into the moss-filled bower, she tried not to jump at every night sound. Nyri comforted herself, knowing that if the Woves were closing, the sentries would sound the alert.

Kyaati lay motionless beside her. She wanted to say something, to offer words of comfort, but all thoughts lodged in her throat. Nyri sighed and turned over, seeking release in sleep. She could not remember ever feeling more exhausted, but peace would not be granted.

Decide soon or it will be too late. You must act!

Nyri, Nyri, Nyriaana...

Her heart contracted, yearning to answer the call, fighting against her control. It was now almost too powerful to contain.

Follow your heart.

Nyri...

Do not be a coward. Be brave like your mother...

As if in answer, her mother's voice rose to join Sefaan's. *Nyri, I want you to meet Juaan... We have to look after him now because no one else will.*

No one else will...

I promise to look after you, too, Juaan. We look after each other now.

By the time Ninmah rose, Nyri had crumbled. Scrubbing dry, sleep-deprived eyes, she threw herself out of the bower to pace fiercely back and forth. Waves of nervous energy rolled through her body, but she did not bother to control it.

Nyriaana.

"Stop!" she burst out. "Ninmah, so help me!" But Ninmah did not answer, and no clarity was forthcoming.

The choice you make could change everything...

Nyri growled, clenching her fists. She stopped pacing to stare down at the unmoving Kyaati. She had always been able to tell her anything. Kyaati had never held any love for Juaan, either, but there would be no harm in sharing this secret with her now. If it snapped her out of this frightening stupor, then so much the better. Nothing else had worked.

"Kyaati, I don't know what to do. I know you don't want to respond, but please listen. When I ran on the night you lost your baby, I ended up near the Pits. I-I found a Wove. He'd fallen into one of the traps. I turned to run but... before I got away, I-I thought I heard a voice whispering something, something only one other person besides me should know."

Nyri's thoughts swirled as the impossible fought to make itself a reality in her mind. "That person was Juaan, Kya! The Wove said something only Juaan could know." She realised her hands were shaking and clenched her fists. "But how can I let myself believe that... *thing* down there is him? I've done my best to convince myself that I imagined what I heard and forget. A Wove deserves nothing but death."

She blew out a breath and forced herself to relax her fingers. "Every time I close my eyes, I see him there. I see the boy I knew dying in the woods alone. I hear his voice, calling me from the dark. I can't stand it! I know I promised I wouldn't leave you again, Kyaati, but I *have* to go back. I have to know the truth if I am ever going to know peace. I owe it to the boy who saved my life."

Nyri sucked in a sharp breath, the cold biting at her lungs. Now that she had voiced her turmoil, her path was clear. She could not hide from this. Sefaan was right; Juaan or mindless Wove, she had to know. She had to act now or she would be tormented forever. Time was running out.

"Have you slept at all?" A voice came from the entrance-way. Baarias was there, observing her ragged state. He appeared only a little more rested than he had the day before.

"I have to go, Baarias."

"Where?" He was taken aback by Nyri's sharp tone. She could feel him probing her state of mind.

"I can't say." She moved past him, her stride conveying her determination. "There is something I have to do. I'll be back. I promise. Please watch over Kyaati for me."

Nyri swept out of the dwelling before Baarias could stop her and demand that she explain. She could not stop. If she did, she might falter, and she needed to know this one thing.

Her very sanity depended on it.

15

Friend or Foe?

Nyri was running before she even left the *eshaara* grove. Now that she had come to her decision, the sense of urgency she had been trying to suppress was almost unbearable. She *had* to get back to the Pits, right now. Something was tugging at her, telling her all would be lost if she did not hurry. Strange, disembodied images of savaging fangs and the spilling of blood flickered through her mind, goading her flight.

She was careful to keep her senses thrown out as far as they would go. The thought of the Woves lurking in the trees threatened to overcome her need. She pushed her legs faster. The hardened ground hurt her feet. She had eaten so little her body threatened to rebel against the misuse.

Just as she thought her body and courage would take her no further, Nyri reached her destination and the reason for her sense of urgency became terribly clear.

"Batai! No!" She rushed towards the wolf pack surrounding the Pit holding her answers. The young wolf had been preparing to leap to the bottom, lips peeling from his thick fangs.

No! Nyri threw out her command. Batai leaped back from the edge, lupine surprise registering on his face. He looked at Nyri, along with the rest of the pack. A few snarls of frustration broke out.

Nyri cringed. Trying to take a wolf pack's kill was not usually in anyone's best interest. It was downright stupid. Times were lean for all of them. But Nyri had no choice. Lifting her chin, she approached purposefully, claiming the area with her energy and posture. Nyri conveyed herself as the strongest member; an alpha, not to be questioned.

They allowed her approach. She singled out the alpha male. He bit back on his impatience and consented to let Nyri touch his grey-brown head. *He's with me.* She didn't think the words; words meant nothing to wolves. Nyri radiated the energies and instincts that he would understand; the language of the earth. The figure down there was a part of her pack and therefore off the menu. He listened, then huffed consentingly. Releasing his pent up energy with a sharp shake of his dark fur, he walked away. Most of the pack followed except Batai, who lay down at the Pit edge watching Nyri.

"I promise, Batai," she whispered, "if he is not Juaan, you have my permission to eat him."

The wolf cocked his head at the sounds she made, uncomprehending, but he waited respectfully for her next move.

Nyri hesitated, unsure of what that should be. Now that she was here, the uncertainty and doubt had returned. They clutched at her throat, pulling her back. She was more frightened than she could say. *Juaan,* she reminded her shrinking courage. *You owe it to him.*

Everything was in her heart as she stepped up to the rocky edge. Wove or Juaan, her Juaan, returned from the dead? She did not know in that moment which thought scared her the most. There was no sound coming from the Pit, and Nyri dared to lean further over. Her breath caught in her throat as the dark form came into view.

He wasn't moving.

Nyri reached out with her higher senses. *Please don't be gone,* she thought as she searched for his energy. His life force was barely there. He wasn't gone, but he was close.

Nyri sank to her haunches at the edge of the precipice, gnawing on a ragged fingernail. For a few moments, she just sat there watching the form in the Pit. She was clueless as to how she should proceed and find her answers. The empty eye socket of the skull stared up at her, sending a chill down her spine. She thought of Juaan's face as she remembered it, set with beloved green eyes. She would know those eyes anywhere. She must be losing her mind to even consider that this skull-headed demon could be him.

Nyri cast around. Picking up a pebble, she aimed and dropped it into the depths. It bounced off the body below and rattled across the ground. Nyri flinched and leaned back, ready to run, but he did not even stir.

"Hey," she dared to breathe. "Hey."

Nothing. Frustrated, she got to her feet and paced up and down the edge. Did she dare go down there? Her steps faltered at the very thought, but it seemed there was no other option. She could not go home without her answers, and time was slipping away. She would have to lower herself down and face the potential viper in the Pit.

Before her common sense could talk her out of the suicidal

idea, Nyri searched the immediate area. First problem: getting down. It was a long way to the bottom. The stone walls were smooth and concave. She could not climb down by scrambling on the rocks. She spied a long, thin root running along the surface of the earth. The idea formed as Nyri followed the root's course to its end.

Digging into the soil, she pulled it up. It was thin but strong; Nyri believed it would take her weight. She retraced her steps, pulling and heaving the root out of the ground as she went. At points the ground was still too hard and Nyri had to strike it with a rock to make it yield its powerful grip on her root-rope.

Before she knew it, she was back at the edge of the Pit with the length of root clasped in her fists. Nyri stared warily at the figure below and then threw the root down with a trembling hand. The dark form remained motionless, and her confidence lifted.

Even so, it was still a few more moments and quite a few more deep breaths before Nyri could bring herself to follow her rope's path. Memories of past death and destruction flickered at the edges of her consciousness, fur clad figures burning at the centre. She balled her fists; her palms were slick with sweat.

Damn you, Sefaan. Nyri wiped her tingling palms dry and swung her legs over the side of the hole, watching the figure below as she would a venomous snake. It was now or never. With one last prayer to Ninmah for protection, Nyri took hold of the root and began to lower herself down. Her entire body was a mass of nerves. If that figure so much as twitched, she would be climbing back up as fast as she could go. He could not be let to escape.

But he did not move and before she knew it, Nyri's toes were touching cold, unyielding rock. She looked up at the sky above. Batai was staring down at her. A soft whine sounded from his throat as his ears tilted towards his neck.

"Stay there," she breathed.

It was even worse now that she was down. Paralysed by fear, Nyri stood with her hands fixed upon the root. This went against every instinct she possessed.

Dropping into a defensive half-crouch, she backed away from the figure lying on the ground. She stopped only when her back contacted the wall of the Pit and she could go no further. Sinking back onto her heels, she pressed her body against the unrelenting stone, wishing she could disappear into it. She did not even dare to breathe.

As she struggled to relocate her courage, Nyri made a quick study. Black furs covered the body from head to toe. Broken shards of bone protruded from the limbs here and there. The thought struck that this was the very demon who had approached Kyaati at the base of that fateful tree; the leader of the band that had raided her tribe.

Anger and hate flared inside of her. The urge to drop a heavy rock on his bleached white head in vengeance for what they had done was almost overwhelming. Nyri had to keep the thought of Juaan firmly in her head at that moment.

There was nothing for it. Nyri had to move. Hesitantly, she stole along on both hands and feet until she was right next to the Wove. She was so close she could smell the dirty furs; Nyri wrinkled her nose in distaste. Without touching him, she made a cursory sweep of his physical condition. His right leg was broken, the calf bloodied and torn by a nasty wolf bite. She could not be sure without contact, but she suspected that two of his ribs were cracked.

What pain he must be in. Nyri felt a quiver of pity, Wove or no. She was a healer, after all. She cocked her head. Did evil spirits feel pain?

She scrutinised the grisly garments. She had never had the opportunity to study a Wove up close before. No one had. Everyone was always too busy running away. Her gaze travelled reluctantly up to the skull and Nyri flinched back in astonishment. The hideous head had twisted into an unnatural angle, but the neck had not snapped. Instead, hair and skin had been revealed beneath the bone. Nyri reached out with tentative fingers and gave the stinking skull an experimental nudge.

It shifted beneath her touch, exposing a human chin and jawbone. Nyri gasped. A mask! Her heart pounded as she made another sweep of the body, finding other falsehoods as she did. The terrifying, jutting bones covering the arms and legs were nothing more than animal bones tied into place. With the lies revealed, Nyri found this form before her to be strikingly similar to her own People. She could detect no power, no dark magic. It was then that an object tied at the fur-wrapped waist caught her eye, and her breath froze inside her chest.

It couldn't be!

It was an object out of place amidst all the foreign furs. A leaf-leather pouch. A Ninkuraaja pouch. It was battered and old, but Nyri remembered it. She remembered it so very well. Her hands shook as they went to her mouth, tears of disbelief starting in her eyes. She hadn't dared, hadn't truly dared to believe until this moment. Nyri lifted the leather bag—

162

She was on the ground before she could think. Long fingers grabbed her wrist, yanking her hand away from the pouch with irresistible strength. She was thrown to the hard rock like a leaf, knocking the air from her lungs. She couldn't breathe. Then another hand was closing around her throat, cutting off her airway. "No, no," she croaked.

The world blurred. Nyri's hands went to the fingers choking the life from her battered body. A face appeared above her, the concealing skull tumbling away completely. The features were rough, hairy, foreign, but in the midst of it all, staring balefully down, were a pair of green green eyes.

The sharp edge of a blade joined the hand at her throat. A shot of adrenaline lent Nyri vital strength. She managed to pry the fingers away enough to scream.

"Juaan! No!"

16

Stranger

"No, Juaan!"

Her mother's sharp command stopped the boy in his tracks. Nyriaana stood, trembling and frightened, arms still outstretched from where the boy had twisted free of them. She shrank down, terrified by the anger and hate he was radiating. He was facing away from her, readying to launch himself at a group of Elders who had arrived on the scene, their voices raised and full of revulsion as they demanded to know her mother's business.

They took a half a step back from Juaan's violent reaction, but otherwise showed no other sign of surprise. A pair of arms scooped her from the ground as her father rushed her to a safe distance.

"Jaai!" He called. "Get away from him."

Her mother ignored him. "Juaan," she said again. "Don't. Don't give them an excuse." She turned her gaze to the Elders, her expression cold. "You ought to be ashamed of yourselves!" Nyri felt her father draw a breath of shock. "The boy is grieving. His mother joined the Great Spirit last night. Have you no heart?"

"The heathen is dead," Aardn, the youngest of the Elders spoke, eyeing Nyri's mother with distaste. "I see no reason why... that," she gestured to the tall boy, "should stay now."

Nyri watched as the boy balled his fists. He was shaking. He could barely contain his rage. Jaai put her hand out in a blocking motion and calming energy rolled out, cocooning him. The trembling eased.

"Rebaa was no traitor," her mother spoke. "She was a loyal daughter of Ninmah. Juaan carries her blood, and you gave her your word. Would you dishonour the promise you made before Ninmah herself to one of her own, exulted Elders?" She shamed them with her words.

"Watch yourself, Jaai."

"Would you?"

Their annoyance was palpable, but they could not fight her mother's words. Aardn curled her lip. "Who is going to keep him now? No one in their-"

"I will look after him," Jaai said firmly. "I gave my promise to Rebaa, too, and I intend to honour it. I will raise her son as my own."

Aardn hissed between her teeth. "You're as crazy as Rebaa."

Jaai held her ground. "Even so, I will not break a promise made before Ninmah. Sefaan herself ordained it is meant to be. I cannot go against the Kamaali."

Aardn's jaw worked in frustration. "And we all must honour the Kamaali's wishes," she ground out. "Alright, keep the abomination. He is yours until our word binds us no longer. Prepare yourself for that day. We will be waiting." With that stark promise, the Elders turned away, skirting around the green-eyed boy in their midst as if his very presence sullied them.

Jaai let out a breath and turned to Nyri and her father. "It is

165

all right, Telaan. Let her back down."

"No," her father refused, gripping her tighter. "Jaai, that thing is dangerous. Would you risk your own child so readily?"

Her mother snarled, and Nyri felt her father flinch. "How dare you, Telaan? You know very well Nyri means more to me than life itself!"

Nyri was watching the boy they called Juaan. She wondered why he was causing such trouble. Now his anger had burned out. He didn't look that frightening to her. He had collapsed to his knees and was crying openly. Just a boy who had lost his mama. Her heart bled for him.

She struggled in her father's arms. "Put me down, papa!" He only held her tighter. She stopped struggling and put her hand to his face, letting him feel what she did. "Please. Mama says he is safe. He not hurt me. I know." She could not say how she knew that. She just did.

Her father's eyes flickered to her and then her mother. Under both their dark indigo stares, he gave in. He placed Nyri on the ground, but he did not stay. He walked away and climbed back into their tree and out of sight. Her mother's gaze followed him, face tightening with concern.

Nyri paid them no more mind. She tottered back to the strange boy who was now part of her family. She plopped herself next to him.

"Why they hate you?"

"Different." His face was buried in his long hands.

"Oh." She didn't really understand.

Reaching out, she toyed with a little leather bag that was tied to his waist. "What this?"

His tear-streaked face came out from behind the hands to glare at her. "My mother gave it to me. Leave it." He shifted his hip, moving the pouch out of her reach.

Nyri put her hands behind her back. She stared at his eyes; the colour was unnerving. Different. Different? They hated him because he was different. Nyri dropped her gaze. She scratched a little in the soil with her fingers, frowning. She stopped when her nails came up against the hard, unrelenting surface of a rock. The stone was smooth and round and would fit into her palm nicely. She dug the pebble from the earth, intent on collecting it.

Wiping off the dirt, Nyri held it up to Ninmah to study her find. She gasped as the light caught it. It was green, like his eyes, glinting so prettily in the golden rays. She closed her fist around her new treasure and looked up at the weeping boy next to her. His mother had given him a gift. She was gone now, so Nyri would give him a gift instead.

"Look. For you." She nudged his arm. "For you." He peeked down at her little outstretched hand. "Pretty rock. Pretty... like your eyes."

He paused, then reached out and plucked the pebble from her palm, blinking at Nyri in wonder. "Pretty?"

She nodded, grinning shyly under her lashes. "Yes."

He gave her a slow, tremulous smile. "Thank you," he whispered.

She glanced up to where her father had disappeared, frowning. "You no hurt me?"

Juaan shook his head, hand closing around her gift. "Never."

* * *

"Juaan! No!"

He was gone from above her in an instant. Released from his strangling hold, Nyri doubled up on herself, choking and heaving. She gulped the frigid air into her starved lungs. Her neck felt bruised. It was a few moments before she recovered enough strength to raise her head. On all fours, she stared across the Pit. The fur-wrapped figure was now pressed against the furthest wall, watching Nyri with startled, wary eyes.

None of it mattered. Not his demon disguise, not her pain or his attack. Nothing. Motionless, she drank in the sight of him. Nyri could not describe the emotion she was feeling; it was too great to be comprehended.

What should she say? She opened her mouth several times, but in the end, all she could do was whisper his name. "Juaan. My Juaan." For it was him. Alive. He had come back to her. After all this time, he had come back.

Joy filled her heart, glowing like *girru* moss until the light of it spread to every fibre of her being and could no longer be contained; she would surely burst. Nyri started forward, the child within rising from the forgotten regions of her soul, fully intent on throwing herself into his arms. Alone no longer.

The raising of the bone blade in his fist stopped her short and punctured the moment. She rocked back. "Juaan. It's me! It's Nyri."

The blade did not waver. He did not relax his tense posture. He stared at her, and she stared back. She stared right into familiar eyes, housing the soul of a perfect stranger.

"My name is Khalvir." He spoke, and his voice was not that of the boy that had haunted her through all the passing seasons. It was the deep and discomfortingly unfamiliar voice of a man. "If you dare to come near me again, I *will* kill you."

Nyri recoiled. The sight of the blade raised against her cut at her heart. "Juaan. It's Nyriaana," she repeated. "Don't you know me?"

For the briefest moment, the hatred in his gaze clouded with confusion, pain and... fear. She took a step towards him, reaching out with a trembling hand; he *had* to know her. The knife held steady against her approach, but he tried to shift to the side to put more distance between them.

"Keep away, she-elf," he threatened.

He transferred his weight onto his broken leg. Nyri winced as she heard the bones shift. He did not make a sound, but she saw the blood drain from his face. He collapsed, the ground rushing up to punch his broken ribs, and then he did cry out. He fought hard to rise again, struggling to keep Nyri in his sights, but his depleted body betrayed him. His eyes rolled back into his head, and he collapsed in a motionless heap.

Nyri rushed forward without a thought. "Juaan! Juaan?"

No answer; he had lost consciousness again. Timidly, Nyri touched his dark brow, studying his face, trying to see past the strange hair covering the lower half. She stroked at it with tentative fingers, weeping over every dearly familiar feature, morphed and hardened by time but still, every bit of him, her Juaan.

She was overcome; unable to hold back any longer, Nyri threw herself on his chest and cried long tears. It felt as if every shred of pain she had experienced since the Woves had taken him from her, every moment she had missed him, was pouring from her soul in this dreadful, blessed Pit.

Questions flew through her mind. How could he not know her? The hostility in his eyes had been almost more than she could bear. Juaan had never looked at her in such a way.

Khalvir, he had called himself. Nyri dragged her fingers through the hideous fur coverings on Juaan's chest, wet now with her tears. He *must* remember her; she told herself. He had spoken her name in the depths of unconsciousness. Therefore, the memories were there, somewhere. He was just weak and bewildered right now, drunk with pain. Once he was healed and in his right mind, he would know her.

At least now she knew why he appeared so normal with no trace of evil spirit; this was no Wove. He had disguised himself to survive among the enemy until he could return.

Nyri sniffed, scrubbing her eyes as she sat up. She could not take her gaze from his face. By and by, Nyri began to see past her glowing wonder and saw the signs of severe deprivation. Cringing at the thought of how long she had left him here while she wrestled with her inner demons, Nyri vowed to do all that she could for him now.

Thirst had cracked his lips while hunger hollowed his cheeks. On top of the deprivation, were the injuries. Nyri drew a breath. Even with Ninkuraaja skills, broken bones could take a while to heal fully. Baarias had taught her how, but Nyri had to admit, she had had little practice at it.

She wasn't sure if she trusted herself, but she had little choice. She could not involve Baarias in this. He might be the only one who would not come down here with a pack of wolves set to kill, but she could not guarantee his reaction if he believed she was putting herself in danger. Daajir could never, ever find out. Juaan's true identity would not protect him from Daajir. Daajir had hated Juaan even as a child.

Nyri refused to let the reason for that hatred register, though the evidence lay before her.

Forbidden....

She banished the thought down deep and placed her hands on his temples. Her mind and body were still buzzing with a mix of fear and excitement, but seasons of practice made it easy for her to quiet it all and focus her energy on what was needed. He was alien and familiar all at once.

The flow of energy was sluggish; unused to being directed or used. Buried. Merging her life force with and directing a fellow Ninkuraa's energy was like breathing air; this felt like wading through mud. The energy did not flow smoothly under her direction.

As a child, Juaan had struggled to harness Ninmah's Gift, the vital connection in the mind given to all Ninkuraaja. He had always seemed so... frightened of it. Now it lay entirely dormant and forgotten. Sweat beaded on Nyri's brow from the extra effort. She increased the blood flow to the affected areas, threw the Great Spirit's energy at the broken bones, encouraging them to knit and merge once more.

Ninmah was high in the sky when Nyri finally withdrew. The golden light filtered through the trees to dance over them both. She had done as much as she could. Now she needed some materials. She climbed back out of the Pit and collected some of the tough leaves growing close by, along with a couple of slim, flexible stems before carrying her finds back into the Pit. With them, Nyri bound the broken leg; they would give the limb extra support until it had healed completely.

As she tied the last stem tightly in place, she spotted an object on the ground. It was the knife; lying where Juaan had

171

dropped it when he collapsed. For a moment, Nyri dared not touch the object. It was a Wove weapon, most likely soaked with terrible magic and unknown power; a killer. It appeared to be made from the tooth of a *grishnaa* cat and carved with mysterious markings.

Nyri hated it. It had to go. Screwing up her courage, she took it between a thumb and forefinger, careful not to waken its power, and then hurled it as far and as fast away from her as she could. It flew up out of the Pit and thudded into the undergrowth, somewhere out of sight.

Relieved by its absence, she went back to watching the man lying beside her. A part of her was still trying to convince itself that this was not an illusion. Her fingers kept stretching out to touch him, a hand, his brow. Real. So very real. And so very hard to accept, even now. She did not know how this was possible.

Ninmah passed higher overhead, and an awareness for the rest of the outside world came stealing upon her. She had to leave. The very thought of it caused her pain, but if she did not return to her tribe soon, they would come looking for her. She could not let them find Juaan. She had to leave for his sake if nothing else; they would kill him.

There was Kyaati to consider, too. She leaned down and whispered in his ear. "I'll come back soon. I'll bring food and water." She had to make sure he survived. Nyri would not lose him again.

With that promise fixed in mind, she tore herself from his side and moved back to the Pit wall. She took hold of her root-rope and scrambled back to the surface. Batai was still waiting at the edge.

"Keep him safe for me," Nyri spoke to him in a low tone

as she coiled the rope. She placed it next to the Pit, allowing herself a last lingering look over the edge and the figure sleeping there. She took care to re-cover the hole before she walked back into the forest.

She did not run; she had done enough running these past days. Maybe this *was* all a vivid, cruel dream that she would have to wake from at any moment, but she did not care. She wanted to live in the dream for as long as she was able. Only one thought existed and it shone so brightly it burned away all else.

Juaan was alive!

* * *

17

Recovery

"Nyriaana!" The cry cut through the silence of the tree.

Baarias leaped to his feet, heart hammering in his chest as it roused him from his sleep. He blinked, trying to clear his mind. He knew that voice. "Kyaati?"

It couldn't be.

"*Nyriaana!*" The cry sounded again. "No! Don't go!"

"Kyaati!" Baarias dashed from his personal chamber into the part of the tree where Kyaati had lain in her death sleep. His stride faltered at the sight of her sitting up in her bower, her face alive and animated as her eyes darted around the chamber. Distress radiated from her in waves.

"Kyaati! Shhh!" Baarias recovered himself and rushed to her side. He needed to keep her calm. "Nyri is safe. She came back. She came back. Relax, dear one. She has been here with you. She's…" Where had Nyri gone? She had left in such a hurry she had not stopped to tell him what had been so urgent to her.

"No!" Kyaati refused to be assuaged. "She is in danger. She

said—" Kyaati's eyes continued to rove around the chamber. "She said…"

"Shhh," Baarias placed a hand upon her tense shoulder. "I will find her for you, just try to stay calm. She will be relieved to know that you are awake. Stay here, Kyaati, rest. I will find Nyriaana and bring her to you."

She resisted for a moment as he tried to lean her back into the leaves, but she did not have the strength to fight and gave in. "Nyri… Wove."

"She returned after the Woves attacked, Kyaati. She is safe. I will find her, please, try to stay calm, young one."

Baarias left the chamber. Sweet relief coursed through his veins. He had almost given up hope. He lifted his eyes towards Ninmah. *Thank you…* He didn't think his heart could have taken another death. The situation was far from over, but he couldn't let such concerns trouble him in this shining moment.

A presence brushed against his senses, getting closer, and his heart leaped. He wouldn't have to track Nyri down after all.

His young charge entered the tree before him. Distracted, she did not notice him waiting in the shadows. Her face was twitching, as though she was trying very hard to control her expression. Her emotions gave her away, however. She was elated. Overjoyed. Her aura glowed against his senses.

Baarias would learn the reason behind this elation later. Right now he had other news to add to her joy. Unable to resist, he darted forward and caught her in his arms, crushing her to him.

"Oof! Baarias! What's the matter with you?"

"Nyri, she's awake! She's awake!"

175

Nyri blinked, then gripped his forearms as his words took meaning. He felt her heart soar. "When? How? What did you do?"

"Nothing. She woke just moments ago. She seemed most agitated as to your whereabouts. I struggled to keep her down." His smile widened into a grin. He couldn't remember smiling this much in a very long time. "I *knew* you were the key to bringing her back to us."

To his surprise, Nyriaana's face became somewhat fixed as he said this; a sharp crease formed between her brows, wrinkling the Mark of Ninmah. "Can I see her?" She asked. "*Please*, Baarias."

He laughed. "Yes." Of course she would be eager to see this miraculous recovery for herself. He took in her appearance fully for the first time and noticed the dirty streaks on her face. "What's the matter? You've been crying."

Her eyes widened at the observation, and she wiped hastily at her cheeks. "I was just… worrying about Kyaati. I'd lost hope that she'd ever come back to us." She kept her eyes down as a flush crept into her cheeks.

Baarias patted her shoulder in sympathy. She should not be embarrassed about her tears. "Cry no longer, my dear Nyriaana. Come, she has been asking for you. Just be mindful that she is still very weak."

"Of course," Nyri agreed. "I won't tire her."

Baarias could feel her tension mounting as he led her back to the chamber where Kyaati waited. He was anxious himself, afraid that Kyaati would have lapsed into her stupor again in the short time he had been away.

He needn't have feared.

"Kyaati?" Nyriaana's voice came upon a sigh of air as her

friend's face turned towards them. "Kyaati!" His student rushed past him and threw her arms around the other girl. Smiling, Baarias leaned against the wall of the tree. He ought to leave them to have their reunion in private, but after all the sorrow, he couldn't help gravitating towards this joyous scene.

"Nyri," Kyaati's voice cracked. "You're safe?" Her hands fluttered up and down Nyriaana's back.

"Yes, I'm safe," Nyri reassured her. "I'm here."

"W-where did you go?" Kyaati asked. "I remember you talking. I could hear you b-but it was like a dream. You were telling me about a Wove in a Pit and... you were going to see it." She pulled away and rubbing at her forehead.

Nyri's shoulders stiffened. "You were dreaming, Kyaati." Was her quick reply. "Why would I be going to see a Wove in a Pit? Even I am not that reckless." She gave a half grin, but Baarias could tell it was forced. "Daajir would never again let me leave my tree."

Baarias frowned. What Kyaati was saying was indeed absurd, but something was wrong. He would ask Nyriaana the cause of her agitation later when they were away from Kyaati. She knew she could confide in him for anything.

"I-I don't know." Kyaati's face clouded. "I don't know where I've been." She was exhausted.

Baarias stepped forward. He took Kyaati's shoulders and laid her back down. "Rest now, dear one. All that matters is that you have returned to us. I shall fetch your father."

Kyaati did not resist him this time; she laid down and curled in on herself. Silent tears slipped down her face. "I did not want to come back," she murmured so low Baarias strained to hear her. "I did not feel pain wherever I was."

Baarias felt his breath catch as the words punctured the joy he had been floating on. Here was the reality he had been trying to hold at bay for as long as possible. Nyri's breath hitched beside him. Her face was agonised as she stared down at her friend. Baarias sighed as he put a hand on her shoulder and guided her from the room. He, at least, had been prepared for this.

Give her a few moments, he thought.

Nyriaana gripped his hand, clutching at his presence. The glow he had felt in her heart had dimmed. She was coming to terms with the terrible challenge that lay ahead of them.

"Will you be all right here while I find Pelaan?"

Nyri nodded, straightening her shoulders as she accepted the burden. His pride swelled.

Pelaan was not hard to find. He was on the farthest side of the grove, tending to the plants around the roots of his home. He had evidently not felt the change in his daughter's condition; he was not even paying close enough attention to feel Baarias' approach. His every movement was heavy with defeat. He had given up hope.

Baarias cleared his throat. The surprise on the Elder's face as he glanced up turned into a scowl. "Baarias," he said stiffly. Baarias knew the Elders had not yet forgiven him for his outburst at the auscult. Worse still, Pelaan blamed him for his inability to revive Kyaati's baby. The Elder's animosity twisted like thorns inside Baarias' chest. Didn't Pelaan realise that he would have done anything to save that infant if it had been within his power?

"Kyaati has awoken," he said. "I have come to take you to her."

The Elder's brows rose into his silver hairline as his

pale eyes widened. Without waiting for another word, Pelaan dodged around him and ran towards the healer's tree, leaving Baarias to follow in his wake.

He caught up to the Elder outside of Kyaati's chamber. The sight of his revived daughter had frozen Pelaan to the spot.

"Nyri?" Baarias heard Kyaati's voice call.

From behind Pelaan, he watched as Nyriaana moved to her side. "Yes?"

"Where is my baby? Why isn't she here with me?"

Shock rolled through Baarias. Surely Kyaati remembered what had happened on that terrible night?

"Kyaati, don't you...?" But the rest of Nyri's words were cut short as Pelaan recovered from his amazement and rushed into the chamber. Nyri made room for him beside the bower and retreated to Baarias' side. Together, they stepped into the adjoining chamber, leaving father and daughter alone. Baarias felt a twinge of unease as he did so. He knew what would be forefront in Pelaan's mind now, and he hoped the Elder would have the tact to keep it to himself until a more appropriate time.

"Baarias... please tell me she's going to be alright." Nyri's voice broke into his thoughts as soon as they were out of earshot.

Baarias grimaced. "It will not be easy. It will take her a long time to recover and... she might not want to."

"Is this an 'I told you so'?"

"I always do my best to avoid those." He shook his head. "Do not misunderstand, Nyriaana. I am overjoyed to have Kyaati back, but that is because her return has fulfilled my own selfish desires. I warned you it might be kinder to just let her go. Pelaan will want to make another match for her, mark my words. I ask you, if you could choose between release and living only to face more death, what would you decide?"

Nyri pressed her lips together and refused to grace him with an answer.

Baarias regretted that he had to be so blunt with her. "We will do all we can. We will not give up hope." He studied his young akaabi's face. The weight of her cares had lined her smooth features. "Rest, Nyriaana. You need your strength, too. Kyaati will be safe with her father for now."

To his relief, she lifted her chin once in agreement, groaning as she stretched her back.

"No!"

The wave of pain and despair ripped through the air before Baarias even heard the scream. Nyri's eyes flew to his in alarm, and they ran back towards the chamber beyond.

Baarias stumbled as he beheld the scene before him. Pelaan had both Kyaati's wrists locked in his grasp as she writhed against him, wailing.

"You're lying!" she screeched at her father. "You're lying! You are hiding her from me! Give her to me!"

"Kyaati!" Pelaan's face was ashen as he tried to calm her. She only fought harder.

Baarias whirled into action, drawing water from an aquilem vine into a *haala* nutshell. The heady aroma of the herbs filled the air as he crushed them into the water. A strong sleeping draught.

"Kyaati, here," Baarias urged, kneeling by her side. "Drink this, drink this, it will help."

Under his direction, Kyaati quieted enough to take the

shell and down its contents. She then grasped Baarias' arm.

"Baarias, where is my baby…?" Her eyelids drooped.

"Shhh," he soothed, struggling to keep the anguish from his face. "Just rest, just rest."

Kyaati looked as if she wanted to say more but could not fight the effect of the herbs. Pelaan released her wrists as she fell back into the bower, unconscious.

Baarias stared down at the recumbent form with Nyri and Pelaan. He had expected Kyaati's recovery would be hard. He had not expected this.

"W-what?" Pelaan broke the terrible silence first. "Baarias, what is the matter with her? She has gone mad! She accused me of hiding her baby."

Baarias could not speak. The mind was a complex entity beyond his understanding. He could feel the weight of Nyri's gaze upon him, trusting that he would have the answers. He drew a long, steadying breath. This was what it meant to be a healer; it was a burden he had accepted long ago. "We must wait and see." Even he could hear that his voice lacked its usual conviction. "Rest might ease her confusion. L-leave her with me, Pelaan, and I will do all I can."

Pelaan was silent in his agreement.

The sound of the summoning horns broke the bubble of tension inside Baarias' tree. The Elders were gathering the tribe.

"An auscult?" Nyri asked, dismayed.

Pelaan tore his gaze away from Kyaati. His eyes were raw, but the muscles in his face were working to keep his expression smooth and free of emotion. He always liked to believe he was above such things. "Yes, the rest of the Elders and I have been debating our situation," he said. "It is time to put the choices we face to the tribe."

"What about Kyaati?" Nyri asked, hesitating at her friend's side.

Baarias put his fingers to Kyaati's temples and closed his eyes, probing. "She will be safe here," he said. "She will not wake until morning."

He could feel that Nyri was far from appeased, but she followed him out into the waning light willingly enough. Baarias curled his fingers into his palms. He did not know what was going to happen now. Whatever this auscult was about, it couldn't be good, and the last thing any of them needed to hear was more doom and gloom from the Elders.

* * *

18

Impossible

Nyri followed Baarias as they made their way towards the clearing.

The heady, carefree joy she had felt at the return of Juaan evaporated as true reality crushed the happy dream she had been existing in. Kyaati was not well. She was awake, but it didn't change the fact that she had lost her baby and she might not want to live with that.

A long and difficult path of seeing her friend through her grief twisted out before them; the end unseen. Finding Juaan had pulled Nyri's heart and mind from the suffering of her people for a few precious moments. Now, feeling Kyaati's broken spirit and hearing her wish to be gone once more, Nyri could feel the grip of despair trying to re-establish its choke-hold.

She wanted to cling to Baarias for strength but she could not; not anymore. She had to face this alone. She had to be here for Kyaati, help feed her people through the looming Fury and, she wondered just what in Ninmah's name she was going to do with Juaan now that she had found him.

Nyri frowned, he was drifting once more into an unreality; nothing more than a desperate vision out in the woods. She fought to hold on to her certainty.

He would need food, water, and most of all she needed to keep him secret for as long as she was able. She could not release him; not until he remembered who she was and who he had been. If Nyri released him before then... there was no telling what he would do. He could attack them out of fear or worse still, return to the Woves, bringing them back in force. But, when he remembered her, and she refused to think that he would not, what then? There was nowhere for him to go. Her people would never accept him. She imagined a Forbidden living among them and gave a humourless laugh.

For that was what he was. Forbidden. She could not hide from that knowledge any longer; the innocence of childhood no longer protected her. Juaan was Forbidden.

Nyri trembled in the face of her predicament. The Golden Mother forbade the existence of such beings. Nyri herself had fought with Baarias over this very issue not two days past. Forbidden children went against all teachings. A heresy.

Nyri chewed a fingernail as everything she believed in clashed with the feelings she bore for Juaan. She did not want to offend the great Ninmah anymore than the Elders did but, no matter what, she could not leave Juaan to die. She had made a solemn promise long ago to look after him. Surely the Golden Mother could forgive Juaan. His heritage, whatever it was, was not his fault. His mother was the one who had committed the heresy; Juaan was innocent.

But Nyri knew others would not see it that way. Forbidden was Forbidden. The tenets of their lores were too

184

ingrained; there could be no exceptions. She was defying Ninmah Herself by her very actions, no matter how she tried to justify it. She risked bringing a curse down on the entire tribe by keeping him. Anyone who had ever tried to accept Juaan had perished. His mother, her mother. The knowledge was unsettling.

Nyri rubbed her forehead. Her mind worked, but she had no solutions. She did not know what would happen now. The future suddenly loomed more dangerous and uncertain than ever before, and Nyri could feel herself crumbling under the weight of it.

She wrenched her thoughts back to the present as they reached the clearing. The tall rock in the centre was casting a long shadow across the waving grass. The rest of the tribe had an edgy vibe as they gathered, very much like deer on a game trail.

The last time they had been here, they had fled for their very lives and Kyaati's baby had died. The threat of the Woves' return hung in the air; it was at the forefront of everyone's thoughts. Nyri felt a thrill of fear. Maybe she wouldn't be the one who released Juaan from that Pit after all.

"My People," Aardn called their attention to her once they were all gathered. "We have called you together to address the grave situation we now face. Imaani has been searching—"

"Have they left?" Raanya interrupted, her good hand twisting in her woven garments. "Have the Woves gone?"

Aardn's expression was grim. "No, they have not left."

Cries of dismay swept around the group. Nyri put her hand to her mouth as the blood drained from her face. She had been out in the woods and their enemies were still in the area.

Aardn lifted her hand for quiet. "Imaani informed us that when climbing the tallest trees, their glowing spirits can be seen burning in the distance on the edge of the plains."

"But what are they doing?" Umaa asked, tightening her arms around Omaal in her lap.

"We do not know. Waiting, licking their wounds. They have not yet made another attempt to cross back into our territory. We are keeping a careful watch."

Nyri dug her nails into her palms. The Woves were camped on their border, regrouping. She forced her hands to relax when she felt blood trickling from her palms; the air was suddenly too thin.

"What are we going to do?"

"This is what we have called the auscult to discuss. The decision is yours. We have debated at length as to the best path we should take. Some of us," the senior Elder's voice gave away her opinion on this, "would have us leave this place and take the chance of finding a new home before the approaching Fury sets in."

A wave of dread swept around the circle. All but the youngest remembered the Dark Days of the homeless wandering and the suffering they had endured. So many souls had been lost.

"We can't do that." A few voices protested. "We will die."

Oraan, Naaya's father and the most junior of the Elders, interjected. "When the Woves return, we most surely will. They know we are here and now they sit poised on our borders, biding their time. We need to leave before they decide to return. This place is no longer safe."

"What does the Kamaali say?" someone demanded.

Aardn pressed her lips together in irritation. "Sefaan *claims* the will of the Great Spirit is unclear. She will not commit to a path. She remains in communion with Him as she searches for an answer."

Discontented muttering broke out. The lack of a Kamaali's guidance was a disaster. Without it, the tribe would remain divided. Arguments raged back and forth. Nyri chewed a fingernail, her insides twisting; dead one way, surely dead another. What could they do? What would *she* do if they left? She had just found Juaan again; she could not abandon him. The arguments went on around her, but she barely heard.

"We cannot leave!"

"We cannot stay!"

"We could *fight!*"

Daajir's voice cut into her thoughts. He rose to his feet from where he had been sitting beside Pelaan. "Haven't we done enough running? Haven't we lost enough to these monsters?" He thumped his chest. "Well, I say enough! We must fight back!"

If a leaf had dropped then, Nyri would have heard it. She couldn't believe he had just voiced his wish to fight the Woves in front of the entire tribe. It was one thing to vent his emotions in front of her, another to do so before the Elders. She tested his intent and was stunned to feel that he was adamant. The rest of the tribe echoed her disbelief. Aardn was the first to recover.

"And how do you propose we do this, young Daajir?" She gave an incredulous laugh. "Their powers are beyond us. To fight them would be the most certain way to get us all killed."

"Maybe not," Daajir returned. "We always knew this day would come, and I have been preparing. I may have found a way to repel the beasts. I beg of the Elders and my people time and I will prove to you how we might exact our revenge and break their curse once and for all."

Aardn and the Elders were silent as they regarded Daajir. He raised his chin, his eyes steady and unflinching. They reached deeper, assessing his soundness of mind; testing his certainty.

Whatever they found obviously satisfied them.

"You really believe you have found a way to do this?" Aardn asked.

"Yes. Please just hold on making a decision until I am ready."

Aardn looked at her peers. Their faces were unreadable, but as the moments passed, it became clear to Nyri that they had come to an agreement. Perhaps they didn't really have another choice with the tribe so divided. Whatever the reason, they agreed to Daajir's impossible plan.

"Your proposal opens an intriguing new path," Aardn mused. "It is agreed. We will hold on our decision until you prove to us that standing our ground is our best chance for survival."

Daajir bowed. "Thank you, Aardn."

She inclined her head.

Nyri eyed Daajir. It was impossible to believe he had found a way to defend against the Woves. But like the Elders, she wanted to hope all the same. What a victory it would be to break their curse at last. Possible or not, the ruling Daajir's claim had brought about relieved Nyri. It would give her more time to figure out her situation; they were staying. For now.

"Let us pray the Woves do not decide to return before then," Oraan mumbled. A glare from Aardn silenced him.

"In light of that possibility," Aardn continued, "we ask you all to remain close. We may have to flee with little to no warning and will not have time to find those of you who stray. We must stay together. I permit nobody to wander alone beyond the boundary of the *eshaara* grove." Her eyes seemed to flicker in Nyri's direction. "It is not safe. The watch will be doubled. Nothing will move without us knowing. If the Woves cross our border before we meet again, we shall flee without question, which brings us to our next concern. Food."

More discontented murmurs broke out. Many were angry, others despondent.

Aardn raised one hand for calm. "I know many of you will find the strict ration we have had to impose hard—"

"Hard?" Umaa's face was raw, an expression reflected by all those with children. "Do you know the sentence you are passing on many of our heads, *respected* Elder?"

Aardn did not even flinch. "There is no choice, Umaa. I will not shade the truth; the food we have left will barely be enough to see us through the Fury that approaches. The times of Ninsiku's power have grown longer than I have ever known in my lifetime. Perhaps the longest since the passing of the Great Fury.

"Unless Ninmah re-establishes her strength and banishes Ninsiku back to his rightful place, our situation is grave. We are under attack from two fronts, the Woves and starvation. We must face both with equal gravity and as one People.

Everyone must make sacrifices for the good of the whole."

Aardn's energy rolled out in stark warning so that none could fail to heed her will and the consequences for crossing it. "No one is to take more than one item of food from the stores per day. One. The supplies will be watched. I will not tolerate any selfish attempt to take more than this. We will face the hardship equally, come what may."

Umaa buried her face in her crippled son's hair as her shoulders shook. Imaani put an arm around them both, his face grave.

Nyri's mouth had gone dry. She had already acknowledged that visiting Juaan and keeping him supplied with food was going to be difficult. Now it seemed out of the question. Nobody was permitted to leave the tribe, and nobody could take more than it would take to keep a maamit alive.

Nyri ran her hands through her hair. She would have to figure out a way to slip by the sentries. That would be almost impossible. Even harder would be getting the food she needed; one item per tribe member. Nyri chewed her lip. She had a few personal rations left in her own tree, but after that…

"Nyriaana." Baarias shook her shoulder. Nyri started under his touch. She realised they had been dismissed and she had been staring into space as she wrestled with her dilemma. "Come, child. You need rest."

"Kyaati—"

"Will not need you until morning and you will be no good to her if you do not rest yourself."

Nyri nodded, too exhausted to argue. She bid Baarias a peaceful night and parted company with him. Let him think that her troubled air was because of the situation that had just been outlined to them. It was partly the truth.

She started for her tree, feeling dead on her feet. In the morning, she would face the challenge of disobeying the Elders for the first time in her life. And with the Woves so close, she was putting her own life in serious jeopardy. She did not know if she possessed the courage. She had to hope that she did.

Juaan's very survival depended on it.

19

Bravery

"Nyriaana."

She was almost back to her tree when a soft but firm voice called her name. Her heart skipped a beat as she turned to face Aardn. Nyri did her best to keep her features smooth and Juaan far from her mind as the Elder approached.

"Walk with me."

"But—"

Her protest died on her lips. Aardn was already moving away, leaving Nyri with no choice but to follow. Struggling to gather her thoughts, she gripped her elbows in both hands. Aardn never usually singled her out.

Fortunately, Aardn came straight to the point. "I wish to praise you for the bravery you have shown in the past days, Nyriaana."

Nyri blinked. "Th-thank you, my Elder. Though, I do not understand what I have done to earn such praise." Most of what she remembered from the past days was being scared out of her wits and nearly dying. Twice. Daajir would have another description for her actions, and it wouldn't be brave. Idiotic would be more likely.

"I have known many in my lifetime, young Nyriaana, and there are few I could name who would run into the jaws of a *grishnaa* to save another's child. Omaal told me of what you did. If it wasn't for you, he would be dead at the bottom of a Pit and our tribe would have one more soul to mourn."

Nyri shifted, at a loss for a response. She felt a cold sweat prickle over her skin at the memory of that day. She hadn't really stopped to think of what she was doing; she had just acted out of fear and instinct.

"For his life. I thank you."

"All I did was pull him from the Pit. It was Batai that showed the real bravery." Nyri kept her eyes fixed on the ground, embarrassed by the attention she was being shown by an Elder.

"Look at me, Nyriaana." Aardn's quiet command forced Nyri's eyes up. "I also thank you for Kyaati's life. Pelaan will be forever indebted to you. We all saw you face down that demon alone. You inspired our People to take a stand against our enemies. Never have the Woves fled before us. Because of you, I now have hope. A hope that whatever plan Daajir brings before us will drive our enemies from our borders and our people will be free of their dark magic. I have you to thank for that hope."

"I do not deserve such thanks," Nyri said. She, for one, could not look back on that terrible night with hope. "I was not thinking when I faced that Wove. And Kyaati's baby still died. I could not save her."

Aardn's lips thinned. "Not even Baarias could have saved Kyaati's baby, Nyriaana. The curse of the Woves is getting stronger. They are to blame for Kyaati's loss, not you. Because of you, she lives and can bring more children into the world. We will Join her—"

Nyri gasped. "But she does not want to! She swore."

Aardn's eyes widened in the face of her outburst. Nyri felt the backlash of her anger at such a contradiction from a junior member of the tribe. "She may feel that way now. But, when she recovers, we will make her a new, stronger match. It was a mark of Sefaan's growing madness that she Joined Kyaati and Yaanth in secret. It was not Ninmah's will. Once Kyaati knows that a true Joining awaits her, she will rejoice and remember her duty to our People's survival."

Nyri blanched. She remembered the emptiness in Kyaati's face and could not share the Elder's confidence. When she looked up, she found Aardn was now regarding her appraisingly, her vexation with Nyri's outburst forgotten.

"You have grown, Nyriaana. I had not noticed until this moment. You are a child no longer."

The cold sweat was back. Nyri glanced around for an avenue of escape. She did not like the turn this conversation was taking.

"Baarias says you are the strongest and brightest akaabi that he has ever guided. Stronger even than he." Her expression was that of a proud grandmother. "High praise indeed."

"Thank you, Aardn," Nyri said, but her voice was wooden. Ordinarily, she would have glowed under such commendation but, in this moment, she wished Baarias had told Aardn she had been the least talented *akaabi* he had ever had the misfortune to know.

"Yes, you have grown, indeed. It may be time to find

you a mate." The Elder smiled widely; a rare sight. Nyri shuddered, concealing her revulsion with an effort. "It would certainly prove a task to find one worthy of *you*. Even Daajir—"

This time there was no hiding her reaction. Nyri stepped back, throat closing as the colour drained from her face.

"What is the matter?" Aardn demanded. "Does this not make you happy?"

Nyri screwed up her courage. She had betrayed her emotions, and now she had no choice but to forge ahead. "No, respected Elder. Do not misunderstand. I am overwhelmed that you see so much potential in me but, I admit, the thought of being Joined terrifies me." Nyri hesitated. "The thought of children terrifies me more."

The Elder's frown was cutting. "And what causes you such fear? There could be no greater glory and honour than ensuring the continuation of our People. You would stand defiant before a Wove and yet tremble at this?" Aardn's face turned towards the great tree where Baarias lived. Nyri was quick to guess the direction of her thoughts. The Elder's eyes flashed. "It's him, isn't it? He is losing his senses, just like Sefaan. Filling your head with misguided—"

"No. No!" Nyri defended her teacher. She didn't want to get him into further trouble. He was not losing his senses. "I believe in Ninmah's teachings. Please. I simply... do not feel ready."

Aardn eyed her for a moment, then relaxed, satisfied by the truth in her soul. "Good. If I thought he was poisoning your mind with heresy, I would end his guidance of you, whether or not he saw fit. Baarias was wrong to say what he did. I forgave him because of his skill, but I cannot have him turning our most promising off the path we must follow. The power Ninmah has blessed you with is a Gift that we cannot waste. Hold on to your bravery, Nyriaana. You have your mother's courage and that will never see you fail."

Aardn's face gentled. "Jaai and I might not have seen eye to eye on many things, but she was one of the bravest women I ever knew. She would never turn away from what she believed to be right. If only she had possessed the sense of your father..." The Elder shook her head. "I pray you inherited that from him. We will need all of your strength if we are to overcome our enemies. You cannot waver. It is those like you who will return our true People to greatness!"

Nyri wanted to take another step back, but forced herself to remain.

"Nyriaana. Aardn."

Nyri could have wept with relief at the sound of Baarias' politely intrusive voice.

"Baarias." Aardn acknowledged him coolly without turning, still staring at Nyri as a hungry wolf would stare at a haunch of meat.

Baarias stood in the shadows with his arms held behind his back, his silver-white hair billowing in the breeze. "Could I borrow my *akaabi*, respected Elder? I have an important lesson that she may find illuminating."

At last, Aardn turned her head from Nyri to regard him. The interruption clearly annoyed her, but she could not deny the master *akaab* his request. "Very well. Go." She waved at Nyri without taking her eyes off Baarias. "But do not keep her too long. It is late, and she is exhausted."

"Just so," he said as Nyri all but ran to his side. "Ninmah's blessings be with you this night, Aardn."

"Blessings to you," she responded, sour-faced, and turned to walk away. "I will speak with you again soon, Nyriaana," she called over her shoulder.

Nyri shuddered and looked up at Baarias. Her teacher was staring after Aardn, a grim set to his lined face.

"What was it you wanted to show me?" Nyri prompted. She did not think she could take much more before her head burst.

"Nothing," he said, a smile playing on his lips as he looked down at her.

"Oh." Nyri rubbed her eyes.

"It just seemed like you needed rescuing."

"Ah." She stifled a yawn. "Kyaati?" She ought to check on her friend, but Baarias' tree seemed so very far away right now.

"Still sleeping," he said. "I told you, she will not wake until morning. Go." Baarias patted her shoulder. "There'll be time enough for lessons when you are not asleep on your feet. Do not worry about Aardn. I will do what I can to keep her distracted for as long as I am able."

Nyri smiled wanly, knowing he would do just that for her, no matter how futile the effort. She stretched out with her energy, wrapping it around Baarias' own in an embrace. "Blessings," she murmured to him. Baarias smiled before disappearing back into the shadows as he made his way home.

Nyri climbed her tree and threw herself into her bower, leaves and moss billowing out, then lay there unmoving.

So, Aardn thought her as brave as her mother? A laugh bubbled from Nyri's throat. She certainly did not feel that way. From what little she remembered of her mother, Jaai had been a force of nature. Nyri had never seen her mother afraid. Nyri was afraid; she trembled before the future and all that it might bring.

Aardn had also hoped that she had inherited her father's good sense. Nyri thought of Juaan in the Pit and smiled dizzily. Aardn would be disappointed.

Good sense seemed to be the last thing she was capable of.

* * *

Aardn moved through the *eshaara* grove on her way back to her tree. She turned over the conversation with Nyriaana in her mind. Such strength. In the wake of Kyaati's loss, the need to see this girl Joined was now stronger than ever. The tribe needed hope.

A presence brushing against her senses in the darkness ahead pulled her from her thoughts. Someone was waiting for her.

"Daajir," Aardn greeted.

The young man stepped from the shadows before her. "Respected Elder." He bowed his head.

Here was one Aardn knew she could always rely on. Daajir's heart was steadfast in the need to uphold the sacred teachings of Ninmah and keep their People true to Her vision. Nevertheless, she had been surprised by his declaration at the *auscult.* Had such a proposal come from anyone but him…

Daajir appeared to read her thoughts. "With your permission, Aardn, I wish to show you my plans."

Aardn could not deny her intrigue, and she gestured for him to lead the way. Daajir smiled and started toward the outer forest. "Daajir!" Aardn admonished. "There were to be no exceptions to wandering beyond the *eshaara* grove."

He lowered his head. "Forgive me. I mean no disrespect, but I hope that when you see what I have to show you, you will grant me permission to do what is needed. And I am not going alone now, you are accompanying me."

Aardn scowled for a moment, but her curiosity won out. "Very well," she said. "Continue."

He waited until she was beside him, and together they set off into the darkness. Daajir took the lead, travelling unerringly along a route he seemed to know well.

"Pelaan tells me that Kyaati has awoken from her death sleep," the boy ventured after a few moments of silence.

Aardn's lips twitched as she tasted the concealed hope behind his probing. "Yes," she said. "Though she is a long way from recovery. The Woves have wounded us yet again."

She felt him struggle with himself before he screwed up the courage to speak. "If she recovers, I would like to propose a Joining between us."

Aardn chuckled. "Ah, Daajir. That would be something for the Elders to decide. There is another possibility. One that may make an even greater match."

She could almost hear him scowl as he rubbed at a tight wrapping on his arm. "If that is what the Elders decide, I will of course bow to your wishes."

"If it is any consolation, boy, she is no more happy about a Joining than you are." Aardn's mouth twisted as she recalled the conversation she had just had with Nyriaana. "I fear

Baarias is poisoning her mind."

Daajir's shoulders stiffened. "You do?"

Aardn lifted her chin. "I believe we need to keep a closer watch on the master *akaab.* The slightest slip and I will have the excuse to end his guidance of Nyriaana. We cannot have this heresy spreading any further."

Daajir raised his head. "I will keep watch, Aardn. Sefaan, too."

Aardn snorted, bile rising in her throat as she thought of the old woman. She who had brought a curse down on them with her heresy. "It is past time to be rid of her. A new Kamaali is needed. I pray to Ninmah every day for such a miracle."

Daajir lifted his chin in agreement as he came to a halt. Evidently, he had reached his destination. The scent of rotting earth and leaf decay filled Aardn's nostrils. The night sounds of the forest were more muted here. Before them lay a damp, shallow hollow. Daajir beckoned to her and started down into the dell. At the centre was a small collection of *haala* nutshells, all filled with varying shades of dark liquid. Daajir lifted the closest shell and presented it to Aardn.

"I have developed a poison effective against the Woves," he whispered. "A combination of snake venom, night berries and the crippling influence of the *vaash* plant."

Aardn raised an eyebrow as she swirled the contents before her. "A potent mix."

Daajir's eyes gleamed in the darkness. "I assure you, death is long, painful, and slow. If I get the Elders' permission to use this against our enemies, they will not dare come near our forests again. I will lift their curse!"

Aardn shifted her gaze from the poison to study his

shadowed face. "You are certain of the effects?"

A grimace contorted the young man's features as his eyes lowered. "Yes. I am certain."

"How?" Aardn could taste his reluctance, his fear, and his guilt. This was a question he had been hoping she would not ask.

"I—forgive me, Aardn." He turned his head, indicating a place at the far side of the hollow. Aardn followed his gaze, and her heart lodged in her throat. Piled in the mud were three twisted bodies. Boar, deer, all Children of the Great Spirit.

"Ninmah preserve us!" she gasped. "What have you *done?*"

"What I had to!" Daajir removed the *haala* nutshell from her frozen fingers.

Aardn fell back a step. "No, Daajir, I cannot allow this. What you have done—"

"—is what I have had to do! I take my soul as the price. Can we willingly stand by when this could save our people? Surely it is against Ninmah's will for us to wither and die! She fought for us against Her own mate. She would want us to take up that fight! Tell me, respected Elder, what are a few lives against the survival of our People?"

His words struck home. Aardn wanted to argue, to denounce what he had done here, but in the end she could not. The survival of their people was all there could be. It was her duty as an Elder to ensure their continued existence and if this was the only way...

"And... how do you intend to get close enough to a Wove to deliver this poison of yours?" she asked without looking at him.

His excitement vibrated in the air, encouraged by her

further interest. "I do not intend to get close. I am working on a solution to deliver the poison at a distance. I do not want them to see this coming."

Ninmah forgive me. "You… have my blessing to continue with your study," Aardn said. "I will tell the sentries that they are to let you by unchallenged."

His lips curled into a triumphant smile. "Thank you, respected Elder."

"But Daajir," she warned. "You have until the next dark night to find a solution, and that is all. No one must ever know. If the others find out what you have done, I will not help you. May the Great Spirit forgive us all."

20

Time

"**C**ome and play, Juaan!" *Nyriaana bounced before the mournful boy. She wanted to cheer him up. It had been days now since her mama had brought him into their family. Nothing she tried worked. She had brought him more gifts, talked to him, slept by him and yet he still just sat there, brooding, green eyes distant. He would not speak. He would not even eat. "Do you wanna find some* haala *nuts?" she tempted. He must be starving. "They my favourite!"*

Nothing. He just shook his head in a silent gesture; he did not even look up.

Nyri hung her own head in defeat. She went to the back of their tree where her mother sat watching.

"Juaan won' play with me," she whined. "He won' talk. Doesn't he like me?" Tears started in her eyes at the thought.

Her mother smiled down at her. "Of course he likes you, my little cub. He is just sad. You carry on being there for him and he will get better. Just give him some time..."

* * *

Time. Nyri woke. She did not remember dreaming, and that was unusual. She glanced across her tree to the deeper darkness waiting outside; it was still long before dawn. Exhaustion pulled at her, dragging her back down, but she fought it. It was a blessing she had woken early. Baarias had assured her that Kyaati would not wake until light, and she wanted—*needed*—to see Juaan again.

The longer she was away, the harder it was to accept that he was real; his return from death too much of an impossibility. And despite the new fears and confusion his presence brought her, the distraction was a relief. This was the only chance she would get to sneak away. Most of the tribe would still be sleeping—except for the watch, she assumed. Baarias would not miss her yet.

Nyri pulled herself upright, combing her fingers quickly through her hair to rid it of any stray pieces of moss. Every moment counted; she must have returned by Ninmah's rise, otherwise her absence would be noticed.

Digging out the last of the food from her own ration, she stowed one honey fruit and a large *haala* nut. She imagined the giant frame of the man in the pit and cringed. How much food would it take to keep him? She pushed the thought away and grabbed an empty *haala* nutshell half as an afterthought.

The cool air swept across her hands and face as she slipped down her tree. A thick mist was swirling between the forest's tangled feet. She blessed it; it would hide her that much better.

Nyri hesitated at the edge of the black outer forest. If the Woves had re-entered the borders, the sentries would have sounded the alert. Only the familiar shrill whistles and chirrups of the night met Nyri's straining ears. Comforted, she drew a breath and struck out into the darkness.

The trees closed around her. Now and then, Nyri paused in the dim pre-light. Her every sense hummed, tasting the energies of the forest, checking for watchful eyes. She couldn't silence the small, guilty voice that told her she shouldn't be out here; she was selfishly putting her entire tribe at risk. *I have no choice,* she told the voice. *I can't let him die.*

She was barely out of sight from the *eshaara* trees when she came up against the first sentry. Perched high in a tree, Imaani scrutinised the forest beyond, his senses tasting the vibrations of life ahead of him.

Nyri crouched out of sight. She was not the best at masking her presence; it was her weakest talent. Imaani would pick her up as soon as she moved into his range. Far-seeing, Omaal's father was their best sentry. It was just her luck to have run into *him*.

She waited for him to move away. And waited. But Imaani did not leave. One idea after another passed through Nyri's mind; each one more futile than the last.

Disappointment thudded through her. She would have to abandon the attempt. She could not get past. Nyri felt the food she had brought keenly against her skin and her heart twisted. Juaan could not last much longer without nourishment, but she could not risk getting caught. She would have to figure out another way to get to him, and soon.

She had just shifted her weight back, intent on returning to her tree to think, when a browsing boar lumbered through the undergrowth close to where she crouched. An idea rekindled the hope in her heart. It was an old trick of Baarias' and it might just work. Nyri merged her will with the massive creature and sent him an overwhelming sense of fear; he would think a predator was on him.

The effort paid off. With a sudden squeal of terror, the boar crashed away through the undergrowth; running as though its very life depended on it. Nyri was sorry to have caused him such alarm, but the plan worked. Startled by the creature's unexplained behaviour, the boar distracted Imaani for a few vital moments. On cat's paws, Nyri evaded him and ran.

Ninmah was with her and she met no one else. The way to the Pits appeared lightly guarded. No doubt the sentries considered the great hidden maws to be sufficient protection on their own. Nyri thanked Ninmah for that.

A stiffening breeze hissed through the shadowed leaves above and blew strands of dark hair across her face; Nyri brushed them away with sweat-slicked palms. Her insides writhed at the thought of seeing him again, in turns both excited and terrified. Nyri tried to think of what she should say, what he would say now that they were finally together again.

Her breath caught in her throat as she reached the Pit. A part of her still expected to find the hole empty. With fumbling hands, Nyri removed the coverings and peered into the gloom below with a mix of dread and hope.

He was there; a large, dark form sitting in the depths. Nyri blew out a breath of relief. But, as his eyes came to rest upon her, all her carefully planned words turned to ash inside her mouth. They were vicious in their hostility.

"H-hello." Her voice caught.

He did not respond; the frightening expression only intensified. Nyri had to call upon all of her will to remain in place.

"Um. I-I brought you some food. Are you hungry?"

Until now, Nyri had imagined going into the Pit again, of him recognising her at once now that he was more lucid. She had imagined their joyous reunion. She saw now that this would not be.

Whatever was preventing him from remembering her went deeper than the mere stun from his fall. There was not one flicker of familiarity in that gaze, and there was no way Nyri was going into that Pit when he was looking at her in such a way. A sick feeling took hold in the pit of her stomach. The Woves had bewitched him.

But he has *to remember. He spoke our rhyme. He still speaks our tongue.* Whenever Nyri had been unfortunate enough to hear a Wove speak, their Ninkuraaja words had been fractured and halting; Juaan appeared fluent. His memories were still there. Somewhere.

Time. Time. He needs time. She would not reach him in just a few moments. It had been many seasons since they had taken him from her. Seasons upon seasons under the evil influence of the Woves. Nyri controlled another wave of hatred for their enemies and lowered herself to sit upon the edge of the pit. She worked to keep her expression smooth.

"Here." She pulled the honey fruit out into the faint light. She thanked Ninmah he could still understand the Ninkuraaja tongue. This was going to be difficult enough;

it would be impossible if he had forgotten how to hear her. "This is sweet. Try it." Nyri threw the golden globe down to him. The tough fruit bounced once on the ground and rolled to a slight distance away from where he sat. Nyri looked on hopefully, but he made no move to pick it up. His piercing gaze did not so much as flicker from hers.

Her face fell in disappointment. Pulling out the *haala* nut, she broke open its shell and picked at the offering inside. She chewed, savouring the creamy texture, thinking. Juaan watched every motion, and Nyri saw him swallow visibly. His gaze left hers for the briefest of moments to flick to where the honey fruit rested. Then he regained his composure and returned his warning glare towards Nyri with a heavy scowl.

He didn't even trust her enough to eat the food she brought.

A new fear twisted her stomach; a fear that she would be forced to witness his painful demise as he faded towards death. The set of his face promised that starvation would be preferable to submitting. Nyri shuddered. She *had* to reach him.

"I healed your wounds. You were badly hurt from your fall."

His face contorted, and he withdrew his hands from the brace on the healing limb as though it may bite.

"It's all right, Juaan. It will heal. I wouldn't do anything to harm you."

He flinched at the mention of his name. It hurt; Nyri fell silent, finding that she had run out of things to say. Feeling increasingly helpless, she filled the silence with action. She got up and moved around the Pit. His gaze followed her, but she ignored him with an effort and turned her mind to fulfilling his immediate needs. She needed to provide a water supply; if she had to carry water here from the river, it would draw unwanted attention.

Studying the area, Nyri spotted what she needed clinging to a mossy trunk. An *aquilem.* The water vine was delicate and would not hold any weight. Perfect. Nyri tugged it from the hosting tree and peeled it carefully along until she had a substantial enough length, then she threw it down the side of the Pit. One problem solved. She was glad to note the sandy areas dotting the bottom of the Pit, too. It wasn't all solid rock. That solved another dilemma; he could dig holes. Nyri wrinkled her nose.

Juaan was eyeing the vine she had just thrown down with keen interest.

"It won't hold your weight," Nyri warned. "It supplies water. Here." She tossed him the empty nutshell half she had brought. He wouldn't be able to use the vine like a Ninkuraa would, but he could get a little from it until she gained his trust enough to get down there again.

Nyri realised she could see him far more clearly now. Ninmah was rising; her brief time had run out.

"I have to go." She tried to keep the despondency out of her voice. "I will return when I can with more food. Take this for now." She threw down the rest of the half eaten *haala* nut. "It's going to be hard for me to come here often, but I will come back. Trust me."

An eyebrow raised; it wasn't much, but it was a reaction. A very Juaan-like reaction. Coupled as it was with the hate in his eyes, it was almost more than she could bear. Nyri tried her best to ignore the pain and let it reassure her that

Juaan was still there, somewhere. "You will remember me, Juaan. I promise."

As the flare of hatred burned across the space that separated them, she did not know in that moment which one of them she was attempting to convince.

21

Poisoned

Dawn was breaking as Nyri made her way back towards the safety of the *eshaara* grove. She scowled at nothing in particular. She had never thought it possible to loathe the Woves any more than she had; how wrong she had been. The beasts had taken the most precious person she had ever known and filled him with the blackness of hate, taking his memories, taking his heart.

No further doubt lingered as to Juaan's impossible return. A dream would be happier. Anger ripped through her despair. Nyri struck out at a rock in her path with her foot, sending it flying into the trees.

The fit of childish temper was an outlet for her building frustration, and she lashed out at a few more rocks until she stubbed her toe and had to gate a cry of agony between her teeth.

It did nothing to improve her mood.

Imaani was unfortunate enough to be the first person to cross her path. Releasing her frustration and bitter disappointment, Nyri unleashed a flock of birds upon the watchful sentry. Imaani leaped from his perch with a cry of surprise, shielding his face from the angry barrage of flapping wings. Nyri dodged round him and slipped back into the safety of the *eshaara* grove.

It seemed getting in and out of the tribe unseen would be the easiest part of her challenge. She had not factored Juaan's memory loss into her plan. She thought of their enemies waiting just outside of the trees. How long did she have before they breached her tribe's borders again? When they did, her tribe would flee, forcing her to leave Juaan behind.

Nyri took a few deep breaths, calming her nerves enough to get a hold of herself before she faced Baarias. She certainly could not present negative emotion in front of Kyaati.

Her people were emerging to the rise of Ninmah. They moved with furtive caution; parents keeping their children close to their sides. The knowledge of the Woves poised upon the border harried at their nerves. A few wore dazed expressions, as though they could not comprehend how they had lived through another night to see the light of a new day. The air was tainted with fear.

Making her way to Baarias' tree, Nyri ran through ways to break through the spell Juaan had been placed under. If she could just earn enough of his trust to get back into the Pit with him...

She cut the thought off as she reached the threshold of Baarias' home. Her teacher was already awake and expecting her. Nyri hesitated at the entrance, overcome by the irrational feeling that her morning activities were scrawled on her forehead for all to see. She was holding her breath when she stepped inside.

"Could you wake Kyaati please, Nyriaana?" Baarias asked as he moved around the first chamber of his tree, gathering supplies for the day. He did not even look up. Nyri let out her breath. It had been foolish to fear that he would be waiting to fling accusations at her, but Nyri could not help feeling self-conscious of her wrongdoing. "I need to go to the stores for some food," Baarias continued. "There are some duties I want you to attend to, but I will discuss them with you when I get back." He glanced towards the chamber where Kyaati slept.

Nyri acknowledged this with a tilt of her chin. "H-has there been any news from the sentries?" She was careful to keep her tone even.

"No. The Woves have yet to make their next move. My guess is that they are waiting for reinforcements before they challenge us again."

"Reinforcements?" Nyri asked, her knees going weak at the thought.

Baarias rubbed his forehead. "They won't risk sending so small a force against us again. Their confidence was shaken, but I doubt their caution will last for long once more of them arrive."

A knot formed in Nyri's stomach, making it hard to breathe for a moment. She struggled to release it as she watched Baarias leave the tree.

Kyaati was curled upon herself inside the bower where she slept, staring off into space as tears dried upon her reddened skin. Nyri's breath caught at the sight of the crumpled expression on her face. She cleared her throat with difficulty.

"Kyaati," she said. "Ninmah is risen. It is time to get up. Baarias is bringing food."

The lavender eyes flickered in her direction; an accusing gleam glowed from their depths as Kyaati pushed herself upright. "You know where my baby is, Nyri." Her voice was so rough, it was almost unrecognisable. "You ran into the forest on the night she was born. Where did you take her? *Where* did you hide her?"

"Kyaati!" Nyri took a step back. Sleep had not cured her friend's confusion. *Your baby died, Kyaati. How could you accuse me of such a thing?* The words burned on her lips, but she hesitated to speak them, afraid of her friend's reaction. "Kyaati, *no.*"

Kyaati's gaze burned into her for a moment longer. Then she shook her head, making a disgusted sound in the back of her throat as she rose to her feet. "You, too. I can't believe you of all people would be a part of this."

Nyri backed out of the chamber without another word, unable to bear such accusations. She swallowed against her dry throat. The Woves. The Woves had twisted Kyaati's mind, too! She watched apprehensively as Kyaati followed in her wake.

As they emerged from the chamber, she saw to her relief that Baarias had returned. She wanted to tell him of her thoughts, but she knew he would never believe her. He did not think the Woves capable of such dark magic. But he had not seen what she had. He had not seen what they had done to Juaan.

"I trust you have eaten, Nyriaana?" he inquired as he produced two pieces of fruit.

"Yes." Her traitorous stomach chose that moment to

protest into the silence. She had eaten little of her *haala* nut before she had sacrificed the rest to Juaan.

Baarias frowned, but let it pass. "Kyaati." He handed her a honey fruit. The fruit was her favourite. Baarias knew that; the entire tribe knew that, but Kyaati made a face as if she had just been given night berries. She sank her teeth into the sweet, golden flesh without enthusiasm. Nyri's own mouth watered; her stomach threatening another noisy objection.

"I don't care what any of you say," Kyaati declared out of nowhere, throwing the fruit down. "I am going to find my baby. I will find out what you have done with her."

Baarias' face was pale as he turned to Nyri. "Would you be good enough to check on our people today, *akaabi*?"

"You want me to go alone?" Nyri's eyebrows shot towards her hairline. As an *akaabi*, a learner of her art, she had never been permitted to tend to the tribe without the guidance of Baarias.

"Yes." Baarias flicked his gaze towards Kyaati. "There are chores I need to attend to here. Herbs and such."

"Ah." Understanding blossomed. Kyaati was in no condition to be exposed to the curiosity and the pity of their people. They could not be allowed to see what the Woves had done to her mind lest it spread further panic. And one wrong word could shatter Kyaati completely.

"I am grateful that you think I am ready for this, master *akaab*." Nyri took up Baarias' charade.

Baarias smiled, his eyes crinkling, and held his healer's staff out to her. "You are."

Nyri glowed under his praise, but then caught sight of Kyaati's face and her pride drained away. "Be careful with her," she whispered to Baarias, then left the *akaab*'s tree, feeling the weight of the healer's staff in her hand.

It surprised Nyri to find Daajir waiting outside. She was further taken aback by his appearance. It was as if he had aged seasons since she had last seen him. New, deep lines of strain were carved into his face. His dark eyes were hollow, haunted, though there was an odd gleam there that Nyri could not place.

"How is she?" he asked without wasting time on greetings. "Baarias will not let me in to see her."

Nyri shook her head once in answer and his worn face twisted.

"Is there anything I can do?"

"No. I doubt there is anything any of us could do right now, Dar. Not even Baarias knows how to reach her." She paused and then decided Daajir had a right to know. He was one of Kyaati's closest friends, just as she was. "She thinks her baby is alive, and we have all plotted to hide her away. It is like her memories have been twisted and turned against us—"

Daajir's outrage flared satisfyingly alongside hers, understanding in an instant what Nyri knew Baarias would refuse to see. His hands balled into fists. "Wove curses! Ninmah help me, I will make them *suffer* for what they have done!"

Her brief sense of camaraderie fled at these words. "How?" Nyri bit out between her teeth. "Tell me, Daajir, how will you do that? Please, stop this! No one can defeat the Woves."

His lips curled into a fierce smile. "I can." His breath hissed through bared teeth as he stared off into the surrounding forest. "I'm *glad* that raiding party chose to stay. Soon enough, they will feel the sting of revenge!" The strange gleam in his eyes burned. "I will try to check on Kyaati later.

For now, I have work that cannot wait. I must be ready for them when they decide to make their move." He turned on his heel and strode away.

Nyri watched him go, her eyebrows pinching together. Daajir could never resist a flair for the dramatic. She scuffed her toes in the earth.

Omaal was the first patient she visited. She was about to climb into the branches of his family's tree when a hand grabbed her arm, halting her ascent before it could begin.

Umaa stood scowling beside her as she prevented Nyri from entering her home.

It's all right, Umaa, she thought through their contact. *I have come to check on Omaal's progress.*

Where is Baarias? The tension in the other woman did not ease.

He is occupied with other matters. He sent me in his stead.

Umaa relaxed slightly, but her eyes darted to the entrance of her home and Nyri spied a tightening around her thin lips.

"Can I go up and see your son?" she pressed.

Umaa shook her head, and Nyri felt a flash of distress from the other woman before it was tempered. "Omaal is not up there," she said. "He's playing with Batai." The boy's mother gestured around her tree. As though in answer, an excited squeal floated to them from a short distance away.

Nyri smiled carefully and nodded as she stepped around the trunk of Umaa's home and followed the sound of laughter. From what she could hear, Omaal seemed to have made a full recovery from his brush with the *grishnaa*.

The boy and the wolf were wrestling together. Batai was writhing on his back, mouth opened playfully as little huffs and growls emerged from his throat; his head whipped back and forth. Omaal lay across the wolf's chest, hands buried in the thick fur as he tickled.

Nyri's lips twitched at the scene. At least someone around here was happy. "What are you doing, Omaal?" she asked.

"I a wolf!" Omaal giggled. "I fighting evil Wove in woods!" He renewed his attack on his friend.

"Evil Wove?" Nyri's heart skipped a beat. The last thing she needed was visions of Woves waiting in the woods.

"He had a nightmare," Umaa murmured a quiet explanation as she came up behind. "He's been having them ever since that... night. Those filthy monsters scared him to death!" she spat. "Why can't they just leave us alone!"

Nyri grew cold as she remembered the night the wolf pack had chased the Woves from the forest, the real Woves, dead eyes rolling in their skull faces. Her stomach squeezed.

"Evil Wove in woods!" Omaal declared again

"Omaal, can you come here a moment? I need to look at your shoulders."

The little boy stopped playing with a long-suffering sigh. He rolled off Batai and caught hold of his fur, seeing through the wolf's eyes through their contact as they made their way towards Nyri.

Forcing down the fears clawing to get loose inside her chest, she examined the wounds the grishnaa had inflicted upon him. Baarias had done his work well; the wounds had healed. There was no sign the wound had become cursed. Nyri released the pair to continue with their game.

As she left, she did her best to banish the vision Omaal's words had put into her head—that of a skull-faced monster lurking in the woods.

* * *

Baarias was lighting the *girru* moss inside his tree when Nyri returned. He was glad to see some of the tension leave her shoulders as the warmth and light of the moss fell upon her drawn features. Her face appeared to have hardened over the past days since the raid, the girlish softness leaving it at last. Baarias did not like the change.

Kyaati lay restlessly upon her bower as he finished crushing his sleeping herbs into a *haala* nut filled with water. "This should help you rest better," he murmured to her. He could not ease her agitation; the best he could do was to keep her calm in the only way he knew how.

Kyaati drank greedily, though her eyes darted, lacking any of her usual cool reason. Baarias' stomach tightened at the sight. He turned to Nyriaana. "All finished?"

Nyri jerked her chin in an affirmative gesture as she sank down beside Kyaati, her creased brow reflecting his own concern. She reached out and took Kyaati's hand, but Kyaati tore away from her grip. Pain contracted across Nyri's face. Kyaati did not see it. She hadn't even spared her tribe-sister a single glance.

"Is there anything I should know about?" Baarias asked, covering the uncomfortable moment.

"No," Nyri answered. "Omaal is having nightmares, but that is all."

"Nightmares?"

"About Woves in the woods." His young charge gave a delicate shiver. "A reaction to the attack, Umaa suspects."

Baarias lifted his chin in agreement. "Understandable. If

219

the trauma does not ease on its own, I'll mix him some herbs to help him rest."

"Your sleep remedies could knock out a boar." Nyri attempted a teasing tone. "I remember drinking them after Juaan—" She cut off abruptly.

Baarias's brows rose. Nyri had never mentioned the Forbidden's name voluntarily since she was a tiny girl. He felt his own heart shiver at the unexpected reminder of his sister's sin. Nyri's face flushed as she ducked her head. Tears had started around the edges of her eyes.

In the ensuing silence, Kyaati was quick to pounce. Battling the influence of the herbs Baarias had given her, her gleaming eyes narrowed. "Do not tell me you still mourn for that Forbidden half-breed?"

Nyri hunched her shoulders. "He was my friend."

"*Friend*," Kyaati snorted with cutting sarcasm.

"Kyaati…" Baarias warned. Nyri was fighting to keep herself composed as he had taught her, but she had not yet mastered the skill and he could not bear to see her pain.

"What?" Kyaati lashed out at him. "She should not mourn such a creature! He was nothing. An abomination. A *monster*."

"He was *not*!" Nyri snapped back, her tenuous control failing. Her chest heaved as she tried to regain it.

Kyaati had no such compunction. "Oh yes, he was," she continued without mercy. "You were a naïve *baby*, Nyriaana, easily fooled by the poison that came from his mouth. You did not see what he was. It was a blessing the Woves killed him. A *blessing*!"

"Shut up!" Nyriaana's face flushed. "*I'm* not the one who has been poisoned, Kyaati! Don't you see what's happening here? Don't you understand what they have done to you? You—"

"Nyriaana!" Baarias scolded. A healer could not afford such a lapse. "Kyaati does not mean what she is saying." It was her pain causing her to lash out, making her want to hurt the nearest person she could reach.

"Yes, I do!" Kyaati spat. "He deserved to die, my baby—" Kyaati's voice broke at the end and she buried her face in her hands. "My baby. My little baby," her voice came in muffled, racking sobs. "Where is she? Where is she?"

Baarias' heart shattered at the sight of her grief. He knew he would be rejected, but he couldn't help trying to offer what comfort he could. "Shh, shh." He placed a hand on her shoulder.

"No!" The maniacal gleam blazed back to full strength, and Kyaati shoved him away. "My baby!" she screeched as she fled into the other chamber.

Nyri jumped to her feet and started after her, but Baarias caught her arm and shook his head. "No, don't. Give her space. There is nothing you can say right now that will help and *you* need to get a better hold on your temper."

Shame coloured her cheeks. "Baarias, I…"

"Never mind. Go home, Nyri. I will take care of her."

For once, Nyri did not argue and shuffled from the tree. The combined pain from both young women ripped across Baarias' senses and he cringed, at a loss how to comfort either of them.

* * *

22

Enemy

"Mama, Juaan is sick," Nyriaana tugged on her mother's arm.

"I know, little one," her mother reached down to touch the boy's sweaty brow as he writhed deliriously. She closed her eyes, frowning. "This is beyond me. Nyri, get Baarias."

Nyri moved to obey. Juaan was never sick. A bite from the ushaa spider usually spelled a quick death unless treated immediately.

"Stay right where you are, Nyriaana," her father's angry voice cut in. He rounded on her mother. "This is nonsense, Jaai. If he is to die, then let him go. It pleases Ninmah. I don't know why you are wasting your time. He is a monster who doesn't belong. He dies now, or he dies later. His fate is—"

"Telaan!" Her mother glared at him. Nyri was quick to emulate her fierce energy. She had grown tired of her papa's dislike for Juaan. She raised her chin in defiance.

"I get Baarias, mama," she said, and scooted out of the tree before her father could stop her.

The healer was easy to find, and she dragged him back to her

222

home. *"Come! Sick!"* she told him over and over. Baarias was confused but did not resist.

"Who's sick?"

She didn't answer and made him follow her up the tree. She noticed her father had disappeared when she entered; she could taste the aftershock of a fight on the air. He and her mother had argued. Again.

Baarias stopped dead when he saw Juaan lying in the bower. Nyri pointed hopefully. Her mother got up from where she had been sitting by his head and extended her hands to the healer.

Baarias backed away. *"No, Jaai!"* he whispered. *"You know I cannot. Do not ask this of me."*

"Pleeaaase!" Nyri begged, tugging on his coverings and widening her tear-filled eyes. Fellow tribe members always gave way to her when she did this and quickly surrendered whatever she wanted.

"Baarias," her mother's voice was insistent. *"He got bitten by an ushaa spider while protecting Nyri."*

"But, Daajir said he attacked..."

"I do not care what that weasel pup said! Juaan saved Nyri. Now you must save him."

Baarias stood, agony scrawled across his face as he put a hand to his mouth. It appeared as though he was trying not to cry. Strange for an adult such as him, Nyri thought.

"Baarias!" her mother snapped. *"He put himself in harm's way to save Nyriaana's life. Do something!"*

The healer pulled his hand away from his face. *"You know the consequence I would face if they ever found out."*

"To Ninsiku with them!" Her mother cried. *"Show some courage, Baarias, for Rebaa's sake. He is just a boy. He does not deserve to die. He cannot help his heritage."*

"It is because of his heritage that he is already doomed. We have no way of knowing what he may become. It may be safer for all our sakes just to let him go."

Nyri did not know what they were talking about. She moved over to clutch Juaan's hand. His eyes fixed on her briefly as they rolled deliriously in his head. He smiled. "Nyri, Nyri, Nyriaana... "

"I here." Terror washed through her. She wished she were a healer. Then she could make him better herself.

Behind them, her mother continued to argue with Baarias. "You cannot know that. We do not know what his fate may be. The future isn't certain. We can only do what is in our power now, and it is within your power to help this child. Your own sister-son!"

But fear was the only expression on the healer's face as he stared at the stricken Juaan. "You truly do not know what you ask of me, Jaai. I do not have your courage, Jaai. I cannot help you. It is wrong. Daajir said that he sensed something from him... a dangerous energy..." There was a pause. "You know about that?" the healer demanded.

"Th-there is a power within him, yes." Nyri heard the reluctance in her mother's tone. "I cannot tell you what it is. All I know is that Juaan is no monster. Not unless we make him one."

Make Juaan a monster? Nyri frowned at the adults. How could they make her friend into a monster? What dangerous power were they talking about?

"It might already be too late." Baarias said.

Nyri's mother dropped her arms in defeat and Nyri began to cry. Juaan was going to die.

Baarias shifted uncomfortably in the face of her sobs. "Here."

He thrust out a bundle of herbs. "I will not heal him. It goes against my better judgement, but these might help. If you can break his fever, he may have a chance; he is... uncommonly strong. He should be dead already."

"Thank you," her mother whispered, taking his offering.

The healer squeezed her hand. "The boy is lucky to have you watching over him," he murmured. "Your courage may see him through yet; Rebaa would be pleased. I just hope your sacrifice does not lead to the same hardship and despair that hers did..."

* * *

Nyri felt like she had only blinked when she awoke before the dawn. Exhaustion sucked at her. She lay for a while in the cocoon of darkness, trying to sort through the turmoil of her thoughts. She cringed at the memory of her fight with Kyaati. Such a lapse on her part was unforgivable, she should know better. The disappointment on Baarias' face had been a slap across the cheek. He was right. She had to get a hold of herself. She would be of no use to anybody if she kept falling apart.

Her mind turned to the outer forest. Juaan had resided in the Pit for four days. Four days without food. If she did not get through to him, he was going to die. The last vestiges of sleep fell away, and Nyri scrambled to her feet.

First things first, she needed more food. Cautiously, she made her way towards the nearest store. None of the rest of the tribe was awake yet.

Or so she had thought.

Umaa was descending from the store ahead of her. Omaal's mother touched the ground and then flinched when she saw Nyri.

"It's only me, Umaa," Nyri soothed as she approached. "You're awake early." She tried to sound conversational, though she was dismayed to find another up and alert before dawn. She had hoped she would be alone.

Umaa shifted. "Omaal had another nightmare. He will not go back to sleep."

"Another? About the Woves?"

"Woves, yes." Umaa edged away. "I'd best get back to him. Imaani is on watch."

Nyri's throat tightened at the thought of what Umaa's mate was watching for. "The Woves...?" She was almost afraid of the answer.

"Still on the plains," Umaa said before all but running in the other direction back to her unprotected son. Nyri watched her go, noting that the other woman's gait appeared awkward. She shrugged it off. If Umaa had been injured, she would have come to Baarias.

Shivering from standing in the chill mist, Nyri leaped into the branches of the store tree. One item. That was the limit. Her lips pulled down; one piece of food per day would not keep two people fed. She needed to take two.

It's worth it, it's Juaan, she chanted in her mind, *it's worth it.* She stole the extra ration without another thought.

Imaani was in another part of the forest that morning, and it surprised Nyri how much easier it was to evade Javaan.

As she ran, she tried to put from her mind the words Kyaati had spoken. She had *not* been a naïve baby. Nyri remembered the love and affection in Juaan's eyes whenever

226

he had looked at her and knew it had not been a lie. She let the warmth of the memory carry her along.

Upon reaching the Pit, Nyri lifted back the coverings. He was waiting in the dimness.

"I came back!" she panted.

If she had hoped to see a change from the day before, she was disappointed. His posture remained aggressive; a cornered animal waiting for his enemy to strike. The same terrible hatred filled his eyes.

Forcing the words past the lump forming in her throat, Nyri asked, "How are your injuries? Are you in any pain?"

His hands tightened around his healing leg.

Where are you? Nyri thought, searching his eyes for a spark, anything that would let her break through. *You are him, so you must be in there somewhere. Whatever has made you forget, fight it!*

"Please, try to remember," she begged. "It's me. It's your Nyri."

His eyes narrowed.

Nyri's breath hitched. It was becoming obvious that any mention of his true name or their childhood would only make matters worse. She decided she must avoid such subjects until he was ready to hear them. Nyri shifted under his forbidding glare and tried another course. The food that she had thrown to him on her last visit remained untouched. "Aren't you going to eat?"

His chin lifted in defiance.

Forcing down her rising despair, she assessed his condition. His life force felt so weak. She did not know how he was still upright, though the rock wall at his back seemed to have a lot to do with that. Despite herself, Nyri could not help but feel awed by the strength of will it must be taking. It also unnerved her. She needed to break that will before it was too late.

His rigid face was hollow with exhaustion. The green eyes were growing dull, yet he still gave out his warning. *Don't come near. Leave me.*

No! Nyri dug her nails into her palms. "Please, eat. *Please,*" she appealed. "You are dying. You cannot go on like this. Please."

It did no good. The fading stare remained unyielding, and tears stung her eyes as Nyri faced the reality of losing him for a second time. She did not know how she would bear the pain. Nyri reached out a hand, wishing she could bridge the distance and touch him. "Please. What can I do to prove myself to you? I do not mean you harm. Let me help, I need to help *someone*—"

The emotions she was fighting so hard to hold in check in the face of her tribe's plight, Kyaati's curse and now Juaan's slow demise got the better of her, and the tears spilled down her cold cheeks. She was losing everybody, and her world was falling around her.

A movement caught her eye. Juaan had shifted, hate and confusion warring for dominance on his face. Nyri blinked to clear her blurring vision. Her tears had affected him. *Juaan, Juaan, please.*

He watched her with the same torn expression for a moment longer, then closed his eyes to block her out. He leaned back, dropping his head against the rock wall behind.

Maybe he was just too exhausted to fight anymore and didn't care what she did now. Whatever the reason, Nyri felt hope surge at this small gesture. Closed eyes suggested a certain amount of trust, surely. It bolstered her waning confidence. Perhaps he had decided that if she were going to hurt him or betray his presence to the rest of her tribe, she would have done it by now. Whatever the reason, she would take the opening.

Wiping her face dry, Nyri began to talk. It felt stupid just to sit there saying nothing. Now that he wasn't glaring at her, the words came easily. "My tribe posted extra watch. It is very important that you do not draw attention to yourself. Do you hear me?"

He half opened his eyes, regarding her with a raised eyebrow. She got the uncomfortable impression that he was questioning her sanity.

The shadows of the predawn were receding, and Nyri realised that her time was running out. She had to press this tiny advantage she had gained. She pulled the food she had brought out from concealment. "Maybe you'd prefer these." She displayed a bunch of fleshy vine roots. "Try them."

The longing on his face was obvious. His hunger was breaking his will; he *wanted* to give in. Nyri's heart quickened and in the spur of the moment, she forgot herself.

"Juaan—"

It was a mistake. The hostility blazed back to life. Fury rolled from him such as never before. The hairs stood up on the back of Nyri's neck as the air grew cold.

"Get away from here, witch!" He uncoiled from the ground like a *grishnaa* preparing to strike. "Get. *Away!*"

The food dropped from her numb fingers and toppled away into the depths.

"Get away from here!" he snarled. "Elf *witch*! My kin will find me and when they do, you had better pray to the gods I do not find you!"

He swept a jagged rock from the ground and swung back his arm. Nyri stumbled away from the edge only just in time, feeling the sear of wind as the rock grazed her ear. Had the blow connected, it would have been fatal. Nyri gasped but did not feel the air in her lungs. He had tried to kill her! She fled, hot tears of betrayal blinding her vision.

The trees swept by as she ran, whipping and cutting her face. She heeded nothing. Wrong. She had been so wrong. All of her childhood memories flashed through her mind, every word, every shared moment. Lies, all of it, lies.

Kyaati's words echoed with merciless clarity. *You were a naïve baby, Nyriaana, easily fooled by the poison that came from his mouth. You did not see what he was.*

Now she saw it. Ninmah had been right to forbid such half-breed creatures. All that resided in that Pit was a vicious, bloodthirsty monster. Nyri choked, feeling the blood ooze from her wounded ear. She only ran faster.

23

Missing

Nyri was gasping for breath when she reached the border of the *eshaara* grove. She skidded to a halt and back-peddled, sensing the sentries before her. With a thrill of panic, she realised it would not be as easy getting back into the settlement this time.

Four of her tribesmen were concealed on the outskirts, evenly spaced. Fighting against the hysterical sobs that wanted to break loose from her chest, she crouched in the undergrowth to wait. She hoped they might move after a time to monitor other areas.

But the moments slipped by and the sentries remained. Nyri dug her nails into the earth in frustration. *Oh, come on!* Ninmah's warmth crept up her back. She would soon be missed and her actions questioned. Once that happened, they would find her out in a heartbeat.

Not that she really cared about that now. What did it matter if they found him? He was nothing but a monster. Baarias had been right that day all those seasons ago. He had seen it as he had stood over the dying boy. But if they caught her, what would they do to her? Nyri did not know what the punishment would be for doing what she had.

If she made it through without being detected, she vowed she would never disobey the Elders again. There was nothing out here for her but heartbreak.

Drawing a steadying breath, Nyri started forward, willing herself invisible. Time to put her woeful skills at concealment to the test.

"Raanya!" A familiar voice broke the stillness. "Come and help an old woman, will you?"

The sentry nearest to Nyri abandoned her place of concealment and rushed away. Unable to believe her luck, Nyri was quick to take advantage of the hole in the defence. She slipped back into the protection of the *eshaara* trees.

She was in time to see Raanya aiding Sefaan with a basketful of goods.

"Thank you, thank you!" The Kamaali thanked her. Then, even though she had not yet reached her destination, she brushed Raanya off. Nyri paused in her escape to listen. "No, I've got it from here. No, I'm fine. You get back to your watch. Anyone could have slipped by while you had your back turned!" Nyri could have sworn Sefaan's eyes flickered to hers.

Exasperated but obedient, Raanya disappeared back into the outer trees, and Nyri hastened to continue her own escape. The way Sefaan was looking at her made her uncomfortable. She could feel the ancient eyes burning into her back all the way to Baarias' tree. Nyri forced her pace to remain even until she ducked into the healer's tree.

Concealed from scrutiny at last, she collapsed back against the tree wall and buried her flushed face in her hands, the full weight of her grief washing over her. *None* of it had been true. She had indeed been a lonely child, desperate for somebody to love her. Easy prey for the monster hatched in their midst. Now she had let that need ruin her again.

Why is Ninmah doing this to me? She knew the answer. It was a punishment. She had knowingly committed a sin by aiding a Forbidden creature. Ninmah was teaching her a lesson. The jagged shards of her heart sliced through her chest. She had failed everyone. She wished with all her might that her mother had never accepted him into her family.

With a growl, Nyri pushed herself away from the wall. She would not fall apart like she had the first time she had lost him; she was not a child anymore. She would wait until she retired to her own tree to allow herself the luxury of breaking down.

She found Baarias sitting with Kyaati. Her tribe-sister clutched an untouched piece of honey fruit in her hands.

"Ah, Nyriaana has arrived at last." Baarias seized upon her appearance. "Now the day can begin."

If he had thought Nyri's presence would raise Kyaati's spirits, however, her mentor was sadly mistaken. Kyaati did not look up from her fruit. The wild gleam in her eyes was still there as she stared hard into space, her lips moving as though she were speaking to herself in her mind. Nyri ignored that and crossed the space to squeeze her shoulder. Even bewitched, Kyaati had seen to the truth before she had.

"What happened to your ear?"

Nyri clamped a hand over the wound Juaan had inflicted on her, feeling its sting afresh. "Nothing. I grazed it climbing down my tree. Careless."

"Nyri," Baarias admonished. "There is no need to show off every time you leave your home. Try to be more steady for once." He reached a hand towards her injury.

"Leave it!" She thrust his hand away and Baarias recoiled. Seeing the shock on his face, Nyri drew a deep breath and forced a smile onto her lips. "Let it stand as a reminder for me to be more careful from now on."

Baarias lowered his hand and acquiesced silently, though a frown still marked his face as he watched her.

The morning meal was stifled. Kyaati refused to speak, and Nyri offered no conversation. It was almost a relief when Pelaan came in and broke the protracted silence. "Baarias," he called. "I would like to spend some time with my daughter. I am sure you have much to do."

Baarias' lips pulled down. Nyri could tell he was not happy to leave Kyaati in anyone's care but his own. He could not deny an Elder's request, however, and inclined his head.

"If you need me, I will not be far."

Apprehension shivered down Nyri's own spine as she recalled the last time they had left father and daughter alone together.

"Nyri." Baarias rose to his feet. "We must go."

Nyri trailed along as Baarias visited the most infirm members of the tribe. She responded to questions and smiled whenever it was required of her. As much as she was hurting, she still had to function and perform her duties.

It was a sad business. The shortening of food rations and the constant threat of the Woves' return were already taking their toll. Nyri felt an echo of Kyaati's craze sink into her own mind, threatening to take a hold. She struggled to see how she could carry on with her life as she had before. She

234

had not realised how much of a distraction Juaan's return had provided, giving her a reason to rise in the morning. Naïve baby, indeed.

Little Naaya had fallen and broken her wrist. The tiny girl's frame had been spare before; now she was gaunt. Despite Baarias' ministrations, her injury was not healing as it should. Nyri emulated Baarias' impassive expression in front of Naaya's anxious mother as her teacher gave his assurances and bound the wounded arm. Only Nyri knew him well enough to detect his concern. The child's condition was not promising.

"You must keep it still for a while, little one," Baarias told the starving child in a light voice. "I'll do all I can to make it better."

Naaya smiled at him, blinking sleepily. She barely had the energy to keep her eyes open.

Nyri was glad when they left Naaya's family tree. Baarias squeezed her shoulder in silent support as they walked away; he said nothing. There was nothing to say.

Naaya was not the only one suffering. Nyri's own stomach ached. She had not eaten with Baarias and Kyaati; she had lost her ration to the Pit. Before she could stop herself, she wondered if Juaan had finally eaten or if he still faded towards his own demise.

Why should I care! She raged at herself. *He is your enemy. That is all that there is, now. All there ever was.*

But as the day passed, her shock and her anger at what had happened began to fade. To her dismay, the strange pull in her heart drew her once again towards the outer trees. Familiar green eyes overshadowed her every thought. Her stomach gave a little lurch as it occurred to her that she would never see them again.

We have got to look after him now because no one else will...

Nyri shook the voice away. *I cannot risk my life or those of my People, mother, and you were* wrong *for doing so. He made his true nature clear. I* will *look after my tribe. That is my duty.* Her father had possessed the better sense after all. Nyri's foolish heart, however, remained unconvinced.

They retreated to Baarias' dwelling as evening closed. Nyri was so preoccupied that she almost didn't notice when Baarias came to an abrupt halt. The sudden tension rolling from him alarmed Nyri. His eyes fixed on a point ahead of them. She followed his gaze.

Pelaan was crossing the *eshaara* grove to his own tree. The Elder was alone. Baarias gave a soft gasp and broke into a run towards Kyaati's father. He grabbed the Elder's arm, looking very much like he wanted to shake him. "Pelaan! Where is Kyaati?"

No! Nyri rushed to Baarias' side, wanting to shake Pelaan herself.

The Elder yanked his arm free of the healer's grasp. "In your tree where I left her! I tried to reason with her, to rid her of this senseless idea that her baby is still alive. She has to move on. She all but attacked me when I suggested another Joining would help. She has lost her mind! I refuse to see her again until she returns to her senses."

"She is not the one who is foolish, Pelaan!" Baarias threw the words into the Elder's stunned face before racing towards the healer tree.

Kyaati! Nyri chased after him, catching her teacher at the entrance to his home. Baarias had already stopped, his arms dropping to his sides in defeat. He had seen with his eyes what Nyri already knew in her heart.

Kyaati was gone.

24

Search

"N o!" The denial slipped from Nyri's mouth.

"Pelaan!" Baarias ran back to the Elder still standing away in the deepening gloom. "Pelaan! Gather the tribe. Now! Your daughter is gone."

"Gone?" Pelaan drew himself up in surprise. "Where has she gone?"

"I don't *know*!" Baarias snapped. "She—"

"Well, she can't have gone very—"

"Naaya!" Another voice cut across their debate. Nyri watched as Naaya's mother came running through the *eshaara* grove. "Naaya! *Where are you?*" She skidded to a halt in front of their group. "Please, please help, my little Naaya is gone." Haana fell to her knees and clutched at Pelaan's coverings. "Please, respected Elder, I only left to collect more moss for her bedding. When I got back, she was gone! Please, I must find her, she is so weak!" The frantic sobs bubbled in her chest. "Why would she run away? She knows how dangerous it is! *Naaya!*"

There was no answer to her piercing cry.

Pelaan raised his hands for calm. "She must be somewhere, Haana."

The commotion was drawing the rest of the tribe. Daajir stalked to Nyri's side, his dark gaze questioning.

"Kyaati," Nyri clutched at him. "She's gone. And so has Naaya." Two vulnerable tribe members missing without explanation.

With a snapping of branches, the answer came.

"Aardn!" Imaani flew in from the outer forest. "We must leave. Now. Javaan saw two of the Woves leave the main raiding party and cross into the trees; he tracked them but lost them somewhere north of the river. They could be anywhere by now."

The colour drained from Pelaan's face. Haana's mouth fell into a silent scream, her hands clawing at her skin. Nyri caught hold of Baarias as the strength went out of her legs. The Woves. The Woves had used their dark power to slip past the watch and taken Kyaati and Naaya. There would be no direct attack this time. They were going to pick them off one by one, unseen and unheard, like the devils they were.

Daajir hissed and made as if to fly into the forest on the kidnapper's heels. Nyri grabbed his elbow. She would not lose another member of her family.

Oraan's lips were white as he gathered his mate into his arms.

"Our baby," Haana sobbed into his chest as his hands rubbed up and down her back. "They came and took our baby!"

Oraan glared at Aardn. "I warned you! I told you it was too dangerous to stay with those beasts camped on our border. You would not listen. Now my daughter is in their clutches!"

A howl of grief from Haana punctuated his words.

The lead Elder ignored Oraan's accusations. Instead, she rounded on Imaani. "How could you have let them by you!"

"I-I don't know. Javaan had them, but then they evaded him."

Aardn growled and took a step towards him. Nyri thought the Elder was going to strike the sentry.

Umaa planted herself at her mate's side, Omaal clutched tight in her arms. The boy's eyes were wide with terror, Batai ghosted along beside them, his hackles raised in response to the tension in the air.

"It's not Imaani's fault!" Umaa snapped. "We all know the power those beasts possess. What makes you think they couldn't make it past the watch unseen if they wanted?"

Nyri stifled a cry of impatience. What did it matter how the Woves had got in? What mattered was that Kyaati and Naaya had been taken and were slipping further away with every passing moment.

Aardn closed her eyes, composing herself. Her expression was smooth when she faced Imaani again. "Go with the rest of the sentries to the last place Javaan saw the Woves. Make sure no others cross our border to help the trespassers. Summon the wolves if you must."

Imaani nodded once and bounded back into the trees as Aardn dipped her head to look into his son's blind eyes. Umaa shifted as if she wanted to pull Omaal away from the Elder's scrutiny.

"Umaa, we need to use your Omaal's bond with Batai to track the Woves who came here. There is no more time to waste."

Umaa gasped, clutching Omaal tighter. "You would go

after them? I thought you said we would flee at the first sign of their return!"

"They've taken my daughter! I will not abandon her!" Pelaan snapped. "Of course we're going after them!"

Umaa's gaze hardened into flint. "If the Woves have her, then it is already too late. Why risk the rest of us? Your child is no more important than mine, *respected* Elder. We should run for our lives before they all decide to come back!"

Pelaan's face reddened as he opened his mouth to respond, but Aardn cut him off. "Imaani said that only two crossed the border, the rest remain at camp. A weak force. If we catch them before they make their camp, we may be able to rescue Kyaati and Naaya before it is too late. I will lose no more of our family to Ninsiku's Children!"

The Elder's tone ended any further discussion. Her eyes flickered to Daajir for the briefest of moments, and Nyri could have sworn he raised his chin infinitesimally in response. Aardn then addressed Omaal before anyone else could raise a protest. "Omaal, listen. I want you to tell Batai to track down the Woves. We will follow him."

Omaal's small face twisted in terror as it turned unerringly towards the outer trees. "Out there? I no go out there. Evil Wove waits!"

Nyri wanted to fall to her knees and beg the child herself. *Please, for Kyaati!* The thought of her friend in their enemy's grasp was almost more than she could stand.

"Yes, Omaal," Aardn said. "We must go after the evil Woves and stop them. We have to go now. Please. Nothing is going to happen to you. Send Batai, now."

Omaal shuddered, but tilted his head to stare down at his wolf. Nyri felt the energy flow and then Batai took off, bounding into the trees, his nose to the ground.

"Follow him!" Aardn barked. "We all go together. Do not get separated!"

As one, they followed Umaa, carrying Omaal as the boy directed them through the trees on the path his wolf had taken.

"Baarias," Nyri whispered. "Please tell me we'll find them."

Her teacher gazed down at her but gave no reassurance. He would not lie to her.

Twice Batai doubled back on himself to read the scent anew. Nyri could have screamed whenever he did this, but the wolf continued to lead them on into the night, following on the heels of their enemies. Haana had to be supported between Oraan and Pelaan; she stumbled and fell often; her legs giving out.

"Be careful!" Aardn's warning came from ahead. "The Pits are close! Keep your wits about you."

The Pits! Nyri's stride faltered. Batai had been told to follow the scent of the Woves, and now he was taking them to the one place where the Wove scent would be strongest.

No! Nyri screamed inside her head. *Please, no, stop! Batai is following the wrong scent! Don't go that way.*

"What's the matter?" Daajir was frowning at her.

All she could manage was an incoherent gurgle.

He misunderstood. "Don't worry, we will get her back. Batai is getting close. I can feel it!"

Yes, he is, Nyri thought desperately. *But not to what we seek! We are going to lose Kyaati!*

And they would find Juaan. The ground lurched nastily beneath her feet. She had convinced herself that she no longer cared what became of him, but faced with the reality, she found she did not truly wish him dead. It did not matter that everything that had once been sacred to her was now a lie. Nyri knew she could not live through seeing him put to death, torn apart by wolves.

The realisation came too late. The Pits opened out before them and Batai came to a halt, sniffing intently around the nearest hole. Nyri fought the urge to rush forward and push him away.

"Everybody, down. They're close." She heard Aardn breathe as though from a great distance.

"But I can't feel my daughter!" Haana cried. "How can she be close?"

No one spoke. If the Woves were nearby, but neither Kyaati's nor Naaya's presence could be felt, there could only be one answer. An answer no one was willing to voice to the little girl's mother.

Daajir was pushing about in the undergrowth, searching for tracks. "Ninmah's mercy!" He thrust the leaves aside and bent to pluck an object from the ground. When he came up, he was holding Juaan's bone knife before him. Nyri bit down on her lip to gate the cry of denial that slid between her clenched teeth.

The rest of the tribe gasped at the sight of the Wove weapon and collectively took a step back from Daajir.

"They *are* here." Aardn glowered. "Find the murdering monsters!"

Batai whined and started scratching at the earth next to the nearest Pit. Nyri could only watch, helpless to prevent it, as Omaal pointed with one trembling hand.

A rustle of leaves was their only warning. A dark figure stepped out from behind a tree. Daajir lifted the knife he held awkwardly in defence, ready to strike as the rest of the tribe stumbled back. Nyri's eyes widened. He got out? *Impossible!*

"You're in the wrong place." The dark form shrank down in Nyri's mind's eye as a calm, familiar voice called from the silhouette.

"*Sefaan!*" Aardn gasped. "Wh-what in Ninmah's name are you *doing* out here?"

The Kamaali limped forward and the veil that had shielded her presence rolled back. Her lined features were sharp in the darkness. "That is none of your concern, Aardn. My business is my own. But I will tell you, you are following the wrong scent. She is not here."

Aardn's temper flared. "The Woves have infiltrated our home and taken off with two of our number! I have no time for your games, Sefaan!"

A smile tugged at the ancient mouth. "Of course not. You never truly listen to the Great Spirit, Aardn. Here." She reached down and touched Batai's furry head. His nose lifted from the Pit, immediately turning in another direction. He trotted to the edge of the collected tribe and sat on his haunches, waiting. "Come with me and you will see for yourself. He is on the right scent now."

The old Kamaali started after Batai without so much as a backwards glance. Nyri could almost hear Aardn's teeth grinding together. To her surprise, Baarias was the first to follow Sefaan, an understanding seeming to pass between them.

"I believe I know what you mean, Revered One," he said in a low voice.

Sefaan dipped her head once, and she and Batai set off on

the new trail. The *akaab* healer followed close behind. Nyri waited until the rest of the confused tribe set off in their wake. Daajir was the last to go. He was staring at the bone knife in his hand, running his fingers over it again and again. Nyri would not move from the Pits until he did.

"Ninmah has blessed me with a gift." His voice was speculative. "Now I know I am truly following Her path." With that cryptic comment, he tucked the weapon into his coverings and followed the tribe, leaving Nyri alone next to the damning Pit.

Nyri blew out the breath she had been holding and braced herself on her knees. She glared at the concealed hole. "You are lucky, Forbidden," she hissed in his direction before turning her back and following in the wake of her tribe. She vowed that would be the last bit of pain he ever caused her. She would never return to this place. His presence may yet have cost Kyaati her life.

Her tribe had disappeared into the trees and Nyri ran to catch up. Being alone only got her into trouble. *Kyaati!* Her heart cried out. *Where are you?* She watched the two figures leading the way behind the form of the forest wolf. They did not appear to be hurrying anymore as they wove around the maze of hidden Pits. Indeed, Baarias was calm.

Nyri wanted to scream at their apparent unconcern that Kyaati was in the hands of the Woves and getting further out of reach with every moment that passed. They had already wasted enough time on the Forbidden. She itched to blast past them and chase after her tribe-sister herself if they would not.

Nyri gathered herself to do just that when the procession came to an abrupt halt.

245

"Kyaati!" Baarias breathed.

Nyri's stomach dropped as she pushed her way to his side, preparing herself for the worst. Pelaan was right beside her.

They stopped dead at the sight that greeted them, and Nyri understood what Sefaan had meant about Batai following the wrong scent.

There were no Woves here. Kyaati was sitting alone amid several Pits. She did not look up. Indeed, she appeared quite oblivious to their presence. She bent protectively over a bundle in her arms, crooning as she rocked back and forth. The bundle was struggling, trying to get away from her hold.

"Mama!" Nyri recognised Naaya's thin voice. Her hand went to her mouth as the enormity of what had truly happened struck home.

"Naaya!" Haana stumbled forward in response to her daughter's plea. Oraan was at her side. Fury replaced the mother's panic as she took in the scene playing out before her. A snarl burst from her lips. "*She* took my baby?"

Baarias caught her arm. "Please, Haana, let me deal with this. *Let me*! I will get your daughter back."

Haana fumed, but complied with the *akaab*'s wishes.

Nyri gnawed on a fingernail as Baarias stepped forward, moving as though he was trying not to spook a flighty animal. "Kyaati? Kyaati, it's Baarias."

Sefaan was shadowing Baarias' steps as they picked their way around the maws in the ground.

Kyaati lifted her head and saw the healer approaching. "Baarias. Look. I told you I'd find where they were hiding her. I knew I'd find her. My baby, isn't she beautiful?" A proud grin broke over her face.

Naaya whimpered.

Haana let out a strangled cry, and Nyri put a hand on her arm to restrain her. She had never been more frightened for Kyaati. They had to let Baarias get to her.

"Yes, she is beautiful, Kyaati," Baarias agreed, edging closer to where Kyaati sat. Nyri held her breath. If Baarias made the slightest wrong move, Kyaati might take flight. The empty spaces gaped on all sides as Baarias sank onto his haunches next to her friend. "May I have a hold?"

Mistrust flickered across Kyaati's glowing face.

"Please." Baarias held out his hands. "I won't do anything to harm her, Kyaati."

Kyaati's arms tightened. "You are going to take her away from me again."

Baarias shook his head. "I will not take her away from you, Kyaati. I am here to take care of you both but... I think we both know that she is not your child. I think deep down, you know where your baby is."

Kyaati's face clouded. "My baby..."

"Kyaati," Baarias said. "Dear one, it is time to stop. Let me look at Naaya. She has a broken arm. She is in pain."

"Pain?" Kyaati's forehead creased in distress as she looked down at the child.

"Yes. Please. I am here, Kyaati. I know what you are going through. Let me take care of Naaya."

Tears started in Kyaati's eyes as she looked up into Baarias' steady countenance, her face twisting through a range of wild emotions. Nyri could see the sobs building in her chest. Kyaati held Naaya tighter, leaning away. The maw behind her beckoned...

Then Sefaan was there. She cupped her hands around Kyaati's face. "Let her go, child," she said. "She is not yours to keep. Baarias is right, you know where your child is. Let go."

Under Sefaan's touch, the Wove spell of madness shattered. With a brokenhearted wail, Kyaati thrust Naaya into Baarias' waiting arms and collapsed into Sefaan's embrace. The Kamaali pulled Kyaati from the edge of the Pit and stroked at the silver hair as she screamed to the night. "I've got you, child," Sefaan whispered. "That's right, let it all out. Let it go. It is time to accept."

Haana and Oraan rushed to take their daughter from Baarias. Pelaan moved to hover over Kyaati as a hiss of angry voices broke out from the rest of the tribe. Nyri was dimly aware of Daajir at her side. His face was grim.

"This isn't good," he whispered in a tight voice. "She took a child. What was she *thinking*?"

"I don't think she was," Nyri murmured. "The Woves had control of her mind. It is not her fault."

"She's alright." Baarias was reassuring Haana as he handed Naaya over.

Haana hugged her squalling daughter close, trying to quiet her. "You!" She jabbed a finger at Kyaati where she lay crumpled in Sefaan's arms. "*You* stole my daughter. *You* took her—!"

Aardn thrust her arm out, cutting her off. "Stop! Now is not the time for this, Haana! Your daughter is safe, but she may not remain so if we do not move. The Woves are still out here and we do not know where they are. We must return home and await news from the sentries. This night is not over yet!"

The tribe huddled closer together, knowing tonight may be the night they had to flee, leaving their lives behind.

Without waiting for the still fuming Haana to argue, Aardn turned and led them in the direction of the *eshaara* grove.

Pelaan stooped to get his daughter to her feet, but Sefaan warned him away with a fierce glare. Pelaan stepped back as Sefaan allowed Baarias to approach. Nyri hurried forward at his side. "Come on, Kyaati," she murmured in her friend's ear. "We have to go home."

Kyaati did not resist as they pulled her up and supported her between them as they set off after the tribe. Sefaan released her and followed behind.

"Baarias," Nyri whispered. "What can we do?" She would do anything to ease her friend's pain, even for a moment.

"There is nothing you can do, child." It was Sefaan who answered. "She has accepted the truth, but a lot more needs to happen before she heals."

Some of the tension left Nyri's muscles when they reached the safety of the *eshaara* grove and Baarias' tree came into view. The tribe gathered inside, Aardn keeping them together until the sentries returned with news. Nyri trailed Baarias as he guided Kyaati straight to the centre chamber, out from under Haana's murderous glare. Laying her in her bower, he made her drink a whole dose of his sleep remedy. Her lavender eyes closed almost immediately, too exhausted to fight or maybe all too willing to go. Nyri suspected both.

She remained by Kyaati's side for a long time, stroking her hair. She feared the consequences to follow. Daajir's words echoed around her head. *She took a child...*

The night passed. The tribe took turns sleeping. Those on watch waited for the alert. It never came. Nyri hoped the sentries were safe; if they had been captured or killed, then there would be no warning. The thought banished any hope of sleep. She almost envied Kyaati's soft breathing as her friend lay unaware of the tension mounting in the air. Nyri was tempted to ask Baarias for her own remedy. Oblivion would be preferable than this interminable waiting.

The memories of the night flashed through her mind: Baarias' vacant tree; Kyaati, her eyes half crazed, holding the kidnapped Naaya in her arms, the Woves in the woods. The Forbidden in the Pit.

As though the very thought had summoned it, his voice echoed through her mind.

Nyri, Nyri, Nyriaana.

Nyri shuddered, wrapping her arms around herself.

Nyri.

Leave me alone!

She paced into the outer chamber, releasing Kyaati's care to Baarias. She re-settled close to the outer entrance, gazing into the darkness, willing the sentries to return with news that the Woves had left the forest, but no news came. It seemed like forever had passed before Ninmah broke into the sky. Most of the tribe were now sleeping, or at least dozing fitfully. Nyri's head was just beginning to nod forward when movement flickered in the corner of her eye. Something was moving outside of Baarias' tree. Her head snapped up in time to see a lean form step into the entranceway.

He appeared so fast Nyri didn't even have time to raise the alarm.

25

Zykiel

"Imaani!"

Aardn leaped to her feet and rushed to the exhausted sentry as he stumbled inside the tree. "Baarias, get him some water!"

Umaa ran to her mate's side as Imaani sank to the ground. Baarias drew water from the nearest aquilem vine and handed the filled shell to the watchman. The tribe pressed close as they waited for the news he had brought.

"The Woves?" Aardn pressed as Imaani drained the *hala* shell. "Where are they?"

"Gone," Imaani gasped as soon as his lips were free.

"*Gone?*"

Imaani nodded. "We found the pair who breached our borders, but they did not come near the settlement. We tracked them and they returned to their camp as soon as dawn broke. They are no longer in the forest."

Aardn's brow shot up. "They just left?"

"Yes." Imaani was just as perplexed as the Elder.

"What are they *doing?*" Aardn paced the ground.

"I can't be sure, my Elder, but to me it seemed as if they were searching for something."

"Searching for what? They already know where we are."

Nyri grew very still as she listened to this.

"Well, whatever it was, I don't think they found it."

Aardn's frown slashed her brow. "What could they be after if not us...?" she pondered aloud, then shook herself. "You're sure none remain within our borders?"

"Quite sure. There are five of them, all that remained after the wolves attacked them. We can see all five moving within their camp."

Aardn blew out a breath. "Good. Go with Umaa, Imaani, and rest. I will call on you when I have need."

Imaani staggered to his feet and, using Umaa for support, disappeared outside with his family.

"I suggest the rest of you do the same," Aardn addressed the gathered tribe. "It's been a long—"

"Aardn," Haana's voice cut across her. "I cannot hold my silence any longer. This is not over."

Aardn's face tightened. "Haana—"

Haana ignored the warning in the Elder's tone. "My child was taken from me, Aardn, taken out into the woods where monsters were lurking. Such a crime I cannot forgive." She jabbed an accusing finger towards the chamber where Kyaati still slept. "I want her to know the pain she caused me. I demand the right of *Zykiel*."

"No!" Nyri rushed to stand between Haana and Kyaati's chamber.

The Ritual of Transference would force Kyaati to take the fear and pain Haana had experienced as her own. Kyaati would not survive this punishment. As fragile as she was, it would shatter her. Surely Haana could see that. Baarias rose to his feet and came to stand by Nyri's side in support. His face was stiff with disapproval.

"I am sure she already understands your distress, Haana," he said. "I am sure she understands it better than you. You have your daughter. She does not."

Aardn seemed inclined to agree. "Haana…"

Haana's expression was unrelenting. Anger had driven out her compassion. "I do not care! I want justice for what she did to my family. I want the one responsible to know the pain she caused me."

"Then punish me!" Baarias bowed to his knees.

A collective gasp went around the tribe.

"Baarias," Nyri gripped his arm. "No."

Baarias stayed her hands. "What happened last night was my fault and mine alone. I left Kyaati against my better judgement. She was my responsibility. I am the one who deserves punishment."

Aardn was outwardly impassive, but Nyri could taste her relief on the air as Baarias offered himself in Kyaati's place. "Do you accept Baarias' offer, Haana?"

Haana glared at the healer, her jaw working furiously. Nyri gripped Baarias' shoulder.

"Yes," Haana replied through her teeth. "That is acceptable."

"Then it is decided." Aardn was quick to move the situation along. "Sefaan."

All eyes turned to where the ancient Kamaali had been sitting at the edge of the gathering. Raanya aided her as she pushed herself to her feet; the large seed bound to her throat swayed with the awkward movement. Nyri felt a tightening in the collective atmosphere as they all witnessed Sefaan's increasing frailty.

Aardn bowed her head stiffly, making it clear her respect was only a formality. Somehow Nyri knew that if she had had any other choice, Aardn would have excluded Sefaan. Only the tribe Kamaali could only carry out the Ritual. Not only did the process take a lot of skill and strength, but to hold such power over someone's life was a responsibility to be trusted only to the wisest of hands. "*Revered* Kamaali." The Elder's lips barely moved around the words. "The Ritual of *Zykiel* has been demanded and now must be evoked. I place the lives of this victim and the perpetrator in your hands."

Sefaan nodded, appearing not to notice the forced edge to Aardn's tone. "Who calls for the right of *Zykiel*?"

"I do," Haana lifted her chin.

"And whom do you call against?"

"This man, so that he might know the pain I have suffered, pain inflicted by his own negligence."

Sefaan raised a hand. "And do you accept her right?" she asked of Baarias.

The healer's shoulders were straight, his head high. "I do, for the sake of Kyaati."

"Both have agreed to the Ritual. You will kneel before me."

Haana sank to her knees beside Baarias, and Sefaan placed a hand upon both their heads.

Nyri felt hands clamp around her arms as Daajir pulled her away from Baarias.

"No!" She struggled, but Daajir held her firm, his fingers cutting into her skin.

Sefaan grew still, her eyes emptying. She was a conduit,

her own soul and emotions removed. Nyri could almost see the energy move up through the arm reaching down to Haana, contracting through her and finally moving into Baarias.

The healer shuddered and gasped as the full force of Haana's desperation, anger and fear were forced upon him. Nyri fought harder against Daajir's grip as Baarias bent double, his arms wrapping around his chest as he fought to contain the onslaught. A whimper escaped through his teeth.

Nyri echoed the sound.

At last it was over. Sefaan blinked and returned to herself. She staggered, drained by the effort she had put forth. Baarias gasped and opened eyes that were wet with tears. He knew now what it was like to lose a child. He reached a trembling hand towards Haana. "I am sorry," he rasped. "I am so sorry."

Haana only turned her back and moved to stand with her mate and her daughter.

Daajir released Nyri, and she rushed to where Baarias knelt, bowed under his ordeal.

"Justice has been given," Aardn barked a dismissal. "Go to your own trees now, all of you,"

A babble rose as the rest of the tribe moved to obey. Some glanced curiously towards where Kyaati slept, others spoke in hushed whispers about what had just happened. The last to leave was Sefaan. The Kamaali's eyes lingered on Nyri before she followed the rest of the tribe.

"Baarias…"

He did not raise his head. "Please, I-I just need to be alone for a little while. Can you keep watch over Kyaati?"

His control was tenuous, Nyri could feel him fighting to hold his composure together in front of her. Her mentor pulled himself to his feet and disappeared into his personal chamber without a backwards glance.

Nyri raged against his suffering, but there was nothing she could do for him. He had to work through the ordeal himself, balancing the new emotions and sensations within his mind and soul before he could accept them.

Nyri shuffled to where Kyaati rested and collapsed next to her inside the bower. Nyri wondered if Baarias would ever tell her what he had done. She hoped what he had just suffered was worth it. She hoped Sefaan had been right and Kyaati would now heal...

"Nyri."

Nyri jolted upright, disorientated. Evening rays of light were slanting through the tree. She had fallen asleep. The entire day had passed. Kyaati was awake and regarding her solemnly. Nyri tensed, but the manic gleam that had haunted her tribe-sister's eyes since losing her baby was gone.

Nyri took her hand. "Yes?"

"Why did my baby have to die?"

Nyri swallowed, pausing for a moment until she could keep her voice steady. Baarias would not tremble before someone who needed his strength. "She was born malformed, Kyaati. It was not your fault."

Kyaati's hand tightened on Nyri's as she choked. "What Baarias said at the auscult, do you think he is right? Are we doing this to ourselves? Are we killing our own children in the name of an absent deity?" Her tortured eyes met Nyri's.

"No Kyaati." Nyri was vehement. "It cannot be. Ninmah taught us our ways, and we were strong for generations before the Woves came with their dark magic."

"But, if it is true…"

Nyri took her friend's face between her palms. "No. We did not do this. *You* did not do this. None of this is your fault. This is happening because of the curses the Woves have placed upon us. Now stop. Leave the worrying to the Elders. You concentrate on getting better. You need to be strong before the Fury. You need to survive."

"Why?" Kyaati mocked. "What are we surviving for, Nyri? Tell me one thing worth going on for?"

To her dismay, Nyri could not think of an answer.

Baarias entered the chamber. Nyri got up and went to him, taking his hands. They trembled within hers, but he appeared to have regained a measure of his usual composure.

Thank you, my akaabi. *I am able to take over now.*

"How long must I stay here?" Kyaati's voice broke into their exchange.

Baarias shifted, his expression carefully composed. "I do not think it is wise to return home yet, Kyaati."

"I do not wish to go back." Her deadened eyes sparked with some of her old fire.

Baarias reached out to squeeze her arm. "You do not have to return to your father until you are ready."

Her drawn face eased slightly. It wasn't long before she returned to sleep's embrace.

"Her senses have recovered," Baarias murmured, "but her heart still has a way to go. Are you alright?" Baarias was studying Nyri's pale face.

"You're asking me? Baarias, I am more worried about you."

"I can manage this, Kyaati cannot. I had to do it." He touched her face. "Go home, Nyriaana. I will keep watch

257

now."

Nyri hesitated. His eyes crinkled reassuringly.

"I'll be back in the morning," she promised and turned to leave. She had taken but a step when dizziness swamped her and she almost fell.

Baarias caught and steadied her. "Nyri!"

"I'm alright." Nyri tried to push him away. He didn't let her get away so easily. She felt his energy probe against hers, assessing.

"When did you last eat?" he demanded.

Nyri shrugged. She knew exactly when, but she would not admit that to Baarias.

He glowered at her. "I'm calling Daajir to help you to the stores, you need to eat."

"No." Nyri straightened up with an effort. "You don't have to do that. I can make my own way to the stores."

Baarias' face was stern. "Go. Now. You help no one by weakening yourself in this way. It is unwise."

"I know." Nyri attempted a weak smile. "Don't worry, Baarias, I promise it won't happen again." She meant it.

Calling on her last reserves of strength, she made her way to the store tree and picked out a ration for herself. It had been two days since she had eaten; she recalled the previous day's ration tumbling away into the Pit when—

My kin will find me and when they do, you had better pray to the gods for mercy!

Imaani had said the Woves had been searching for something last night. She knew what that something was.

Nyri dropped the fruit core she had been eating. He was drawing the predators right to the flock. She should tell the Elders and let them kill him. She flinched at her own thought and pushed it aside. Killing him would not make a difference. Dead or not, the Woves would still be searching.

The only answer was to release him. If he went back to the raiding party, perhaps they would leave. She huffed out a breath. That was a false hope. She thought of the terrible green eyes and knew for certain that if she released him, he would kill her. Once he had achieved that wish, he would summon the Woves and they would slaughter her tribe.

Nyri dropped her head into her hands.

Nyri, Nyri, Nyriaana...

Nyri growled to herself. It was still there, the pull inside her heart, the yearning to run to him. She couldn't believe after all that had happened, his call still held any power over her. He hated her and wanted her dead. His very presence was putting her people in danger. He had almost cost them Kyaati. Nyri shivered to think of what would have happened had Sefaan not appeared last night.

Nyri...

Stop it!

Why? Her heart joined the fray. *You will not let the Elders kill him, but you will murder him yourself by abandoning him to starvation? He is going to* die *out there.*

Nyri lifted her chin, ignoring the pain. *He made his choice when he tried to kill me.*

Did he? Her heart taunted. *Did you ever know Juaan to miss when he threw a rock? He is still in there, and you are abandoning him! You are a coward, hiding like a child behind your fear!*

* * *

26

No Turning Back

The girl was coming home. Sefaan could feel her approach. She was agitated and hurting, desperate for the familiarity of her tree.

Sefaan kept to the shadows as Nyriaana leaped lightly into her living space. That the girl did not notice she had company was an indication of her emotional state. Sefaan knew she had come at the right time.

"Hello, Nyriaana," she spoke as she stepped from the shadows. "I am glad to see you home at last."

The girl let out a soft yelp. "Revered Kamaali!"

It gave Sefaan a small sense of comfort to know that at least one person still regarded her so. She hid her smile, however. They had bigger issues to attend to. "Not stealing out tonight, child?"

Nyriaana stiffened. "W-what do you mean?"

"I think you know what I mean." The time for playing games was over.

"I—" The girl floundered, opening and closing her fists in a tense motion, appearing very much like a disobedient child who had been caught pulling heads off blossoms.

Sefaan almost laughed. "You look as guilty as one sentenced to *Zykiel*."

Nyriaana fell back a step as the panic contracted across her face, and Sefaan instantly regretted her choice of words. The memory of her teacher's recent punishment was still fresh in her mind.

"Relax, child," Sefaan soothed. "No one is going to punish you."

The girl attempted to compose her features as she studied Sefaan's own. The tension eased from her shoulders somewhat when she saw no anger upon Sefaan's face.

"I take from your flouting of the Elders' wishes, that there was an important reason for going out into the forest alone, young one?"

Nyriaana opened her mouth.

Sefaan waved a hand. "No. Do not speak. You do not have to tell me, and I will tell no one of your secret excursions. Fear not. You obviously felt it was worth the risk! You took my advice."

The girl jerked her chin once in acknowledgement.

"Good. I told you to follow your heart. I came only to ask, why are you fighting it now?"

Colour flared across Nyriaana's cheeks. "Because it is not right! Sefaan, *please*. The path I started down… it was wrong. It would not have ended well." She blinked rapidly and looked away.

Sefaan touched her arm, drawing the girl's attention back. "A path does not have to end well to be the right one, child. Just ask yourself this; could you truly turn from the path you speak of, now that you have embarked upon it? Even if you knew for certain it would end in despair?"

The tears were threatening to spill. Sefaan could read her thoughts. So many who had followed this path had already ended their lives in despair. Rebaa, Jaai. Sefaan's sorrow rose for those sad but necessary losses as the warm wetness flowed down the girl's face.

"Sefaan, I can't."

"Not even for *him*?"

The blood drained from Nyriaana's face. "H-him?"

"His return seems quite impossible, does it not? But there he is. The Great Spirit works in mysterious ways." Sefaan chuckled.

"You *know*!" Nyriaana staggered back. "You *know* Juaan is out there!"

"Oh, come, girl. How do you think you have been getting by the sentries so easily? Your skills in concealment are improving, but not by *that* much."

Sefaan recalled her visit to the boy on the night Kyaati had stolen Haana's infant. She had needed to see the girl's secret for herself, hoping it would provide more clarity to the visions the Great Spirit whispered. Her instincts had proven correct.

The boy had been unconscious, but the Great Spirit's energy had swirled around him stronger than ever. Sefaan could not guess the reason for KI's need for this Forbidden boy, but his importance was clear. As was the need for this girl's continued involvement. She watched as Nyriaana raked her fingers through her hair, pacing back and forth in the face of Sefaan's revelation.

"Are you going back to him?" Sefaan did not give her time to recover.

The girl halted and fixed her with an incredulous stare. "No!"

"Why not?"

"Because he is not Juaan anymore! The Woves have twisted his mind!" The last shreds of Nyriaana's composure broke. "Juaan is *dead*."

"No, he is not." Sefaan jabbed a finger towards the outer forest. "Out there he sits. I would not have thought you could abandon him so easily, Nyriaana."

The girl's temper flared hot inside the tree. "It's not easy! He tricked me into caring for him I was a child who did not know any better. He is nothing but a Forbidden monster. By Ninmah, he should not even *exist*."

"And yet he does. That means something."

Nyriaana snorted, ignoring her. "And what of the Woves? They are out there searching for him and when they find him, you know as well as I what will happen!"

Sefaan let the girl's rage play out before countering. "Then you must reach him before they do. You must make him remember you."

"And what good would that do?"

All the good in the world! Sefaan could not explain all the half visions and truths that the Great Spirit whispered, not in this moment. Instead, she gave another, more defined reason. "Did he not lead the Woves when they attacked? They followed him. He was in a position of power."

Sefaan watched as the meaning of her words struck home. "Is that what this is about?" The girl's brow pinched together. "You actually believe he would help us?"

Sefaan shrugged. "That depends upon him, child. I cannot say for certain, but I know you *must* continue to try."

Nyri groaned. "No. I have had enough of this. I'm tired, Sefaan. Fate can do without me. I want no more part of it." She turned to leave.

"Nyri, Nyri, Nyriaana."

Nyri halted mid-stride at the sound of the familiar rhyme falling from strange lips. "What did you say?"

"You know what I said."

"How did you know about that?"

"Nyriaana." Sefaan reproved. "You forget I am Kamaali. Surely you aren't blinded by the lies Aardn spread about my failing sanity." She tapped the Mark on her forehead. "I see all. Listen to me now. If anyone can reach him, it is you. Our fate sits in your hands. Yours alone. Are you still going to give up?"

Nyriaana buried her face in her palms. "Why me? Does the Great Spirit hate me so much that he wants me to die?"

"I do not think that will be your fate. The love that boy bore for you was more powerful than the love for his own life. Such a bond was meant for something."

Nyri brushed at a wound on her ear with trembling fingers, and winced. "It was a lie. Kyaati saw it."

"It was no lie."

"Sefaan. He tried to kill me!"

"And yet here you stand. He could not have tried very hard."

"Ninmah was with me."

The girl's rebuff came swiftly, but Sefaan could detect the waver in her certainty. She needed something. A reminder. Reaching into her garments, Sefaan pulled forth a green pebble. It had caught her eye as she had travelled to the girl's tree. For some reason it had seemed significant, and Sefaan was never one to ignore an instinct. She rolled it across to where the girl knelt. A frown pinched Nyriaana's brow as she reached to pick it up. Her eyes widened as it glinted dimly in front of her face.

The memory that rose in the girl's mind then was so strong Sefaan saw it all as if it was her own: the sorrowful boy peeking out from behind his hands as her younger self presented him with a gift. *Pretty rock, pretty, like your eyes...*

You no hurt me?

Never.

"Oh!" The gasp shuddered from Nyriaana's throat as she wrapped her fingers around the pebble and clutched it to her heart. Her anger and resistance crumbled away as silent tears slipped down her cheeks.

"You loved him."

"Yes."

"And no matter what he has done, you love him still."

Nyriaana took another shuddering breath. "Yes."

"And knowing that, knowing there is a possibility that he can change our fate, will you still turn from the path? Will you let him die?"

With a muffled cry of defeat, Nyriaana dropped her hands. "No," she whispered. "By Ninmah, I cannot. Even though he does not remember, *I* remember, Sefaan. I am bound to him. It seems I have always been." She gave a little humourless laugh. "And if there is the slightest chance he can save our People, what choice does that leave me? Fate has decided that I must remain by his side even if it means my doom."

"Then cast your doubt aside!" Sefaan placed her hands on either side of the girl's face. "The Great Spirit has brought him back to you and He will lend you the strength to find

265

your way, no matter where it may lead."

Nyriaana's hands came up to close around her own. "I hope you're right, Sefaan."

"Have faith, child. The future is waiting and you must do all that you can."

* * *

27

Protector

"Are you hungry?" Nyriaana cocked her head.

"No." The long arms folded.

"Yes, you are."

"No, I am not."

"Yes, you are. I can tell."

"Can you?" The tone was dry as dead grass.

"Yes. You're grumpy. You're always grumpy when you're hungry."

"No, it's because you're such a menace. Go away and bother someone else for a while."

Nyri giggled. She knew he didn't mean it. She crawled across the space of the tree and plopped cross-legged before him. Green eyes regarded her beneath the mop of dark brown hair.

"What are you up to?" he asked suspiciously.

He knew her too well. She smiled. "I wanna go and play."

"Well, go on then." And leave me in peace, you little monster. She almost heard him think.

Nyri pouted. "I want you to come, too. It's no fun on my own."

"Nyri!" he protested.

"Please."

"Go and play with a wolf. As you say, I'm grumpy. What do you want me for?"

"Pleeeaaase!" Nyri pulled on his hand, bouncing up and down. She knew he would give in. Patience wasn't one of his strong points when he was hungry.

"You are the bane of my life, you know that?" He pulled his hand from hers but rose to his feet. "Alright. If it will make you happy."

She had him. "Come on! It'll be dark soon."

"Good. Let's make this quick."

"Don't go far!" Her mother's admonishment came from somewhere above.

Nyri didn't bother to answer and jumped from the tree. She tumbled through the air before grabbing the branch growing beneath the entrance to their home and swung nimbly down; she loved doing that. Juaan had scolded her so badly the first time she had attempted it. He thought she would end up breaking her neck. He forgot she was Ninkuraaja. She was made to climb trees. Juaan could run fast, but he could not climb as well as she could. She was proud of that fact.

As she waited for Juaan to make his way down, Nyri stared into the darkening trees. Away from the safety of her lofty home, she felt the first faint thrill of trepidation. Her mind conjured all kinds of danger and monsters. Maybe this wasn't such a good idea after all. Perhaps they should wait until morning. But if she did, her surprise might be ruined by thieving maamits. She gripped her friend's large hand as he came to stand beside her.

"Will you protect me, Juaan?" she asked, facing the shadows.

"To the end."

Her fear left her. "Come on then, clumsy!"

"I'll give you clumsy!"

Squealing, Nyri dodged away as he tried to grab her. She barely noticed the looks of disgust and disapproval from the rest of the tribe as they ran among them. She sprinted from the settlement, using her smaller size and agility to stay one step ahead. She jumped into trees and ran across branches that were too small to take Juaan's weight. All the while she led him towards her target.

They were getting close when Nyri stopped, leaped down, and spun to face him. He had not expected this move and scrambled to prevent himself from colliding with her. His feet skidded from under him in the dark loam and he ended up on his back. She could not resist. She pounced. His stomach was the most ticklish, and she targeted it mercilessly. Juaan squirmed and twisted, trying to escape her fingers.

"Stop!" he choked in a tortured voice. "Stop it!"

"Say please," Nyri giggled, keeping up her relentless attack.

"Please, please, you little monster!"

Nyri sprang off him, laughing. "Close your eyes."

Juaan rolled to his feet, brushing the leaf mould from his back. "Why? What are you going to do with me now?"

His suspicion hurt. "Nothing! I've got a surprise for you."

He eyed her. "Like what?"

She sighed. "Close your eyes and you'll find out!"

He folded his arms, stubborn as always.

She folded hers right back and thrust her chin out. "I'm not leaving until you close your eyes." She stamped her foot for emphasis.

Nyri watched Juaan glance at the deepening shadows with her own earlier trepidation and decide that it wasn't worth the fight. "Alright, have it your way!" He closed his eyes.

"No peeking!" She bounced up and down in triumph and then

scrambled a short way into the trees where she had hidden her prize. The stash of ripe red berries was still there. They were Juaan's favourite. She had found them and kept them secret just for him. Juaan never got to choose what he wanted to eat. He always had to wait until everyone else had taken their pick. Sometimes there was nothing left. Nyri didn't understand, and it upset her.

"Surprise!" she announced as she lifted his hand and laid her gift across his palm. "For you."

Juaan's eyes widened when he saw the full bunch of sweet red berries. "Where did you get these? You didn't risk going into the stores again? Aardn will kill you!"

She shrugged. "Aardn no catch me. Wanted you to have them. You never get what you want to eat."

She would get into serious trouble if Aardn did catch her near the stores again, but as a smile broke across his face like Ninmah through the rain clouds, Nyri knew any amount of trouble was worth this one moment in time.

He caught her up in his arms and swung her around. "Thank you, Nyri, Nyri, Nyriaana."

* * *

Nyri opened her eyes and stared into the dark. She would not find more sleep; dawn was not far away. Doubt continued to plague her as she considered everything Sefaan had said. There were people who needed her here. Baarias, Kyaati... She should not be running off into the trees to aid the man who had sentenced her tribe to starvation through the Fury.

Our fate sits in your hands. Are you so willing to give up?

Nyri turned her head to stare out towards the forest. *Could he save them?*

Nyri, Nyri, Nyriaana...

She clutched at the little pebble in her hand, letting it lend her the strength she needed. For her People's sake, if nothing else, she would face him again.

Rolling to her feet, she climbed from her tree and made her way to the nearest food store. She hoped she wasn't already too late and this impossible path had met its end before it had even begun. The thought pushed her into a flat out sprint.

Reaching the store, Nyri cast around. The forest rested around her, dim and silent. She climbed into the branches and disappeared inside. She paused, once again absorbing the sight of the depleted stores. Even with everyone taking the barest minimum, there was already a noticeable drop in supplies. The sight made her empty stomach plunge to towards her feet.

In her mind's eye, she saw Naaya's pinched little face and almost wept. Did Sefaan grasp the full consequences of what it would take to keep Juaan alive? Granted, she was only taking one extra ration, but it was still wrong.

Nyri had no time to dwell upon that fact. She could not turn back now. She had made her promise. Taking one last look around to make sure she was alone, Nyri bent to search through the baskets and suspended nets for something enough for Juaan. She drew out a large ripe honey fruit. A fruit this size would be enough for both of them. She turned to leave, but as she did, her foot caught a stray gora root. She stumbled and came face to face with some very familiar red berries dangling from a woven net.

Despite everything, a laugh bubbled from Nyri's throat. For years, she had not been able to look at such fruit without feeling the sting of loss. Now she saw the berries and felt hope, hope that maybe what Sefaan said was true; the Great Spirit was indeed with her.

Dare she take them? She should only take what was necessary to keep her and Juaan on their feet. The giant fruit was more than enough for two. Nyri stood, shifting from foot to foot. In the end, she could not resist. She vowed to go hungry the next day to make up for it.

Hungrier, her mind corrected itself. Nyri stuffed the honey fruit into her clothing and reached out to collect the berries.

"Nyriaana!"

She almost hit the twisted branches above her head. "Daajir!"

He was there in the entranceway. His dark eyes studied her face as her cheeks flushed traitorously. "What's the matter with you?"

Nyri fought to compose herself. "You startled me! Don't do that again." She hoped he hadn't seen her transgression.

He smirked. "Do what? I wasn't sneaking. You just weren't paying attention."

"I suppose not." He hadn't seen, but he had almost caught her.

"Are you sure you're alright?" He pressed. "You seem... flustered."

"Yes, yes," she said. "What are you doing up so early?"

He held up a pot of honey for her to see. "I came to replace this. Sefaan demanded that I find it for her. I did not want to be distracted, but she insisted." He gave an exasperated sigh. "But now she does not want it."

"Really?" Nyri asked, trying to cover the flutter of her heart at the mention of Sefaan. "Why is that?"

"Your guess is as good as mine. You know Sefaan."

Nyri nodded absently

"I didn't think you liked that fruit."

"Excuse me?"

Daajir pointed at the berries clutched in Nyri's hand. "You have refused to look at them since you were a child."

"Oh! I... just decided it was time to try them. We can't afford to be picky now, can we?" She gave a weak half laugh. *You're going to have to get better at lying,* she thought to herself. *You'll have the entire tribe knowing full well you're up to something.* Daajir wasn't looking convinced.

"Have you visited Kyaati?" Nyri distracted him.

"No." His mouth turned down. "Baarias would not let me. How is she?"

"She is herself again, her mind has recovered."

Daajir cast his eyes towards Ninmah. "Thank you," he whispered.

"Perhaps Baarias will let you see her today," Nyri encouraged. "Perhaps you could tell her about your plans—"

Daajir grabbed Nyri by the shoulders and planted a kiss on her forehead. "Yes!" He bounded off before she had a chance to be shocked. "I believe I am about to make an important breakthrough. Maybe if she knows I can protect us..."

"Um, perhaps you should wait," Nyri called after him, wishing now that she had held her tongue. "She's still fragile. You need to be careful."

"I can be tactful," he said, and was gone.

"Since when?" Nyri muttered to the empty air. She hoped Baarias would not be angry with her for sending Daajir his way. At least her distraction had worked better than she hoped; she was now free to do what she needed. Nyri moved to the edge of the tree and looked down. Daajir had disappeared. She dropped to the ground.

To her surprise, Sefaan was waiting on the edge of the outer forest.

"They are more wary since the attack, girl." She gestured into the darkness, and Nyri could feel the presences of the sentries shadowed in the trees. She took a quick breath. "Don't worry." Sefaan touched her arm. "I will deal with them. You do your best to hide your presence and I will do the rest."

"Thank you, revered Kamaali." Nyri plucked up the courage to squeeze the ancient one's hand and asked. "I just met Daajir. Why did you send him on a blind errand?"

"Because he is another that needs distracting," Sefaan answered cryptically. "Now go, there is no more time to lose. May the Great Spirit guide you."

Stealing herself, Nyri set off into the forest. She fought to concentrate as she neared the sentries, doing her best to blend in to her surroundings. The sudden screeching of a maamit troop burst into life overhead, almost shattering her effort. The tiny creatures leaped and swung through the canopy. Cries of surprise told her the maamits had startled the sentries even more than her. Taking that as her signal, Nyri ran.

As soon as she was away from the borders, her pace slowed to a crawl. She was not looking forward to what was coming in the slightest. Her anger might have dissipated, Sefaan might have given her renewed purpose, but that did not mean her fear of him was any less. She remembered the blaze of hate lashing against her senses and shuddered, clutching the red berries close. *You must try*, she told her quailing heart.

She hesitated before the Pit before screwing up the courage to pull back the coverings.

The snap of a twig behind her made her start violently. Golden eyes peered out of the foliage before the entire furry form emerged from the trees. Batai. Nyri let out a breath of relief and almost chuckled.

The wolf trotted over and nuzzled her hand as she scratched his ears. He was curious about what she was doing. She should send him away but couldn't find it in herself to do so. She felt very much alone, and she was terrified of what she was about to face. Batai was familiar and comforting. She faced the Pit again. "Well, here goes nothing, Batai."

The wolf blinked and lay down, watching Nyri in his usual pose. Bolstered by his patient presence, Nyri finished pulling the covers back from the Pit. *For my People*, she vowed as her muscles tensed, bracing for the onslaught.

It never came.

A gasp of horror choked off in Nyri's throat at the sight that greeted her.

Juaan was lying face down on the ground, unmoving. At first glance, Nyri thought him dead. *No!* Pain lashed through her. Her own blinding, personal pain. The conviction that she was doing this only for her People's sake slipped. *Juaan...*

Then her higher senses came to bear, and she breathed once again. His life force was still there. Barely. The deprivation had overwhelmed him; every bit of food she had brought remained untouched, lying where it had fallen. She cursed. *Foolish, stubborn...!*

She paced up and down the edge of the Pit. He was slipping away before her eyes, and there was nothing she could do to prevent it.

Not if she didn't go down there.

To Ninsiku with it all!

Before she could think, she found her root, still coiled where she had left it and threw it over the edge. After the slightest hesitation, she started down.

She was under no illusion that she was gambling with her life. Even weakened, he could kill her. He had threatened to do just that if she ever came near him again. She pushed her apprehension away and placed her feet on the ground. If she was to save his life and save her people, she must put his threat to the test. Nyri could hear the faint brush of his breath as it passed his cracked lips; his life force was so weak it was frightening.

Grabbing the nutshell she had given him from where it lay untouched, she rushed to the *aquilem* vine. Extending her will, Nyri caused the plant to draw water through the fleshy tube; it poured forth into the waiting bowl. She returned to Juaan's prone form.

His face was turned to the side. She dripped the water onto his mouth. His parched lips twitched and then started to move, unconsciously seeking the nourishment. He swallowed, slow at first, then more eagerly.

His eyes snapped open.

This time Nyri was prepared and dodged backwards as his arm shot out. Quick as she was, his fingers still managed to brush her shoulder. She bounded away, sure he would follow and catch her. But he made no further move; he hissed in pain as his lunge proved too much for his tender body. He rolled over and doubled up on himself.

"Careful," Nyri said as she stood tense by her root. "You haven't fully healed yet."

Green eyes fixed upon her as he propped himself into a sitting position. His hand moved to his ribs, and he winced, almost doubling up again.

"Juaan." Nyri stepped forward. "Are—"

He was on his feet before Nyri could draw breath. "I warned you!"

And he hurled himself at her.

For her own life, Nyri could not move. She watched as he came, unable to take her eyes from his. *So, this is what death looks like.* In a different situation, the cause of her demise would have been laughable. Juaan was going to kill her. Juaan was...

He was but a stride away when something inside Nyri snapped. All of her fear, all of her anger, all of her love and pain broke loose. Defiant, she set her feet.

"Kill me then!" she screamed up at him. "Go on! Be rid of me!"

Her rage brought him up short. One hand stretched forward as it reached for her throat. Nyri lifted her chin, inviting.

"Go *on*," she hissed. "Free me from my bond, there is no other way."

His fingers brushed against her flesh. She felt them quiver, somehow unable to take their deadly hold. The green eyes flickered. Nyri kept her own locked upon them, challenging him with all her might. If he was going to kill her, then so be it; she would not fight. She took half a step forward into his grip.

And he stepped back. The green resolve shattered before her steady gaze. His hand fell from her throat as he collapsed to the ground, huddling back against the Pit wall at her feet. His head bowed between his arms, as if he no longer had the strength to hold it up.

"What spell have you cast on me, she-elf?" His voice cracked. "Who *are* you?"

Nyri's muscles were still locked in position. For a moment, she could not move so much as a finger. She found her voice first. "I told you. I am Nyri."

His fists tightened around his knees at the sound of her name. "And why do you insist on tormenting me like this?"

He sounded so vulnerable in that moment it tore at her heart. *Oh, Juaan...* "Please, I do not mean to torment you. I only want you to recover."

"You are an elf." He lifted his head and eyed her wearily. That look was back. The one that questioned her sanity. "I am nothing but an abomination in your eyes. I know that well enough."

"You're wrong!" she blurted. "You are *everything* to me, Juaan!"

"I told you before," he snapped as harshly as he could manage. "My name is not Juaan. I do not know who you have mistaken me for. My name is—"

"Khalvir. Yes, I know." *Careful. You can't let your heart run away with you. This is for your People only.* She had just gambled with her life. There was no need to take further risks.

They stared at each other in loaded silence. She watched

as his eyes went from her face to the dangling root and back. He was assessing his chances. Nyri became dreadfully aware of just how very alone she was down here with a being almost half again her size and who knew how many times her strength. She could not stop him if he tried to escape. She watched as he came to the same terrible conclusion.

Her mind worked quickly, and she took another gamble. "Do not attempt to escape," she said. "I have a pack of wolves up there who do not take kindly to strangers in their territory. It took all of my skill to prevent them from coming down here to chew your head off. You wouldn't make it two strides." To drive her point home, Nyri stretched out her will. Batai's answering howl echoed through the trees above.

His rich skin paled as his face turned towards the surface, but he composed himself in the flicker of an eye. His fists clenched and Nyri took half a step back from the murderous scowl.

"Are you going to hurt me?" Her voice came out childlike, small with vulnerability. It was the same question she had asked when they had first met. Was he too the same? The same boy who had always vowed to protect her to the end? Had it been a lie, as Kyaati claimed, or did Sefaan have the truth of it? She had to believe in the Kamaali's words. Her father was no longer here to sweep her away, her mother not here to calm him. If he attacked her again now, it would be over. Even if she got away, she could never return. Not this time. She would truly have lost.

It felt like forever before he sighed. "No. I won't hurt you. I can't, it seems. For the love of Ea, I do not know why."

Relief washed through her. The hope that she might yet overcome the impossible rose in her heart. Nyri reached a hand towards him. He leaned away, and she withdrew. She tasted the surrounding energies, trying to read his emotions and gauge how best to behave, and felt a ripple of shock. He wasn't angry now. He was fearful. Confusion flooded her mind; surely, she had more reason to fear *him*. "Don't worry," she said. "I won't hurt you, either."

He did not look convinced, so Nyri did not push her luck. A fearful animal was the most dangerous of all. She squatted down at a safe distance of two strides. This was a strange truce, but she'd take it. Nyri stared at him, taking in this familiar, foreign face. She did not like all that she saw.

"What?" he asked brusquely. He might have accepted her presence, but he was making it clear that he didn't have to like it.

Nyri shook herself. "I'm sorry. I was just thinking, now that we have established we will not hurt one another, are you hungry?"

His face set. "No."

Nyri blinked against the sudden moisture starting in her eyes. How many times had they played this game and he couldn't even remember. "Don't be stubborn."

His mouth opened and closed, shocked by her audacity. "I'm not being stubborn!" he snapped. "Why should I trust you? It is in your best interest to kill me."

"And it is in *your* best interest to kill me," Nyri countered. "You could do so so easily. That first time I came here, you had me pinned to the ground and at your mercy. And again, just now. You could have hurt me, killed me, but you didn't. You let me go. Why?"

His fists tightened once more in frustration and... pain. "I. Don't. Know." He ground each word from between his teeth. "By the Sky Gods, I have reason enough."

"Well, *I* know," Nyri said. "And it is for the same reason I will never hurt you."

His green eyes sparked. "Will you stop that, I am not—"

"Look," she cut him off. Nyri saw she would have to win this with cold, hard logic. "It does not matter who I might have mistaken you for or who you think you are. You either trust me or you die. You *are* dying. I can feel it. I am offering you survival. The choice is yours." She cringed at the bluntness of her ultimatum.

He glowered at her, frighteningly so. Nyri had to remind herself once again that this was a stranger sitting opposite her. She was baiting an adopted Wove in a Pit.

"I have a surprise for you," she blurted. She reached into the folds of her garments for the berries she had brought and had a sudden, childish urge to tell him to close his eyes. Nyri quashed it. He had never trusted that instruction, even when he had known her. She pulled the fruit out for him to see. He recoiled and had to look twice at what was in her hand before he relaxed. Nyri rolled her eyes. "What? Did you think I was going to pull a snake out of there?"

He snorted. "Who knows with your kind."

"My kind?" She was getting annoyed. "The Woves are worse than any snake!"

"Woves?"

"Yes. Woves. The murderous dark spirits who followed you here. By all rights, I should pull a snake on you. Now, do you want this fruit or not?"

He fell silent, regarding Nyri with his head cocked to the side. He was smiling; she realised. Not visibly, but he was. "You are a spirited one."

281

"Do you want them or not?" Nyri grouched.

He eyed the fruit. He wanted to resist; so stubborn, even now. Nyri waited, not daring to breathe as slowly, oh so slowly, he leaned forward, reaching out towards the berries she offered. Then he stopped.

"Alright, have it your way," he said. "First, put them on the ground and move away."

"Why? I won't bite you."

"That's the least of my worries." The bitter expression returned. "You have the gall to call me a murderer? I know what you could do if you touched me."

"Like what exactly?"

"You tell me, elf-witch. If you indeed have the power to do this," he indicated his leg. "What else are you capable of?"

"Elf? Witch?" Nyri frowned. "That's rather ungrateful. Would you rather I had left your leg snapped in two?"

His jaws ground together. "Even so. Move away."

"Oh, for Ninmah's sake!" Nyri placed the berries on the ground and backed away.

He watched her move to a safe distance and then stared at the fruit. He could resist no longer. Juaan descended on the berries, tasting the first tentatively. His eyes widened at the flavour, and the rest were gone in moments.

"They were always your favourite," she said. Nyri wasn't sure if he was paying attention. She felt a wave of sadness. His tastes hadn't changed, but he was no longer the Juaan she had known. This man was too hard, too angry. Her heart cried out for the boy she had loved. *What were you hoping for?* She admonished. *He has been raised in the company of Woves. Your task is to reach him enough to order the demons away, that is all. He is no longer your friend.*

282

Leaving the last half of the honey fruit for him, she picked up the half nutshell and drew some more water from the vine, speaking in a louder voice as she did so. "I need to go now before I'm missed."

He searched her face. She tried to imagine what was going through his mind. Here he was, trapped with an enemy whom he hated, but for reasons beyond his comprehension, he could not bring himself to harm. A stranger who held his entire fate in her hands.

"What is it you want from me?"

For you to remember me. For you to save us. I need you still, Juaan. But she couldn't tell him that. He couldn't know that she was using him.

"Nothing." She started for the rope.

"Nothing?" His tone was sceptical. "Well, just how long are you planning to keep me down here?"

"I don't know that, either." *Long enough for me to get through to you, I hope.* "We'll just have to see what the future brings."

He grumbled, frustrated. "Has anyone ever told you that you are a little monster?"

His eyes widened in alarm when Nyri started to laugh and cry at the same time. "Yes. *You.* Several times." He stared at her as though concluding that she was indeed mad. Nyri composed herself. "I must go." She needed to get back. She needed to see that Kyaati and Baarias were as well as they could be. "Rest," she called over her shoulder. "You need to get your strength back. I'll return with more food, but I have to be careful. I cannot let my people become suspicious. They *would* let the wolves chew your head off."

She felt his eyes on her back. "Why?"

"Why what?"

283

"Are you protecting me from your own?"

Nyri turned. Those green eyes were so familiar they made her forget herself. She spoke. "Because no matter what has happened or who you have become, you are still my Juaan and I will protect you to the end."

With that, she scrambled back to the surface and was gone.

* * *

28

Promises

Sefaan hobbled to where Aardn had called the tribe to attention. She kept a low profile. Nyriaana was still out in the forest trying to get past the sentries. Distracted by the Elder's call, Sefaan had not been ready for her return. Quickly, she extended her will, dulling the sentries' senses and concealing the girl as Nyriaana covered her passage with a flock of birds.

She was through. Sefaan saw her emerge from the trees, flushed and panting. She straightened at the sight of the gathered tribe and made her way over to them.

"The Woves have made another breach of our borders," Aardn announced, drawing Sefaan's attention back to the centre of the gathering.

"Then why are we not running?" someone demanded.

"They did not come near the settlement," Aardn assured. "Once again, we were not their target. Something else is drawing them. I will not abandon our home until it is absolutely necessary."

"What are they searching for?"

"We do not know."

Sefaan caught Nyriaana's eye across the restless crowd. The girl's mouth thinned into a grim line as they shared the same thought. The days she had to bring the boy back to them were numbered.

"They have returned to their camp." Aardn said. "We will continue to watch."

Grumbling in discontentment, everyone dispersed, and Sefaan made her way to Nyriaana's side. "Well?"

"He has accepted food and promised not to harm me."

Sefaan let out a breath. It was a step forward, at least. "Good."

"But that is all, Sefaan. He still does not remember, and he does not trust me." She rubbed at her forehead, glancing to where Aardn had made her announcement, letting her dismay leak into her emotions. "They are searching for him. I do not have enough time. They'll find him long before—"

Sefaan waved a hand. "We have to trust the Great Spirit, young one. It is a large forest and only five Woves. Keep trying."

Nyriaana sighed. "I promised I would, Sefaan, but I cannot help feeling that it might not be enough."

* * *

It was fully light when Nyri showed up in Baarias' dwelling.

"Nyri, where have you been?" he scolded. "I've been looking everywhere for you."

Absent-minded, Nyri brandished the herbs she had collected on the way home, thanking Ninmah that she had thought to do so. "You were running low on these, Baarias. I thought I'd pick some for you to save you the trouble. Kyaati needs your undivided attention." She turned away, still wrestling with what she had just heard from Aardn.

"What's wrong?" he asked, picking up on her subdued state. He had not joined the gathering outside and had not yet heard the news. Nyri enlightened him.

"The Woves breached the border again."

His intake of breath rasped the air.

"Don't worry, they didn't come near."

Baarias grumbled low in his throat. "What are they doing? Their behaviour makes no sense..."

Nyri kept her eyes down.

"Where did you go for those?" Baarias frowned at the herbs in her hand.

"I was at the river, washing," she said. "I wanted some privacy." Nyri brushed past him before he could probe any further, intent on checking on Kyaati. He knew she did not like to bathe in front of others. Kyaati had always found her need for privacy amusing.

"You shouldn't be straying from the tribe!" he admonished. "Those Woves could decide to return at any moment!"

"If they return, it will not matter where I am, Baarias." Nyri kept walking.

He grabbed her arm, yanking her around. "Nyriaana, *promise* me! I don't want you out there alone. You do not know where they might be. *Promise* me!"

Nyri stared at him in alarm. His rough treatment was out of character. She saw in his face an echo of how Haana had looked on the night she believed her daughter lost to the Woves. Nyri was witnessing firsthand the consequences of *Zykiel*. He was terrified of her being in danger and having to experience such things again.

"Promise me."

Nyri clutched at the herbs in her hand as her heart sank. She had just given her promise to Sefaan. If she made this promise to Baarias, she would betray him. But her teacher did not know that. Baarias wanted her safe, and she knew he would not rest easy until he had her word. He needed to rest.

She closed her eyes, breathed in through her nose, and lied to him for the first time in her life. "I promise, Baarias. I will not go out alone."

Guilt shot through her as she glanced up into his readily accepting face, his fear draining away as he released his grip on her arm. "I'm sorry, Nyri," he said, releasing her bruised arm. "I'm... still adjusting. I just want you safe."

Safe was the last thing she could stay. Juaan needed her, and she needed him to command the Woves.

"I need you."

Nyri's heart leaped, terrified that he had somehow heard her thoughts.

"I need you to take care of Kyaati," Baarias continued and Nyri breathed again. "Her mind might have healed, but that is all. This place is doing nothing to aid her recovery; all it does is remind her of sickness and death. And... as you just saw, I am probably not the best person to be around at the moment." Nyri could see how much the admittance cost him. "I need you to take her into your home, let her accompany you at all times as you go about your day—"

"Can't Pelaan look after her?" Nyri blurted, then realised how awful that had sounded. The situation was going from bad to worse. "I mean," she added, "surely her father will want to be the one to take care of her. He's her father."

"He did want to take care of her." Baarias' face tensed. "But, honestly, Nyri, I don't want Pelaan to be the one to take care of her. You saw what he did the last time he was alone with her. He lost the grandchild he still so desperately craves. It won't help Kyaati being around someone who is focusing on the loss as much as she is. She'll have to feel that from her father every day, along with the pressure he will put on her to rectify the problem. You remember what Aardn told you after the auscult. They will not stop to consider the cost to Kyaati."

"We can't let them!" Nyri burst out. "She cannot stand it."

Her teacher gave a humourless laughed. "If you have any ideas how we would stop Pelaan seeking a new match for her, I'm all ears, *akaabi*."

Nyri cringed at her own selfishness. Baarias was already doing all he could to keep their focus off her, and now he was also struggling against the aftereffects of *Zykiel*. She could not let him bear this burden alone. "I'll take care of her, Baarias," she said. She would do all she could to keep Kyaati away from her father and Aardn. "But, how did you ever get Pelaan to agree to hand her care over to me?"

"It wasn't easy. In the end, I had to promise..." Her teacher grimaced as his grip tightened on her shoulder. Was it guilt she could feel?

"Promise what, Baarias?" Nyri asked with a mounting sense of foreboding.

"That if you succeeded in caring for Kyaati, then I would

deem you a full *akaab* healer in your own right. My teaching of you would be over."

Nyri gasped and took a step back from him, a myriad of emotions sweeping through her.

Betrayal. Baarias knew what it would mean for her when her teaching was complete.

Elation. He thought her ready. She imagined the pride in Baarias' lilac eyes when he completed the mark of the *akaab* healer over her brow.

Fear. Kyaati's recovery was now in her hands, and she wasn't sure if she was ready for such a task.

Resolution. She had to do this. If she refused to take care of Kyaati, she could remain safe behind Baarias' protection for a little longer, but it would mean that her friend would have to go back to her father where her heart and mind would shatter.

The sense of betrayal evaporated. Baarias had made the only choice he could.

Nyri squared her shoulders and lifted her chin, facing the fear. "I will not let you down, Baarias. I will complete my journey as your *akaabi* and make you proud of me."

His eyes crinkled with relief. He reached out and squeezed her shoulder. "Thank you. But I could not be prouder of you than I am in this moment. I know Kyaati will be safe with you."

Nyri smiled at him, hiding her racing thoughts. She could not stop in her mission to free Juaan's mind from the Wove's hold. It was too important. The raiding party was prowling, closing. If they reached him first, her tribe was finished. Now she would also have Kyaati to consider. She bit her lip.

Baarias sent her on his daily rounds again, but there was

only one visit to make that morning. Omaal's nightmares were keeping him from resting and Umaa was growing concerned for his health.

"He keeps having the same dream," Umaa said as they stood before her tree.

"Evil Wove, evil Wove," Omaal muttered over and over.

Nyri crouched before him. "Where is the evil Wove?"

"In the woods." The boy shivered.

Banishing her own fear at the thought, Nyri let soothing energy roll out. "The Woves are not in the woods, Omaal. Your father and the other sentries are watching. We will know if they decide to come back. You are safe."

Omaal shook his head, fear scrawled across his pinched face.

"Aardn made it worse, forcing him to track down Kyaati," Umaa said. "He's scared to death. That girl has a lot to answer for."

"That's not fair, Umaa," Nyri admonished as she pulled some herbs from the pouches on the *akaab* staff. She handed them to Omaal's mother. "Mix these with water, they will help him rest."

Sitting close by in his usual place next to Omaal, Batai's tongue lolled out. Nyri eyed the furry form. *I'm so glad you can't talk.* Besides herself and Sefaan, Batai was the only other being who knew of Juaan's presence. The wolf cocked his head at her stare. *Yes, you just keep your thoughts to yourself, young wolf.*

After she had done all she could for Omaal, Nyri returned to the healer's tree.

"I have nothing for you to learn today," Baarias said. "I will keep Kyaati for a few more days until you have made

291

your preparations. Your tree is young. Ask Daajir to help you, it'll keep him away from here and you may need to go out into the forest for supplies. Do *not* go alone."

Nyri ground her teeth at the thought of asking Daajir for help, but obeyed her teacher.

Daajir was easy to find. He had just finished his turn on watch and was looking tired and irritable.

Well, join the tribe, Nyri thought.

"What?" he asked when he saw her approaching.

"Hello to you, too," she said. "Baarias wishes for Kyaati to stay with me while she recovers. I need to prepare my home. I could use some help."

His tiredness lifted, and he puffed himself up, just as she had imagined he would. Nyri had to remind herself how he would want to do anything to help Kyaati.

"What do you need first?" he asked.

"I suppose a second bower is most important." Nyri considered. "Mine is too small for both of us. Let's go back to my tree and see what we can do."

Together, they headed to the young *eshaara*. She might not like it, but Nyri was secretly glad of Daajir's help. She did not believe she had the energy to complete the tasks that were needed alone.

Daajir helped her as she selected the best shoots from the interlocking branches above. Together they drew them down, influencing them to grow, weaving them together into a cosy and secure, tear-drop shaped bower beside Nyri's. They worked in silence, both lost in their own thoughts as they focused their will on the newly forming structure.

In the end, Nyri could do no more. Exhausted, she looked out of her tree to see that Ninmah was low in the sky. The new bower would require a few days of careful attention before it was strong enough to be used.

Daajir settled on a branch outside of the main chamber and pulled a fruit from a fold in his garments. Nyri went out and sat beside him as her eyes drooped. Her stomach snarled.

"Aren't you going to eat something?" Daajir asked.

"I have nothing," Nyri said without thinking.

He turned to her, askance. "What happened to all of those berries you had this morning?"

Nyri blanched, realising her blunder too late. "I ate them."

"All of them? Already?" He frowned at her, as though preparing to scold an errant child. "Did you not plan for the rest of the day?"

"Obviously not." Nyri folded her arms and stared straight ahead. Daajir really knew how to get on her nerves, and she had precious few of those left.

There was a long pause. "Here." Daajir broke the piece of fruit he had in half and offered one part to her. He could see she was in no mood for a lecture.

"I will not take your ration," Nyri refused. "I'm the one who foolishly ate mine in one go. I'll live." As long as she didn't faint and humiliate herself first.

He did not withdraw his hand. "You look like you are going to fall from your branch. Take it this once. Just be more careful next time."

Huh. Nyri took what he offered. She wolfed the fruit down and instantly felt better.

"I wish I knew what those Woves were after!" Daajir burst out, à propos of nothing.

The core of Nyri's fruit froze halfway to her mouth as her

face grew cold.

Thankfully, Daajir did not notice. "I tracked them earlier with the other sentries. If I could find out what it was, we could use it as bait." His face grew thoughtful. "If you were a Wove, Nyri, what would be so important to you that you would search the forest for it ignoring your primary prey? What would you care so much about that you would give up your hunt for us?"

"Daajir, could we continue tomorrow?" She needed him to leave. "I'm too tired to carry on today."

His eyebrows shot up at her dismissal. "Alright, I'll work it out on my own, since you are not interested." He swung down from the tree. "Somebody has got to do something." He shot back over his shoulder before disappearing into the gloom below.

Nyri wrapped her arms around herself as she blocked out the sound of his voice.

"Ninmah, help me," she whispered into the darkness.

29

Traitor on the Inside

"Where are you going, Nyriaana?"

She had just crept from her tree and was about to steal into the forest. She froze at the sound of Baarias' voice; he had seen her. She had hidden from Juaan. She could not hide from the others, it seemed.

"To find my mama," she whimpered.

"Little one..." he said. "You cannot find her. She was lost to the Woves. I'm sorry."

"No," she tried to cover her ears to block out what he was saying. "Mama!" Baarias came over and tried to gather her to him, but she fought him off. "No! I find her! No!"

"Nyri!" Juaan appeared out of the trees and Baarias back stepped quickly. Juaan's face had been panic-stricken, but it quickly subsided at the sight of Nyri standing there safe and sound. "Where have you been? I've been looking everywhere—"

She threw herself at him, wrapping her arms around his waist. She could feel his shock and embarrassment at her actions. He attempted to free himself, but she clung on and he quickly gave up. He had been in this position many times over the last few *days and he knew better. Instead, he simply stood, awkward and silent, and let her cling. His warmth spread through her shivering body. "What is it?"*

Baarias took another step back from them. "She's just—"

Juaan acknowledged the healer's presence with an icy glare. "You do not need to trouble yourself," he snapped. "Go. We are none of your concern." Furious, Juaan pulled Nyri after him and out of Baarias' sight. Glancing back, Nyri was in time to see pain contract across the healer's face before he became lost in the trees. As soon as they were alone, Juaan composed himself and crouched before her. "What's wrong, Nyri, Nyri, Nyriaana."

"Baarias," she whimpered. "He-he said mama was not coming back!"

Juaan sighed as he gripped her arms. "It's true," he said gently. There were tears in his eyes. "She was lost, Nyri. I'm sorry."

The words brought the full truth crashing down upon her at last. She knew Juaan would not lie. Burying her face in his chest, she wailed until she thought her heart would burst. "I want my mama!"

He caught her up in his arms, murmuring comfortingly, whispering his rhyme for her. She clung to his neck as he carried her back into their tree, more clumsily than her mother would have. By and by, she became aware that he was crying, too. Her mama had become his mama. They had both lost her. This knowledge only made Nyri cry harder. She tightened her arms through the fresh onslaught of grief.

Finally, the tears ran out. Nyri wiped at her puffy eyes and nose. Her head throbbed.

"It's alright," he said as he set her down. "Your mama told me to look after you and that is exactly what I am going to do, Nyri, Nyri, Nyriaana."

"She did?"

"Yes."

She touched his face, running her fingers over skin that was always slightly too dark. Her mama had wanted Juaan to look after her. Her sadness and pain did not lift, but her uncertainty evaporated. She frowned then, tracing his tears. Who had promised to look after him? She remembered her mother's words on that very first day. "Juaan lost his mama last night. We have to look after him now because no one else will." *Mama might be gone, but she was still here. That meant the responsibility to take care of Juaan like her mother had wanted was hers alone now. She patted his cheek softly.* "I promise I look after you, too, Juaan. We got to look after each other now."

He nodded solemnly. "To the end."

* * *

"You're quiet today, elf." Cool green eyes stared from across the Pit, shaking Nyri from her reverie.

"I thought you did not like me talking." She kept her eyes down so she wouldn't have to see the bitterness in his eyes. Days had passed and Nyri hadn't got any further than this uneasy truce. Each morning before dawn she would go to the stores, fearful and on watch to take her forbidden ration, stealing it out into the forest, using every trick she possessed to get past the watch to spend a few precious moments with Juaan.

His appetite was insatiable. After taking just a few bites herself, Nyri would often give him her whole ration along with the little extra she had dared to take just to keep him sustained. And all for nothing. He still hated her. "It's not as if you talk back much."

He shrugged and turned the fruit he held over in his hands, frowning. "I suppose if you have to be here, listening to you chatter breaks the tedium."

His words made Nyri lift her head to peek at him. "Well, what do you want to talk about?"

She had learned that she could not mention their forgotten past without provoking his temper, and she could not afford setbacks in their uneasy truce. She needed to find something else to breakthrough. It didn't help that his glowering presence intimidated her enough to make talking almost impossible. Her brow pinched together as she tried to form a coherent thought inside her overwrought mind.

"How many are in your tribe?" he asked.

"Fifteen," she supplied automatically.

His eyes widened. "So few?"

Nyri felt her shortening temper flare. "Yes, thanks to the Woves. It is only by the grace of Ninmah that we survive at all."

His face remained composed in the face of her outburst, but his eyes were thoughtful.

"Are there other tribes?"

"Not that we have found." She kept her stare fixed on the ground.

He continued to turn the fruit, the fruit that should be with her People, over in his long hands, apparently lost in thought.

"What would your tribe do if they found out you were coming here?"

A bitter laugh found its way past her lips. "That is something I try hard not to think about." The Elders would never understand her purpose here. She didn't think there could be a punishment great enough.

The silence stretched. Nyri looked up to find him studying her with a peculiar expression. "I am your enemy," he said. "The enemy you say threatens your People's very survival and yet here you are, risking capture and probably death to keep me alive. A Forbidden abomination. *Why?*"

"I have told you why." Part of the reason, anyway.

He ground his teeth together. "He must have been very dear to you, this boy you knew, for you to risk yourself in such a way."

"Yes. He was."

He searched her face and Nyri fought to smooth the pain from her features with little success. After a few moments, his expression became almost pitying. "I am sorry you lost such a person. Let me ask, would he have wanted you to risk yourself in such a way?"

Nyri drew a deep breath. She could see what he was trying to do, and it would not work. She couldn't let him go. "Probably not," she admitted. "But it is no less than he would have done for me if the situation was reversed, so what choice do I have? We promised to look after each other. I will not break that vow."

He shook his head, incredulous. "And this boy was like me?" He gestured to his appearance.

Nyri did not know how to answer that without upsetting him, but he took her silence as confirmation. His gaze softened. "You... are not what I expected from an elf."

She offered a sad smile. "Probably not, but here I am,

foolish as it may seem."

He looked her right in the face and Nyri felt her heart give a strange little jolt as his eyes locked on hers. "You should not be putting yourself at risk. You..." he hesitated, "I do not think you are someone who deserves death."

Nyri could see how much the admittance cost him, but her spirits lifted. Maybe, just maybe, she wasn't doing all of this for nothing.

"I can take care of myself," she said. "I know what I am doing and it is the right thing to do." *For everyone, whether they accept that or not.*

He growled in response and lapsed back into the familiar silence. He was not happy with her answer; a heavy frown slashed at his brow. Nyri tried to divine if he was truly concerned for her, or just disappointed that his tactic hadn't worked. She hoped for the former.

The dark sky above the canopy turned to grey, and she knew it was time for her to leave. She rose reluctantly to her feet. "I promise to come back tomorrow. Please stay quiet and wait for me."

His eyes lifted. "Tomorrow," he said. "I'll be here."

Nyri's lips lifted half-heartedly as she climbed out of the Pit and set off through the forest. The strangest of bird calls whistled out behind her.

* * *

Daajir paced outside Nyriaana's home. Where was she? Didn't she realise he had better things to do than to help rearrange a tree? Aardn was losing patience with his lack of progress in administering his poison at a distance. The knife he had found had been a gift indeed, but he needed more. Another way...

When at last Nyri arrived, she had the audacity to smile at him. Following the way she had treated him the last time he had helped her, Daajir felt like walking away.

"You're in a better mood today," he said, letting her know by his cool tone that she was not yet forgiven.

"I might be." There was a palpable lift in her mood since the previous day when she had all but chased him from her tree in a fit of pique. "I wouldn't push your luck, though. Just keep to your own side today."

"I was only trying to help," he grumbled.

"Well, I don't need your help," she said, climbing up into her tree to start work.

"You could have fooled me." Daajir followed her. The sight of the half completed bower helped belie her words. The branches on the side he had been working on were thick and strong enough to support his weight. In contrast, her side appeared much the same as it had when they started. She at least had the grace to flush.

"Huh. Well, just keep out of it."

"If you insist—!"

His words were cut off as the summoning horn rolled out.

Daajir swung around as a wave of energy hit them. He recognised the tenor of the energy. It was Aardn, and she was *angry*.

"What? What is it?" Bewildered, Nyri rushed to his side. Then her breath hitched as she felt it, too.

"Come on!" Daajir flew down the tree with Nyri following

in his wake.

Aardn was standing at the foot of the main store tree. The Elder's expression was contorted with fury. Daajir saw Nyri's eyes dart from the tree to the Elder's face and back again. Her own face became ashen beneath her red-gold skin.

"We have a traitor in our midst!" Aardn's voice broke over them all. "Food has been stolen."

Daajir stiffened as the shock travelled down his spine. A collective intake of breath swept around the gathered tribe. For a moment he felt nothing, then rage like he had never felt burned through his chest, releasing in a hiss through his throat.

Nyriaana was silent at his side. A nauseous, greenish tint had crept under her skin as though she was about to vomit. He shifted away from her, then movement caught his eye; Umaa had staggered against Imaani. Omaal's mother's face was a mask of horror, her eyes large in her head as tears spilled down her cheeks; so great was the shock that a Ninkuraa would betray their own.

Daajir shook with fury. All the effort. All the sacrifices he had made at the cost of his own soul. To know one of those he had paid such a price for had betrayed them was almost more than he could bear.

"I warned you," Aardn said. "I warned you I would not tolerate such selfishness. When I catch the one responsible—." Her voice had been rising in volume and she cut herself off to draw a steadying breath then, with the composure more befitting an Elder, she faced them all.

"I had hoped that it wouldn't come to this, but rations must be halved."

"No!" The voice was Haana's. The child, Naaya, was clinging to her mother. The infant was weaving on her feet. The spirit that had existed in her eyes when she had followed Daajir and his group on the Gathering, a lifetime ago it seemed, had died. He ground his teeth together. Death would be too light a punishment for the one responsible for this. If he was the one to catch them... perhaps a Wove would not be the first to taste the effects of his poison.

Nyriaana pitched into him at Aardn's ruling, and he grabbed her arm in a firm grip as her knees almost gave out.

Angry tears stood in Haana's eyes. "You cannot do this to us, Aardn." Her accusing gaze flickered to her mate in Aardn's shadow. Oraan's face remained composed as he stood beside his fellow Elder, but Daajir could not miss the strain on his face.

"I must!" Spittle flew from Aardn's mouth, and Daajir's heart lifted in agreement. What was one life when action was needed to save the many?

"Then you are sentencing us to death," Haana spat. She stared Oraan down. "Just know that if my daughter dies, I will too."

"If it comes to that, then the blame lies with the traitor standing hidden among you." Aardn's words hung in the air. "This time, I cannot even say that it was a Wove who did this to us."

Daajir narrowed his eyes as he scanned the small crowd around him, looking for the merest hint of guilt. How he would love to be the one to catch the traitor.

"Go!" Aardn barked. "There is no more to be said."

Daajir yanked Nyriaana away, for she seemed unable to

303

move under her own power. He resisted the urge to shake her. What good was despondency now? Now was the time for strength and to bring those responsible for this horror to account: the monsters without and now those from within.

"Ninmah above!" Daajir burst out once they were back inside Nyriaana's tree. "Isn't it enough that we are being stalked by the Woves without having to watch for betrayal within our own family?"

Nyri's skin was clammy under his hand and she did not respond to his question. Her face was blank, eyes unseeing. Well, if she was too weak to do anything other than stare into the abyss, he would go on alone.

"I'm leaving," he said. "I cannot sit here making a bower while a traitor hides in our midst. I must speak with Aardn and know what is to be done."

Nyri jerked her head once in acknowledgment. Daajir sighed. She could not help being weak. She was young and frightened. What she needed was a show of strength. Biting down on his impatience, he placed a hand on her shoulder.

"Do not worry, Nyriaana, we will catch whoever it is and I will make them suffer."

* * *

30

Vision

I *will make them suffer.*

Nyri descended from her tree, holding herself together by her fingernails. She couldn't concentrate on the bower any more than Daajir. She needed to go somewhere, anywhere. Automatically, she made her way to Baarias' home.

The news food was being stolen had hit her teacher as hard as everyone else. Nyri could feel his anger at the betrayal burning just beneath the surface. She could not look him in the face. Coming here had been a mistake.

"H-how is Kyaati?" she asked in a strangled voice. Her palms were still sweating from what she had just heard. *Traitor.*

"Still sleeping," Baarias answered her question, a frown marring his brow. "She retired before Ninmah last night. You must hurry with your preparations, Nyriaana."

"We're working as fast as we can, Baarias."

"Good. See if you can wake her. I'll visit the stores." The

catch in his voice at the end closed Nyri's throat.

She shuffled into the next chamber where Kyaati slept and shook one thin shoulder. "Kyaati?"

The lavender eyes opened. "So, Baarias has sent *you* to wake me from my refuge this morning?"

Nyri tried not to shiver at her bitter tone. "He is getting food."

"You should not be wasting rations on me," Kyaati muttered. "Save them for someone who actually has an interest in living."

"Kyaati!" Nyri's tenuous composure shook.

Kyaati waved a hand. "It doesn't matter. You feed me or you don't. No one is going to live through the Fury now, even if they wish it. It is over."

"Kyaati, stop, please," Nyri begged. "Don't say that! It is not over." There had to be a way. A reason for it all.

"Yes, it is."

"Baarias!" A shout tore through the healer's tree. "Baarias!"

Nyri rushed out of the chamber to greet Haana. "Haana, Baarias isn't here, he's—"

"I need him!" The other woman beseeched. "Please, he is the only one who can help."

"Haana?" To Nyri's relief, Baarias had appeared in the entranceway.

Haana turned from Nyri and threw herself on her knees before the healer, clutching at the woven fibres around his waist as the tears spilled from her eyes. "Wise *akaab*, please help me. You must help me." She lifted a shaking hand to reveal one small chunk of gora root. "This is all I may take. It is not enough. My daughter… Baarias, speak to Aardn! She will listen to you. Please make her see sense! My family needs more."

Nyri felt like she would die right there. Agony ripped across Baarias's worn face as he bent to take Haana by the elbows with shaking hands. When he spoke, his voice sounded as old as Sefaan's. "Haana, understand, there is nothing I can do. Aardn will not relent on her ruling; not for me, not for anyone."

"Baarias, I cannot watch her die! She is starving. She is in pain. Help me, help me."

"I-I'm sorry." Nyri could feel his fragile composure breaking in the face of her pain. She almost did not recognise this man who had always been such a rock to her. "H-here. Take this. I-It is as much as I can give."

Haana appeared to shrink before him, the last of the hope dying in her eyes. She took the ration he offered. "Thank you, master *akaab*," she said and left without another word, moving as one who knew her days were numbered.

Vomit rose in Nyri's mouth. She could not bear the expression on Baarias' face. "Excuse me," she said and ran from Baarias' home. Blinded by tears, she tore across the *eshaara* grove and burst into Sefaan's tree without announcement.

The old Kamaali was sitting in the shadows, idly toying with the *enu* seed around her neck. She did not appear surprised by Nyri's arrival.

"I can't do this, Sefaan! I want to save our people. But how can I go on doing what I am? In trying to save them this way, I am only bringing about their doom! Please, tell me what to do! Please. I am lost!"

"The boy must live." There was no waver in the ancient voice.

"But what good is it for him to save us, only for us to starve to death? Why do I have to be the one to make this choice?"

"I cannot help you, Nyriaana. I only know as much as the Great Spirit whispers. Our fate is in your hands. You must choose between your love for him or loyalty to your people."

Nyri dropped to the ground and put her head between her knees, gripping her hair in her hands.

Sefaan's touch ghosted across her right elbow. "I believe that aiding this boy is the right path. You are the one who has been chosen for this task and you are the one who has to bear the burden in the end, whatever that may be."

Nyri sniffed through her tears. "How in Ninmah do I choose, Sefaan?"

"Listen to the Great Spirit for yourself, and perhaps it will help you decide. I will show you what I see." The old Kamaali reached up to place a hand on Nyri's heart. Nyri felt the energy around them gather and seep through her skin. *Follow me.* Tentatively, Nyri reached out to join Sefaan in the flow of KI.

Visions flickered through her mind. She saw a woman stumbling through the snow on open ground. She was racing for her life, running from dark enemies behind her. Nyri knew instinctively that she was a Ninkuraa, though she was wrapped in a mixture of dark grey and brown furs. In one hand she held a spear and, in a sling around her body, her other arm clutched a green-eyed baby to her breast.

The Great Spirit swirled lovingly around the image for a moment before the vision shattered to be replaced by pictures that Nyri recognised, images of her and Juaan as children, images of Juaan sitting trapped in the Pit and with it a sense of certainty that if he died, all hope for her People's future would die, too.

But why?

The vision shifted, becoming unfamiliar. She was no longer in the forest. Nyri found herself flanked on both sides by faces of sheer rock. Strange white rain swirled in this cold and desolate place, and she shivered as though she were truly there.

Where are the trees? Nyri's breathing hitched in panic. A dark, flat expanse stretched out before her. It was water. Steam rose from the black surface.

Nyri focused and saw a fur-clad figure crouched at the waterside. The figure stiffened, though Nyri had not made a sound; seeming to sense it was being watched. Nyri held her breath as the figure straightened up. She was female. Her dark hair billowed out in the wind. Nyri gasped as the figure turned. A familiar coiling symbol ran between her brows. The *enu* seed of an *eshaara* tree rested at her throat.

A Kamaali!

As though the realisation had called her by name, the stranger abruptly lifted her head. Green eyes pierced Nyri's soul. The girl smiled in recognition and reached out with a hand, beckoning her...

"Ah!" Nyri yanked herself away from the vision, breaking contact with Sefaan. The Kamaali's tree re-materialised around her. She shook her head, but the green eyes continued to stare from behind her lids, calling for her.

"Who was *that?*"

"Ariyaana," Sefaan replied. "Now you see her, too, and only you can find her. Her fate is tied to yours, and she is waiting for you. I am not the Last."

"Not the Last?" Nyri was still breathless from the intensity of the vision. "Is *she* the one the stories speak of?"

"I believe she is the one we have been waiting for, yes."

"But… she is not Ninkuraaja. She is like Juaan. Forbidden. How can she be Kamaali?"

Sefaan shook her head. "I do not know. I only know what I see. You have to find her and this boy can help you."

Nyri pictured Haana's despairing face, the depleted stores, a Fury of starvation that stretched before them and how she was the cause. She thought of the Woves and their Forbidden leader trapped inside the Pit.

Nyri closed her eyes and found the strange girl smiling at her from behind her lids, as though she were the keeper of the most sacred secret. Vestiges of KI swirled around the image. *You have to find her and this boy can help you…* Her Juaan. They still needed each other, perhaps now more than ever. It was *necessary*.

Nyri lifted her face to meet Sefaan's gaze. "May Ninmah have mercy on us."

"You are your mother's daughter." Sefaan touched her cheek.

Nyri sighed. "But… I cannot do this alone, Sefaan. I need help. Can I at least tell Baarias? I can't bear lying to him. He wants me to care for Kyaati but I don't know how I am going to do that—"

"You must not tell Baarias!" Sefaan's voice was hard. "He cannot know. Even if he was in his right mind. If you tell him, all will be lost."

The vehemence of her tone took Nyri aback, but she nodded her understanding, remembering the anguish on her teacher's face as Haana had beseeched him. There was no telling what he might do if he knew the extent of the danger she was putting herself in. Baarias had changed since the Ritual. He was more protective, more liable to break.

Nyri clutched on to the Kamaali's presence for strength. "At least I have you on my side, Sefaan. It helps to know there is one person who does not think me a traitor for my actions. If I know that, I can walk this path. Never leave me."

Sefaan smiled, looking more ancient than ever. "Ah, my dear Nyriaana, you must find your own strength, for that is one thing I cannot promise."

That night Nyri's sleep was broken. She tried to keep her experience with KI firmly in her mind, clinging to the sense of *rightness* she had felt within the vision.

The Woves were hunting for Juaan, and now her own tribe was hunting for her. There was no more time. She had to make it right and do as the Great Spirit wished. Giving up on sleep, Nyri pulled herself from her bower. She still felt sick at the thought of what she must do to walk the path that had been put before her, but she forced herself to continue.

The air outside was bitter; Nyri's fingers grew numb as she emerged from her home and crept to the nearest store. Her senses hummed, every nerve ending alert as she climbed inside. She paused, feeling the currents of energy around her. After several moments of holding her breath, she relaxed. She was alone. There was no time to waste. Nyri picked a large gora root and stashed it inside her clothing before turning to pick up a fresh set of berries.

She was unprepared when the hand came down on her shoulder.

DAUGHTER OF NINMAH

* * *

31

Caught!

The wave of desperation hit Baarias full in the chest. Kyaati was sleeping beside him as he leaped up from his vigil.

Nyriaana!

The ever present panic simmering beneath his reason shot through him like *vaash* barbs. Baarias gritted his teeth, trying to control the wave of adrenaline. Nyriaana was in trouble. With only a glance at Kyaati, he dashed from his tree, following the direction of his charge's desperate plea, as the blood pounded in his ears.

Baarias' stride faltered as he caught sight of the scene unfolding at the store tree in the distance. Imaani had hold of Nyri by the arm and was dragging her back to the ground. Rage burned in Baarias' chest, and he fought against the urge to run forward and knock the other man to the ground.

"You're lying. I can feel it. Thief!" Imaani's voice carried on the wind. "I was praying I would be the one to catch you."

"No, please. I'm taking the ration to Kyaati. I am not stealing. Please, believe me!"

Umaa was waiting for them at the base of the tree. Baarias felt the energy swirl between her and Imaani. The Bonded pair were communicating with each other.

"Watch the tree while I'm gone," Imaani told his mate. "I won't be long." Then he continued to drag Nyri, who stumbled in his wake, towards Aardn's tree.

Baarias rushed forward. "*What* is the meaning of this?"

"I caught her stealing food, Baarias." Imaani did not slow his pace, appearing determined to reach Aardn before Baarias could stop him. He held up the gora root and some berries in his free hand as proof. "This is enough for three! *She* is our thief."

Shock doused Baarias' anger, rendering him speechless.

"No, please, I can explain!" Nyri was digging her heels in.

"You have already explained!" Imaani snapped. "I do not believe you. You are hiding something. Your mind is closed."

Recovering himself, Baarias lengthened his step enough to place himself between Imaani and the Elder's tree. He raised an eyebrow at the younger man. "What was her explanation?"

"She told me she was collecting a ration for herself and Kyaati." Imaani's tone was begrudging. He did not want Baarias to interfere, that much was clear. "Only, I know you always collect the extra ration for Kyaati."

Baarias' eyes flickered to his akaabi. Imaani was right. Nyriaana was not telling the truth. He did not want to believe it. He *couldn't* believe it. Not his Nyriaana. She would never betray her people so.

Help me. She appealed with her eyes. *Please.*

Baarias held her gaze for a moment longer. She had a lot of explaining to do. He faced Imaani. "What she tells you is true," he said, no hint of waver in his voice. "I had some important work to do and sent Nyri to collect our rations. I apologise for not informing you, Imaani."

Baarias reached forward and took Nyri's other arm, tugging her out of Imaani's still determined grip. He placed himself between her and the sentry. "You have my word that she is not your thief, Imaani. Nyri would not steal from her own tribe. I trust her with my life."

He heard Nyriaana sniff back tears behind him.

"I was only doing my job." Imaani's demeanour was sullen as he handed back Nyri's food.

"I respect that," Baarias inclined his head, "but do not be overly zealous. Next time, learn the truth of someone's story before you march them to Aardn."

With that, he towed Nyri away.

"Would you care to explain yourself?" he asked as soon as they were out of earshot.

She didn't appear capable of speaking. Her ashen face was downcast, and her fists clenched, he guessed to prevent her hands from shaking. "I couldn't sleep," she said at last, her voice almost inaudible. "You have so much on your mind at the moment, Baarias, I thought I'd help you by collecting our rations for the day."

She was lying again. He could feel it. Thorns contracted inside Baarias' heart. She had never lied to him before. He felt the walls closing about her mind, shutting him out. She had changed. He could not believe she could betray her people, but something was wrong, and it was clear that he was not going to get the answers he sought from her lips.

And so Baarias pretended to accept her words. "I thank you for your kind gesture, Nyriaana, but next time, please inform us of your actions before you act. The Elders are extremely twitchy at the moment. You can't afford to raise suspicion. If their focus falls on you, the actual thief will walk away unpunished."

Her lips pressed together and said nothing, confirming his thoughts. She would not speak to him. He could feel a rift opening up between them. For some reason, she did not trust him anymore. He should never have revealed his secret beliefs to her. That was when all this had started. He had been a fool.

Baarias led her back to the healer's tree in stifled silence. Kyaati was waiting for them. Pale and still trembling slightly from her ordeal, Nyri shared out the rations she had taken from the store tree. Kyaati did not speak as she chewed; she had shrunken to skin and bone. Baarias rubbed restlessly at his forehead. He hoped Nyriaana would soon be ready to take over her care. It was taking all of his willpower to face Kyaati's constant despair, knowing he was failing to save yet another life.

A furtive movement caught his eye, and he was in time to catch Nyri trying to conceal her own ration behind her back without eating it. Seeing he had caught her, she flushed and quickly brought the food to her lips.

What are you doing, *Nyri?* Baarias thought as one more stone sank deep into his heart.

* * *

Daajir paced the hollow. In his hands he held a cut length of an *aquilem* vine. He had stiffened its flesh with *tyraa* sap, and now he was ready to test his latest idea. If it did not work.... Aardn was not a patient woman. If he failed this time, she would wash her hands of him. She would not present his plans to the rest of the Elders.

It *had* to work.

Sending a prayer to Ninmah Herself, Daajir fitted a *vaash* barb into the end of his invention, then lifted it to his lips. Drawing a deep breath, he blew one short sharp blast into the *aquilem* pipe. The *vaash* barb flashed out of the other end, whistling through the darkness. With a dull thud, it embedded itself into the rotting flesh of his latest victim.

Daajir blinked, shocked. It had worked! Ninmah had answered his prayer! He had found the way at last. Unable to contain his elation, he threw his head back and crowed his triumph to the night.

A grin split his face in two as he stared down at the vine in his hand. Now all he needed was a Wove to cross his path.

* * *

32

Finding Trust

It was almost impossible for Nyri to make herself approach the store tree the next morning. The memories of the previous day had kept her from sleep. Imaani had caught her. If it hadn't been for Baarias...

Baarias.

She stifled a moan, thinking of the pain on his face when he had realised she was lying to him. Something had broken between them. An essential trust had been lost. This path was exacting a heavy price.

Gathering her courage, Nyri ascended into the store tree. Sure enough, Imaani was waiting for her. She cringed at the sight of him. He did not seem pleased to see her, either. Sour-faced, he broke a gora root in two and thrust the meagre half into her hands. Nyri quailed at just how little was in her hand. She got the impression Imaani was daring her to complain. Without giving him the satisfaction, she left the tree and walked far enough to be sure she was out of Imaani's sight before cutting into the outer forest.

At least if Imaani was guarding the stores, he was not out

here. The other sentries were easier to deal with. She could not tell if Sefaan was still helping her.

Nyri reached the Pits and pulled back the coverings from Juaan's prison. She could see nothing in the pre-dawn dimness. She paused before lowering herself down into the misty depths, still hesitant about how she would be received. Following her near capture, she had not been able to return the previous morning, as she had promised him.

The mist was thicker at the bottom; the icy blanket curled around her. She stood on the damp rock, shivering and on guard. "Juaan?" Her voice fell dead in the damp air. Water dripped from the stone walls. There was no answer. "Juaan?"

The shadows swirled, threatening. Nyri held her breath, not daring to move. *He promised not to hurt you,* she told herself. But he was so much stronger now. He might have changed his mind in the wake of her absence. Her palms were awash with nerves, Nyri swore if he was waiting to pounce, he would find her by her heartbeat; it was the only sound.

Finally, and to her relief, Nyri caught his essence. His muted energy had the stillness of sleep. He was a couple of strides to her right.

Now that she knew he was there, Nyri could just detect a darker shape in the mist. She stepped closer until he became clear. He did not wake. He was sitting propped against the Pit wall. Nyri crouched before him, alarmed to see fresh cuts and bruises littering the deep red-gold flesh. His hairy chin was propped against his chest, brown hair falling across his face, brushing the high cheekbones, darkened by the damp. The long hands draped carelessly, one in his lap, the other lying on the freezing ground. Nyri could see that at least

319

one finger was broken, and the skin was bluish from the cold. What had he been *doing*? She took the wounded hand between her palms. It dwarfed her own, but she did her best to warm it. She traced the rough and smooth paths with her fingers as she studied the damage.

"Don't."

Nyri flinched at the sound of his voice and looked up. She hadn't noticed him wake. His eyes were half open now, watching her. The green gaze sent a thrill through her, reminding her of the vision Sefaan had shown her. She let go, and the hand flashed out of sight beneath the furs.

"Don't what?"

"Creep up on me. I don't like it. I could hurt you and I gave you my word that I would not."

"I'm sorry. I did not mean to." Nyri nodded at the hand he had hidden from her, frowning. "What have you been doing?"

He straightened up as her question shattered the quiet moment, backing her off. "What do you think? You don't expect me to just sit here, do you, waiting placidly for you to come back?"

"You tried to climb out? You can't climb out of this Pit. It's sheer rock!" Nyri couldn't help but feel a sting of agony at the fact that he was trying to get away from her. She was nothing more than an enemy, one who was keeping him prisoner and entirely dependent on her. He did not strike her as a man who liked to depend on anyone.

"So I found," he said, closing his eyes and leaning his head back.

Nyri shifted. "I'm sorry I did not come yesterday." She decided not to tell him the reason behind her absence. She was doing her best to banish the memory from her own mind. "Here," she said, pulling forth the half root. Half was hers, but she couldn't bring herself to take it. He was already noticeably leaner than when he had first fallen into the Pit.

He stared down at the offering for a moment, frowning. "Thank you, she-elf," he muttered.

"Nyriaana," Nyri reminded him. "It's Nyri. Can't you remember, Juaan?"

"Khalvir," he reminded her in return. "And of course I don't."

He picked up the root and took a bite. She watched him struggle not to spit it out. He pulled a face as he chewed and swallowed.

"This is awful! What is this?"

Despite herself, Nyri's lips twitched. "Gora root. It's very good for you. Makes you big and strong." She nodded sagely.

His face was askance. "Whoever told you that complete and total—?"

"Never mind." Nyri shook her head. "It's a private joke. Just eat."

And he did so, though he made a face at every bite.

"*What?*" he asked irritably after a few moments.

Nyri realised she had been staring at his face again, or more specifically, his chin. She reached out to touch the hair growth. He shied away from her hand and she dropped it, embarrassed. She really needed to stop forgetting herself around him. The years apart had not diminished the attachment or the familiarity. Not for her. She touched her own chin instead. "You have hair here."

"Yes." His tone once again questioned her sanity.

"It's... strange. I've seen nothing like it before."

His eyebrows rose. "Your people don't grow beards?"

"Beards?" She tested the word. The entire concept of someone growing hair on the chin was very unnatural. Nyri shook her head, still studying his face.

This seemed to amuse him. "You are strange, elf."

Nyri frowned. "What is this *elf*?"

"That's what you are, aren't you?" he threw her previous words to him back at her. "It's what we call you. The People of Ninhursag."

Nyri lifted her chin. "I am not an *elf*. My People are the sacred Ninkuraaja, created by the holy Ninmah."

"Oh, really?"

He was mocking her. She heard the pompousness of her own statement and got defensive. "So what do *Woves* call themselves?"

The edge returned. "We have clan names." He studied the last remains of the *gora* root in his hand. Nyri's mouth watered as her empty stomach snarled. "Is this all you can bring to eat?"

That was the last thing he should have asked so flippantly. In an instant, Nyri was on her feet, standing over him, vibrating with anger. "Yes, as a matter of fact, it is! Thanks to your *clan,* we now no longer have enough food to get us through the Fury. You took most everything. You are lucky to get that, believe me, *Forbidden*."

He rocked backwards in the face of her rage. His eyes flickered and then, to Nyri's surprise, he apologised. "I'm sorry. That was wrong of me."

"Huh. Small comfort that is to the old and the young who will die this Fury from starvation." Her voice cracked. *Stop.* She thought to herself. *Don't break down in front of him.*

"I'm sorry," he said again, and Nyri felt the last thing she expected—remorse. It reminded her of what she had forgotten in the last few moments. This was Juaan here with her, not a mindless Wove. He would never have taken their food. Their dark magic had twisted his mind in order to make him serve them. Her anger drained away. She collapsed back down before him, exhausted.

"No, I'm sorry." She stared at the ground. "You don't need to hear."

The silence stretched.

"Are you hungry?" he asked. She looked up to see the most gentle of expressions on his face. He seemed to be truly seeing her for the first time.

Nyri's mouth fell open. Removed of the bitterness, his countenance was breathtaking. She hadn't really noticed until this moment. Nyri closed her mouth and shook her head in response to his question. He needed everything she could provide, even if it meant sacrificing her own needs. What she had told him was true. It was no less than he had always done for her. "No," she answered.

His eyes gleamed with amusement at the role reversal. "Here." He moved to break off a piece of the root for her. She saw him wince as he used his broken fingers.

"Let me heal that." She held out her hand.

He instantly withdrew, the anger and mistrust returning to his gaze.

"Please, I don't like to see you in pain."

His eyes moved to his hand and back to hers again as he warred with his better judgement. Some deep-set instinct was compelling him to trust her with his very life, while his entire life experience was telling him to fear and mistrust

323

the *elf*-witch. Nyri had to reach that deeper part of him.

"Please. Please, trust me." She extended her hand out further, displaying how small and vulnerable it was next to his.

His fingers made an involuntary twitch towards hers, then stopped, trembling in the air. Conflict flitted through those green depths. *Come on, Juaan. I know you're in there.*

He made his decision. "I'll let you heal me, but only if you eat something. You look like the wind could blow you away." And he placed his hand in hers.

How was it that amid so much fear and uncertainty, all Nyri could feel in that moment was the purest joy? Juaan was still with her, somewhere beneath the depths of this Wove facade. He was there, and Nyri felt whole. His hand was warm and solid in hers. Everything she was sacrificing was suddenly worth every moment of the agony it cost her.

She healed the bones. He held stone-still the entire time. Nyri didn't even hear him breathe. It was easier for her this time; she understood more of the muted energy hidden within his body. He was Ninkuraaja, but not. She teased his energy free, moving it along under her guidance.

He pulled his hand from her as soon as she finished and stared at his fingers, a range of emotions playing across his face. "Never believed it…"

"Never believed what?" she asked.

He shook his head, covering the unguarded moment. "It doesn't matter. You have a great power, young elf."

"I'm not an *elf*. I am of the Ninkuraaja." Nyri reminded him.

"Yes. That's a bit of a mouthful."

She grinned. "It took you a long time to teach me how to

say it." She waved a hand at his reproachful frown. "Never mind."

"Thank you." It was a sincere sentiment.

"You're welcome." Nyri felt warmth on her forehead and experienced a jolt as she realised it was the light of Ninmah touching her. She had to go. She had lost track of time. Baarias would be awake soon, if he wasn't already. She could not afford to raise his suspicions any more than she already had.

It tugged at her heart to leave Juaan. She felt closer to him now than she had since before she had lost him. He was undeniably different from the Juaan she had known, and she was slowly accepting that. She herself had changed from the girl she had been. Their relationship was beginning anew, for better or worse.

Juaan was still studying his hand, a brooding expression on his face. "Thank me for that by not trying to escape again," she admonished.

He glanced up and raised his eyebrows at her. Nyri might not have seen him since he was a boy. He may have lost all the memories of his childhood, but she could still read that expression as readily as her own. "I mean it. Please promise me you'll stay here and keep quiet. I wasn't lying when I said the Elders had posted extra watch. They may patrol around close by. You cannot do anything to attract their attention. Please, for me, stay quiet and wait for my return. I will not leave you to die. Trust me."

Nyri could not guess why he should do that. All she had done was heal his hand and bring him scraps of food. She was still the one keeping him prisoner here, frightened and uncertain, and yet she saw something about her impassioned plea stir something deep within his soul.

He fought it for a moment, then gave up. "What is it about you, elf?" he grumbled. "I promise."

"Thank you." Nyri had needed to hear it, otherwise she wasn't sure if she could have left him. "They *will* kill you if they find you, and I could not bear it if they did." She reached out a hand, ignoring him as he flinched back, and touched her fingers to his cheek, letting her emotion flow. She did not know if he would feel it. "I can't lose you again. Ever. You mean too much to me."

His eyes were wide as he pulled back from her touch. Nyri could not hold his gaze. Embarrassed, she tore herself away.

33

Selfish

"Kyaati, why don't you join Nyri and fetch me some more *haarif* herbs. You need air. You have been sitting in here for days."

Kyaati turned sullen eyes upon Baarias. "Do you really think air is going to cure me, master *akaab*?"

Nyri was careful to keep her head down to escape notice. Baarias' words were firm. "Nevertheless, I wish for you to go out. Nyri, do *not* go far. The herbs are growing near Imaani's tree. I saw them a few days ago."

Nyri set aside the roots she had been crushing and rose to her feet. She wavered as she did so; the world taking a few moments to right itself. It had been two days since Imaani had caught her in the store tree and denied her extra rations.

Baarias caught her arm, steadying her. "Are you well?" His brow pinched together as Nyri felt him probe along the edges of her consciousness. His lips turned down when she raised her defences. "Have you eaten?"

Yes, about two days ago, Nyri thought to herself. Irritated by her lapse, she shook him off with a little more vehemence

327

than she intended. She needed to be stronger. "I am well, Baarias. Please, don't fuss!"

His frown deepened, and she realised her outburst had only made things worse. She rarely snapped at him. She had to get out before he demanded that she explain or her thoughts gave her away. Her powers of concentration were deteriorating. "How much do you need?"

"A basketful should do."

Nyri grabbed one from the corner of the chamber. Then, more gently, she took Kyaati's hand. Her friend did not resist. "Come," she beckoned. "We won't be long. Baarias is right. You need to get out."

Without a word, Kyaati let her lead her from the healer's tree.

The herbs were not hard to find, covering the ground around the roots of Imaani's eshaara, and they set about gathering what was needed. A face caught Nyri's eye from above. Umaa was looking down from her tree. She scowled and then disappeared back inside. Nyri sighed. Imaani and Umaa had not given up on their suspicion, it seemed.

"Have you seen Daajir?" It was clear she didn't really care about the answer and was only making a lacklustre effort to talk. Baarias must have been lecturing her.

"Y-Yes," Nyri answered. She did not know if she should mention to Kyaati that Daajir was helping her every day to get her tree prepared for a new occupant. She wondered whether Baarias had told her of the new arrangement. She decided not to risk Kyaati's wrath, if not. "He disappears a lot. He believes he has a plan to repel the Woves. He won't say what it is, though," Nyri barked a mirthless laugh. "You know Daajir. All wrapped up in his own self-importance. It is not for the likes of *us* to know."

She had hoped Kyaati might join her in the disparaging assessment of Daajir's ego, but she did not. Her tribe-sister lapsed back into silence, obviously satisfied that she had made enough of an effort to interact for one day. The emptiness in her soul sucked at Nyri's dwindling energy. She did not know how Baarias was enduring it, but she would find out soon enough when she was the one to take over Kyaati's full care.

It was a relief to return to Baarias' tree. As Nyri took her leave, Baarias halted her at the threshold.

"How soon do you think your tree will be ready?"

Nyri thought about it. "We only need to line the new bower. Daajir and I should finish tonight."

Nyri could taste Baarias' relief. "I will let Kyaati know you will take over her care from tomorrow." The wind picked up around them. Icy and ominous. Baarias hunched his shoulders. "You had better hurry. I fear there is a storm coming."

Nyri looked to the rippling canopy above and shivered. She had not missed the drop in temperature. The wind was gathering its strength.

Baarias disappeared back inside his tree without another word. Nyri was glad of it, for at that moment, another wave of dizziness overcame her. She doubled over and braced herself on her knees, fighting down the queasiness brought on by her empty stomach. It had only been two days, and she was failing already. The next ration would have to be hers.

"Nyri?" Daajir rushed up, misreading her pale and ragged appearance. "What's wrong. Is Kyaati—?"

"Kyaati's well," she told him, straightening up. *Alive, at least.* "Let us go. We need to finish the bower before this storm hits." She had to focus on something, anything. He agreed silently, glancing towards the healer tree before Nyri led him away.

Daajir predicted they would need several trips to fill the bower and so they wasted no time moving out into the forest beyond the *eshaara* grove. The sentries let them through when Daajir explained their purpose.

"Any signs?" he asked Javaan in passing.

"No," the older man replied. "The forest is quiet. You are safe to go out. They have not set foot away from their camp in days. But… stay on your guard. There is something out there that sends a chill down my spine." He shuddered. Nyri stared into the thick trees beyond and tried to quell the thrill of apprehension she felt at his words.

"The animals are acting strange of late, too," Javaan pondered on. "Just this morning, a flock of birds chased me from my watch. The others have experienced similar incidents. Mark my words, there is Wove mischief still afoot."

Ah, Nyri thought, keeping her eyes down. Woves had nothing to do with it. Only herself and one wily Kamaali.

"And…" Javaan continued. "There is a new call that I cannot place. I thought I knew the voice of every bird in this forest, but this one is new, I have yet to sight it. No doubt Ninsiku's tightening hold has driven it here."

Something tugged at Nyri's memory as she listened to this, but could not place it inside her hazing mind.

Daajir patted Javaan's shoulder. "Keep sharp. Their darkness will linger for a good while yet until we can drive them from our borders." He patted at his garments as though reassuring himself that something vital was present before leading Nyri on. She shivered as the light grew dim, the dark clouds gathering above the canopy.

"What's wrong?" Daajir asked once they had left Javaan behind and were alone.

Nyri fought through the increasing muddle of dizziness. "Nothing. I just don't like the thought that a Wove could be close by, watching us. Makes me edgy."

To her surprise, Daajir placed a protective arm around her shoulders. She fought the urge to shrug it off, but such an action would ruin her charade of vulnerability. It was so easy to play on Daajir's ego.

"They will not trouble us for much longer, Nyriaana. Trust me. I promised the Elders I had found a way to defend us, and that is exactly what I have done. They will not crouch on our borders, tormenting us when they have a taste of what I have in store for them." His hand twitched towards his garments again and his eyes swept around, as if longing for a Wove to appear before them.

Right, Nyri fought the urge to roll her eyes. She was grateful when the conversation lapsed as they searched the groves, this time for moss and leaves rather than food; the trees were bare of edible offerings. The tribe and the rest of the forest inhabitants had stripped them to prepare for the Fury.

As Daajir had predicted, it took several trips to fill Kyaati's new bower. There were anxious moments when their foraging took them close to the Pits. Nyri tried to keep her furtive glances towards the area to a minimum. Thankfully, Juaan appeared to be keeping his promise, and the Pits remained still and silent.

The effort of travelling back and forth, however, took a heavy toll on Nyri. On the last trip, her strength gave out. Foraging near a fallen tree, she bent to lift her full basket onto her shoulders when the ground lurched beneath her feet. Falling to her knees in the undergrowth, Nyri tried to clear the dark spots that swam before her eyes. She had to get up. She could not let Daajir see! But her body refused to obey. Her empty stomach convulsed, and she retched into the earth.

As Nyri battled the darkness sucking at the edges of her vision, her eyes fell on something beside her on the ground. At first she thought she was seeing things. A gathering basket should not be lying abandoned on the forest floor this far from the tribe. And not just any gathering basket, but a gathering basket stuffed with food.

Now she knew she was hallucinating.

Her need was such that she could not help extending her fingers, wishing for the vision to be true. A jolt shot up her arm when instead of passing straight through the vision as she expected, her fingers came up against cold, solid fibres. She gasped. *Real!*

Her hands plunged into the woven net, pulling out the first thing she could reach. She stuffed the berries into her mouth, groaning in relief as they filled her empty stomach. She pulled out another piece and another, unable to stop until her belly was bursting. Satiated, she lay unmoving in the soft dark soil, savouring the strength returning to her limbs. Her vision cleared.

As Nyri recovered, her thoughts untangled. She pushed herself into a sitting position and saw with a thrill that there was not just one, but two gathering baskets lying next to her, hidden beneath the undergrowth. *Where had they come from?*

The answer struck like a bolt of lightning. They were *hers*. The very baskets she had dropped when the *grishnaa* had attacked Omaal. Nyri descended on them, unable to believe most of her gathering was still there, untouched.

She had assumed when she hadn't returned for them straight away, maamits would have stripped the unprotected contents bare. Then Juaan and everything that had happened since that day had driven them from her mind. Ninmah Herself must have been watching over these baskets to offer a gift in her greatest time of need.

Or a test.

Nyri glanced around for Daajir, but he was a long way off, absorbed in gathering the moss from a tree for Kyaati's bower. He had detected nothing amiss with her.

Nyri turned back to the baskets. She knew the right thing to do; her people needed this food. She saw Haana's broken face in her mind's eye, begging Baarias for her starving daughter's life. Every day drew them closer to the brink. She should alert Daajir and carry these baskets back to the tribe in triumph. And yet...

A selfish thought flickered through her mind. She was failing. She and Juaan could not survive much longer on a single half ration. If she hadn't found these baskets, she would have succumbed right here on the forest floor. And if she succumbed, then so would Juaan. The vision of the green-eyed girl bearing the marks of the Kamaali danced before Nyri's eyes. Sefaan had said she must find her and she could not do that if she died of starvation—

"Nyri!" Daajir's voice broke into her deliberation. "I've

gathered as much as I can carry. Have you finished? That storm is about to break."

"Yes!" Nyri called back and made her choice right there. Staggering to her feet, she kicked the undergrowth back into place over the baskets and rushed to where Daajir stood, waiting.

"What were you looking at?" he asked.

"Nothing," Nyri said.

He raised an eyebrow, then shook his head, amused. "You are getting very strange, you know."

Nyri forced a laugh, shrugged, and walked on. They started back towards the tribe with their baskets of collected bedding. The other two baskets and their infinitely more precious load remained behind.

34

The Branch and the Mountain

Nyri did not sleep again that night. The storm that had been promised came. It lashed against her tree; the wind tearing through the branches. But the noise had nothing to do with her wakefulness. Her guilt raged louder than the storm. She tossed and turned in her bedding, unable to escape the torment.

She was frightening herself; her growing list of crimes marched relentlessly through her mind. She was disobeying her Elders; she was committing a sin against the Holy Creator herself; she had lied to Baarias and everyone she cared about, and now she was withholding vital resources. Nyri shuddered, wondering just how far into Ninsiku's damnation this path would take her.

As soon as the storm had blown itself out, she rose. She could not remain alone with her inner demons any longer. She needed to see him. She needed to look into his eyes and be reassured once again that what she was doing was right. That it was all worth it.

A chill mist had settled over the ground. Nyri's fingers

grew numb as she emerged from her tree and crept into the forest. She waited for the first sentry, but was not surprised when she found no one in place. The storm had driven everybody under shelter. They hadn't yet returned.

The trees dripped mournfully as Nyri made her way through, their branches hanging low. Even they seemed judgemental as she passed. She hunched her shoulders and hurried to where she had left the baskets. It was hard in the blanketing mist, but she found them. Nyri figured they would keep Juaan supplied for a good while. She would no longer have to starve herself to keep him supplied. Her conscience took a fresh battering. Her people were starving. By rights, these baskets should be *in* the stores.

Nyri picked them up and carried them with her. They weren't as full as she remembered; no doubt raided by maamits. She would have to smuggle them back to her tree and keep them safe from further pilfering.

Juaan had been oddly careful with her since she had healed his fingers, and Nyri felt awkward remembering how much emotion she had revealed to him on that visit. He avoided her eyes as she handed him his food. The time passed in almost silence. At least he appeared pleased by the increased ration.

"I have to leave now," she said as the sky turned grey. "I'm not sure when I can return. Things are about to get a little complicated." She still hadn't figured out the problem of having to look after both Juaan and Kyaati.

Nyri fancied she saw a flash of disappointment in his eyes, but knew that was just a figment of her wishful imagination.

"Why?" he asked.

She paused. Even now it was almost too hard to speak of.

Would he even care? "My... kinswoman lost her baby on the night your clan came—"

His frown interrupted her. "The girl who fell from the tree?"

"Yes," Nyri bit out, trying to push away the images his words evoked. It amazed her to feel another flash of remorse; perhaps he did care. She drew a breath. "I have been bound by my teacher to care for her. She cannot yet be left alone, she is grieving too deeply."

"Your teacher?"

"Yes. In the art of healing. Baarias—"

Nyri broke off when he let out a soft hiss. "Baarias? That is his name?"

"Y-yes. What of it?" She felt a stab of resentment. *He remembers Baarias, but not me?* The evil spell that the Woves had cast over him worked in strange ways indeed.

He just shrugged and began running the fingers of his left hand back and forth across the finger that had been broken, deep in thought. "He must be a skilful master."

"Yes, he is," Nyri said. His behaviour confused her but knew from his expression that she would get no further, not today. She had to leave. "I promise I will come back. Wait for me."

He did not answer, still lost in contemplation.

Nyri left him and set out towards home, hefting her two baskets upon her back. It was time for her to take over Kyaati's care and all the difficulties that would entail. She had to run some of the way, still being careful not to be detected.

When she reached the borders of her home, her heart plummeted. Everywhere she probed, sentries hid, waiting for anything that might approach or pass them by. Around and around Nyri circled, looking for an opening in their defence.

There wasn't one, and there was nothing that she could use this time. Not a single maamit quivered on the edges of her senses, just a couple of roosting birds, and they would not get her very far. She had been practising at hiding her presence, but she doubted her skills were yet strong enough to get her past four of her people. Nyri sank down on her haunches and put her head in her hands.

Golden light was now touching the ground. Baarias would be awake and wondering why she was not there to collect Kyaati. *Where are you, Sefaan?* But Sefaan was not coming to her aid this time.

There was nothing for it. Nyri crept forward, hoping her improving skills would be enough.

"Who's there?" Imaani's voice snapped out.

Nyri froze, scrunching her eyes shut. That answered that question. Her skills were woefully inadequate; they knew somebody was here.

"Over there," another voice answered a question. "Something moved."

They began to converge on her position.

It was no use. The baskets she carried felt like flamboyant birds displaying themselves upon her back, announcing their presence to the world.

Nyri was preparing to turn tail and flee when the tension was shattered by a sharp whistle of alert from further off inside the forest.

"Woves!" Nyri heard Imaani hiss. "They've breached the border again!"

"Where?" Raanya asked.

"That was Javaan's signal. They're coming from the west. Warn the tribe. I will help Javaan track them."

Both sentries dodged away. Nyri's heart was in her throat. She had to fight the urge to run back to the Pit. The Woves were hunting again. Looking for him. What if they found him this time? Nyri twitched, almost dropping her baskets. She stopped herself before she could make the foolish move. Even if she went back to him, there would be nothing she could do. All she could do was hold tight.

Going against her will, Nyri ran forward, ducking between the trees, keeping her head low until she was back in the confines of the *eshaara* grove.

She wove around the edges of home, staying out of sight until she reached her tree and swung herself up into the branches. She stuffed the gathering baskets into her bower and buried them in the moss of her bedding.

Breathless, she glanced out of her tree. The tribe was gathering around as Raanya talked with Aardn far below. Nyri bolted back to earth in time to gather with her people. For better or worse, she needed to know what was happening. "Go, Raanya!" Aardn was saying. "We need as many eyes on them as possible!"

The Elder faced the rest of their fearful gazes. "We will wait. They have crossed the border many times now and have not come near. I can't see why this time would be any different. Stay close and keep alert. We will trust in the sentries to alert us to danger."

Please. Nyri prayed to Ninmah. *Please don't let them find him.* After everything she had gone through, this could not be the end. She would live one moment to the next on the edge until the sentries gave the all clear.

Baarias was expecting her when she arrived in his tree. He was sitting inside his favourite chamber, bundling his precious roots and herbs. "I'm sorry I've taken so long, Baarias."

He nodded, his face tense. "They're in the forest again."

The reality of the Woves' presence hit Nyri afresh, and she leaned back against a wall for support, breathing against her rising panic. If they found Juaan... it was all over. *Ninmah, please!*

Baarias was at her side in an instant, the breach between them disappearing for a few moments. "Nyri, Nyri, do not fear. The sentries are watching them. They are not coming here. They are searching in the west. Do not fear."

Nyri continued to take long breaths, trying to control the cold sweat that had broken out over her body. To the west. They were a long way from Juaan. Her breathing came more easily.

She reached a hand out to Baarias, attempting a shaky smile, relieved by the closure of the distance between them, however brief. "I'm alright. Just give me a moment."

"Are you sure you're fit to take on Kyaati today?"

"Yes." Nyri straightened up. "I will do my duty, Baarias." She needed to do something to make up in some small way for her crimes. "Does she know?"

"Yes, she does," Kyaati answered for herself, appearing from the other chamber. Her tone was peevish.

"How are you feeling?" Baarias asked.

The look in her tribe-sister's eyes chilled Nyri.

"Have you eaten?"

Again, silence. She gave an almost imperceptible shrug

before her eyes found Nyri's. "So, you're the one who is going to babysit me." She slumped down beside Baarias and stared up at Nyri with her pale eyes, silver hair hanging limp and lifeless around her face.

Nyri was stricken by the sight of how painfully thin she looked, not even feeling the sting of her words or the hostility rolling from her. Baarias sighed. "She's not babysitting you, Kyaati."

"Oh yes, she is. I wish everyone would just leave me alone."

"Kyaati, *please*." Baarias pressed his fingers into his eyes. "Alone is not good. You need your kin around you."

"For as long as they'll all last."

"Enough! I am the healer of this tribe, and you will respect my judgement. You will stay with Nyriaana until such a time as I see fit. Now, Nyri, come with me, I need to speak with you."

With an effort, Nyri tore her thoughts away from what might be happening in the outer forest with the Woves and moved with Baarias into the next chamber. She noted he was careful to keep Kyaati firmly in his sight. He caught her wrist. *Never let her out of your sight. Not for a moment. I'm trusting you with this task, Nyriaana. I dislike what I feel there.*

What do you mean? Nyri asked, a new foreboding starting in the pit of her stomach.

I don't know. It's just a feeling. Never *leave her alone.*

Nyri hesitated. To promise him that would mean lying to him again. Another piece of her soul tore loose at the thought. She should tell Baarias she couldn't be the one to take care of Kyaati. She couldn't fulfil even her first need. If they survived this latest Wove raid unscathed, she could hardly take Kyaati with her to the Pits to break fruit with

Juaan every day. But to refuse would mean explaining her reasons for being an unsuitable carer.

Instead, she imagined telling Baarias she had found Juaan, but he had become their enemy, that she was the thief and was making her people suffer in favour of a Forbidden abomination, all because of some vague vision from the Great Spirit. Nyri shuddered. She had no choice. Nyri had to lie to him and face walking the thinnest of branches, hoping she didn't fall one way or the other. *I promise I won't leave her alone, Baarias,* she swore.

He smiled. *I... have always been able to count on you, Nyri. Between us, we will bring her back. I am sure of it.*

She squeezed his hand, but could not meet his eyes.

The sentries returned when Ninmah was at her zenith and reported that once again the Woves had left the forest. They had followed the same pattern, breach and retreat, except this time only one beast had crossed the border instead of the usual pair. This news mattered little to Nyri; they had left the forest empty-handed, and that was all she cared about.

She left Baarias' dwelling sometime later in the company of the sullen Kyaati. She was almost afraid to be alone with her. She did not know what to say. Kyaati remained closed, her feelings frighteningly silent. Nyri tried to provoke one or two conversations, but each one fell on deaf ears. There were not that many topics open to her at present that would lighten anyone's mood, much less Kyaati's and Nyri was the furthest she could be from feeling lighthearted. This was going to be a hard time for both of them.

How could Nyri even attempt to remove that empty look from Kyaati's eyes, the void that should have been filled with the love for a child? The answer was simple. She could not.

And she did not know of anyone who could. Helplessness threatened to drown her. She had lost Juaan, and she had lost Kyaati, too. It felt like she was dragging them both up a mountain with their heels dug in.

Nyri would just have to keep her eyes on her feet, not on the climb, follow her instincts and hope Kyaati found some reason to live again. Unless, of course, the Woves came back to finish them first or starvation took them mid-Fury. Nyri shook her head. She needed to banish such thoughts if she was to be any sort of rock to Kyaati during her fragile time.

Nyri set Kyaati to work mending old clothes and gathering baskets, they went to the river to wash, anything Nyri could think of to keep Kyaati from lapsing into a hopeless stupor and to keep her own mind from dwelling on the morning's events and the damning food inside her tree.

Nyri worried Juaan would go back on his word and attempt to escape again, that he might guess that the Woves were searching for him. She had to trust that he would keep his promise.

She set her mind to the problem of how she was going to get away from Kyaati to visit him again. The dead of night would have to be her only opportunity to see him now, when she could be sure Kyaati was sleeping and safe to leave.

Nyri resigned herself to no sleep as well as almost no food. The thin branch rattled beneath her feet, threatening to throw her already.

The day was drawing dusk behind it when Nyri ran out of tasks. Kyaati appeared exhausted, though no more talkative. Nyri herself struggled to keep her eyes open. She had been awake since before Ninmah's rise and hadn't eaten since then either. She was steering them back towards her tree

343

when Daajir appeared at their sides. Nyri almost groaned out loud.

His energy felt odd, and it took her a moment to understand why. It hit Nyri that he was the only person she had seen today who did not have an aura of despair or outright fear clinging to him. Quite the opposite. Did she sense... hope? Nyri tilted her head, wondering what he could be concocting for the Elders and why it gave him such purpose. He caught her unguarded thoughts and grinned.

"Not yet, Nyriaana," he said. "Just know that was the last raid they will walk away from."

Nyri was too tired to wonder or give him the satisfaction of her curiosity. She knew there was nothing Daajir could do to protect them, but she would leave him to his delusions.

He held out a hand to Kyaati. "How are you feeling?"

Oh, no. Dar! Nyri cringed. Kyaati ignored his hand, and Nyri felt a stab of hurt and annoyance from Daajir as her rejection wounded his pride. "Baarias has given the task of watching me to Nyriaana. I do not need two caretakers, thank you." She walked past him and started up into Nyri's tree.

"Wha—" The fool went up after her. Nyri put her hands on her hips. Did she have no privacy now? Then she blanched as she thought of what she had hidden inside her home. She hoped she had been thorough enough in hiding the baskets. That morning, she had been in no fit state of mind. She jumped into the tree behind the other two. If Daajir found them...

"Well, forgive me for being concerned!" Daajir was snapping at Kyaati when she caught up with them. Nyri moved to stand in front of her bower to hide any signs she might have missed.

"I'm tired of everyone's concern," Kyaati was sitting on her newly made resting place, slender arms wrapped around her thin chest. "No one, not one of you can bring my baby back." Tears started in her eyes. She hid her face in her hands, gulping the air. "When will you understand I don't want any of you! I want *her*!"

Nyri could sense a storm was about to break.

So could Daajir. He held up his hands, backing up a step. "I'm sorry, Kyaati, I just wanted to see if there was anything you needed. I want you to look forward again. Think of the future, not back at the past. Have faith that Ninmah—"

"Faith is for the faithful, Daajir." Her voice was dead. "I have none. I do not believe in anything anymore." She turned her face away and rolled over, giving them her back. Daajir stood there helpless and not a little upset by her continued rebuff.

Nyri put a hand on his arm. *Patience,* she thought to him, *she's hurting so badly.*

He turned his dark eyes on her. Patience was not one of his strengths. *She needs to stop this. She could have more children. It's not the end of the world.*

Nyri drew a sharp breath. *You are such an insensitive boar, sometimes! You really are. Have you no empathy? She lost her* baby, *not a toy.*

"Huh." He turned away and started to step around her towards her bower.

"Hey!" she said, putting a hand on his chest. "What are you doing?"

His gaze roved around the inside of the tree. "Aardn has ordered a search of the trees to try to catch whoever is hoarding food. That is what I came here to do. We must catch the thief."

Nyri's blood ran cold. "And… you are going to search now?"

"Yes." He tried to move around her again. Nyri blocked his path a second time, her mouth dry. If Daajir found the gathering baskets hidden within her bower, she was finished. Baarias could not protect her this time.

"Daajir." She struggled to keep the panic from her voice and inject the right amount of indignation. "Do you really believe I am the thief? How could you even *think* that of me?"

"It does not matter what I believe, Nyri," he said. "Aardn told me to search every home, no exceptions."

"Daajir, please, be reasonable. You have been with me every day, inside this tree making the bower. You would have seen if I had been hoarding food. I am *not* the thief. Please, Daajir, Kyaati needs her rest." She pressed her hand to his shoulder. *She is very fragile. Please don't upset her anymore.*

He hesitated, thinking through her logic. His eyes flickered to where Kyaati lay, distant and brooding, and he relented. "Fine, I suppose you're right." He looked Nyri up and down. "The thief certainly would look better fed than you do right now. I'm sorry."

"Forget it," Nyri said, willing to say anything to get him to leave. "Thank you for understanding, Dar."

"Here." He shoved two small honey fruits into Nyri's hand. "I brought these for the two of you." He turned his face away, cheeks flaming.

"Thank you," Nyri said, this time with genuine gratitude.

"How did you get so much?"

"It's the whole of my ration for the last two days, I've been saving it."

Nyri tried to push the fruit back into his hand, but he backed away.

"Take it. I want you to have it. You two look like you need it more than me. I can't lose you—" he cut himself off, blinking hard.

This rare show of emotion took Nyri aback. "Thank you," she said again and, without thinking, leaned up to kiss his cheek.

Daajir's eyes burned with sudden elation. With an unpleasant jolt, Nyri realised what she had done and grew uncomfortable. The silence stretched, and she watched as Daajir became acutely aware that he was in the home of two Unjoined women about to prepare for sleep.

"Goodnight, Dar," Nyri said, flicking her eyes towards the way down.

"Ah, yes, sleep well," he said, flushing again as he took his leave.

She couldn't help but smirk as she turned to Kyaati. It wasn't often Daajir got embarrassed.

"You shouldn't have done that," Kyaati murmured as Nyri handed her one of the fruits. "You shouldn't encourage him. Remember what I told you before. He is the greatest danger to us. The Elders cannot afford to waste our strength and he is the strongest... Daajir knows it. He is simply waiting. He wishes to have one of us for his own."

Nyri shuddered as she thought back to the night Aardn had walked with her. She had done her best to lose herself in other worries so she wouldn't have to face what the Elder had promised. "It's not Daajir's fault, Kyaati. He's just trying to look out for us."

"Nyri, all Daajir really cares about is Daajir and the glory of the lost past. He is prime Elder material. The rest of us are just leaves in the wind to him. I see it. He'll be in full agreement with the Elders when they make their ruling. He will not think twice of our feelings."

Nyri knew deep down that Kyaati was right. "No," she said. "I will not let them do it to us. I won't let them do it to you."

Her tribe-sister smiled wanly. "Oh, how I wish..." she whispered as exhaustion caught her and she drifted into unconsciousness.

Nyri rolled the fruit Daajir had given her between her hands. Hungry as she was, she couldn't eat. Nyri put the fruit aside to supplement Juaan's stash and curled up into her own bower, wishing she could find the peace she needed.

She had been foolish and vowed not to give Daajir even the slightest encouragement from now on. She would not accept any more gifts. She would not, *could* not, become his mate. Nyri cringed even as she drifted towards oblivion, imagining how Daajir would react if he ever found out the gift he had just given would keep a Forbidden alive for another day...

35

Shaken

"Nyriaana, stop this foolishness."

The voice was angry. Nyri did not care. She was angrier and they would not win. Her mama was gone. But before she had joined the Great Spirit, she had made Juaan promise to take care of her. They had promised to take care of each other, and this was the third time the Elders had dragged her away.

Nyri lay weakly upon the pile of moss. Pelaan pushed the fruit towards her. Her stomach growled. She was starving, but she would not take anything they offered. She did not want them to care for her. That was not what her mama had wanted. She rolled over, turning her back. She thought of Juaan alone in their tree without her. She saw again the pain in his eyes as they had dragged her away again, knowing he was powerless to stop them. Tears slipped down her face. Why couldn't they just leave them alone?

"You will not change her mind, Pelaan." It was the healer's voice. Baarias' tone was heavy.

"I must," the Elder's voice rang with determination but Nyri

349

was pleased to hear a vibration of doubt. "It's for her own good. It's what my brother would have wanted. I owe it to him. I must protect her from herself."

"She's not seeing it that way, I'm afraid."

"I did not ask for your opinion, master akaab. I called you here because she is sick. What do you make of it?"

There was a sigh, and Baarias came forward to examine her. She balled up stubbornly, hindering his examination. Go away! *She fancied she felt a brief flash of amusement at her antics before it disappeared beneath a wave of concern.*

"There is nothing wrong with her except severe malnutrition. Pelaan, if you don't give this up soon, she will succumb."

Silence.

"Let her go back to the boy."

"It's not a boy!" The Elder spat. "She is not safe."

"She seems to have done well enough in his care so far. Better than she is now, at any rate. I keep a close eye. Accept that you cannot control this, Pelaan. You are not going to break her will."

"I cannot accept it!"

"You must. Forgive me, Elder, but you are going to lose her. Are you willing to risk that?"

Nyri felt the storm of Pelaan's frustration. It battered against the truth Baarias had just laid bare before him. For it was true, she would die before she let them separate her from Juaan.

The storm blew out. Pelaan conceded. "Very well," he growled. "She is a foolish child, just like her mother. I have my own to look out for. She may return to the Forbidden... for now."

Weak as she was, Nyri grinned to herself. She had won. She knew now they would think twice before taking her away again. She and Juaan could stay together forever! Happy in her triumph, she let herself drift to sleep. She really was very tired...

* * *

Nyri rolled over with a groan after what felt like mere moments. Ninsiku's squinting eye was riding high overhead. It was time. She rose silently, cursing in her exhaustion that she had a Forbidden in her care that needed feeding. Kyaati was still sleeping. It wouldn't hurt to leave her now.

To be sure, Nyri touched her fingers to her friend's temples and pushed her into a deeper level of unconsciousness. Reassured that she would not wake, Nyri stole from her tree and into the black outer forest, flitting around the patches of silver light where Ninsiku's searching stare touched the ground. Dangerous.

It took her longer to reach the Pit than usual. The sentries were even more vigilant at night than they were in the early morning. There were tense moments where Nyri could do no more than lie low in the undergrowth until the eyes of a watcher had moved away. Her practice was paying off, however, and finally she got away.

"Juaan," she whispered into the surrounding blackness of the Pit once she had climbed down. He was cloaked to her, his presence too murky to pinpoint. "Juaan?"

"Khalvir." His voice floated from the darkness. Bodiless. The hairs rose on Nyri's neck. His voice was deeper than any man of her tribe. It had never bothered her until this moment. Detached from the sight of his familiar face, the sound of it was terrifying. The only voice she had heard deeper than this...

Suddenly, Nyri was back inside another dark night. She could almost smell the smoke, feel the sear of heat on her flesh… *you do nicely…* Nyri shivered as her skin crawled over her body. She balled her trembling hands into fists, screwing her eyes shut against the memory of the Wove demon.

A touch on her shoulder made her flinch and almost cry out.

"It's all right," the deep voice said. Nyri spun around and stared up into green eyes. The fear fled. Quite suddenly, she felt as safe as anyone could ever be. "Don't be alarmed, elf. I promised I would not hurt you." He lifted his long hand away from Nyri's shoulder and held both up in the air to demonstrate his meaning.

She recovered herself. "Nyri."

"Khalvir, then." He turned away, morphing into the blackness once more. Nyri heard the soft scraping of rock that told her he had lowered himself to the ground. She followed carefully. Not carefully enough. She trod on something soft. "That was my foot."

"Well," Nyri danced backwards and landed the soft part of her foot on a loose stone. "Ow! Don't clothe yourself in damned black, then."

A soft noise. He was chuckling to himself. "I have little choice, really. It's that or go naked down here."

Nyri flushed. "If you were Ninkuraaja, I'd know exactly where every part of you was without having to see you."

"Truly?" He sounded intrigued. "You cannot sense me, then?"

"Well, I can, but not exactly." Nyri sank down, as close to him as she dared. "It's like a part of you… an energy… for want of a better word, is not there or lies dormant, if you see what I mean."

"Not really."

She sighed. "It is hard to explain. How do you describe seeing to a blind man?"

"How indeed." Nyri could feel him appraising her in the dark. She could barely see him. Experimenting, she pulled out the gora root she had brought and held it out to the darkness. He took it deftly from her fingers, confirming that his eyes were far superior to hers.

"Not this again," he complained.

"Eat and be grateful."

He grumbled to himself, but chewed in silence. She guessed he had learned that food was a subject best left alone.

A strange chirping whistle came floating through the air. Nyri lifted her head. "What is that?" she wondered out loud, listening for it again. "I've never heard such a bird before." A memory tugged, and Nyri realised she *had* heard it once before, days ago, as she had left the Pit. This must be the new bird that Javaan had spoken of.

Juaan shrugged, hunching deeper into himself, and made no answer.

"So, what have you been up to today?" Nyri cringed as soon as the words were out. What a ridiculous question. But the silence had stretched, and she had felt compelled to break it.

"Not climbing if that's what you're worried about." She could almost see the sardonic twist to his mouth.

Nyri snorted. "I'm always worried. You're just the latest on top of a great pile of concerns."

A sudden howl split the air in the distance, long, mournful and piercing. Juaan was on his feet in an instant, but Nyri remained seated, unperturbed.

"It's only the wolves," she murmured. "They are hunting."

"That's what scares me." Nyri could feel his tension faintly on the air.

"They do not hunt us. The wolves, like every Child of the Great Spirit of KI, are our cousins and teachers. They do no harm."

"Not to you, perhaps, with your witch magic. But I have known those beasts to take the old and the very young and devour them if the strong are not watchful. They are one of our most bitter enemies and we will kill them in turn."

The cold telling of such savagery sickened Nyri. "The Woves are the unnatural creation of Ninsiku. I'm not surprised KI sends his Children to kill them. All of Ninsiku's creations are bloodthirsty abominations. They are not the People of Ninmah. They do not have the Gift. They do not hear."

"So all the losses we have suffered are our own fault? Just for being who we are? Typical elf. Such creatures are monsters who cannot be reasoned with, only their savage hunger drives them. They cannot speak. They do not think!"

"Of course they do! They speak with the voice and truth of the earth. How can you look at everything around you and say there is no thought behind it? The world is alive with the greatest of intelligence. We are blind to it unless we learn to use Ninmah's Gift to us. The Woves are the ones who do not know how to speak. They are abominations on the earth and they have blinded you, too. You *used* to understand."

He ignored the allusion to his forgotten past, as was becoming his wont. "Who is this KI?" he asked instead. "And Ninmah and Ninsiku? More elven superstition?"

354

One part of her hated his disrespectful tone. He was a complete stranger to her in these instances, and she loathed it. It made her feel like Juaan was truly lost, replaced by her enemy, by Khalvir. The other part of Nyri jolted. "You do not know of Ninmah or Ninsiku?" That was not possible. They were the very fabric of the heavens. She wondered if he could be trying to trick her. "You do not know who Ninsiku is? He is the very power that created the Woves."

"Well, if he did, he's kept silent about it."

Nyri got to her feet and paced the dark. He was lying. He must be lying. *But why?*

"What's wrong?" he asked.

"You *must* know Ninsiku," Nyri hissed. "It is the Woves who give him his power. It is they who are providing him with the strength to overthrow Ninmah, to wipe us out, and bring about the End of Days where eternal cold and darkness hold sway." Nyri had always believed this truth with all her heart, learned from her first breaths. Baarias' words came whispering back to her. Niggling. She shook her head to clear it. No, Juaan was lying and Baarias was wrong. The Woves were demons.

He shook his head. "I have never heard of Ninsiku. We do not do his bidding, nor do we worship him."

"Then *why* are we suffering?" She burst out. "It has only happened since the Woves arrived. If Ninsiku does not command them, why do they hunt us? Why do they come and take our young to devour in the night?"

He gave a short, incredulous laugh. "We do not 'devour' you. What a ridiculous notion. Is that what you believe?"

"What else are we supposed to believe?" Nyri shot back. "The Woves come. They sacrifice our homes to their burning spirits. They kill and kidnap. Flesh eaters! If they do not devour us, if Ninsiku does not send them, why do they come?"

He was silent for a while, studying his hands. "You truly do not know?"

"What is there to know? All we know is that they come and kill us."

He shook his head again and dropped his hands. "Please, sit," his voice was placating now. "Talk to me. Who is KI? We know little of your superstitions."

Nyri stared suspiciously in his direction, trying to calm herself down. "That's a very long story," she growled out, irritated.

He snorted. "It's not like I've got anywhere to go, thanks to you. What do you think I have to do between your little visits? At least give me something to think about."

Nyri sighed. Try as she might, she could not see what harm it would do to humour him a little. He must be lonely down here, Nyri realised. Whenever she left him, she had so much else to think about. He was right. What did he have to do but sit and stare at these stone walls awaiting his captor's return? She glanced upwards. The night air was sharp. Ninmah's rise was still far off.

"Is KI your People's guiding light?" he prompted.

"KI is everything," Nyri replied, settling back down by his side. Her tone became hushed as she spoke. "He is the Great Spirit of the earth. He exists in the rocks and the ground beneath our feet, flowing in great Rivers that criss-cross the land, guiding his Children on their journeys. He lives in the trees that surround us. He moves as the wolf and the deer. He is Life itself."

"Ah," he said thoughtfully. "And how do you know this? Do you see him?"

"*Feel* him is probably a better way to speak of it. Though… when I am still, with my eyes closed, he usually appears as a golden energy flowing through everything that exists. He can be felt the strongest when close to the Rivers. This forest lies along one such Line. Everything is a part of the great power that flows through the earth."

"Interesting," he murmured. "Does that include you and I?"

Nyri shook her head. "We are different. We are not the Great Spirit's children. The Ninkuraaja are the People of Ninmah, the great Queen and Healer and She made the essence of the Great Spirit a part of us. She alone knew how to give her People Sight. Only by using Ninmah's Gift are we able to glimpse the Great Spirit, to learn and look after his secrets. Ninmah made us for that purpose."

"Ninmah's gift?"

Nyri pinched the bridge of her nose. She would have to tell the entire tale. Settling herself as comfortably as possible, she began. He listened to the story of her people's beginnings. He was a surprisingly good audience, and Nyri enjoyed weaving the tale for him. She found the tension leaving her. It was as much of a distraction for her as much as it was for him. Nyri sang the song of how Ninmah brought the first Ninkuraa, Ninsaar, into being. It was her favourite.

"Ninmah's Gift is our higher being," Nyri concluded, "a connection between mind and soul. Ninmah showed us how to reach out to the Children of the Great Spirit and his world by using his essence to create the Ninkuraaja soul." Nyri placed a hand over her heart. "We are blessed to hear the Great Spirit's song."

Nyri could just make out his face in the dimness. He almost looked like her Juaan sitting there, watching her with a faint smile. For the first time, his face was devoid of suspicion or hostility. His voice was filled with a soft wonder that was for her alone. "You tell a good story. It's... nice... listening to your voice."

Unable to take her eyes from his, Nyri's fingers tingled with the need to reach out and touch his face. She saw his hand twitch where it lay next to him on the ground, and Nyri fancied he was fighting the same compulsion. Her breath caught.

In the distance, the wolves were still singing. "Listen," she said, tearing her gaze away as the pack's voices came together in a harmonious cacophony. The power and the wildness of it thrilled through her heart. The hairs prickled on her skin. "It's beautiful, isn't it? Can't you hear Him?"

"No," he whispered back, his voice strangely rough. "You said we *Woves* are Ninsiku's creation? And you believe us to be evil."

Nyri gave a firm nod. "Yes, they are. Ninmah's brethren created their own Peoples, but they were born Blind. They could not know the Great Spirit, and so they were made powerful in other ways. Ninsiku was Ninmah's mate, and he grew full of jealousy and spite. He created the Woves with dark energies to oppose Ninmah's People. They are nothing but evil spirits clothed in flesh."

"I suppose I can see why you would believe that." He looked Nyri in the eye. "And what do you think now? Do you still see me as an evil spirit clothed in flesh? I am one of your *Woves*. What do you think now?"

Nyri shook her head. "You are no Wove, Juaan. They took you and made you their servant. Your mother was Ninkuraaja. Your father was…" Nyri trailed off, frowning. A Cro, he had claimed once. She did not know who they were. She thought of the girl in her vision, Ariyaana, her features so strikingly similar to Juaan's own. Nyri realised that she too must carry the blood of this mysterious race. Perhaps if Nyri could find out who they were, she would know where to look for the girl.

Juaan had turned his face to the sky at her mention of his true beginnings. He was still refusing to believe her version of his past. "What became of Ninsiku and Ninmah?" he asked, changing the subject before it led to an argument.

"Ninsiku came to destroy us, and Ninmah fought him. The power of their battle would have destroyed the earth. Ninmah saw that the only way to make us safe was to leave with Her erstwhile mate. She imprisoned him in the heavens and exiled Herself along with him to hold his dark power in balance. For time out of memory, they have continued to chase one another through the sky. Ninmah's spirit appears as the Golden Mother by day until She has to give way to Ninsiku. The night is his." Nyri pointed warily to the silver disc in the sky. "His eye watches us in the darkness, surrounded by the lights of the souls he has stolen. We are best to avoid him lest he see us and send his dark servants."

Juaan rose to his feet. Nyri heard the softest of footsteps before he stepped into a pool of Ninsiku's light that had spilled into the Pit. He was bathed in silver, every feature thrown into sharp, haunting relief. Where there usually sat the beloved green eyes, there were now only emotionless pits, making him appear like a true skull-headed Wove. Nyri shrank away, fearful.

"This is your Ninsiku?" He raised a hand before him, studying the play of light and dark upon it.

"Yes," Nyri whispered. "He sees all. Ready to steal away the unwary."

Juaan frowned and moved out of the chilling light with a shrug. "Best not to be caught in his stare then." He sat beside her again, closer this time. "I never realised what interesting beliefs you elves had."

"What beliefs do the Woves have?" Nyri whispered. "What powers do they possess?" He had not heard of Ninsiku. Perhaps the Woves knew him by a different name.

Juaan was silent for a long time, considering. "Our beliefs are not entirely dissimilar. We believe that gods that came from the sky created our People. Ea created our People to serve him as Ninhursag, his twin sister of the Sky, created yours. But unlike you, we don't believe our creators left for our best interests.

"In our legends, they left to live in the mountains where no man can tread and forsook all contact, aside from descending occasionally to kidnap women. We had grown tiresome to them. Yet still we continued to cling loyally to the wisdom they had taught us for many generations.

"But then the Great Winter of Sorrow came and nearly wiped us all out. Ea did not return. Lost and without hope, we turned our backs on the teachings of the traitorous gods. It served us well, and we have grown strong enough to survive without them. But now, once again, the world is shifting." Juaan gave a bitter laugh, and his expression grew sad. "I'm sorry to shatter your cosy illusion of blame, but we have no power to lend a supposed god who brings the cold, elf. We pray for Ninmah, as you call her, to regain strength and push back the winter. But she does not listen any more than Ea.

"Perhaps we are being punished for having the audacity to survive when they clearly did not wish it but, either way, I fear the world we know is dying and there is nothing that you or I or anyone else can do to stop it."

Nyri did not respond. It was all too much to take in. What he had just revealed went against everything she had ever been taught. Now, as she listened to the wolves' song, she tried to cling to what she heard there. A single point of focus in the turmoil of uncertainty.

* * *

Kyaati opened her eyes. It was dark, but she knew in an instant that Nyri was gone. Her friend had attempted to push her into a deeper sleep, but that suggestion had been easy to throw off. Nyriaana had been distracted.

She wondered idly at her friend's whereabouts and what could be so important to make her take off into the night before realising that she did not care. Nothing mattered anymore.

Wrapping her arms around her empty chest, Kyaati pushed herself from the bower Nyri had made for her. She was alone at last; free to do as she wished without someone hovering, someone incessantly trying to convince her that there were things in this worthless world still to live for. She had tried to stop the relentless beat of her own heart, but her body's keen sense of self-preservation thwarted her efforts every time.

Kyaati wandered back and forth, not really seeing where her feet were taking her until she found herself poised at the entrance to Nyri's home. She leaned over, peering down at the ground far below.

Her numb heart leaped. It would be so easy, so easy to take one more step. The void beckoned, offering release. Kyaati lifted a foot and her balance wavered.

She cried out softly, adrenaline shooting through her fingers as she caught the side of the tree, steadying herself before stepping quickly back into the dark chamber. Her courage was not great enough. Not tonight.

Not yet. Soon, but not yet.

Tightening her arms over her chest, Kyaati returned to the bower.

* * *

36

Eyes Open

"*Juaan!*" *Nyri called. "Where are you?"*

His muted essence had led her to the edges of the eshaara *grove, right to the foot of an abandoned tree. Juaan was above. She scrambled up into the branches without hesitation.*

Inside, the tree was dark. The walls were damp and decaying. She could see that no one had lived here for a long time. Why would Juaan come here? Her eyes roved around the unfamiliar space. The leaves and moss inside the one small bower had rotted away. The girru moss on the walls was long gone.

By and by, Nyri's eyes lighted on different objects. Unfamiliar objects. The walls were covered in carvings. Never had she seen such things; no other Ninkuraaja dwelling had them. No Ninkuraa would dare defile a tree so. Nyri frowned disapprovingly.

The most prominent carving was that of a mother and baby. She started forward to take a closer look, but almost tripped as her feet became tangled in something hairy and coarse. Nyri danced backwards to save herself, and she bit back a cry when she saw what had hindered her. It was a skin. The fur of the dead animal was thick and dark brown, though much of it had fallen out in patches. It had been fashioned into some sort of sling. Nyri reached out to touch it with flinching fingers. Poor thing.

A soft murmur from the far side of the tree drew her attention. Juaan was sitting propped against the rough wall. He was asleep, the tracks of tears drying upon his face. Nyri stepped around the skin sling but stopped short at the sight of what her friend clutched to him in unconsciousness.

A spear. The weapon looked similar to those carried by the Woves. Nyri recoiled. The unnaturally shaped branch that formed the shaft was stout and long. She would not be able to get her hands around it. Near the top were bands of strange carvings. She took another step back. What was Juaan doing with such a thing?

At that moment, he woke. His eyes widened when he saw her standing there and hastily tried to push the spear he held into a pile of leaves. He gave up just as quickly, shoulders slumping in defeat.

"What are you doing here, Nyriaana," he growled, his tone sullen.

"I-I wanted to be with you." She wrapped her arms around her chest. "It hurts. I miss my mama so much."

He looked up, anger warring with sorrow as he took in her face. Finally he blew out a long breath, his ire draining away; evidently, she was forgiven for intruding. He beckoned to her. "Come here."

Nyri hesitated, afraid, eyeing the spear in his hand.

"It's ok," he soothed. "It won't hurt you."

Nyri scooted to his other side, as far away from the weapon as she could get. Juaan put his arm around her shoulders and she leaned into him, letting his presence calm her. "What is this place?" she whispered.

"This was my mother's home. I come here sometimes."

Nyri gasped as she took in the tree with new eyes. Rebaa was a complete mystery to her. Seeing the inside of where she had lived only deepened the intrigue. Questions flew through her mind, questions she would never dare ask him.

"Do you miss your mama, Juaan?" she asked instead. "Is that why you come here?"

He sighed into her hair. "Yes. I don't think that will ever change."

Her eyes welled with tears at his words, despair adding itself to the pain in her heart. She had hoped he would tell her this agony would stop. She wanted it to stop. They were silent for a long moment, both lost in their memories of loved ones lost.

"What of your papa? Do you remember him?"

Juaan stiffened. "No."

"Who was he?" Again a forbidden subject, but she could not help herself.

"My mother told me he was a tribal chief."

"Oh!" Nyri was impressed. "Which tribe?"

He angled his face away. "Mother wouldn't speak of it much. She said they called themselves the Cro."

"The Cro? What are they?"

Juaan just shrugged, keeping his focus on the far wall.

Nyri studied him for a moment, and could tell by the set of his mouth that he would speak no more of it. She sighed in disappointment.

He shifted the spear in his other hand, and Nyri stiffened. "Why have you got a Wove weapon?"

He pulled it nearer, causing her to flinch away. "It isn't a Wove weapon," he said. "It was made by a Thal."

Curiosity held Nyri in its grip, and she dared to lean around Juaan to study the weapon more closely. The Thals passed by the forests sometimes, but did not bother her People.

"Where did you get it?"

"My mother gave it to me. It saved her life once. She seemed to think I may need it some day to save my own."

Nyri eyed the weapon. She couldn't imagine why Juaan would need such a thing.

Her friend rose to his feet, his face twisting as he fought to keep his emotions in check. "I need to leave here now." He turned to bury the spear back into the pile of leaves. "I have to keep this hidden. The Elders must never find it. This is our secret, Nyri. Promise me you will tell no one."

"I promise," she vowed, as they left the cold and abandoned tree. She could see how much all of this meant to Juaan. It was a part of him. She would never betray it.

As they walked hand in hand back towards home, Nyri's mind buzzed like a swarm of restless bees. Juaan's father was a tribal chief. And who on earth were the Cro?

"How did your mother get that spear?" she risked one last question. "Did a Thal give it to her? The Elders say all the other Peoples are not to be trusted. That they are vicious, only put on this earth to kill."

His voice when he answered was hard and bitter. "The Elders are wrong about many things, Nyriaana. Do not listen to all they say."

* * *

"When will you be back?" Juaan asked when Nyri rose to leave. The tone in his voice was one she had not heard before. It did not hold the bitter resentment it usually did. Instead, there was a note of longing.

The need to reach out and touch him was stronger than ever before. Nyri resisted, folding her fingers into fists. "When Ninsiku rises again, I will return." She could not bear the thought of being away from him any longer than that. "Wait for me."

A smile tugged at his lips. "For as long as these walls stand... Nyriaana." His face became serious. "Keep the wolves close."

Her heart had skipped a beat at the sound of her name on his lips, and she barely heard the rest of what he said. Dazed, Nyri clambered up her root, feeling his eyes on her back until she summited the wall of the Pit and disappeared.

She travelled a way into the trees, then paused, attempting to return her pulse to normal. *Nyriaana.* He had said her name. A shiver ran down her spine and it took her a moment to realise that she was standing with the most foolish grin stretching across her face. *Nyriaana.* Her smile widened.

She was so distracted that she almost missed the presence that brushed against her senses far to her right. Her smile vanished.

It was not the presence of a Ninkuraa.

Freezing in place, Nyri turned her head to the side and saw what her higher sense had already told her.

The dark, skull-headed figure of a Wove was waiting in the blackness.

Nyri dropped to her haunches in the undergrowth. Her fingers sank into the soft ground, tearing at it in her terror.

A Wove was in the woods and she was out here with it.

Why hadn't the sentries sounded the alarm? Adrenaline pumped through her veins, bringing every thought into sharp focus. Earlier that day, the Woves had broken their search pattern. They had sent only one of their number into the forest to search for Juaan. Nyri understood the reason for that now. That one had been a distraction, sent to keep the sentries distracted while the other invaded the forest unseen. And it had never left.

What was it doing? Trying to control her trembling, Nyri dared to lift her head to peer above the undergrowth.

The demon had vanished.

Nyri's heart thudded. She had thought seeing the Wove was bad enough, now she found that not seeing it was worse. At this very instant, it could be circling around behind her for the ambush. Nyri latched on to the tree beside her and leaped into the branches.

The height was natural, a comfort. Concealed in the boughs, Nyri made a search for her enemy. The darkness pressed in on her eyes as she strained to see. Tentatively, she stretched out with her senses, tasting the surrounding energies.

She found the demon in an instant, a muted presence against the vibrancy of the forest glowing around it. It was moving away from her. Moving towards the Pits.

No!

Once, she would have rejoiced in its direction and willed the demon to fall to its death in the hungry maws that awaited. Not now. She had to lead it off somehow.

Screwing up her courage, she followed her quarry along the swaying boughs; invisible as a tree cat above its head.

The Wove was tall. The typical dark furs covered it from head to foot. One scarred, dark-skinned hand was exposed as it clutched at its weapon. Nyri tried to make sense of it; sharpened prongs of a stag's antlers burst into a curving array from either side of the fist. The demon swung the strange weapon back and forth in a guarded motion, as though expecting an enemy to spring at any moment.

Such wariness had puzzled Nyri when she and Kyaati had first seen the Woves on that fateful night when Juaan had fallen into the Pit. Nothing could be more dangerous than the Woves themselves. Her time with Juaan had taught her the answer. They were superstitious of the *elf magic*.

A tight smile curled across her face. If it was elf magic this demon feared, then she would willingly give it a taste. *You are not getting anywhere near those Pits, monster!*

She drew the power of the Great Spirit to her. The trees and the essence of the earth readily lent her their strength. Drawing a breath, she prepared to do battle with the evil spirit dwelling inside Ninsiku's creation. Here stood a true Wove, the very creature who had stolen Juaan's memories and made him believe he was one of them.

She bared her teeth and unleashed her will.

And met nothing.

Startled, Nyri rocked back on her haunches. She reached out again and again, but there was nothing to feel. This creature before her felt no different to Juaan.

It was a trick. She hissed through her teeth. The power of Ninsiku was hidden somewhere, taunting her with its elusiveness. She gripped onto her branch, concentrating harder.

The cry that split the air shattered her focus. Nyri recoiled as the Wove before her doubled up. Another shout joined his and Nyri's eyes widened as a second, bigger Wove burst from concealment, its bony head crowned with ox horns. It flew to its stricken companion's side. There was no expression to be seen on the white face, but its energy vibrated with fear, fear for its *friend.*

Nyri watched the second figure pull an object from the first creature's belly and her shock deepened. It was a thorn as long and thick as her own finger. There was only one plant that grew such thorns, and they grew in this forest. The barbs of the carnivorous *vaash* plant. The barb that had pierced the Wove dripped red. Mortal red.

The second Wove flung the bloody barb down, grabbed its companion's arm and stumbled off into the night away from the Pits, disappearing into the blackness.

Nyri remained frozen, stunned and confused by what had just unfolded, until a sudden movement in her periphery brought her eyes around and she stiffened, shielding herself hastily. Sitting low, half hidden in the trees, was Daajir. Nyri stared as his hands lowered a long narrow object from his mouth; a mouth twisted in a wicked smile of satisfaction.

"Where have you been, Nyri?"

Nyri flinched at the sound of Kyaati's voice as it broke the stillness. It wasn't yet light, but to her dismay, Kyaati was lying awake, waiting in the shadows as she re-entered her home. Nyri guessed she must have been so exhausted when she woke, she hadn't pushed Kyaati into a deep enough sleep. She couldn't make that mistake again.

"I-I had to relieve myself," she mumbled as she threw herself down and buried herself in her bedding to hide the fact that she was still shaking. She was too overwhelmed by what she had witnessed to think of a better excuse. Kyaati didn't reply and to Nyri's relief her friend soon drifted back to sleep.

There would be no more sleep for her. Confusion smothered her brain like a cloying smoke. Daajir had been in the woods stalking the Woves and he had injured one. *Injured a Wove.* She rubbed her forehead, seeing again the second monster coming to the aid of its companion, same as any of her people would if a friend was in danger. Only... monsters should not have friends.

Nyri pinched the bridge of her nose. She felt like the roots of her teachings had been severed, and every belief she had clung to was withering away.

You must know Ninsiku...

I have never heard of Ninsiku. We do not do his bidding, nor do we worship him.

There was only one person she could talk to, and once Ninmah had at last peeked into the sky, Nyri rose and started for the healer's tree. The only problem was Kyaati. Nyri could not ask the questions she needed answers to in Kyaati's presence.

Baarias was already about his day, as Nyri knew he would be. He was organising the remedies he would need, drawing water for mixtures from the *aquilem* vines clinging to the walls of his home.

"Nyri," he greeted without looking up as he finished crushing the last handful of herbs into a basin. "You're early." He turned then to regard her and frowned. "What's wrong?"

Nyri could only imagine how pale and ragged she appeared, but she brushed him off. "It's nothing," she said.

371

"How did you rest, Kyaati?" Baarias turned to her silent companion. "Is Nyri's home to your liking?" He got a mere shrug in response. Her teacher pressed his lips together in disapproval. "Hmmm." He turned back to Nyri. "Nyri, please fetch us some food. And, don't worry, I told Imaani you would be coming." His lips twitched, but Nyri only grimaced at his words. Her almost capture at Imaani's hands was not a laughing matter. "Once we have eaten, there are a few matters we need to attend to."

Nyri toyed with her breakfast. She was anxious about raising her thoughts with her teacher but, at the same time, impatient for the opportunity to rise. Kyaati picked at as much as would appease Baarias. While he scolded her, Nyri used the unguarded moment to stash half of her ration inside her coverings.

She couldn't eat. She was too nervous, but also admitted that part of her self-denial was to ease the guilt she lived with. Eating even less than everyone else somehow made her feel like she was making amends for the food she had stolen and had now hidden from her people. She should suffer for what she was doing.

The rest of the morning passed without incident, but Nyri struggled to keep her mind on the tasks at hand. They were attending young Omaal, who was feeling unwell, when Nyri lapsed badly.

"Nyriaana!" Baarias had to snap his fingers at her. She jumped from her waking dream. He frowned, uncharacteristically sharp. "Go with Kyaati to fetch me some *haarif* herbs, quickly!"

The day did not improve after that. Nyri ended it miserable and frustrated. She needed sleep, and she needed clarity.

"What is wrong, Nyriaana?" Baarias asked her once they had returned to his dwelling, their duties complete.

It was now or never. Nyri glanced sideways at Kyaati, who had been busied with the task of tidying away Baarias' remedies. She did not appear to be paying attention. She hadn't truly been with them all day. Nyri was concerned she was getting worse, not better.

"I-I just wanted to ask you," Nyri hesitated, then the rest came out in a rush, "why you believe the Woves are not the demons the Elders convince us they are."

His hands tightened upon the gathering basket he was re-hanging. She could feel his reluctance and anxiety as he turned to face her. He was obviously assessing the risk of where this might lead. Nyri could not blame him. Their last exchange on this subject had not gone well.

"Why do you ask?"

Nyri ignored the question. "You truly believe that it is not the Woves unleashing the fury of Ninsiku upon us, don't you? That the Elders are wrong."

He shook his head. "Forgive me, Nyri. I should not have said what I did. Please forgive me."

"No! You were right to tell me. I want to know now, how is it you are so certain? What convinced you?" She had been so hell bent on convincing herself that Baarias was mistaken, that she had never given this one possibility much thought. The possibility that he *might* be right.

Juaan had said that the Woves did not worship Ninsiku. Indeed, Juaan claimed they prayed to Ninmah herself, prayed for the end of the cold times, just as the Ninkuraaja did. She wrestled with the concept.

Baarias had denied the Woves' central involvement in their People's downfall. So strongly convicted was he in this belief that he had been willing to challenge the Elders themselves. Nyri could scarcely guess his reasons, but she needed to know if she was to believe that what she had seen and heard last night was more than the trick of evil spirits.

Baarias' hands closed into fists, then relaxed. His eyes travelled to Kyaati before he took Nyri by the arm and pulled her into the adjacent chamber. He was agitated. "Why do you want to know such things, Nyriaana? When I tried to tell you before, you closed your eyes on me. You did not want to hear."

Nyri shifted her feet, ashamed of her previous behaviour. As he had so rightly said, she had been too wrapped up in her hatred of the Woves to listen. She still hated them very much. The misery they had brought to her people, demons or not, could never be forgiven. But her eyes were opening on impossible new truths, and no matter how much she might want to, she could not close them again. She *had* to know the truth.

"You told me to think," she told her teacher. "And I have. I have always trusted you, Baarias. Our Elders say they are leading us back to strength but everything they do just brings us further death and misery. Look at what has befallen Kyaati. How much more must we suffer? Something is wrong and I am ready now to listen to what you have to say."

He regarded her for a long moment. Nyri could still feel a reluctance, a secret he wasn't quite ready to impart.

"I don't know, Nyriaana," he said. "Maybe it is for the best that you keep your eyes shut, after all. You will only hate me for what I say, and such knowledge will only bring you misery and put you at risk. Nothing will ever change. My outburst at the auscult was a mistake. You were right. If the Elders ever found out that I—"

"Please, Baarias," Nyri begged. "I was the one who was wrong. You can't lose courage now. How did you come to be so certain that the Woves do not have the power to manipulate Ninsiku? How do you *know*? I promise I will not hate you for it."

"Do you? I would not be so quick to give a promise you may not be able to keep."

He could not know how making promises she could not keep had become the story of Nyri's life of late, but she frowned at his words, unsure of how to respond.

Baarias sat down upon the ground and motioned for Nyri to sit next to him; he was silent for a long time, deciding upon his words. At last, he spoke. "I had a couple of... encounters with the men we call Woves when I was a foolish young healer," he said. "This was back even before the raids began."

"And these encounters were enough to convince you?" Nyri said sceptically. There were few of her tribe she could name that had not had an 'encounter' with a Wove at some unfortunate point in their lives and they were still convinced that these men were the embodiment of evil, tendrils of Ninsiku, stalking the land and unbalancing all that was natural.

Baarias shifted, but his flash of discomfort was gone so fast Nyri thought she must have been mistaken. He rubbed his scarred jaw. "You do not remember my sister, do you?"

The question was not what she had expected. Surprised, Nyri shook her head. She only knew little pieces of what

Juaan had told her, and that wasn't very much.

"No, you wouldn't. She died when you were very young," he said. "But you already know that because that is how Juaan came to join your family. What you do not know is that Rebaa was taken by Wove raiders when she was a young girl. You have never been told this, the Elders forbade anyone to speak of it."

Nyri's shock reverberated through the air. Rebaa had been taken by *Woves*?

"She was taken many Blessings before you were born. The Woves... had taken up their special interest in our People by that time." His lips twisted around the words. "I thought I had lost her; all that was left of my family. I grieved. I was sure she was dead. But then... in the depths of a Fury, she returned to us. Half dead, she stumbled back into the trees carrying a green-eyed baby in her arms."

Juaan. Nyri struggled to find her voice. "How-how did she escape from the Woves?" Juaan's father must have rescued her. The Cro must be a powerful People indeed to defeat Woves. She thought of Ariyaana. A Forbidden. A Kamaali.

"She did not escape, Nyriaana. The Wove chief fell in love with her. He took Rebaa as his mate."

Baarias' words dropped like a rock inside Nyri's chest. The air was suddenly too thin. "A-and so... J-Juaan's father..."

"Was a Wove, yes."

Denial cleaved through the haze, and Nyri shot to her feet. "No! That *cannot* be! Juaan told me his father was part of a Cro clan. He can't—couldn't have been half Wove! Woves are demons," she clutched at the last straw, falling back on the security her lifelong teachings offered. "Demons can't sire children!"

"And therein lies the answer you seek, Nyri. Demons can't have children, and yet Juaan existed. What does that tell you?"

"Juaan never lied to me! His father was Cro!"

Baarias gave a humourless laugh. "My dear Nyriaana. The Woves *are* the Cro. He didn't have to lie. Wove is simply the name we gave them. They do not name themselves so."

The world seemed to tilt, turning itself over as the enormity of what Baarias was saying crashed down upon her. The Cro. The Woves. One and the same. Shades of Ninsiku, their bitterest enemies, the men who slaughtered her People. Juaan was one of *them*. The man she was trying to save at the expense of her family. Ariyaana. The Kamaali of the future. All Woves.

Why did you never tell me? But the answer to that was clear. Would she have been his friend if she had known he was a Son of Ninsiku? The same as those who were murdering her tribe, who had murdered her family? She did not know the answer to that question.

"Did Rebaa hate him?" Nyri finally forced between her teeth. "Did the chief take her against her will?"

"No," Baarias' eyes were overbright. "She loved him back. She loved him with all of her heart."

The words came as another stunning blow. A Ninkuraa falling in love with a Wove raider? It was not possible, an unnatural thing that went against everything her People believed in. Conceiving a *child* with him. A Forbidden act above all else. A betrayal of Ninmah. Nyri regained her voice and ran with the unbelievable scenario Baarias was painting. "Then... why did she leave him and return? Surely she knew what our People would think of her baby?"

"I learned after she stumbled back to us, barely alive, that monstrous beings from the distant mountains attacked the Wove tribe she was with. Juaan's father got Rebaa to safety and told her to run. She begged him to escape the bloodbath with her but he was the clan's chief, he could not leave his People. Rebaa escaped and after a horrendous journey that nearly killed her, she returned to the only other place of safety she knew.

"The Elders wanted to kill Juaan of course and tried to tear the baby from her. Dying though she was, she hung on to him. The Elders threatened to cast her back out if she did not give the baby up. They were adamant there could be no such stain on the tribe. She screamed for my help, but I could not. I could not. I was afraid. The beliefs of our People are too strong. The baby was sentenced to death."

"So what happened?" Nyri breathed. "Why were Juaan and his mother allowed to stay?" It seemed unbelievable now that Juaan had ever been a part of her life.

The ghost of a smile touched Baarias' mouth. "Sefaan. She waded in with all of her might and threatened to leave with Rebaa if the Elders threw her from the tribe. She bent their will to hers and forged a promise that the boy could remain until he was old enough to fend for himself. Aardn has never forgiven her actions from that day and has done her best to undermine Sefaan's influence ever since."

"Is that how the rumours over her state of mind started?"

"Yes."

"Oh." Nyri ran through her childhood memories in the light of this revelation. The Kamaali had always been especially kind to her and Juaan, slipping them food, making sure they were cared for at a distance. Now all of that made sense. But those memories did nothing to ease the anger and sense of betrayal that were swiftly rising. Sefaan had known Juaan's heritage and that of the girl in the vision. The Kamaali had known, and she had not told her. Nyri balled her fists. Hadn't she deserved to know the truth? Didn't she have the right to make up her own mind?

"But that's all even Sefaan could do." Baarias continued. If he sensed her outrage, he was choosing to ignore it. "Our people will not tolerate such blemishes to Ninmah's creation. Rebaa might have been allowed to stay with her abominable offspring, but the Elders forbade anyone from helping her under the threat of the same treatment as the child. They shunned her to the fringes of the tribe.

"During the first long Fury, she nearly starved trying to keep Juaan alive. I did not have the courage to stand against the Elders, and I feared the sin she had committed. I did not help her and she never recovered. You don't know how much guilt I have had to carry through all these seasons, knowing I did not have the courage to save my own sister. Sefaan certainly has never forgiven me, nor let me forget my weakness.

"Even after Rebaa was gone, I turned my back on her offspring, terrified of what he might become and angry at the loss of my sister. I blamed him for it, and he hated me in return. Your mother was the only one who reached out and showed true courage."

"My mother knew what he was?"

"Yes."

Nyri pressed her face into her hands. The most important person in her life was a half Wove, and everybody had known it but her. He had lied to her; everyone had lied to her. She felt so foolish. So blind.

"It was through studying Juaan at a distance that I was forced to reconsider certain things. He was strong, with no hint of physical deformity. He never got sick apart from the time he was bitten by that spider. Such a poison would have killed a Ninkuraa; he recovered with hardly any treatment. There *had* to be something in that." Baarias frowned, frustrated. "Nobody else sees the possibilities."

They were silent for a long while. Nyri did not know how to go forward; trapped in the moment. She was angry and heartbroken by the terrible truth that Baarias had just revealed. But in doing so, he had indeed given her the answer to the very truth she had come here to seek. Juaan was a Wove by blood as well as by upbringing. She had healed him and when healing, it was impossible for her to be any closer to a person. Their body became hers; there was nothing that could be hidden.

Baarias had been right all along. The Woves were not evil spirits; they possessed no dark power. It was almost incomprehensible but undeniably the truth. Of that one thing, Nyri was now certain.

One question forced itself to the forefront of her mind. "If you could speak to one of them, would you? Do you think they could ever be reasoned with?"

Baarias' reply came swift and sharp. "No, Nyriaana, never! I might be certain that the Woves are not wholly responsible for the dire changes to our people and the greater world, but they are still a dangerous, bloodthirsty race. You have no idea how close an eye I kept on you with that boy. I could never be certain just how much Wove savagery he might have inherited or when it might surface. To trust a Wove is to entertain danger and death."

Nyri bit her lip. She was trusting one with her very life. "But what about Rebaa?" she asked desperately. "How could she fall in love with such a being?"

Baarias' face clouded. "I do not know. He must've been a rare thing, this Wove, to earn the love of a Ninkuraa and make her defy all she was ever taught."

Nyri drew a shaky breath. "He must indeed."

Their quiet contemplation was interrupted by Pelaan. "Baarias," he said as he pushed into the chamber. "I am to watch our borders until Ninmah sleeps. I am taking my daughter with me." His tone was final; he was informing Baarias, not asking. Aardn must have truly been desperate for Nyri to finish her teaching to get Pelaan to agree to put Kyaati into her care.

Baarias did not look at all happy but could do nothing. He nodded his assent and Pelaan left without another word.

"Do you think he heard us?" Nyri asked in sudden concern. She had been so wrapped up in what she had learned; she had not been paying any attention to her surroundings.

Neither had Baarias. He looked worried. "I do not think so. I don't think he would have been able to hold his tongue if he had. I would be wandering the wilderness already." He shrugged.

"What can we do, Baarias?" Nyri looked to him, like she had so often in the past. "How can we convince others of the truth you have found? The Elders are killing us. We cannot just sit by and do nothing."

He looked back at her, the heavy weight of experience in his eyes. "We must. I have tried, Nyriaana, but it is impossible. Unless we are sent a miracle, we are doomed.

All we can do is stand by our people until the very end."

Nyri thought of her vision and the mysterious green-eyed girl that Sefaan named Ariyaana. Was this half-Wove child their miracle? The Last Kamaali fabled to save them all? She did not know what to believe anymore.

Nyri blinked back frustrated tears. "I don't know how you have endured this for so many years. I am so sorry for how I acted, Baarias."

"I have done it because I had to. It was not all down to cowardice, as Sefaan believes. My tribe needed me. *You* needed me, *akaabi*. I have tried to make them see what I do but, as you have witnessed for yourself, they do not take kindly to my words. I could not risk expulsion, or the undermining of respect that Sefaan has suffered, when so many depend on me. They would have taken you from me, too, if they had even a hint that I was imparting my heresy upon you. They will still do so if they realise I have now accomplished that. You must bear it, Nyriaana, as I have. You must keep this to yourself, for my sake, if nothing else. At least my burden will be easier to bear now that I know I am not alone and I have you on my side."

Nyri's smile was bittersweet. "I have always been on your side, Baarias, even when I was being stubborn."

He squeezed her shoulder. "Then we will bear our burden together and pray to Ninmah we will not always be alone."

Nyri was so desperate to tell him in that moment. She did not know why Sefaan had forbidden her from confiding in him. She did not know why she was holding to her promise when the Kamaali had deceived her so badly. Who could she trust if not her teacher, surely she owed more loyalty to him? The distance that had existed between them over the past days had been painful.

"Baarias," she started. "I need to tell you something—"

"Baarias." Now Imaani appeared in the doorway. "Javaan has fallen and broken his fingers. Can you attend him, master healer, he does not want to leave his watch?" He rolled his eyes disparagingly.

Baarias shook himself out of the little bubble they had existed in and forced a smile onto his face. "Of course," he told Imaani. The sentry left at once, avoiding Nyri's gaze. Baarias got up to follow. "You don't have to come for this, Nyriaana. You may do what you will for the rest of the day. Rest. You look exhausted." He touched her cheek and then paused. "You had something to tell me?"

But the moment had passed. Nyri opened her mouth, unsure, and then changed her mind. Maybe later. She smiled reassuringly. "It's nothing important, Baarias. You go. I may visit Sefaan. I haven't seen her in a while." She and the Kamaali were going to have a talk.

"Nor I." Baarias frowned. "She's been acting very strange lately."

"Hasn't she just."

Once Baarias had disappeared, Nyri could contain herself no longer. She headed straight to Sefaan's home. The Kamaali was inside, she could feel it. Nyri strode into the tree without waiting for an invitation.

"You *knew*!" She flung the accusation out. "You knew Juaan was a Wove, and you never told me!"

The Kamaali had been lying upon her bower but rose at Nyri's entrance. "Hello, Nyriaana," she said mildly. Nyri was dismayed by how frail she appeared, far more so than the last time she had seen her, but she did not let it break her momentum.

"How could you have lied to me after all I have done? Did I not have the right to know?"

"Did I ever tell you he wasn't a Wove?" Sefaan was steady in the face of her tirade.

"Don't twist things around. How can I go back to that Pit knowing what he is? How can I carry on feeding the son of murderers?"

"If you don't, you will never find Ariyaana."

"Ariyaana." Nyri threw her head back to stare at the ceiling of the ground-level chamber. "Another Wove. Another Forbidden. How do you know if she is even real? How can she be real?"

"You saw her, too. What do you think?"

Nyri barked an incredulous laugh. "I don't know! I just discovered most of what I was taught is a lie. Tell me, Sefaan, what am I to think?" Nyri dropped her gaze to the Kamaali's. "He may not be a dark spirit, but he is still the son of a vicious enemy."

"But he is also the son of your kin. His heart is his mother's."

"How can you know that?"

Sefaan shook her head. "How can you not know it? Stop letting your hate blind you. Your mother saw it, why do you of all people deny it?"

Nyriaana pinched the bridge of her nose, fighting the confusion roiling through her as her hate for the Woves clashed with her feelings for Juaan. She could not reconcile the two.

"Forget what you were taught," Sefaan's voice broke in. "Forget everything the Elders have said. What do you, *you*,

Nyriaana, know? Did Juaan ever give you any cause to believe that he was a monster?"

Nyri was still so angry she wanted to rebel, to lash out against the lies, but she could not. "No," she choked.

Her admittance vindicated the Kamaali and Sefaan pressed her advantage, mercilessly cutting at the deepest parts of Nyri's heart. "Would a monster have loved you, comforted you, and sacrificed himself for you as he did?"

"Sefaan, please..."

"Answer me." It was a command.

"No!" Nyri burst out. "He would not."

"Then how can you condemn him as the son of murderers?"

"I-I," Nyri sank to the floor. "I don't know." The world she had known no longer existed. She was floating, getting lost in the void. She searched for something to cling to, to pull her back and keep her grounded in this strange new place. Reaching into a fold in her garments, she clutched at the pebble Sefaan had given her, letting the memories flow.

Nyri, Nyri, Nyriaana...

Juaan. The turmoil receded. Nyri closed her eyes to keep the tears from falling. Falling for Juaan, for his mother, for her own ignorance. Who his father had been had never mattered, not to the vulnerable child she had been. Should it matter now? *His heart is his mother's...* And Nyri did know that. She knew it in her bones. Her new knowledge of his true heritage changed nothing. She let her anger go. "Forgive me, Sefaan."

The Kamaali's fingers brushed her cheek. "You are carrying much on your young shoulders, child. It is no shame to waver, but you must not fall. The future is fast arriving and you and he, no matter what he is, must be ready when it does."

Nyri bowed her head. "I promise, Sefaan," she whispered.

"Be strong. Now, please," the Kamaali's trembling hand fell away. "Leave me, girl. There is something important that I must do, and I need to concentrate."

Nyri sniffed and rose to her feet. She bowed to Sefaan and left the Kamaali's home as the world rebalanced itself around her.

She was so lost in thought that she nearly ran straight into the back of the crowd gathered around the foot of an *eshaara* tree.

She looked up, and her heart sank. It was dying. Disease marked the red-gold trunk. The branches that twisted into the nest-like chambers above were rotten and weak; the thick leaves that crowned and covered them were thinning. Gaps in their protection were beginning to show, revealing the skeleton of the structure underneath. She knew what must be done now, and she moved to take up position with her People.

Aardn was closest to the massive tree, and Nyri was careful to keep her head down. The Elder had her hand pressed against the ravaged bark, eyes closed. When she finally turned to the rest of them, her expression downcast. "She is weak. She will not survive another Fury. Already she is preparing to give her essence to her brethren."

Moving closer, everyone placed their own palms against the old tree and Nyri felt clearly what Aardn had. The golden thread of the Great Spirit within ebbed, her days were done; it was time to pass her strength to the rest of the forest. In this harsh time, those of the living needed all the strength they could be gifted.

Along with her People, Nyri drew the life force from the *eshaara*. It came willingly, glad of the assistance, and they helped channel it to where it needed to go. The rest of the trees around them came alive as they received this final gift from their sister. The leaves whispered, becoming greener and more vibrant. They danced on the wind, in celebration, in final farewell.

Then the work was done. When they opened their eyes, they found themselves up to their ankles in shrivelled brown leaves. Nyri shook a few from her hair and lifted her chin. The tree stood naked yet proud somehow, even in death. Nyri felt the poignancy of its passing keenly. The cold wind rattled through the now bare branches and Juaan's words echoed in their voice:

The world we know is dying and there is nothing that you or I or anyone else can do to stop it...

37

Learning

"You need to concentrate, young Juaan," Sefaan admonished gently.

The breeze stirred as Nyriaana sat beside her friend. Sefaan was trying to teach them how to merge their will with a group of maamits. They had been allowed to venture out on their first Gathering, and Nyri was feeling very important. The target was some berries at the top of a tall, tall tree.

Nyri grinned at her growing pile of fruit. This was easy! Any task that was presented to her, she took effortlessly in stride. Her father had often boasted of her talent to the Elders. Her smile broadened. The maamit she worked with jumped back and forth willingly at her bidding.

"Don't exhaust him, Nyri," Sefaan scolded, but a hiss of frustration and a stone bouncing off a tree interrupted her rebuke. Juaan eyed the fruit of Nyri's efforts beside his own woeful pile with an envious scowl. He was finding this hard. Nyri was secretly pleased by that fact. Juaan was better than her at nearly everything else.

Sefaan tutted at his outburst of temper. "That won't get you *very far, boy. I told you to concentrate. Do as I say and it will come to you."*

Pelaan's angry voice cut in. "Don't be foolish, Sefaan! He is no Ninkuraa. He does not bear the Gift. He will never help feed our people; he will never grow an eshaara. I don't know why you are wasting your time. It's not like he'll be—"

"Pelaan!" Sefaan cut off whatever he had been about to say. Her gaze was fierce and Pelaan fell silent. Nyri was growing to like the ancient one more and more. She grew tired of everyone picking on Juaan. Sefaan did not pick on him. She picked on the Elders.

"I'll help you, Juaan," she said, upset by his downcast face. She wished they would leave him alone. She would show them all that Juaan could do it. She sat down beside her friend and took his hand. Together, they turned their eyes towards the canopy and the maamits that danced there.

* * *

"Nyri!"

Daajir was pushing his way towards her, his face alight with excitement. She stiffened at the sight of him. She still had not come to terms with what she had seen last night, the curl of triumph on his lips as he had wounded that Wove.

"Nyri, I did it." He grabbed her arm.

"Did what?" Nyri kept her face blank.

"I drove the Woves from our forest last night."

"You did?" She mustered enough surprise to satisfy him.

"Truly?"

"Yes. Trust me, it'll be awhile before they decide to make another foray into this forest. I have seen to *that*." Nyri could have choked on his self-congratulation.

"I can't believe it."

Daajir's hand flexed on her arm. "Believe it, Nyri. I am going to save us all."

He was still clinging to the misguided belief that killing Woves would be the solution to all their problems. Nyri almost pitied him for the very ignorance that she had shared in until only a short time ago.

Daajir frowned. "What's the matter? I have just told you I can save our People and you don't seem pleased at all."

Nyri forced a smile onto her face. "I *am* happy, Daajir. I am weak with relief. I haven't slept in so long for fear of those beasts coming for us in the night. Knowing what you have done, I can rest easy now."

His self-satisfaction impossibly found new depths. "Rest, Nyri. Leave this to me. I will take care of you."

Nyri's smile dropped as soon as he swaggered away. *Sure you will.*

But not all of what she had said to Daajir had been a deception. Nyri was exhausted to the core of her bones, but she knew she could not rest. Not now. She had to see him. She had to see him in the light of her new learning and know that nothing had changed. Kyaati was still with her father and Baarias had released her for the day. She was free to go where she would. At the first opportunity, she stole out of the *eshaara* grove.

She travelled carefully, exhaustion hunting her every step, both physical and mental. She would have served herself better by returning to her tree and catching up on some much missed sleep, but she did not let herself turn back, even when she tripped over a root in her tiredness.

Her skills at masking her presence must have grown indeed, because she was past the sentries before she even really thought about it.

Juaan was a little surprised at her appearance. She had been careful to call down to him before she lowered herself. He wasn't expecting her in the revealing light of day and she didn't want to catch him unaware. She already had enough bruises.

Without speaking, Nyri handed him the food she had brought. He took it and sat watching her as he ate. Nyri watched him right back, seeing him afresh, knowing that he was indeed a Wove, or at least partly. She must have looked troubled because he asked: "What's wrong? You're looking at me as if I have two heads."

She stopped her restless chewing of a fingernail. "Sorry."

"World on your shoulders?"

"I'm reassessing it. It's difficult."

He swallowed the last bite. "Anything to do with me?"

"Everything to do with you. You've caused me nothing but trouble."

"Then let me go."

Nyri blanched. She had only meant that last in jest, but he was serious. "I can't." It still hurt that all he wanted was to leave her, and that pain was the confirmation she needed. Who his father had been did not matter to her. But her heritage was obviously still repulsive to him.

She bowed her head. She had hoped she had at least come to mean a little something to him by now. *You fool,* her inner self told her scathingly. *How could you expect that? You are nothing to him. Only his keeper; an enemy. He will never help you. Sefaan was wrong.*

Nyri shook the treacherous thought away. *No, I am already showing him I am not. I will win his trust. He will remember me.*

Yes, the traitorous voice argued. *But what then? Once you win his trust and if he remembers you, what will you do? You can't keep him in this Pit forever. Your tribe will never accept him—*

"I'm sorry," Nyri said to him. "I can't let you go."

He was looking up at the sky through the gaps in the coverings. It was raining softly; showers of water sighed through the trees. He let out a soft breath. "I wasn't expecting anything different, though it would be better for us both if you did."

Nyri hesitated, then sat down beside him. He no longer flinched away, but accepted her closeness indifferently. As always, she felt dwarfed. She studied his face in the novelty of the light, picking out certain features, seeing now with her opened eyes. So much of it was foreign.

His hair was a deep brown, a darker shade than when he was a boy. His skin was a rich, earthly colour, a couple of shades darker than her own red-gold flesh. His ears were more rounded. The beard. When he moved his mouth Nyri could see the four teeth behind the incisors were slightly pointed, like a wolf. *Flesh eaters...* she shuddered. And then there were those green eyes, same as the girl in the mountains. Not one of Nyri's race possessed such a colour.

Nyri looked closer, trying to see anything of his mother, of his Ninkuraaja half, fearing that the Wove half had driven it all out, like his captors had driven it from his soul. Reaching out with her senses, she found the part of the Great Spirit that resided in all her people. It was certainly there, buried deep and forgotten but there all the same, the Woves could not have that, and was it her imagination or was there something of Baarias in the shape of his eyes and nose, or rather Rebaa. That was a comfort.

"I can see your mother in you," she murmured. The words came unbidden and Nyri knew he would not react well, but she could not help it. "She was of my tribe."

"I do not care who she was," he returned testily. "And I do not want to know. I may carry elf blood but not gladly, I am nothing of you."

"Yes, you *are*." Nyri had to get him back. "You are more of us than them. I wish you could remember. I wish you could remember *me*." She was met with stubborn silence, so she changed direction. "What do you remember?" Nyri was in parts both curious and resentful of wanting to know what had become of him since he had been taken.

He sighed irritably. "I was found in a forest. My chief told me an elf clan had been about to kill me and used their magic to steal my memories. Elves do not believe in half-breeds. We are named Forbidden by all others. You claim we are the evil ones, but your People would have put me to death simply for who I was. Just because the so-called gods tell you it should be so. To me, *your* People are the murderers. It is a fact I have never forgotten." He gave her a chilling glare. "Luckily we *Woves* have none of your superstitions. We know better. My clan took me in and nursed me back to health. When I was strong enough, I became *raknari*, a position of high honour. I protect my clan from those who would do them harm. That is all I know. All I need to know."

"No," Nyri denied. "That is not what happened. You were lost protecting me from being taken by the Woves. They were going to kill me but you would not let them." Tears started in her eyes. "We were only children. I thought they'd killed you. I thought I'd lost you forever, but now here you are and you remember nothing. Your mother—"

"Abandoned me," he growled. "She would never have kept a Forbidden child. She would've killed me. It's what witches do."

"No!" Nyri hissed. "Your mother never abandoned you. She fought for you. She died keeping you alive through the long Fury. You owe her your life as I owe you mine."

"You owe me nothing," he growled. He got to his feet and walked away from Nyri. His fists opened and closed into tight balls. A very Ninkuraaja way of displaying tension, like he wanted to take to the trees. "Say no more. I will not hear it."

Nyri blew out a frustrated breath. "Well, what shall we talk about, then?"

He tipped back his head, calming himself, and then glanced about at their surroundings. A glint came to his eye. "That rock looks a bit like a wolf if you squint at it long enough," he said.

Nyriaana stared at him for a moment, nonplussed, before laughter bubbled from her throat. His dry comment had been so unexpected. It was something he might have said as a boy. *Ah, my Juaan, how I've missed you.*

"I'm glad my boredom amuses you," he grumbled, though Nyri got the sense her laughter did not truly annoy him.

The rain fell harder, breaking through the coverings over the Pit. Juaan sat and hunkered down. Nyri saw for the first time the dark circles under his eyes. He did not move as smoothly as he had. "Are your injuries bothering you?" she asked in concern. "You look... uncomfortable."

"So would you if you'd been sleeping on bare rock for nights on end."

"But," she hesitated, embarrassed by her own ignorance, "don't Woves usually sleep on the ground?"

Juaan laughed. "Yes, but not on the bare rock. We dark spirits need a few human comforts, you know."

Nyri blushed, mortified. She glanced around the Pit. He had indeed been sleeping on bare rock, shelterless and exposed. The sticks and scattered leaves covering the hole above offered little protection from the elements. How thoughtless she had been. She had thought she had covered everything. Already the rain was soaking his furs through. It sluiced off her waterproof coverings.

Where did Woves usually sleep? It wasn't a question she had ever had cause to ask herself. She had never really entertained the idea that the 'evil spirits' slept in the first place.

"I'll be right back," Nyri told him. Swiftly, she rose and scrambled up and out of the Pit. It was getting harder to manage as her strength waned. She scoured the forest, the sodden ground squishing beneath her feet, collecting what she needed as she went. Nyri wished she had a gathering basket. She did her best with her arms, gathering moss and leaves and throwing the loads down to Juaan bit by bit until there was enough to make a resting place big enough even for him.

"That should make things more comfortable for you," Nyri called down. "But I'm afraid I have nothing for you to shelter under." She wiped a lock of dripping hair out of her face, musing that she could hardly grow an eshaara before Ninmah set.

He looked up at her, frowning. "But you have all the materials you need. Do you elves know nothing?"

Nyri opened her mouth to retort, but he waved a hand. "Find me some sturdy branches. I'll show you."

His dismissive tone annoyed Nyri, but curiosity got the better of her. Instead of planting her feet as she might have wanted, she did as he asked. It took her a while to find as many sturdy branches lying around as would satisfy him. He had wanted her to take them from the trees themselves, but this notion had appalled her.

At last her offerings satisfied Juaan, and Nyri climbed back down into the Pit. "Watch and learn," he said and began arranging the branches, propping them against one another. He grumbled about having nothing to tie the pieces together with, but he was clever and they balanced and interlocked perfectly. When Juaan finished, Nyri could only stare in amazement at what he had made. It had the appearance of a beehive, with a little opening on one side.

"But there are still gaps in it," she pointed out, casting her eye a little smugly over the structure. "That's clever but you are still going to get wet."

"It's not finished yet," he growled. "I need hides but I won't get any of those around here, will I?"

"No! You will not."

He chuckled once at the look of consternation on her face. "Don't worry. I wouldn't dare ask." He glanced at her clothes and the water running off them. "Do you have any more of those leaves?"

A smile spread slowly across Nyri's face. "Wait here."

"Of course." He rolled his eyes.

This time Nyri had to travel a little further, but she found what she wanted. The *aacha* tree had leaves as big and as round as an arm was long. She gathered as many as she could carry. When she returned with them, Juaan looked pleased.

"They'll do." He lifted a leaf and placed it against his new structure. It promptly slipped to the ground. "Hmmm."

Nyri touched his arm as an idea struck. "I think I can solve that problem."

"How?"

"Don't you Woves know anything?" She smiled as he raised an eyebrow at her. "Watch and learn."

She knew what she needed. The silk from the weaver spider would be more than strong enough to hold the leaves in place and give Juaan's strange, dead shelter its skin. The only problem was they were very hard to find. Nyri needed a vision far sharper than she possessed. She turned her eyes to the trees as she extended her will. Moments later, a *kaala* bird lighted onto her waiting hand. The small insectivore watched her intently with his bright black eyes as he queried her with images. Nyri showed him her need and his reward if he succeeded. With a brush of soft blue wings against her fingers, he was gone.

Juaan watched with begrudging wonder. "How are you doing that?"

Nyri smiled. "Ninmah's Gift. We are all family here; the Great Spirit binds us all. I told him what I needed and now he has gone to fetch it for me. Kyaati has a particular talent for birds." At the mention of her friend's name, Nyri's heart twisted.

Her sorrow must have shown on her face. "Kyaati is the girl you are caring for? The girl who lost her baby?"

Nyri nodded mutely.

"How," his voice was careful, as if he didn't want to appear too concerned but couldn't help asking. "How is she recovering?"

"She isn't." Nyri could say no more and she was saved from doing so by the return of her little companion. A brown spider dangled delicately from his beak. He dropped it on the roof of Juaan's shelter, then disappeared to fetch another and then another.

Once he was finished, he swooped around Nyri, twirling in an aerial display, showing off his impressive skills. He landed on her shoulder and started pecking at her ear. He wanted his reward.

"Alright, alright!" She brushed him away. "Here." She drew out a handful of plump seeds from her garments. They were the *kaala* birds' favourite treat. He ate quickly and was gone. It didn't do to be still for long in his busy life. Nyri saw Juaan shake his head and murmur something like *elf magic.*

She turned her attention to the spiders that the little *kaala* had brought her. They sat, legs huddled in defensive crouches, not sure what had happened to them. Insects were so different from Nyri's kind, it was difficult to understand and influence them. It took practice. Sefaan had taught her much with the making of garments. Spider silk was an invaluable material.

Concentrating hard, Nyri bent her will on the three dazed arachnids. She sent them the undeniable urge to eat. They set to work at once and Nyri began placing the leaves ahead of them. They scurried along, weaving their tough and sticky silk, binding the leaves together. Hungry as they were, they would not risk a single morsel getting through their nets. It wasn't long before Juaan's roof was watertight. Nyri let the spiders stay. They deserved to harvest the bounty of their skilled labour.

Finished at last, Nyri sat down and leaned against the rock wall. All the activity and concentration had tired her; she felt light-headed.

Juaan circled the structure they had made. He touched the new skin of his temporary home. "The first Wove-Elf shelter ever made. It's... not bad." He looked sideways at Nyri as a smile spread across his face. "Thank you."

Tired as she was, Nyri's answering grin split her face in two. It was a moment of true camaraderie. Nyri's heart danced as their eyes locked and the world grew still around them. Everything else fell away. He was all that existed. His smile transformed his face. He was beautiful.

A blood-chilling snarl from above shattered the moment. Nyri leaped to her feet as Juaan thrust her behind him. Preoccupied, she had not been aware of an approach. Her eyes fixed upon a large grey form looming above them. Batai was standing on the edge of the Pit staring down. Nyri stiffened as she read his intent. His heart was full of fear and anger. Before she could stop him, he leaped down into the Pit with astounding agility, hackles raised and fangs bared.

"Batai?" Nyri whispered. He ignored her. He had eyes only for Juaan and the look in them chilled Nyri to the bone. There was only one thing on his mind. A low rumble was emitting from the wolf's throat as he scented the air. His lips curled higher as he stalked forward. "Batai, stop," she warned, speaking with both voice and soul. "What's the matter with you? He's a friend."

"I don't think he's seeing it that way," Juaan hissed through clenched teeth. He was half crouched in defence as he backed away, but he could not get far and his back was soon against the unrelenting stone of the Pit wall. The wolf coiled.

"Batai!" Nyri cried.

He did not hear her. He sprang, bared fangs gaping wide for the killing bite. Juaan had no defence. "No!" Nyri screamed, leaping forward.

A wave of power almost bore her to the ground. Wild, uncontrolled and desperate. The sheer strength of it took her breath away.

"Down, wolf!"

Juaan had his hands thrown out, but it was not their mortal flesh that had protected him. Batai twisted in the air, aborting his killing leap, and landed a mere arm's length from the tall man before him. There he lay on his belly, appearing as shocked as Nyri. He licked his lips, panting in wolfish distress.

Nyri recovered first. She put her hands on the wolf's fur. *Batai, return to Omaal,* she thought in images, evoking the same reactions in his brain as Omaal's scent did. He understood. With a last confused stare at the Wove standing against the wall, the wolf turned away with a disdainful huff. Gathering his considerable strength, he leaped towards the lip of the Pit above. It was almost beyond even his abilities. He had to scramble and claw his way back over the top.

For a moment there was silence, then: "What was *that?*" Nyri breathed.

Juaan folded his arms away inside his furs. He looked as close to frightened as Nyri had ever seen him. Out of childhood, at least.

"I-I don't know," he mumbled, avoiding her eyes. "It happens sometimes. I can't control it." He paced away from Nyri. "This is the first time it has happened away from..." he trailed off. "Just consider yourself lucky you are still alive."

"This has happened before? Why didn't you tell me?"

"Why would I tell you," he shot at her. "It is nothing but a curse." He was trembling.

"It is no curse. You are half Ninkuraaja," Nyri said. "You have your mother's blood. The Great Spirit of KI is within you." She thought back to the time she had first healed him. "I didn't think you possessed enough of Ninmah's Gift to control it. You struggled so much as a child. Somehow it came to you in that moment. You were in danger. Perhaps your body responded accordingly. Survival instinct."

He raised his arms and pressed his face and hands into the nearest wall, his back to her. Nyri watched him silently, still shaken by this outburst of raw power, greater than any she had ever felt. She could only imagine how frightening it must be for him. It appeared he had grown up with Ninkuraaja gifts but had no one to teach or guide him.

Nyri seized on a sudden hope. If she could teach him, if she could open his eyes and waken his mind to the Great Spirit, maybe he would come back to her. Maybe he would remember. Batai's confusing attack now seemed a blessing in disguise. Juaan had been impressed enough by what she had demonstrated to him so far.

The power that had been unleashed was gone now, muted once more, but its presence had left its mark. He associated his skill only with fear and was desperate to hide it. Nyri would show him otherwise. She would show him the wonder and the beauty such a Gift offered. Nyri vowed when he next heard the wolves sing, he would hear the Great Spirit ringing in their voices. First, she had to make him see.

"Juaan," she whispered. Nyri spied a stone cast from one of the berries he had eaten. She plucked it from the rocks and placed it at the heart of her left palm. "Juaan."

He turned his head away from the wall, just enough to look at her. His shadowed eyes were haunted.

"Watch. Your abilities are nothing to be feared. I promise. I'll show you." And Nyri focused her will upon that berry stone. She found the waiting life nestled within it and poured forth her energy. Before their eyes, the shell broke open and a tiny shoot reached forth, green with life, struggling skyward to take its first taste of Ninmah's warmth.

When Nyri glanced up moments later, it startled her to find Juaan's face a mere hand's breadth from her own. His eyes were fixed on the newly born plant resting between them on her palm. The doubt and fear that lingered upon his face warred with naked wonder.

"How?" he whispered.

Nyri reached out and took his left hand in her own. He was so absorbed that he did not pull away. His skin was warm and rough against her fingers. She turned the giant hand palm up and spilled the little stone into it.

"Would you like me to teach you? You don't have to be afraid anymore."

He stared down at the tiny shoot for a long while, so long Nyri became fearful that he would throw it down and reject

402

her *elf magic*.

He spoke on a breath. "Please, show me."

* * *

38

The Evil Within

Sefaan sat in the gathering darkness outside of her tree, resting from her excursion into the forest on Nyriaana's heels. The girl did not know it, but Sefaan often followed her on her visits to the boy, helping her evade the sentries. Nyriaana's skill at concealment was improving, however, and Sefaan no longer had to expend as much energy to help her evade detection from the sentries. The time was approaching when the girl would need her no longer.

The knowledge came as a relief. Sefaan gave a soft gasp as she felt her heart skip a beat and then pick up again, labouring inside her chest. Restless, she toyed with the *enu* around her throat. Time was running out. The girl needed to hurry if she was to find Ariyaana.

A movement drew Sefaan's eye to the outer forest. A dark figure was skirting around the trees. Sefaan recognised the silhouette at once.

Daajir. This was what she had been waiting out in the cold for. It was time to find out what the young man was up to.

She watched as he disappeared into the forest.

Go after him... KI whispered in the wind.

Heaving a great sigh, Sefaan struggled to her feet and shuffled off in the direction the boy had taken. She could not keep up with his young legs, but she followed along behind him, trailing his unique essence.

The boy seemed to know the path he was taking well. The sentries let him through without question when he came up against them. Sefaan made sure they did not see her.

The night deepened as Daajir's path became more treacherous, and Sefaan had to stop and rest often. *Old. Too old.*

She caught up to him on the edges of a dank hollow. The scent of decay was thick on the air. This appeared to be the boy's destination, for he had come to a halt in the centre of the hollow. Sefaan sank down to sit upon a fallen tree and watched the boy lift a log from the ground. Coiled underneath was a snake.

Sefaan could taste its fear from where she sat as it cowered away from him. It tried to slither away, but Daajir's will lashed out. Sefaan stifled a gasp as the snake's pain spiked against her senses. Anger flared in her chest. Never in all her time had she known a Ninkuraa abuse the Gift of Ninmah in such a way.

The boy grinned as he extended a *haala* nut shell towards the snake, and it bit meekly down upon it. As soon as the snake let go, Daajir let the log fall back into place before plucking a spine from the nearest *vaash* plant to add its poison to the snake's venom, measuring carefully.

Swirling the *haala* nut between his hands, Daajir then placed it upon the ground beside rows upon rows of other shells. The boy, it seemed, had been gathering his supplies of poison for a long time. Daajir nodded to himself, clearly satisfied with his work.

Reaching behind him, he pulled an object out from under the concealment of his coverings. It was Juaan's knife. Sefaan watched as Daajir turned it over in his hands before swinging his arm back and letting it fly. The blade embedded itself in the nearest tree. The boy let out a whoop as Sefaan's eyebrows raised in surprise. Collecting poison was not the only thing he had been up to, it seemed.

Daajir retrieved the blade from the trunk it had pierced, then dipped it into the nearest bowl of his strange concoction. The liquid looked black in the darkness, and Sefaan shivered at the sight of it. Then the boy was moving again, disappearing into the darkness on the far side of the hollow.

Sefaan waited a few moments, making sure he was a safe distance away, and then rose and limped down into the hollow. What she saw then wrested a gasp of horror from her throat. Now she knew why such an aura of misery had swirled every time she had set eyes on this boy.

Everywhere she looked, the bones or decaying remains of a Child of the Great Spirit lay scattered. The contorted corpse of a stag still had the barb of a *vaash* plant protruding from its throat.

Sefaan shook. In a rage, she grabbed a stick and swiped at the rows of *haala* nut shells, knocking them aside and spilling their contents of death and misery onto the ground.

"Sefaan! What are you *doing?*"

Sefaan spun to face Daajir. Without her notice, the boy had returned. He was frozen in the act of wiping the Cro blade on his sleeve - wiping it clean of blood - as he gazed down at her in horror.

406

"Murderer," Sefaan growled between her teeth as she dropped the branch she held.

Colour blazed across Daajir's face. "What are you doing here, you crazy old fool?" He rushed down the hill towards her. "You cannot be here!"

"I am where I am supposed to be. Stopping a monster before he can do any more evil." Sefaan lifted her chin. "I only wish I could have come sooner."

"No!" The boy saw his spilled bowls and fell to his knees before them. "No! What have you *done*!"

"What the Great Spirit willed."

Snarling, Daajir leaped to his feet and the hairs on the back of Sefaan's neck quivered as she beheld the look in his eyes. The Great Spirit swirled, warning; he was coming to kill her.

"No!" Sefaan summoned her will, extending it to the creature lurking beneath the log behind the boy. All too eagerly, the snake lunged from its concealment and sank its fangs deep into the top of Daajir's right leg.

He howled in pain, twisting in his efforts to dislodge the creature. Sefaan saw what was about to happen, but her old body wasn't fast enough. Daajir barrelled into her, knocking her off her feet. The ground rushed up and knocked the air from her lungs. Sefaan felt the bones in her left elbow splinter upon impact. It was her turn to cry out.

It took a few moments to master the pain and refocus her vision. When she did, Sefaan found Daajir was kneeling over her, panting.

"You shouldn't have come, Sefaan," he ground out from between his teeth. He put a hand around to where the snake had bitten him. His fingers came back bloody, but he only gave a laugh at the sight. "Was that the best you could do? You really are losing your grip."

"You cannot continue down this path, Daajir," Sefaan forced the words out between gasps of pain, fighting to keep conscious. "It will only lead to misery."

"Misery? How is saving our People misery?"

"You… you are not the one who will save us… Nyriaana…" Blackness taunted at the edges of her vision.

"Nyriaana?" Daajir barked a laugh. "That foolish weakling. How could she possibly save us from anything?"

Sefaan closed her eyes. "I will tell the Elders of what you have done here," she rasped. "They will not stand for this heresy!"

Daajir shrugged and rose to his feet. "Heresy? Who are you to lecture anyone about heresy? The Elders will not listen to you. Who would they rather depend on? The man who can rid them of our enemies or the crazy fool who forced them to accept a real monster into our very midst." His eyes turned to the knife that was still in his hand. "You know… I believe Aardn would thank me if I was to silence you for good right here." His eyes gleamed as he lifted the knife.

Sefaan's heart thudded and stuttered. This was not how it was supposed to happen. She closed her eyes as the blade came down.

A thud sounded beside her head.

She opened her eyes again to see the knife embedded in the ground close to her ear. She stared up into Daajir's face and saw that the maniacal gleam had dimmed. "But I won't harm you, Sefaan. No matter what you think of me, I am a true Son of Ninmah. I will not kill one of my own, though I might make an exception for the thief when I discover who they are. Tell whoever you wish, Sefaan, no one will ever believe you and Aardn already approves of my actions. You cannot stop me."

The last thing Sefaan remembered before the darkness claimed her was the boy stepping over her and disappearing into the darkness.

* * *

39

Thief

After an uninterrupted night's sleep, Nyri woke feeling like she was floating on air. Juaan had agreed to learn the Ninkuraaja ways. She had found a way to bring him back. It would be a challenge. She was under no illusions of that. He had struggled as a boy but she was not about to let that dampen her spirits; he wanted to learn. Nyri counted that as another step on the path to his recovery.

Rising in a rush, she descended from her home and ran straight to Sefaan's tree, eager to share the good news with the Kamaali. Perhaps Sefaan would help with Juaan's guidance. Nyri chewed her lip, weighing the benefits of having the Kamaali help against how Juaan might react to another of her tribe. She couldn't risk any setbacks.

Sefaan was lying upon her bower when Nyri entered the Kamaali's tree, and all thoughts of Juaan's progress fled at the sight that met Nyri's eyes.

"Sefaan!" she gasped. "What *happened?*" The side of the ancient woman's face was blackened with bruising and her left arm was fractured.

The Kamaali's deadened eyes rose to meet hers. "I fell."

Nyriaana rushed to her side, but Sefaan warded her away with a glare. "Do not waste your time, girl. I am already mending it myself."

"What can I do?" Nyri hovered anxiously.

"Nothing, you can do nothing. The only thing you can do for anyone is reach that boy before it is too late."

"I am Sefaan," Nyri reassured. "He wants to learn our ways. He is coming back to us."

"Good. Now, please, leave me. I need to rest now and you have much to do. Teaching him will not be easy, not after I was forced—" The Kamaali's eyes rolled closed as she gated a whimper of pain between her teeth.

"Sefaan?"

"Go! Be on your guard. Trust no one."

Biting back on another protest, Nyri obeyed and left the Kamaali's tree. She had never seen such defeated lifelessness in Sefaan's eyes as she had just then. She wondered what could have happened to cause such a look.

"Nyri?" Baarias asked as soon as she entered his home. "What's wrong?"

"It's Sefaan."

"What about her?"

"She's injured and… she's not herself. She says she fell."

Baarias' eyebrows pinched together. "Perhaps I should—"

"No," Nyri said quickly. "She doesn't want help and I doubt she'll take any more kindly to you than she did me."

Baarias blew out a breath. "You're right. You look somewhat brighter than you have in a long time at least."

"I slept well last night," she said by way of explanation.

411

"Huh," Kyaati grunted. Both Nyri and Baarias looked at her, but she offered nothing more as they prepared for the day's duties.

Omaal was the first of their visits. His terrible nightmares persisted, and he was running a fever through lack of rest, but he was faring better than the rest of the children. He didn't look nearly so wasted. Nyri frowned. Perhaps Daajir had been right about him being the strongest, despite his many deformities.

"Batai keeps him strong," Imaani said with a guarded smile.

Javaan's fingers were not so lucky. Baarias sighed as he rebound the fingers.

"Lack of food is not good for healing," he murmured to Nyri as they left.

Nyri pressed her lips together, trying not to feel the sting of these words. "Who is next," she asked before she could dwell.

"No one. Why don't you and Kyaati enjoy yourselves for a while? Maybe you should keep Daajir company."

"Why?" Nyri asked.

Baarias's mouth twitched. "He came to me last night. He'd got himself bitten by a snake."

"Again? How in Ninmah did he manage that?"

Baarias shrugged. "When you're an *akaab*, you learn not to ask too many questions and he certainly wasn't in the mood to entertain any. Suffice to say, he won't be sitting down for a while." Now there was a definite twitch to Baarias' lips.

Nyri had not yet learned such control. She laughed aloud in what felt like the first time in a lifetime. "This I have to see. Let's find Daajir, Kyaati. I never did get revenge on him for making fun of me when I sat on that spine nut."

She had hoped for some small reaction, but Kyaati simply shrugged, no hint of her old humour or quick remark. Nyri's smile slipped.

"Go, go." Baarias shooed them away, covering the moment.

Nyri pulled Kyaati with her as she went in search of Daajir. She found him walking away from the main store tree. There was a pronounced limp to his walk, and he winced with every stride.

"Daajir!" Nyri called, unable to keep the mirth from her voice. "Why don't you come and *sit* with us and have a *bite*!"

The laughter died in her throat as Daajir rounded on her. She took a step back from the fury distorting his features.

She held up her hands. "Daajir, I was only—"

"What? Making fun like a child?" he stormed. "I have no patience for your games, Nyriaana. Why don't you go and bundle some herbs and make yourself useful?"

"Excuse me?" Nyri flared.

"Get out of my way!"

"What for? Maamit stolen your favourite toy?" Nyri cut back in a fit of pique.

Daajir flushed red. "I don't have time for this. Someone was seen running from the stores. If we're quick, we might catch the thief!" He pushed past Nyri and stalked off.

Nyri noticed a group of tribe members hurrying in different directions through the *eshaara* grove, their faces determined. She sighed. They were wasting their energy. There was no longer any thief.

"Never a dull moment," Kyaati remarked. She looked at Nyri. "Don't you want to help?"

Nyri gated a laugh at the thought of helping those searching for the thief. She wouldn't have to look very far. "No. Come on, I'm sure we'll find out what happened sooner or later, whenever Daajir deigns to let us know—"

The rest of her words were cut off as a scream shattered the stillness. An all-consuming wave of grief and loss followed it.

Nyri blanched as she spun around. Kyaati was the first to react and ran in the direction of the sound. Recovering her wits, Nyri followed on her heels. Like them, everyone was converging on Oraan's tree, faces pale. Another wave of grief from above rolled over them all.

Baarias stood at the base of the tree. He met Nyri's eyes with a look of dreadful understanding as he flew up into the tree. "Stay there!" he called back to her.

Nyri shared one terrified look with Kyaati before they both ignored his command and followed on his heels. Nyri's heart was in her mouth as she swung herself into the tree.

As soon as she entered, she wished she had stayed on the ground. All of her elation in making progress with Juaan turned to dust in her mouth as she was faced with the ultimate consequence of her actions.

Little Naaya lay dead inside her bower; her body no more than a pile of bones inside her pallid flesh. Beside her lay Haana, her lifeless hand still clutching her daughter's. Nyri could see that her other hand was stained with the dark juice of night berries. Oraan sat in the corner. His eyes were beyond comprehension.

Nyri fell to her knees, not even feeling the pain of the impact.

"She took her own life," Kyaati's voice was soft, almost reverent, as she moved to crouch beside Haana, closing her sightless eyes. "She found the courage to find her peace."

"Kyaati?" Baarias' tone was uneasy as he regarded her. "Don't—"

"I found them like this." Oraan's toneless voice rose from the corner where he sat slumped. "She told me, she told me she could not live without her daughter."

"Baarias?" Aardn had climbed up into the tree behind them. "What's wrong. I felt—"

The Elder spotted the tragic scene before her. Her lips went white as she stumbled backwards, bracing herself against the tree wall.

"We have lost Naaya," Baarias' voice was as heavy as stone. "And, through her, Haana."

A tightening of thin lips was Aardn's only acknowledgement as she pushed herself upright and went to Oraan in the corner. Aardn took his arm and pulled him after her, leaving the tree and his dead family behind.

Baarias got up to follow. He took hold of both Nyri and Kyaati. "Come," he beckoned. "It is too late. There is nothing more that we can do here."

Nyri felt nothing as she climbed back down the tree. *You did this,* her mind told her over and over. *You.*

The power of Aardn's will rolled over the *eshaara* grove. The rest of the tribe's faces were grim as they felt the tenor of the Elder's energy. Some looked aghast at Oraan, reading the truth of what had happened in the youngest Elder's eyes before Aardn even spoke.

"We have lost two of our family." Aardn's grief barely concealed the fury raging beneath. "To the thief who is responsible for this tragedy, I promise you this. When you are caught, you will not only suffer expulsion from the tribe for your crimes, but I will also call for the right of *zykiel* to be performed for the whole tribe. So help me you will *know* the depth of the pain that you have caused." She pushed the mute Oraan forward. The dead look in the man's eyes was dreadful to behold.

Nyri was glad Baarias was still supporting her by the arm. If he hadn't been, she knew she would have fallen, cowering, to the floor. Most of the tribe gathered around Oraan, touching him, murmuring, supporting the bereaved with their energy, promising vengeance.

"Aardn!" Daajir's voice cut over the soft voices. "Aardn, I need to speak with you."

Vomit threatened in the back of Nyri's throat. "Excuse me, Baarias," she croaked. He took one look at her clammy skin and let her go. She turned and ran, the tears streaming down her face. The deaths of Naaya and Haana were on her hands as much as they were the Woves. She dove into the trees, intent on emptying the contents of her stomach in the undergrowth.

Nyri was so caught up in her pain that she tripped over something warm and solid lying in her path. She crashed to the ground, taking the heavy object with her.

Muffling a cry of surprise, Nyri struggled to right herself. As she got back to her feet, her eyes widened as she saw Umaa crumpled on the ground beside her.

"I'm s-sorry!" She stooped to help Umaa back onto her feet. "I wasn't paying—"

Her words trailed away as she stared down at the other woman. Umaa was snivelling into the undergrowth. An armful of food had spilled from a concealed pouch and scattered upon the ground before Nyri's eyes.

"Umaa… what-what is this?"

A shout went up from the *eshaara* grove. Daajir's voice. "Javaan saw someone run this way! Quickly!"

Umaa grasped Nyri's arm. "P-please, Nyri, don't give me away. If they perform *zykiel*, I will lose my mind."

Nyri's eyes widened as her brain caught up. *"You're* the thief?"

Umaa continued to grip her arm, nodding as her face crumpled, shaking with silent sobs. "I'm sorry, I'm so sorry. The Woves killed that little girl, but I have helped. I have to put it b-back." Her hands fluttered over her spilled load.

Nyri slumped down beside Umaa, dumbstruck. She wasn't the only one. She was not wholly responsible. Now the reason for her own careful takings being noticed so easily made sense. Another far more prolific thief had been at work. No wonder Omaal was still strong. There was food enough here to keep a family fed for days on end.

Nyri dropped her head into her hands, gripping her hair in her fists as the enormity of this discovery hit her.

"Does Imaani know?"

Umaa nodded.

Another piece clicked into place. "That's why he was so eager to take me to the Elders. If I was named the thief…" Anger spiked through Nyri's shock. They had hoped to place the blame on her.

"Nyriaana, please," Umaa begged. "I'm sorry. I'm so sorry. Please don't tell them. I can't face *zykiel* with Oraan and the whole tribe. I can't."

"But, *why*, Umaa, why did you do it? Little Naaya," Nyri's anger was gaining momentum. She had tormented herself all this time. Imaani had tried to turn her over to the Elders in Umaa's place. Juaan could have been—

"Kyaati!" Aardn's voice came from beyond the under-growth, demanding. Umaa's head snapped around. "Have you seen anybody? Has anyone come this way?"

"No." Nyri listened to Kyaati's soft, disinterested voice.

Nyri released her hair and turned her face towards the sound of Aardn's voice. She should call out and turn Umaa over to the Elder to face her rightful punishment. Naaya and her mother were dead because of her selfishness.

There was no way of telling if they would have survived the Fury at all following the consequences of the Wove raid, but their chances would have been greater had it not been for Umaa's actions. The Elders might not have reduced the rations beyond the little girl's endurance. Omaal's mother was guilty of her death. She deserved *zykiel*, to know Oraan's pain as her own.

There was a rustling in the undergrowth close by. "Just wait until I catch you." A voice hissed. It took Nyri several moments to recognise it as Daajir's, so twisted was it with hate. The hairs on her arms rose at the sound of it. "You'll be begging for the Elders' punishment when I am finished."

Umaa's face paled, and she threw herself on her knees before Nyri. "Please Nyriaana," she whispered. "Do not call them. You do not have a child yet. You do not understand. Omaal was hungry. I cannot bear to see him go hungry! Without me, he will die. Please. If someone needed you that badly, if you loved them that much, what would you have done?"

Umaa's plea stole the betraying call from Nyri's lips and left her cold. Nyri knew all too well what she would do. She *had* done it; she was *still* doing it. She might not be taking

418

food from the stores any longer, but she was still keeping vital food from her people. And she wasn't even using it to feed a starving child of her own blood. She was using it to feed their enemy. A Wove. Nyri shuddered. She wasn't as guilty as the woman before her; she was worse.

Staring into Umaa's desperate, tear-stained face, Nyri crumbled. She could not do it. She may as well turn herself in. She sank to the ground in defeat. For better or worse, she could not alert Aardn.

"It's alright, Umaa," she whispered through her own tears. "It's alright. I will not tell them. Just promise me, promise me, you will not do it again."

Umaa's relief washed over her with a fresh outpouring of tears. "I p-promise. I know I was wrong. I just... couldn't help myself. Omaal..."

Nyri nodded, placing a hesitant arm around her companion's trembling shoulders. "I understand, Umaa." She cast her eyes to the sky and took a shuddering breath. "I understand, more than you can know."

40

Raknari

The days following the loss of Naaya and her mother were difficult. Nyri could not let herself rest. Umaa returned her stolen food to the store with Nyri's help. The whole time, Nyri burned with the shame as her own secret rations remained hidden. The lifeless faces of Naaya and her mother haunted her dreams, depriving her of what little sleep she had. Sometimes she could barely think.

She worried for Kyaati. Her dear friend remained withdrawn and untouchable. Nyri's heart broke each morning as she would bring food, only for it to be rejected. Kyaati would not even make eye contact anymore. Nyri could trace the change to the day Pelaan had taken her from Baarias' home and the subsequent deaths within the tribe. Baarias was at a loss, and that scared Nyri the most. The fear sank into her bones that their battle for Kyaati was already lost. She would be forced to watch as her tribe-sister wasted away before her eyes.

Life for the rest of the tribe teetered on the edge. Suspicion ran rife and tempers were strained. The ever-present menace of the Woves' on their borders threatened to bring tensions to breaking point. Panic vibrated just beneath the surface of every waking moment. The Elders were struggling to keep them together. Sometimes it felt that the simple falling of a leaf could blow everything apart.

The only thing that kept Nyri sane was the time she spent with Juaan. Every night she would creep away to the Pits where she attempted to teach Juaan the Ninkuraaja ways. Lessons were difficult and frustrating. They took her to the limits of her patience and far beyond his.

Juaan struggled to evoke the Great Spirit within him. There had been a few colourful outbursts to say the least. Nyri suspected it was his terror of his abilities that was holding him back, for it was only when his fits of temper overcame that fear that his Gift came to the fore. But the results were not what either of them had hoped for. Each time Nyri placed a seed or a plant in his palm, hoping he could influence the life inside, his power would flare and utterly consume it. A pile of blackened plants and seeds now littered the Pit. And each time he failed, his fear and hopelessness deepened.

Nyri was frustrated with herself. She had never had to teach that which came naturally to her People before and never had she known a power such as Juaan's. She must be doing something wrong, and she longed for a wiser mind. She had even asked Sefaan, willing to risk Juaan's reaction to a newcomer if it helped, but the Kamaali had refused to come. Nyri was on her own.

Occasionally, however, when she guided him with her own Gift, Juaan would succeed and his expression in those times was so boyish with wonder, a lump would rise in

Nyri's throat. Despite its unpredictability in use, Juaan's connection with the Great Spirit inside him was becoming honed. He could sense its presence and that of the world around him more readily.

The hard, suspicious look in his eyes existed less and less. The lines of his face became softer. At times, Nyri fancied that when he looked at her, she saw a liking there, the barest hint of fondness. She would even say he was enjoying her company. Nyri admonished herself that it did not mean much. She was his only company. But often a banter would arise between them, and it was as if they had never been apart and he had never lost his memories. Nyri lived for those moments. Their friendship was beginning anew.

"Nyriaana!"

She jolted from her thoughts and stared guiltily up at Baarias. She had drifted and there again was that look upon his worn face, half frustration, half concern. "I'm sorry."

He sighed. "As I was saying, the *brodak* herb can be very effective at drawing poison from wounds should you need to treat anyone who has been bitten by a snake or spider. I used this to great effect on Daajir."

Kyaati was also sitting in on the lesson of herb lore. Nyri did not know if her friend was taking anything in, but she liked to think that listening to their voices helped her. Even if this particular lesson was dull. Nyri's eyes drifted closed once more. Her eyelids felt as though they were weighed down with stones.

At last, Baarias finished his teaching and released them for the day. He caught Nyri's arm as she turned to leave.

"Are you sure you are well?"

"Yes." She attempted a reassuring smile.

He was not swayed. Not this time. He caught her face between his hands and brushed his thumbs against the skin under her eyes where doubtless dark circles lay. His eyes searched hers. Nyri kept her thoughts in a tight ball, out of reach and her expression smooth.

"There is something," he hedged. "Promise me you will come to me if there is anything wrong." His concern tore at Nyri's heart. She wished she could say something to set his mind at rest. Ever since they had been interrupted that day when Baarias had opened her eyes, the urge to tell him of Juaan had not risen again. Sefaan had forbidden it and Nyri could not take the risk. His fear of the Woves was too great.

She caught his hands on her face. "I promise, Baarias. I will always come to you." *But I can't about this.* She hated keeping secrets from him. She was betraying him. Although she knew it was necessary if she wanted Juaan to live, she loathed what she had become.

He didn't let go of her face. "Please. You are all I have now, Nyri. I cannot lose you."

Nyri's breath caught in her throat. She saw the strain and the fear in Baarias' increasingly thin face. He was suffering as much as anyone else.

Nyri bowed her forehead against his. "I promise, Baarias. You are all I have, too." She let him feel the love and respect she felt for him flow through the contact.

When they pulled apart, his eyes were overbright. "Well," he cleared his throat. "You best be off. Take care of Kyaati."

Nyri nodded to him, smiling. "I will."

"Nyri," Kyaati murmured as they took their leave. Nyri started at the sound of her voice; a rare thing to be heard now, for sure. "Can we go home? I want to sleep."

The corners of Nyri's mouth pulled down. Kyaati was retiring earlier and earlier, less and less interested in being a part of life. Wanting to sleep while Ninmah was still in the sky was a new low.

"Don't you want to visit Sefaan?" Nyri tried to think of something that would take her interest. "Her stories always make us smile." Nyri would have liked to visit the Kamaali herself. She needed reassurance, to be told once again that she was doing the right thing.

Kyaati shook her head. "I just want to sleep." There was a bite to her voice that told Nyri that she would be wasting her energy arguing with her.

Nyri acquiesced and led Kyaati back to her tree. Once there, Kyaati lay down inside her bower and said no more. Within moments, her breathing deepened, and she was gone. Nyri was left staring down at her, feeling lost. Her friend's soft breaths lulled her. Sleep begged her to pay it a visit as well, but she could not let herself give in. She could not face her nightmares. She needed something to do.

Her heart gave a little jump as the thought struck. With Kyaati sleeping, she could make a rare daytime visit to Juaan. Nyri longed to see his face out of the shadow of night. It would lift her spirits and she could forget her troubles for a time.

Nyri shifted from foot to foot, deciding. It was risky but her desire to go was overpowering and it soon overcame her better judgement. Taking a familiar precaution, she pressed her fingers against Kyaati's temples and drew her down into that deeper sleep. She would not wake now until Nyri returned.

She left her friend inside her tree and slipped out into

the forest in a well-worn routine. Nyri could guess almost exactly where each of the sentinels stood watch now. Their places had become habit, as had hiding her presence. At least Daajir had been right about one thing: the Woves had not returned since he had pierced one of them with a *vaash* barb.

Juaan raised his eyebrows when she appeared.

"A daytime visit? I am honoured."

"You should be. I'm a busy elf." She had grudgingly come to accept his name for her People, just as he accepted her calling him Juaan. He had given up correcting her.

He tilted his head, concern shadowing his eyes, much as it had Baarias. "You look exhausted. You should take time to rest, you are not getting enough."

Nyri rubbed her scratchy eyes, irritation flaring at his words. *I wish people would stop telling me that!* "I wonder whose fault that is?"

"Yours. I'm not keeping myself down here, you know."

Nyri growled and handed him the food she had brought. He smiled at her annoyance and wolfed down his ration. Nyri sat with her back pressed against the hard rock and rested her eyes. Just for a few moments...

She listened to the soothing bird song above and its accompaniment of whispering leaves. They rattled dryly; their decline proceeding at a rapid pace. The temperature was plummeting ever lower. The nights were uncomfortable and soon would become unforgiving. It wouldn't be long until the tribe moved to Baarias' tree to sleep together for shared warmth.

Often Nyri fancied she tasted the promise of frost, but hoped it was her imagination. She did not like what she felt

425

on the air, in the shift of the earth. Everything murmured that what was to come would be terrible to behold. The leaves shivered.

"What is it?"

Nyri opened her eyes to find Juaan crouched close before her, watching her face. She realised she had been frowning.

"Ninsiku approaches in all his Fury and the world trembles," she whispered.

"You mean the winter?" he asked. It was his term for Ninsiku's Fury.

Nyri nodded. "Yes. Can't you feel it? Every cycle, I feel him approach, but this time, this time," Nyri hunched her shoulders, "I fear it. It feels like the beginning of the end."

He watched her expressionlessly, then raised his hand to the soft breeze, feeling its nip. "Hmmm," he said. "It will be a long and cruel one. I fear you are right."

There was a whine from above their heads. Batai was peering down at them. The wolf often accompanied Nyri on these visits now, seeming to think she needed watching with this strange visitor. He had never repeated his descent into the Pit, however, preferring to observe from a safe distance. Batai lifted a grey lip at Juaan, laying his ears flat against his thick neck.

"He still does not like me."

"Maybe because you wear the fur of his dead kin about your body," Nyri pointed out. The skins he wore were obviously wolf. She cringed. She always tried not to let herself think too much about this fact.

"I'm sorry," Juaan said. "It's not personal, simply a matter of survival." His eyes skirted over her very different garments. "I can't imagine that those leaves offer you much

426

protection."

Nyri ignored that. *They were enough once,* she thought sadly.

He held out his hand and Nyri saw he had saved the last few morsels for her. "Take it," he insisted. "You look as if a gust of wind would blow you away."

Nyri hesitated before giving in to the offering. She would not admit to him she was giving him almost every scrap of her food ration; she had to prolong the supplies in the stashed gathering baskets for as long as possible, for she did not know how long this situation would continue. Nyri did not care how much Juaan had changed or forgotten; she knew at her core if she told him she was going without for him, he would accept no more food from her.

"What else concerns you?" He probed. "It is not just the coming of the winter."

Nyri frowned at him. "I thought you said you didn't know me?"

He shrugged.

Nyri sighed. "It's Kyaati. She is ill and not getting any better. I do not know how to reach her. I fear," her breath caught, "I fear we are going to lose her, too."

He sat, taking this in for a few moments. When he spoke, it was in the most gentle tone she had ever heard from his lips. "Do not give up. You will find a way." Nyri's skin tingled as he reached out to touch her hand. "I remember the night she fell. You flew down like a falcon and tried to beat me with a stick to save her." He smiled ruefully. "I noticed your bravery even then. If you can do that and if she has even half your courage, she will recover."

His words stunned Nyri into silence. She had not expected

them. Warmth filled her. She tried to read his face, but he was looking away from her now, keeping an eye on Batai. His next words sounded strained. "Did the fall...? Was it our fault?"

"No." She blew out a breath. "I wanted to blame you. I wanted it to be the Woves' fault. The baby was born malformed. Whether Kyaati had fallen from that tree or not, the result would have been the same." Her voice lowered. "It is happening more and more frequently, our children born dead or deformed. We have always believed that you," she waved a hand at him, "Woves caused our growing weakness, cursing us with some dark power that we could not understand. I was so certain... But you do not have that power, do you?" Nyri finished with a bitter twist to her lips.

"I'm afraid not," he said. "Only what I've picked up from your People, it seems."

"Well, whatever the cause, we are dying. Soon there won't be any of us left for the Woves to hunt." Nyri fixed him with a stare. "Why do you hunt us? You never did tell me. If the Woves don't eat us and do not aid Ninsiku in his vendetta to see us dead, why do they come?"

Juaan stared back, long and hard. He was debating whether to speak. Nyri wanted to know. If she knew, perhaps she could find a way to stop whatever it was the Woves came for. They could be free of the threat once and for all. Maybe then her People could focus on the true reasons they were dying out.

Juaan appeared to come to a decision, but just as he opened his mouth to speak, there was a flare of intent from above. Nyri looked up. Something had caught Batai's attention.

"What is it?" Juaan asked.

"Deer," she murmured. "There is a small herd browsing away in the trees, upwind from Batai. The breeze just carried their scent to him. He's hungry. He has scarcely left Omaal's side apart from to accompany me here at night."

"Omaal?"

"One of the children." Nyri swiftly explained the remarkable relationship between the blind boy and this wolf.

Juaan shook his head in amazement. "I wonder what it is like to see through a wolf's eyes?" he said as Batai disappeared from view, moving away with a single-minded focus.

"Do you want to try?"

"I can do that?"

"I don't see why not."

"What if I harm him?" Now there was a familiar note of anxiety in his voice.

His concern for Batai touched Nyri and bolstered her confidence. "You won't, I have faith in you." She took his wrist, ignoring the tensing of his muscles as she did so. Another suspicion he could not quite let go of. "Focus. I will help you."

Juaan closed his eyes, and Nyri heard his teeth clench. He could not do it on his own, not when he was calm. Nyri still had to guide him. It made her feel like a failure as a teacher, but it had only been a handful of days, she told herself. Ninkuraaja children breathed this learning from their first steps; it was difficult, if not impossible, to change the way a mind could focus itself.

She drew him to his innermost centre, and the trapped energy that resided there, just waiting to be unbound. With her mind, Nyri bridged the absent connection between

Juaan and his power, releasing it, and directed it to the presence that was Batai. His energy came with her willingly, its wildness tamed by her touch. Not unlike the wolf himself. Batai was getting close to the deer as their thoughts mingled with his. Nyri felt Juaan's awe as his senses became one with the Child of the Great Spirit for the very first time. He was Seeing with her and the knowledge filled her with joy.

The thought of juicy tissues filling one's mouth swamped Batai's mind. Nyri flinched away from the sensation. But in that same instant—it happened.

As Batai pictured his meal, another hungry mind answered his hunter's instinct. Juaan's consciousness exploded forth. Once again, the power of it sent Nyri's own senses reeling. His energy broke from her grasp and rushed forward.

"No!" Such uncontrolled power could destroy Batai's mind. She heard a muffled cry of effort as Juaan fought to pull back. He only marginally succeeded. He did not kill Batai, but his will took over completely. Not just a guiding influence. His power had driven Batai out of his own mind. The wolf was Juaan now.

Frozen in horrified amazement, Nyri felt Juaan's disorientation as he experienced his new body. Four legs instead of two, the ears, the tail, the nose—the smell of the deer. Animal instincts took over his higher thoughts and with a wild howl that ripped through the trees, Juaan the wolf surged forward. In a few clumsy bounds, he fell among the deer herd.

His first inexperienced lunge missed the target, and the herd scattered. Juaan swung around and began driving the deer back towards the Pits at reckless speed. The ground trembled beneath Nyri's feet as they came crashing around the edges of the Pit.

One or two of the terrified animals scrambled around the edge, dislodging stones beneath their hooves. The terrible sense of having death snapping at one's heels washed across her mind and Nyri shrank back against the rock wall, fearing for her own life as she struggled to draw her senses back to her own awareness.

Disorientated, she did not hear the danger until it was too late. The dreadful sound of something heavy tumbling and crunching everything in its wake. Nyri raised her hands as the massive rock came crashing towards her, bringing an avalanche of broken logs and debris with it. Her muscles locked down. She could not move even to save her own life.

"Nyriaana!" She heard the cry just as a hard body hit her, knocking her out of death's reach. It all happened so fast, a blur of motion before her eyes. In midair, he twisted, hitting the ground with her on top. She thought she heard a cry of pain before Juaan was rolling again, this time coming to rest with her beneath him, his arms cradling her head as the killing rock smashed into the very spot where she had been standing. The resounding crack echoed through the forest. Flocks of birds took to the air in a frenzy of flapping wings. Then silence.

Nyri gasped, trembling from head to foot beneath Juaan's protective body. She tried to move, but her limbs rebelled against her commands until a stifled groan of pain in her ear brought her back to her senses.

"Juaan," she breathed. He was hurt. She pulled herself from beneath him. "Juaan."

Nyri sucked in a breath as he sat himself upright with a hiss, rocks and pebbles dislodging from his furs as he moved.

Nyri paid no attention to this. She had eyes only for the heavy branch lying next to him on the ground. A protruding, broken off limb was stained with red. Nyri paled as she realised Juaan had fallen upon it as he saved her. The jagged point had pierced his shoulder, ripping through the furs.

Juaan reached over with his hand and it came back bloody. He raised an eyebrow at the sight, but otherwise showed no other signs of distress.

"Who's there?" A voice called out from above. Imaani's voice.

No! Nyri panicked. The disturbance had alerted the watchers, and they were coming to investigate. Grabbing Juaan, Nyri wrapped herself around him. He struggled against her and started to protest. "Be still!" she hissed. "I've got to hide us. They'll kill you!"

Nyri could feel them approaching. They were almost upon them. She drew on all of her strength, pulling it like a blanket around them both. She camouflaged her energy, mimicking it to the rock and the plant life around them. She had never, ever attempted to shield someone other than herself. She did not know if it could be done. But if she did not, Juaan would be taken from her forever. She had to do it. Nothing else mattered.

Nyri tightened her hold and attuned herself to Juaan until their very breaths and heartbeats came together and his energy merged with hers. Nyri drew on it and blended it with the surrounding Pit. She thought she would pass out from the effort.

Through blurring vision, Nyri looked up to see Imaani's head appear over the lip of the Pit in the gap she had made in the coverings. His eyes scanned the surrounding forest.

She prayed he would not notice the root dangling into the depths at his feet.

She felt Juaan stoop to pick up a rock, prepared to throw and dispatch Imaani as soon as he got close enough. *No! Don't hurt him!*

He stiffened at the sound of her voice in his mind. Nyri watched as her fellow tribesman paced around the Pit. He knew something was wrong, but he couldn't find what. Nyri closed her eyes as she concentrated harder. Their breathing stopped. Only their heartbeats counted the moments.

The sound of brushing undergrowth receded, and then… nothing. A bird flew overhead, its flapping wings breaking the stillness that had fallen around them. The next thing Nyri knew, Juaan was breaking himself from her death hold. "I think he's gone. You can let go now." His voice was strained.

"Are you all right?" she asked tightly. She could feel the heat of his blood soaking against her garments.

"I think so," he said. He rubbed the back of his head. He looked dazed. "Are you unharmed?"

"Of course I am!" she snapped. The shock and the fear were rushing up to drown her now that the danger had passed. "You knocked me out of the way." A sudden fury choked her. "You fool, you could have been killed! They could have found us! How many times have I told you what it would do to me to lose you again!" A couple of tears spilled loose. Nyri wiped at them furiously. She knew she was overreacting, but the shock of the near death experience was heightening her already over-wrought emotional state.

He watched her warily as she struggled to compose herself. "Easy," he said. "You're in shock."

"Of course I am! I nearly died. Again. They nearly found *you!*" she ranted. Then Nyri saw his face. She bowed her head, breathing deeply as she tried to re-find her centre. She was coming apart so easily lately. She did not know herself anymore. "I'm sorry," she said after a few moments. She moved to kneel in front of him. The blood dripped to the rock from his shoulder. "Will you let me heal you?" she asked. "Please. I need to see that there is no serious damage. If a rock struck your head..." Her fists clenched.

He looked down at her, hesitating.

Please, she thought at him. *Haven't I proved to you after all this time that you can at least trust in me? Please.*

He must have seen something in her eyes and guessed her thoughts. The hesitation vanished, and the tension left his body. He gave in. "If you wish," he murmured.

"Thank you." If the situation had been different, her heart would have rejoiced. Wiping the last of the stinging tears from her cheeks, she got to her feet. The furs were now soaked with blood from the wound the branch had dealt him. The hairs clung to the edges of the wound. "I need you to take these off."

The hesitation was back, his body tense once more.

"Please," Nyri asked again. "I need to see."

His lips were tight as he pulled the furs from his torso. Nyri tried not to stare like a child as he did. Other differences from her race became apparent as he removed his coverings. Again, there was more hair under the arms and lightly covering his chest. The biggest difference was the musculature. She could see now where his power came from.

He was not bulky, but the muscles were defined, smooth

434

and strong. His shoulders and chest were broad, his waist narrow and lean. Nyri shut her mouth, realising too late that it was hanging open. He hadn't looked like *this* as a boy. An odd but not unpleasant feeling shivered down her spine.

The reaction confused her, and she averted her eyes, embarrassed. She had seen plenty of male bodies in her life and had never reacted in that way before. Nyri was shocked to find that she was attracted to the raw strength he displayed. She scolded herself, she should not be having such Forbidden thoughts. *Ninmah, forgive me!*

Any thought, Forbidden or otherwise, fled, however, as she saw past the immediate. Nyri gasped at the many scars marring the rich skin. He stared stonily ahead, ignoring her reaction.

With increasing horror, Nyri moved around to stand behind him. Even seated, his head near brushed her breast. More scars slashed his back. Nyri bit her lip, holding back fresh tears that begged to fall. Not all these old injuries could come from the accidents of life. *What have those monsters done to him?* An anger that she had long ago buried rose once more at Baarias for leaving Juaan behind all those seasons ago.

Stolidly, Nyri healed his most recent injuries, starting with the deep wound on his shoulder. While working, she checked for any hidden injuries that the eyes were blind to but could prove life threatening if left untreated. There were none, and Nyri returned her full attention to the task before her. When Juaan's torn skin was whole once more, she could no longer hold her tongue.

"What in Ninmah's name happened to you?" Nyri reached out to touch a long scar on his shoulder. He shifted out of her reach, and she dropped her hand. "What did they do to you? Tell me."

"It is not for you to know," he said, setting his jaw.

"Don't give me that," she growled. "Tell me. Where have all these scars come from? Who did this to you?"

He stared at her with a mix of frustration and reluctance.

She sat down in front of him, letting him know she wasn't going anywhere until she got her answers. She could be stubborn, too. "Please."

"You would not understand."

"Help me understand. I want to help you."

Now there was a definite sadness in the half-smile he gave her. "It is nothing you can fix. Nothing has been *done* to me but life." He drew a breath and Nyri knew he had decided to speak. She was conscious not to make any sound or action that might make him withdraw from her again. "When my clan found me, it surprised them to find that I was half elf. They'd found no one like me before."

"There are no other Forbidden Ninkuraa in your clan?" Nyri asked before she could stop herself. She felt a thud of disappointment. Ariyaana was not with his People.

"No," he said. "I am the only one. I believe my clan chief hoped I would possess the power of my elf heritage. When it became clear that I could not control it or pass on my gifts, he was… disappointed. I had to be found another use. When he witnessed me defeat another clan member in a brawl, he gave me over to the spear master to become *raknari*."

"What is *raknari*?" He had mentioned the word before. A *position of high honour*, he had said.

"A warrior. We are trained to protect the clan from any threat, to do anything it takes, no matter the consequence, the survival of the clan is all."

"No matter the consequence? They would expect you to die for the clan?"

Head high, he dipped his chin once. Nyri could detect his annoyance at her tone of consternation. "It is a great honour to be *raknari* and to protect one's clan."

Nyri bit her tongue. "How do you become *raknari*?"

He shrugged. "It is not easy."

"Tell me."

"Training is brutal and very few survive the *raknari* life for long. You win or you die."

Nyri was aghast. "You mean you fight one another? Other clans?"

"*Yes*," he hissed, losing patience, but she did not miss the haunted light lurking in his eyes. He appeared much older than he was. "Only the strongest survive to become *raknari*. Only the strongest survive *life*. Good territories are getting harder to come by. To secure one, we must be prepared to fight for it and then defend it by any means necessary."

Nyri turned her face away from him to glare at the cold, grey wall of the Pit. Her jaw worked as she tried to contain her emotion. They had hurt him. They had made him fight. They had made him... Nyri wanted to ask, but the hollow look in his eyes was all she needed to know. They had made him *kill*. The answer was obvious. *You win or you die.* He was still very much alive. His opponents were not.

Like Baarias, Nyri had come to the conclusion that the Woves were not the evil servants of Ninsiku but, also like Baarias, she realised they were still murderous savages. Monsters that would kill even their own kind over a scrap of meat.

When she could bring herself to meet his gaze once more, her cheeks were wet with tears. "They hurt you," was all she could whisper.

He frowned and reached out to touch her damp cheek. An array of emotions played over his face. "You weep for me?" he asked. "Why?"

Nyri growled in frustration. "Can you not figure it out?" she hissed, wiping her eyes fiercely, trying to keep the choke out of her voice. "Have I not made it perfectly clear? I love you, Juaan. I always have. I cannot bear to see you hurt. Even to protect me."

A loaded silence fell between them at her declaration. Neither breathed. She dared not look at him.

Fingers brushed her cheek for the second time and this time, the touch was almost shy. Nyri's eyes darted up at the contact, and her breath caught at his expression.

"I... could not see you hurt, either."

Nyri could have melted in his eyes at that moment. She lived in it. Then the moment passed, and he pulled his hand away. He shook his head, hissing out a breath. "What is it about you? I do not know." He stared hard at her face, searching. His own was filled with an unquenchable frustration.

Impulsively, Nyri reached out and caught his hands between her own. She had no hope of holding them there should he decide to pull away. She held her breath, waiting for him to break the contact; her heart beat faster when he did not. He was motionless, his soul searching for an answer beyond his understanding. The world turned around them. Nyri no longer cared that he could save her People, or that she had to find a strange girl who may not exist. She could not bear to let him go back to those savages. She would do anything.

"Please stay with me, Juaan," she whispered. "You do not have to go back there. I cannot let you go back. You are not their killer. They took you from me, now come back."

He looked down at their joined hands. He still did not pull away, but the smile that came to his face was bitter. "How?" he said. "Even if I wanted to, even if what you are saying is true and I am a boy you knew long ago, how can I stay here? My life with my clan may be hard but your People," he glanced up to where Imaani had stood before staring Nyri full in the face, "would kill me."

Nyri kept her gaze locked on his for a long and helpless moment. In the end it was she that pulled away. How could she deny it?

41

Eyes Closed

Nyriaana skirted around the side of the massive family tree. Pausing to catch her breath, she leaned a small hand on the rough bark. She could feel activity within buzzing against her senses. A family was waking as Ninmah rose over the blossoming village. Nyri loved the Blooming. It was when everything was at its most beautiful. All the giant trees around her blushed the prettiest shade of green. The nest-like homes growing from them draped in white blossoms.

There was no time to admire the view this morning, though. Drawing in a lungful of sweet, bloom-scented air, Nyri focused her attention back on her mission. The stranger she was shadowing was getting lost from sight. She was supposed to be getting breakfast. If she returned with nothing, Juaan would be cross with her.

Nyri peeped around the tree. The stranger had disappeared. She could still feel his energy vibrating faintly up ahead among the sleepy presence of the trees, but now he was out of sight. For a second she was torn as her stomach rumbled. Then curiosity won out. She pushed away from the tree and trotted on.

The tribe was coming alive around her. Her People were emerging from their homes to greet the day. Nyri was not the only one taking an interest in the strange man up ahead. She could taste the curiosity filling the air and hear the buzz of mutterings as she went by. Word was spreading fast.

Nyri had been on the outskirts of her home, watching Ninmah rise over the trees, when the stranger arrived. He was similar in appearance to the rest of her People. Honey coloured skin with eyes a light shade of indigo and hair in the rare silver-white shade rather than dark. His clothes were different, the leaves fashioned in a strange design, but that was all. At first, Nyriaana had been disappointed. Juaan's tales of the Cro and the Thals had enthralled her. She would love to see one of them one day.

This man was Ninkuraaja. Not very old. One of his arms appeared misshapen, and his gait was uneven. Again, this was not unusual. More than half of her tribe had such complaints. Some found it difficult to go about their daily life. Even so, he was interesting. He was someone Nyri had not seen before. That was exciting and a little frightening all at once. What was he here for? Where was he from? Two of her tribe who had been on watch quickly trailed him. They followed, but remained relaxed.

Now Nyri watched the man pause as he reached the centre of her tribe's home. Here stood the largest tree. The Elders' tree. The Elders often met here to discuss important matters. The giant limbs of the tree twisted this way and that, forming many spaces within them. Vines supplying water twisted like veins over the great tree's skin. Nyri observed as the stranger and his escort climbed up and disappeared into the nearest chamber.

Dare she follow them in there? She was dying to know what he was here for. He had an air of importance. Usually the Elder Tree was open for everyone to gather and meet in, even the children, unless there were more 'adult' matters to be discussed. Was this an 'adult' matter? Nyriaana twisted the leaves at her waist, debating whether she dared to go inside and try to listen in. She'd come this far, after all.

Nyri started forward before fear could persuade her otherwise and climbed up after the stranger. Inside the Elder Tree, a curving passageway led away to the left. It was nice inside here. She could smell the life and growth of the ancient tree.

Hearing voices down the passage, she started along it until she reached another, larger chamber ahead. Nyri crouched a few steps from the chamber, just out of sight from the five people she knew were inside. One was her stranger along with the two sentries who had escorted him here and two of her tribe's most respected Elders. She held her breath and did her best to mask her presence. Not one of her strongest skills. She hoped they would be too distracted to realise she was hiding just out of sight.

This seemed to work. A low discussion started. Nyri heard snatches of words like Thals... sighted... lands. Nyriaana risked slipping closer to better hear what was said.

The man was from a tribe whose home lay further to the north. He was warning the Elders that Thals had been sighted on his tribe's territory, moving south. The increasingly harsh Fury's ies were driving even the Cold People down from their wastelands.

Upon hearing this, the Elders grew agitated and asked many sharp questions. Nyri's curiosity burned even more hotly than theirs. She had exhausted Juaan's stories of the Cold People of the north. She listened avidly, but was disappointed when the stranger said the Thals had been driven off. No one knew where they were now. The stranger advised a closer watch to be kept on her tribe's borders. The conversation then turned to boring things like Joinings and food. The Elders were quick to seize on *this stranger's presence. Nyri stopped paying attention as she let her imagination run wild. Thals had been close, so close.*

"What are you doing?"

Nyriaana jumped and spun around to face the Elder, who had come up unnoticed behind her. Pelaan raised a stern eyebrow. Nyriaana's mouth went dry. Pelaan was the worst person to have caught her. He wasn't nice. He hated Juaan. It didn't help that the voices in the room beyond had stopped to listen to her telling off as well.

"I-I..."

Pelaan watched her flounder. Then his eyes cast around, clearly looking for someone else. When he saw she was alone, his features softened. His gentler tone surprised her. "You'd better get out of here, Nyri. I understand your curiosity, so there'll be no punishment for your bad manners today, but do not let me catch you doing this again. These concerns are not for your ears. Find Kyaati and play."

Nyriaana shifted her feet shamefully and risked a glance into the chamber next to her. The Elders within were regarding her severely. She could feel the sting of their disapproval. The stranger was looking at her with a faint smile on his thin lips. Nyri shuffled past Pelaan without meeting his gaze, feeling their eyes on her back until she disappeared from sight and out of the tree. She blew out a breath as she touched the ground. She had been lucky to get out of there without punishment. The other Elders had wanted to.

Nyri walked away from the Elder Tree as her heart rate returned to normal. With the shame fading, her excitement burned anew.

She broke into a run, eagerly eating up the distance she had to cover to get home. She could not wait to tell Juaan. But when

443

she climbed into their tree, Juaan wasn't there. Puzzled, Nyri descended and searched the eshaara grove for him, to no avail. She was about to get distressed when the answer came to her. He had gone to his mother's tree.

Nyri raced to the edge of the eshaara grove. Grabbing the first hold on the decaying tree, Nyri suddenly remembered the original purpose for her morning trip. Breakfast. No matter, as soon as Juaan heard her news and the adventure she was plotting in her head, then he would forget all about food. Nyri continued climbing towards the upper chamber. Her friend was inside. She could feel his familiar presence radiating out to her.

She scrambled through the entrance. As always, it was dim inside. As her eyes adjusted to the light, Nyri spotted Juaan sitting curled into a corner, his long arms folded around his knees. He held the Thal spear in his hands.

"Juaan, c'mon!" Nyriaana attempted to be as distracting as possible considering she was breakfast-less.

She did not notice his drawn, serious expression as she pounced, bounced up and down on her toes like the seven-Blessing-old she was and not caring a bit. Juaan's green eyes were bemused under his mess of brown hair.

"What is it this time?" he asked. "Have the wolves had pups again?" He was being deliberately calm in the face of her excitement, provoking her. His lips twitched towards a rare smile, dispelling his sombre expression.

Nyri huffed, too excited to put up with this behaviour. "No, silly." She grabbed a large hand and tugged. "C'mon! We gotta go!"

"Where?" Now he was definitely trying not to laugh at her futile efforts to move him.

Nyri stamped her foot. "To find the Thals! A strange man has

444

come from another tribe. I heard him talking. He saw them! I wanna see! Come with me. He's still here, we can ask him where they went."

Juaan's expression closed down and he pulled his hand from hers with no effort at all, placing it back on the spear. "No, Nyri," he said, his voice flat.

"But I want you to come and see!" Nyri tried to keep the whine from her voice.

"No," he said again. Irritation saturated his tone.

"Why not?" Nyri lost her battle with the whine. Why was he being so stubborn? Juaan always came with her when she wanted to explore. "Why won't you come with me?" she asked again when he didn't answer her the first time.

"Because I can't be seen out there! Baarias came to warn me that the stranger was here. He told me to hide and not be seen under any circumstance."

"Why?" Nyri hid her surprise that Baarias had sought Juaan out. The healer usually avoided him, which Nyri thought strange. Baarias was always such a compassionate person towards everyone. "Of course you can be seen."

He let out a frustrated hiss and stood up. He towered over her. But then, he was twelve Furies old. "Look at me, Nyri." He gestured sharply to his face and body. "Really look at me. Now surely you've noticed after all this time that I don't exactly look the same as everyone else? And don't tell me you still believe the 'I ate my gora roots' story, because it's just not true."

Nyri blinked at him, taking in the familiar large frame, the green eyes, his deep skin. Juaan was different. Of course she'd noticed. She just hadn't thought much about what had always seemed so natural to her. Juaan was her life, as much a part of it as the air that she breathed. She was so confused by his demand *she forgot to be annoyed that he'd been lying to her about the vile roots all this time. She'd get to that later.*

"I'm different, Nyri." Juaan dropped his hands. "I can't be seen by the stranger. Our tribe turns a blind eye because... because of Sefaan. But I can't be seen by an outsider. I can't come with you."

He sank back down into the shadows, folding his long arms around himself, closing off. His expression turned Nyri cold.

"Why aren't you allowed, Juaan?" She was suddenly terrified of the answer, although she could not say why.

Juaan's green eyes were shadowed. But for the first time, he didn't shelter her from something that would hurt. "They will kill me."

Four little words. Four vaash thorns to Nyri's heart. She gasped. The horror of their meaning threatened to choke her. Kill Juaan? No. Not her Juaan. She would not survive without him. He was all she had.

"I'm unclean." The words were bitter. "Forbidden. It's only a matter of time before our tribe... as soon as Sefaan—" He squeezed his eyes shut.

Nyri dropped to her knees beside her best friend. She clung to him and buried her face in his arm to hide her frightened tears. Her fists tightened in his coverings. She would never let him go. She tried to make sense of somebody being killed for being unclean. Juaan wasn't unclean. He made sure they washed often in the stream at the edge of the grove. It kept them strong, he said. The same as those horrible gora roots he was always making her eat. Nyri inhaled his familiar scent, letting it comfort her. No, Juaan wasn't unclean at all. But she didn't want to question him further. She feared the answers he might give.

"Promise you won't go out," she begged. "Promise me you won't

ever leave me."

"Shhh,." He brushed her tears away. "I promise. I'll never leave you."

"Promise."

"Promise." His arm came around her as she folded into his side.

She stayed with Juaan in the dimness of his mother's home for the rest of that bright day. The world outside suddenly seemed like a very frightening place indeed.

* * *

Juaan's blood soaked furs were attracting flies.

"You can't put those on," Nyri told him. "I'm going to have to take them and wash them in the river." She glanced up at the sky. Could she make it there carrying Wove garments? If she was caught with them... There would be no explaining her way out of that. She had no choice. These furs needed to be cleaned.

"Make sure you bring them back," Juaan said, folding his arms. Nyri could see that his skin had already prickled against the chill. He was fighting a shiver.

She smiled at his comment. "I will. They needed a wash anyway. You were beginning to stink." She wrinkled her nose as she lifted the dark furs.

He rolled his eyes and threw his arms wide to indicate the Pit, lifting his eyebrows, the message clear: *and where am I supposed to wash?*

"I know, I know." Nyri looked at the rope that would take her back to the surface and hefted the furs. They were much heavier than he made them appear. She doubted she could climb while carrying them.

"Here," he said, flashing a grin. He bundled his clothes up tight, swung back a long arm and hurled them into the air. Up and over the edge, they flew.

"Show off," she muttered, trying not to stare at his movement and the way it made his muscles move. Nyri climbed back to the surface, pulling her rope with her. She gathered up the bundle and set off towards the river, aiming for a location far from the tribe and little used. Nyri often visited the place when she needed to be alone or to think. The sound of the water and Ninmah's light glinting on the surface were always soothing.

She needed that balm now. Her thoughts played over everything Juaan had told her, and her heart burned. When she reached the river, there were no shafts of light playing on the silken ripples today. Clouds masked Ninmah's golden face from view, but the music of the water was still beautiful as the shallow current scurried over the rounded pebbles. A few of the trees stooped on the bank, trailing the tips of their fingers in the stream, waving serenely with the motion.

Nyri dipped the furs in the water, and the flow turned red brown. Nyri waited until the water ran clear and all traces of Juaan's injury had been cleansed. No scent of blood could remain; there were worse things than flies in the forest.

Nyri splashed her tired face with the cold water and crouched, hugging her knees as she wrestled with her dilemma. She had to keep Juaan with her, but how? He was right. Her People's eyes were closed to him. She chewed a fingernail. Maybe… maybe she could go to Sefaan. The Kamaali had forced her tribe to accept Juaan once. Perhaps she still had the power to do it again. Nyri could not face letting him go for a second time. He could not go back to those killers. She could not bear it.

By the time the furs were clean, her will had hardened. She would go to Sefaan as soon as she was able. Nyri yanked the furs from the river and heaved them over a hidden branch just inside a thicket. The shadows made the perfect disguise so long as no one looked too closely, and there was no reason anyone should. The breeze stroked the damp hairs. Nyri hoped they would be dry by the time she returned to Juaan tonight. If he did not have them, he would succumb to exposure in the cold darkness. Nyri glanced at the sky and the angle of Ninmah's light. She should get back to the tribe. She couldn't risk leaving Kyaati any longer. She'd pushed her luck long enough as it was.

"Nyri?"

She stifled the cry of shock as Daajir materialised out of the trees like a ghost. She swiftly blocked any view of the furs hanging behind her as her heart hammered, unsure of how much he had seen. His voice had been full of consternation.

"What are you *doing* out here?" he demanded.

Nyri floundered, "I-I, Baarias needed some more herbs to treat Omaal's fever."

He frowned at her. "Really? I just checked on Omaal's family and the child was much recovered after Baarias' last visit. Why would Baarias need more ingredients? And why in Ninmah's name would he send you out alone?"

The blood drained from Nyri's face at her misstep. Her overworked brain turned to sludge. She sank to the ground and put her head in her hands. "I-I just needed to get out," she blurted. "I just can't face the despair and the hunger anymore. Naaya and Haana... I n-needed to get away for a while while Kyaati sleeps."

"You left her *unattended?*"

"Baarias is with her," she amended. "Of course I wouldn't leave her alone." Lie after lie. This situation was spinning wildly out of her control, and Nyri started to panic.

Daajir did not look convinced. "I hope not. You're disobeying the Elders being out here alone, regardless, Nyriaana. We're all feeling the strain, but you don't see anyone else running away. What is wrong with you lately? You know better."

He was speaking to her like a child again. "So do you," Nyri shot back. "What are *you* doing out here? You are just as vulnerable as I."

To her surprise, his scolding did not continue. His face became animated, eager.

Nyri stepped away from the thicket containing Juaan's furs, drawing his attention with her in the opposite direction.

"I am ready, Nyri," he gloated, following her a step, then paused. "I was going to wait, to surprise you and Kyaati, but since you are out here, I don't think I can resist any longer."

"Then don't, please, I want to see!" Nyri gushed as if she didn't already know well what he had been up to. The memory of the vaash barb embedding itself inside a Wove's gut was not one she would forget easily.

Daajir's eyes glowed at her feigned enthusiasm, and Nyri knew her words had gained the desired effect. "You won't have to face our People's despair for much longer. I have a plan and Aardn has agreed to it. No one else is going to die this Fury. I will take back what is ours! Come, I will show you. It will ease your cares."

Don't hold your breath, Nyri thought.

He took her by the hand and pulled her along. He squeezed her fingers uncomfortably, frowning as he went. "You are wasting away, Nyriaana. You look almost as bad as Kyaati." He turned his head to give her an accusing stare. "We can't have our most promising women fading away. Once you are Joined, you will need your strength to beat the curse those Woves have placed upon us. It is essential you bear whole children."

Nyri dug her nails into her palms. *It's not a Wove curse, you fool,* she thought but held her silence. She had promised Baarias; arguing would do nothing but get them both into deep trouble.

He led her into the forest, away from the Pits. Nyri cringed at the delay in getting home. She was trapped and time was running out to return to Kyaati. Even with Nyri's sleep suggestion, her tribe-sister would not remain unconscious forever. She needed to get away from Daajir as soon as she could. "Where are we going?" she asked.

"You'll see," he said cryptically, unheeding of her tone.

Nyri bit down on her nerves and impatience and pulled her hand from his. His talk of Joining had made her heart squeeze with fear. He was the very last person she wanted to be with right now. "How much further?"

"Not far."

Nyri could hear the smile in his voice. Finally, he stopped. They were in a darker, danker part of the forest. Fallen tree trunks and stumps littered the swampy ground, which was covered with layers of moss and fungus. The air tasted stale and the black ground squished beneath Nyri's feet and between her toes.

"Nyri, you must promise me you will keep this secret until the next auscult. It is very important that you do this for me."

"Alright," she agreed slowly.

He grinned and started down into the dell. "He's here somewhere."

"Who?"

"You'll see."

Nyri folded her arms. "This had better be good."

"Oh, it is," Daajir gloated. "This could be the greatest discovery within the tales of our People. Ah, here he is." Daajir's voice had trailed to a hushed whisper. He crouched down and beckoned Nyri to his side. As she settled on her heels, Daajir lifted back a lump of fallen wood nestled in the ground. Hunkered in the earth beneath was the coiled form of a snake.

Nyri had not expected this and stepped back automatically as the serpent's eyes fixed on her. Its tongue flicked and a low, spitting hiss began in its chest.

"It's safe," Daajir soothed. He raised a hand, and the snake shrank down. "I have reached an understanding with him."

Despite herself, Nyri was impressed. Like spiders, reptilian minds were so removed from their own way of thinking it was next to impossible to create any sort of bond with them. So this was why Baarias had been treating Daajir for snake bites.

"It's taken me the whole of the Blessing," he conceded, reading Nyri's thoughts. "Baarias has had to draw venom from me once or twice." Daajir drew back the coverings on his arm to reveal the scattering of twin puncture wounds littering his pale red-gold skin.

"Why?" Nyri asked. "Why would you do such a thing?"

"I needed his venom."

Nyri raised an eyebrow.

He illuminated her. "Nyri, have you ever seen a snake kill a rodent?"

She nodded slowly, pondering at his direction.

"They inject their victim with the venom. It kills their prey from the inside out. It's a painful death but quick for the small rodent."

Nyri shuddered at the image he had conjured. "Yes..."

"It got me thinking. What if we could use this? What if we could use it to our advantage?"

She frowned at him, a shiver of apprehension working its way up her spine. The memory of his cruel smile as he injured the Wove was strong in her mind.

"Think, Nyri!" he breathed. "Remember how that spider nearly killed that Forbidden abomination?" Daajir produced a *haala* nut shell half and pushed it towards the snake's blunt snout. Obediently, it opened its mouth, pushing the deadly fangs forward and pressing them into the brown bowl. Fluid leaked out and gathered in a small puddle.

"This venom kills effectively, painfully, but quickly and it can be remedied if treated fast enough." Daajir swirled the venom between his hands. "Those last two parts are what I've worked on rectifying. Fast is merciful. The Woves do not deserve mercy and they do not deserve to be saved!" Daajir reached into a pocket and withdrew a handful of night berries. He squeezed the berries over the bowl, releasing the juice into the waiting snake venom, turning it into a violent, unnatural purple.

"Now come here." He moved further into the under-growth. Pushing aside the green foliage, he revealed a cluster of half-grown plants with blood-red leaves and stems bristling with hollow, razor sharp barbs the length of a finger. The *vaash* plant.

Around the roots of each plant was a slimy, fleshy bowl, an inescapable prison in which to trap the plant's rodent victims. All these features were familiar. What Nyri had never seen before was the purple fluid dripping from the tips of the young plants' barbs. Exactly the same shade as the liquid Daajir held in his hand.

"I have always been fascinated by the *vaash*," Daajir said. "It is cunning, and it is deadly. It absorbs the poisons of any other living thing it comes across and takes it as its own, increasing its potency before secreting it from its thorns. I have experimented with many poisons but the combination of snake venom and night juice is what I have been searching for all this past season." He tipped some of the purple liquid from the bowl into the ground near the plants' roots. "The *vaash* slows down the poison's effects; the victim will take days to die. Long enough for said victim to return to their tribe in agony and spread the word. There is no cure for what I have created," Daajir said.

Nyri gaped. *Days to die... No cure...* Her gut tightened as a terrible thought snaked through her mind. "And how have you found this out?" Nyri forced the question between her teeth. "How did you find out what it does and that it can't be cured?"

His eyes closed. "Best that you do not ask," he said. Nyri caught the wave of regret within him.

"What have you been doing, Daajir?" she asked.

454

"It doesn't matter!" he snapped. "I told you. I will do anything necessary to protect our People. Anything!" He drew a deep breath, calming himself with an effort. Nyri had touched a nerve. "The *vaash* barbs are strong enough to pierce the skin of our enemy. That was the purpose of my test the other night. The barb performed admirably." To demonstrate, he carefully plucked a barb from one of his deadly plants. Holding it between a thumb and forefinger, he produced a pipe made from a cutting of the *aquilem* vine.

Nyri's eyes widened as he pushed the poisoned barb into the pipe, placed it to his lips and blew hard. The barb shot out of the other end and embedded itself in the bark of the nearest tree. "They never even saw it coming," Daajir gloated.

Nyri was numb. "D-did you—Was that barb poisoned?"

"No," Daajir said. "I only wanted to test, not spoil the surprise. I don't want them taking off just yet. They have things of ours that we need to take back." He looked down at his poison barbs. "And I have something else."

Nyri's muscles locked in place as he pulled a very familiar bone knife from his clothes. "Do you remember how I found this by the Pits that night Kyaati ran? That place still reeks of their presence. Javaan was right. It is almost like one of them is still there." He wrinkled his nose and Nyri blanched. "One of the monsters must've dropped it the night they fled the wolves." He smiled darkly, examining the sharpened blade. "I expect even a servant of Ninsiku will not survive being pierced by their own weapon. It is infused with all sorts of dark magic. Tip it with my poison and..." He drew back his arm and let the bone knife fly. It embedded itself next to the poison barb in the nearest tree, though it bit into the bark far more deeply. "I saw a Wove do that once. I have been practising." He grinned, walking over to pull it out. "I am ready. I will go to the Wove camp, I will use my poison upon them, and when they are writhing and screaming in pain, I will step over their bodies and take back the food they stole from us. Their deaths will break the curse!"

Nyri took another step back, away from Daajir this time. Her eyes darted between him and the snake, only a few strides away. In that moment she saw no difference in their cold, flat eyes.

"Dar…" she choked. With a shaky hand, Nyri touched his arm and let her feelings speak for her. She let him feel all of her horror at what he was hoping to do.

Daajir's eyes widened in shock, and then anger slashed her senses.

"I thought you of all people would be happy! You hate the Woves as much as I!" He pulled away from her. "But you're just like Sefaan!"

Sefaan. Nyri's breath caught. "Sefaan was here?"

"Yes. The old fool almost destroyed everything."

"Th-that is how she got injured?" Nyri's heart pounded against her ribs. She was now in the same position, alone and isolated, with an increasingly angry Daajir. The knife was still in his hand. The knowledge that a fellow Ninkuraa would harm her, that Daajir could harm her, was unthinkable. But Nyri found herself searching for avenues of escape, nevertheless. She at least would be faster than Sefaan. "You attacked Sefaan?"

"That wasn't my fault!" Daajir pounded his fist on his chest. "She shouldn't have been meddling. I've discovered a way to save our people and all you and Sefaan can do is feel disgust at *me?*"

"It's despicable!" Nyri hit back, matching his anger. "How could you do that to Sefaan? To your *Kamaali?* Ninmah knows how much I hate the Woves, Daajir. But this... it won't help. It is barbaric!"

"Barbaric?" Daajir raged. "What's barbaric is letting those monsters destroy everything we are. They burn our trees, and we fall back. They deform our children, and we simply stand and weep over their bodies. They kill any of us that get in their way and we can do nothing to stop them. I say, no more! They will regret the day they thought to curse our people."

"But they won't! Just how many do you think you can kill, Daajir? All you will do is cause further suffering. For both our Peoples."

"Have they not made us suffer for years? They have driven us to the brink. We are an animal cornered and it is time to show our teeth." He tilted his head at Nyri, and she hated him more than any monster in that instant. "What is it? Do you have a soft spot for these creatures now? I've always wondered about you. The way you used to cling to that abomination when you were a child. What was his name... the Forbidden filth—"

"Don't you *dare,*" Nyri's anger flamed, matching Daajir's own. Her fury lashed at the man before her, but it wasn't enough to cover her pain. He had torn at her old wounds and she was bleeding. "Don't you dare speak his name! He saved me. He gave his life to save mine! You have no right to speak of him. He was worth ten of you. The Woves took him from me. They took my whole family from me! I have every right to hate them as much as anyone. But this... this is evil and it will not change a thing!"

"*They* are evil! And I will make it stop! All of it. It is because of their dark power that our people are ceasing to *exist*! I will turn it on them and make it stop!"

"It won't stop! It's not *them*!" Nyri burst out. "Open your eyes, Daajir! The Woves are only a small part of what is happening. They did not kill Kyaati's babies! They are not freezing us to death every Fury and killing the plants that feed us." It all came pouring out before Nyri could stop it, and now she had no choice but to follow through. "That knife holds no power. Killing a few Woves with a handful of poison barbs will not save us. All you will do is bring them down harder on our heads in revenge and seal our fate all the faster. We are dying, Daajir, and *nothing* we know can stop it."

"No! *Heresy*! I will not hear it!" His eyes bulged frighteningly. "They are the cause and I will save us from them! You will be made to see!" He swirled the bowl and its deadly contents before Nyri. "In three days' time I will go to their camp and I will make them answer for all they have done! Aardn herself has given me her blessing."

Nyri paled. She reached out to him, placating now, desperate to make him see sense. "Daajir, trust me, please. We are family. I have never lied to you. You must listen to me now. I found all this hard to believe, too, but Baarias has always known. He knows and now I am certain he speaks the truth. They are *not* servants of Ninsiku. They have no more power than we do. I *know* it."

"*How* do you know?"

Nyri snapped her mouth closed.

"How do you *know*?" he demanded again. Nyri's eyes

darted, searching for an escape as she backed slowly away from him. He followed her. "Befriended another one, have you? Is that why you are sneaking around? Meeting a demon friend? Well then, why wait? Maybe I should pay him a visit right now." He waved the bone knife before her horrified face.

It was too much. He did not know how close to the mark he had struck. Lashing out, Nyri struck Daajir hard across the cheek with all the strength she could muster. "How dare you!" she snarled, trying to keep the desperation out of her voice. "How dare you accuse me of such a crime!" She slapped him again, her palm stinging from the force of it.

Stunned, he raised the knife reflexively in defence, and the tip caught the skin of Nyri's arm. Razor sharp, it sliced deep into her flesh. She fell back in shock, closing her hand around the stinging pain. Blood oozed from between her fingers.

"Now look what you made me do! This is all Baarias' fault. Aardn was right," Daajir spat. "It is time his teaching of you ended and you be made to fulfil your ultimate duty. That will take your mind off such nonsense!" With that, he pushed past her and stormed into the trees. "I am true to my people and I will protect us. *You will not get in my way!*"

Then he was gone. The storm passed, leaving only destruction in its wake. The only sounds came from the darkening forest dripping around her and her own ragged gasps. Nyri stared at the blood slipping down her arm from the tear in her skin. The trembling began in her hands, then spread to the rest of her body. The palm she had struck Daajir with stung. It burned.

One thing was now certain. She had just made an enemy.

She had closed Daajir's eyes completely against her. The burning spread. Nyri gasped. Once. Twice. But she could not hold back the tide. She fell to her knees and burst into helpless tears.

What had she *done*?

42

The Truth

Nyri did not see Daajir and the other boys detach themselves from the trees until it was too late. "Where are you going?" Daajir asked her.

"To Juaan," she told him. Her mama had taught her to tell the truth. Even to bullies like him.

All three boys glowered at her. Nyri knew they were not pleased. Daajir grabbed her by the arm. She whimpered. He frightened her. He hissed in her ear. "Do not go to him. He probably plotted your family's deaths. He knew your father hated him. He is evil, you stupid baby. The spawn of a monster. The Elders all say so. You're lucky he does not eat you in your sleep." Daajir let her go with a shove. "I'll be watching him. You tell him that. He doesn't fool me. There is nobody here to protect him anymore. And," he poked her in the chest. "I'll be watching you, too. If you are with him, you are not with us."

They disappeared back into the trees as quick as they had come. As soon as they were out of sight, Nyri broke down and ran. Everyone was staring at her, crying and stumbling through their midst.

Ignoring them, she climbed up into their tree and threw herself at Juaan.

"Nyri!" He attempted to free himself, but she clung on, and he quickly gave up. "What's wrong, Nyri, Nyri, Nyriaana?"

"Daajir was mean," she whimpered, words tumbling out. "He said you were evil. That you're a monster. He told me not to be near you. Th-that you'll eat me in my sleep. He said he was watching. He hurt me." She touched her chest to show her meaning.

There was no mistaking the burn of anger. "Did he now?" He was touching her wrist, and she thought she heard him think... frightening a baby. I'll strangle... *"Do you think I am an evil monster, Nyri?" he asked.*

She shook her head in denial.

"Then that's all that matters. I don't care what Daajir thinks or does. He can't hurt me."

"He won't!" she declared. "I protect you. He is wrong."

He smiled, amused by her vow. "Thank you."

Nyri shivered. Juaan rubbed her shoulder. "Are you cold?" She nodded in answer, tucking her chin into her chest and wrapping her arms around herself as far as they would go. She felt the gentle poke of a finger on her arm. "That's what happens to naughty children that play in puddles." The corners of Nyri's mouth dared to turn up in an almost smile. Juaan plucked an aacha *blanket from the nearest bower and wrapped it around her shoulders.*

"Thank you."

"I have to look after my fierce protector, Nyri, Nyri, Nyriaana."

She giggled, her upset forgotten. She couldn't help it. He sat upon one of the moss piles and she crawled into his lap. It was warmer here.

"C'mon. Sleep."

"Nooo. Not sleepy," she slurred "Tell me a story."

He sighed.

"Please?"

"Will you sleep if I do?"

"Promise."

"What would you like to hear?"

Nyri thought for a moment. "I want the one about the Thal boy and how he tamed the great hairy monster in the ice."

And so Juaan began.

Nyri never heard the end. She didn't even remember hearing the beginning by morning. The only thing she recalled was the sound of a dearly familiar voice wrapping her in a cocoon of safety and warmth as it lulled her to sleep. Daajir was wrong. If she ever had to name anyone as evil, it would never be Juaan.

* * *

Nyriaana ran through the trees. For the second time in her life, it was not towards her People. She was running away. Ninmah was low in the sky. She knew that should mean something, something important, but she could not place the concern now. There was only one thing she wanted. She *needed*.

She did not run to him now because he might somehow save her People. She did not run to him for some half-formed vision. She ran to him for him, just him.

It was only through sheer luck she encountered no one in her present state. The Pits arrived before her. The nearest

463

hole offered comfort. If Nyri had paused for one moment to think, she would have known how crazy her actions were, but an old instinct drove her flight. She threw herself to the bottom.

She was pinned to the ground before she could breathe.

"Juaan," she croaked.

He let her up immediately. "How many times?" he swore. "Don't surpri—" He stopped short. Nyri could only imagine how she appeared. She remained crumpled on the ground, her breath hitching in her throat. "What's wrong?" The wave of concerned energy that rolled from him was as reassuring as it was surprising in its strength. "Did I hurt you?"

Nyri shook her head. "No. But nothing will ever be right again!" She covered her mouth with her hands to stifle her sobs. She had broken her promise to Baarias. She had put him in harm's way. There was no doubting they would take her from him now. "What have I *done?*"

Juaan stared at her, bewildered. He was obviously at a loss at how to handle this situation: his captor sobbing her heart out in his prison. Then he caught sight of her arm. "You're bleeding!" He was at her side in a heartbeat. Nyri did not think he even gave it a thought. She wasn't the only one driven by instinct, it seemed. "What happened?" he hissed.

"Daajir," she choked. "I-I hit him and he cut me with your knife." Nyri flinched as she listened to her own words. What was happening to them all? She stared at her smarting palm as she would a snake. She had never struck anyone before.

Juaan's hand tightened on her arm, her blood slicking his fingers. "Why?" The question was a snarl.

"He is misguided. He wants to do something, something terrible. He's created a poison. He wants to use it on you.

On the Woves. But I can't let him. I can't let him. If he finds *you...*"

"He better hope *I* do not find *him*." The strength of his anger took Nyri aback. He started away from Nyri and she was suddenly terrified he was about to climb out. Threat of wolves be damned.

"No!" Nyri grabbed his arm. "Stay with me. I need you, Juaan. I need you now. Please. Stay. I need..." she trailed off, unsure of what she was asking of him.

His head turned from Nyri to the dangling rope and then back again. Slowly, unsurely, he sank to the ground and sat a little distance away. "What do you need?"

Unthinking, Nyri closed the distance and did what she had wanted to do since finding him again. She threw herself at him and curled into his side. He was so warm against her shivering body, despite his bare skin. She had forgotten his furs, Nyri thought distantly.

Juaan sat, rigid as a stone. Nyri did not think he was even breathing.

"Please," she said before he could pull away. She was tired. She was so so tired. His arm was tentative as it went around her shoulders. Warmth enveloped her. Nyri could not fight anymore. Her eyes grew heavy as she turned her face into his chest, nuzzling the skin there. "Just... speak to me."

"About what?" he said, his low voice tight.

"Anything."

He murmured something about his forgotten furs and the cold. She listened to his voice, letting it soothe away her cares. The last thing she remembered before unconsciousness pulled her under was his lips as they pressed gently into her hair.

When Nyri awoke, it was to the dim light of pre-dawn. She was warm, and that was strange but nice all the same. She couldn't imagine moving from her comfortable cocoon, but she supposed she had better get up. Kyaati needed caring for. Her eyelids were sticky, and it hurt to peel them back. Wincing, Nyri cracked them open, expecting to see Kyaati staring sullenly from across the tree. She blinked, surprised by the sight of a bare stone wall visible in the gap of a fading green skin.

Nyri was alert in an instant. The horror of the previous evening came back in a rush of cold dread. She had hit Daajir, and he had cut at her with a knife. She had run to Juaan and… she was still here! She was inside his make-shift shelter, nestled in the moss.

Nyri tried to scramble to her feet, but her motion was hindered by the heavy arm that covered her side. She stared at it, wide eyed, then at its owner, who was curled around her. Now she knew why she was so warm.

Her motion roused him. He sighed, his arm tightening before the green eyes opened and fixed on hers. His reaction reflected her own. He immediately snatched his arm away and rolled free, turning his back. The sense of loss was highlighted by a wave of cold.

"I'm sorry," he mumbled. "It was cold, and you didn't bring my furs back." His breath plumed on the chill morning air inside the shelter and Nyri noticed that the ground outside was crisp with a thin covering of frost.

Nyri stared at his naked torso as he turned his scarred back on her, feeling guilty and… disappointed. To her, the contact had been for comfort and the need to be near him. For him, it had merely been an act of survival. For a few blessed moments last night, his protective reactions had allowed her the beautiful illusion that he cared for her as much as she cared for him. Now it shattered in the dawn light.

"Juaan?" He did not respond. She could feel his increasing agitation. A quiver of unease snaked through her heart. "Juaan?" She reached out to touch his arm.

He flinched away, becoming furiously animated at her touch. "No! No more. I can't allow it. I am Khalvir. I am not your Juaan. I should not have allowed you to keep coming to me. It would have been better for the both of us if you had just killed me from the start." He crawled from the shelter. His anger burned hot against her senses.

This was almost more than she could take. Nyri followed him in desperation. "Juaan, don't. Don't do this to me! Please, not now, I need you," she half sobbed. "Why are you saying these things?"

"Just *leave*. Get away from me. Go back to your People where you belong."

Nyri's bitter laugh edged upon hysteria. "I'm not sure if I do belong anymore. I struck another Ninkuraa. Such a crime is forbidden."

Her stomach churned at the memory of her fight with Daajir. She thought of the weapon he had made and how he intended to show it to the tribe. Aardn had approved Daajir's work and the rest would follow the Elder's lead. Nyri did not know if Juaan was ready to listen, but the choice had been taken from her. It was time to tell him, to plead with him, to order his clan away before Daajir could carry out his terrible plan. It was now or never.

"Juaan, listen to me. Your clan is still here. They have been searching for you."

His face showed no hint of surprise. He continued to stare at her coldly.

She swallowed. "You are their leader. You have the power to save the lives of my People. You must order them away. Tell them to leave. If you can make my People safe, I-I will leave you alone. I needn't see you again."

Juaan's eyebrows shot towards his hairline. "So that's it?" He barked a laugh and his eyes brightened as though he'd come to an unpleasant, though not entirely unexpected, realisation. "That is why you have been coming here? You thought you could use me to order my men away from your forest?"

Nyri shook her head, reaching for him, but he stepped away, increasing the distance between them. It hurt. "No, no, please, that is not the only reason, I have not lied. I love you, Juaan."

"No more. No more lies." He turned away in disgust. "You have wasted your time, elf. I cannot do what you say. I cannot order my men away."

"Why *not*?" Nyri's last hope died around her.

He turned on her. "Because they will never stop coming, you fool! I am not their true leader. My clan chief will not stop until he gets what he wants."

"Your chief?" Nyri's arms dropped numbly to her sides. "What does this clan chief want? What could we possibly have that he needs?"

Juaan shook his head incredulously. "Have you not figured it out? Do you still cling to the notion that my People pursue you for no other reason than to gobble you up? Are you so blind?" He shoved his hand with the fingers she had healed into Nyri's dazed and confused face. "He covets your witch power! I did not believe its wonders to be real until I witnessed it for myself. Few of us believed our Chief's stories. Now I understand his need." He touched his recently healed leg. "It is your own power that has put you in danger. My clan Chief will never stop until he possesses your skills for himself."

"W-what?"

Juaan didn't answer, just watched with a bitter twist to his lips as her mind caught up with his words.

Nyri sank to the ground. "I-I never thought, we j-just thought—." Mindless spirits killing without reason. Child eaters. Nyri had never felt so foolish. Delusions, all of it. "B-but... if you didn't believe before... how did the chief... why?"

His laugh was bitter. "It seems I was not the first to be healed by one of your kind, elf," he said. "My Chief has always told of how an elf witch brought him back from the brink of death. Spooked in the heat of the moment, he tried to cut the healer's throat, but the witch was too quick. My Chief only wounded his face. The Chief escaped and returned to his clan.

"But as the shock wore off, the memory of that elf festered. My Chief grew hungry to possess this power for his own People and started hunting your People in an effort to capture a live elf. He sought to capture women to breed with, in the hope they would pass on the gift to their offspring. We have taken many, but none of them ever survived away from their forests. They grew sick and failed."

Nyri's hands went to her face, but she could not feel them. A Ninkuraa was responsible for bringing the Woves down on their heads. She dug the heels of her hands into her eyes. "I can't believe it," she whispered. "I can't…"

"Believe it. It is the truth. I am your mortal enemy and I will only bring you death. I am sworn to obey my Chief. I never was your Juaan. I am Khalvir. Now leave before—"

Nyri never really heard the rest of what he said. A powerful wave of urgency and misgiving almost bore her to the ground. She clutched at her chest, suddenly short on breath. Something was wrong. Something was *seriously* wrong. The sense of foreboding hit Nyri again, stronger this time, and she fell forward, catching herself on her hands. Juaan was suddenly there, steadying her.

"What is it?" he asked. The cold facade had slipped, betraying his concern. "What's wrong?"

Nyri gripped his arms, struggling to formulate a single coherent thought. All she knew was that she had to get back to her people. *Now.*

"I have to go." She shoved his hands away. "I have to go." Before he could ask her anything more, she was scrambling up and out of the Pit.

Wave after wave of distress rolled over her as she raced. Nyri tripped and fell, stumbled up and ran again. The sense of urgency she was feeling reached fever pitch. She did not know what had befallen her tribe in her absence. All she knew was that it was *awful.*

43

Death of Hope

Nyri could hear the voices raised in distress before she even came near. She pushed her exhausted body to its limits. She was terrified of what she might find. Had the Woves returned? Her legs faltered at the thought, seizing in fear. *You have to go.* She told herself fiercely. *If this is the end, then you have to be with your People. Maybe if you give yourself up, tell them you are a healer, and they will leave the rest alone. They'll have what they came for.*

Even as she thought it, Nyri knew she did not possess the courage to do it. She did not want to die. If she was taken, that outcome would be a certainty. Juaan told the truth. No one could have survived being taken long enough to be of use, otherwise why would the Woves keep on coming back?

Nyri burst through the undergrowth and into the open space the *eshaara* grove provided. She paused, gasping. There were no signs of a Wove attack. There was no blaze of destruction with monsters driving her People before it. The trees stood untouched in the still dawn air. But the silence was not comforting. It was ominous and as her eyes came to rest upon the crowd gathered at the base of her home, Nyri understood.

A fist closed around her throat so tight no air would pass. *No, no, no. Oh no, no.* Nyri could not see the focus of the crowd, but she knew in her heart what had drawn them and knew that she would never live through the consequences that would follow. She wished the Woves had come.

Stumbling, half on her feet, half on her knees, Nyri dragged herself towards the crowd and pushed her way through. They parted for her, their stares of shock and pain turning to anger and resentment as they recognised who had come among them. She did not have to travel far to witness the horror that had befallen. Baarias was coming towards her, carrying Kyaati's broken body in his arms. Her tribe-sister's arms and legs dangled lifelessly towards the ground.

"No," Nyri whispered. The gasps and the tears clawed their way up her throat, choking her. She screwed her eyes shut to block out the terrible sight. It wasn't true. It *couldn't* be true. This was a bad dream and soon she would wake. But when Nyri reopened her eyes, the nightmare remained unchanging before her.

Baarias shouldered past her. He did not even look at her. The crowd muttered. It seemed all eyes had turned on Nyri, staring down her guilt. Nyri could not look at them, could not raise a defence. In a daze, Nyri dragged herself after Baarias to the healer's tree. She did not know what else to do.

Baarias had laid Kyaati on a bower of moss. He was kneeling by her side, his head bowed.

"Baarias," Nyri's voice was a broken whisper. "W-what?"

His shoulders stiffened at the sound of her voice. He was on his feet in an instant. His face was terrible to behold as he rounded on her. "You left her." Her teacher's voice was unrecognisable. "I trusted you with her care and you left her."

"Baarias," Nyri wished she could die right there. She deserved nothing less. "I-I... I'm sorry."

"You do not know how small a comfort that is, Nyriaana," he seethed.

"Please... forgive me."

"I do not know if I can. I warned you not to leave her, and you have betrayed me. And not only me. You have betrayed us all." He jabbed a finger across the chamber. Nyri turned, and the sight that met her eyes caused her to sway on her feet as the world turned sickeningly. There sat her two gathering baskets. "Daajir found those hidden in your bower."

Nyri could raise no defence. There was nothing she could say.

"You have betrayed Kyaati. You have betrayed our People. Never in all the time I have known you, would I have thought you were capable of this. That you were the thief. I do not know you anymore."

Baarias' every word ripped chunks from her heart. She wanted to tell him it hadn't been her, Umaa had been the thief, but she could not find the words. The evidence was too damning. Why drag somebody else down with her? She was no less guilty. "Please, Baarias," Nyri begged, "I cannot explain why I have done what I have. I only care about Kyaati. Is she...?" She couldn't bring herself to say the word. *Dead.* It lodged like a blade in her throat.

His fists clenched. "No. She lives, but she is badly broken

473

from throwing herself from that tree. I do not think there is any hope this time."

Gasping, Nyri took a step forward, intent on getting to Kyaati's side. She would heal her. Nyri had brought her back before. She would do it again. She had to. Baarias blocked her path.

"No," he denied. "You have done enough. You are no longer my *akaabi*. You will never become a full healer. I do not need you. Please. Leave."

"Baarias..."

"LEAVE!"

Nyri flinched backwards as though struck. With a last look at Baarias' unrelenting figure, she turned and fled. The crowd was still outside. Their accusation and hatred raked over her. *Thief. Traitor.* She wanted to escape, but she had nowhere to go. Juaan had rejected her. There was no one to run to. There was no escape, no shelter from the eyes. They were all around her. Inside her mind. Inside her very soul. They crawled up her back as she climbed up into her tree and hid.

The night passed, and the morning found Nyri sleepless with no more tears left to cry. She did not go out. Throughout her confinement, Nyri wandered back and forth to the edge of her tree and stared down at the ground far below, imagining what must have been going through Kyaati's mind. She thought of how her friend must have needed her and Nyri hadn't been there. Instead, she had been seeking comfort for herself with a Wove, trying to save their enemies. Nyri burned.

Ninmah rose higher in the sky. Nyri knew time was

passing only by the movement of shadows. She did not stir and no one came. In the end, as the day grew late, hunger drove her down. She kept her head bowed as she made her way through the *eshaara* trees, but it did not protect her from the sight of backs being abruptly turned and children being herded away.

"There's the traitorous snake," a voice jeered. Nyri would've given anything, anything in that moment to vanish. She raised her eyes to see Daajir standing with Pelaan and Oraan. Scorn was carved upon his face. The Elders' faces were devoid of any kindness. Their eyes were stone cold as they regarded her. Daajir was drawing further attention; everybody within earshot was listening. "She who would defend Woves and neglect her own."

Oraan started towards Nyri, but Pelaan grabbed his arm. "Wait Oraan. She will suffer for what she has done to us. You'll get your justice, as will I, as will we all."

"Pelaan," Nyri croaked. "I'm..."

The sound of her voice seemed to snap something inside him. The Elder rounded on her. "Do not speak to me! I cannot bear to look at you. Your selfish actions have deprived me of my daughter's life. I should have taken care of her, but Baarias insisted I give her care to you. I should never have agreed, my daughter may still be here if I hadn't." It was clear that he shared Baarias' assessment that Kyaati would not survive her injuries. She was already lost to him. Pelaan turned away from Nyri and walked away, taking Daajir and Oraan with him.

Nyri stared after them, reeling from the blows his words had dealt. She collapsed to the ground on her knees, wrapping her arms around her chest in an attempt to contain the raw agony as she rocked back and forth, choking.

Suddenly, strong hands were lifting her. Nyri fought against them. *No, no, leave me down in the earth,* she thought. *It is where I belong.*

"Come," a familiar voice said. A voice she had felt she could never face again. "Come with me."

"No," Nyri whispered. "Leave me. I deserve it."

He ignored her. Baarias half dragged Nyri back to his dwelling. He set her down and pushed some fruit into her hands. "Eat."

"I'm not hungry."

"Eat!"

Nyri lifted the fruit to her mouth and bit into the flesh. She did not identify the flavour.

"I am s-so sorry."

"Not half as sorry as I," he said. Nyri dared to raise her eyes to look at him. He was rubbing his face with his worn hands. He looked infinitely older than Nyri had ever seen him.

I have done this to him. Nyri thought as the barbs of pain went through her gut. "I'm so sorry. It is all my f-fault." The fruit roiled in her stomach. She wanted to vomit.

"It is as much mine as yours," he sighed bitterly. "I saw that something was wrong, but I left Kyaati in your care anyway," he said. "What has happened to you, Nyriaana?" He crouched before her and took her hand. "You have taken food from the stores, hidden it in your home, but you waste like you never have more than a mouthful. Your eyes are blackened like you never rest. You left Kyaati unattended when she needed you. When I *asked* you never to leave her. You *attacked* Daajir and broke your every promise to me."

"H-he wants to do something terrible. He made me so angry, Baarias. I had to tell him. I had to try to convince him that the path he is on will not help. He will destroy us. I tried to open his eyes as you opened mine."

He glowered at her. "You were foolish."

"Foolish? He is going to get us all killed. You know the truth."

"Yes, and look at where it has led me. All I have is you and now I have lost you, too. They will never listen." He sighed. "Please, Nyriaana. Something more has happened and you will not tell me. Your heart is closed and hidden and I cannot understand why?"

Nyri huddled down deeper into herself. She could not tell him. Even now. She hadn't protected Kyaati, but she would still protect Juaan. No matter what.

Baarias dropped her hand in frustration. "The auscult will take place when Ninmah sets," he reminded her. "We will find out what is to happen then."

Nyri knew what that meant, but she was too weak to care anymore.

"H-how is Kyaati?"

"Unconscious," he said shortly. "The healing process has begun. I have done all I can. It is up to her now, but she is very weak. I hold little hope. Prepare yourself."

"Can I see her?"

"I do not think that wise. If Pelaan catches you—"

"I doubt he can do anything worse than he is already planning to do to me. Please, Baarias," Nyri begged. "I want to see her. Just once."

He appeared torn, but then relented. "Be quick."

Nyri had to steady herself against the walls of the tree

as she made her way towards the chamber where Kyaati rested. When she saw her tribe-sister, she retched. What little food she had in her stomach she caught in her throat as she vomited into the corner. *You did this. You did this. You were not there.* She should have taken better care of her.

Kyaati's skin was deathly pale, marred by hideous bruising and swelling. How many bones broken, Nyri could not count. Her chest hardly moved as she drew one breath, paused frighteningly, then drew another. Nyri took Kyaati's hand, feeling for her life force. She shuddered. It was a trail of mist and one more breath would blow it away. Nyri knew then that Kyaati would never return to her. Her tribe-sister would never recover.

Hope died in her eyes. Let the Elders do what they would.

44

Prophesy

Nyri returned to her tree to await her fate. She thought of Kyaati as she was in her youth and she thought of Juaan. Both lost to her. Kyaati soon to death and Juaan to memory. She was alone. Baarias' anger may have subsided, but she had lost his trust and regard forever. She had lost everything she had ever held dear. Nyri lay there as the shadows lengthened towards the fateful evening.

When Baarias came for her, it was almost a relief. "It's time," he said. Nyri nodded silently and followed him. She wondered if anyone had ever survived *zykiel* with the entire tribe before. *Zykiel* with Pelaan and Oraan alone would be enough for anyone to lose their minds. Without a word, she followed Baarias to the clearing. He supported her by an elbow whenever she stumbled.

"Baarias, what is it like?" she asked.

He looked down at her, eyes tight. His expression was enough. She did not ask again.

There was an air of anticipation as they gathered. Half

good, half bad. Word had spread of Daajir's plan to take back their supplies, and that had sparked a glimmer of hope. The bad… Nyri didn't have to think too far to figure the reason for that.

She settled herself at the rear of the gathering, out of sight and away from the stares that she was still drawing.

"Where is Sefaan?" She had searched for the Kamaali but Sefaan was not there.

"She has shut herself away," Baarias answered. "She is in communion with the Great Spirit. Out of respect, nobody has gone near. Her absence has suited the Elders very much, I have to say."

"Ah." Fixing her eyes upon the ground, Nyri attempted to mask her presence as much as possible. She didn't realise just how skilled she had become at this. There was a curse as someone tripped over her. She received an angry glare before her unintentional victim walked on.

Imaani came to Baarias' side.

"How is Omaal?" Nyri's erstwhile teacher asked.

"Sleeping," Imaani said. "I wish to speak to you, Baarias, about these dreams. I am concerned." He glanced at Nyri with a frown. She stared determinedly at a loose stone by her feet.

"I will attend him following the auscult."

"Thank you."

"What is wrong with Omaal?" she murmured after Imaani moved away.

"The dreams he has been having since the night the Woves attacked will not pass. They keep him awake and the lack of sleep has weakened him."

I know the feeling. "Do his dreams still involve the Woves?"

Baarias shrugged. "It varies between that and the Pits. You were close to the Pits when he was almost killed by the *grishnaa*, were you not?"

Nyri had tensed when Baarias mentioned the Pits. She forced herself to relax her shoulders. "Yes, yes, we were." Nyri agreed quickly.

A hush fell over the tribe as Aardn took her place. "As was promised, we gather once more to decide what our path should be. Flee or fight. Both present a danger to us, but with our enemies remaining camped on our borders, our situation can no longer continue. We must choose.

"To flee means that we face a shelterless Fury. We have endured this before and lost nearly all of our tribe. All would have perished if Ninmah had not blessed us with the home that surrounds you. Will we be so blessed a second time? But to stand means fighting beasts much stronger than we are who carry powerful weapons. We have nothing that can withstand their attacks for long."

"We do now, respected Elder." Daajir stepped into the circle. "I made you a promise, and I have discovered a way to repel our enemies." From inside his coverings, he withdrew Juaan's knife and posed before the tribe as if the weapon lent him some superior power. To Nyri's eyes, he looked foolish, but the rest of her People gasped and those closest leaned away from the Wove weapon. "The power of this weapon is now ours, and I have strengthened it still further with a little of our own. Nothing can withstand it."

"Show us," Pelaan commanded.

Nyri dug her nails into her palms. She couldn't be the only one to see where such a course would lead them?

Daajir revealed his poison with as much satisfaction and

reverence as he had to Nyri out in the forest. Nyri looked to Baarias in helpless supplication. To her surprise, he did not seem to be listening. He did not even appear to see Daajir standing there. His eyes were unfocused, a small frown between his brows as if he were listening to something far away but could not quite make it out. Even as Nyri watched him, he rose to his feet, interrupting Daajir's self-congratulation. Eyes turned in surprise and annoyance.

"Baarias," Aardn barked. "Do you have something to say?"

"No, Elder," he muttered, with the same distant expression upon his face. "Please excuse me. Someone needs me." He turned and left the auscult, heading in the direction of his home. Don't leave me! Nyri's breathing hitched, but he was gone, disappearing without a backwards glance.

Aardn didn't appear fazed. On the contrary, she appeared relieved. Nyri guessed the Elder had expected Baarias to be the most vocal detractor from Daajir's deadly plot. Now he was out of the way. Nyri felt naked without him at her side. She did not want to face her coming ordeal without him.

Daajir finished his speech. "There is no cure. If the victim is pierced, they are doomed to die."

"How long will it take a victim to succumb?"

"Days if they are strong," Daajir said. "Enough time to spread warning among their fellows before dying in agony. The terror will be enough to ward them away."

Mutterings started all around Nyri. The energy in the air was eager, vengeful. No one seemed to see the wrong in this.

"You have the paths before you," Aardn addressed the tribe once the murmuring had subsided. "What say you?"

There was a collective pause. Everyone was testing the air,

testing to see if all were in agreement before venturing an opinion. In the end, it was Imaani who had the courage to rise. "I think I speak for everyone when I say we cannot run any longer. We can all feel it; in the groan of the earth, in the whispers in the wind. The Fury that comes will be like nothing we have ever seen. To leave will mean certain death to us all. We cannot survive without our homes. I do not want to see my son perish unprotected. I want to stand and defend him; I want to drive the Woves from our lands for good! They have cursed Omaal's sight. They have cursed all of our children. We must vanquish Ninsiku's servants once and for all if these ills are to be cured and the Fury to be stopped!"

"No!" It took Nyri a moment to realise the outburst had been hers and that she was on her feet. All faces had turned in her direction. Not one was welcoming; all were resentful. Some were filled with outright loathing. She quailed.

"I have not given you permission to speak," Aardn snarled. "You are Disgraced."

Nyri trembled before the Elder's anger, but forced the words out. "This path is wrong. Even with Daajir's weapon, we will not win. There are more of them than us. Killing these few will not stop the rest. There is no curse to break!"

There was an outbreak of murmuring and shifting of bodies.

"*Please*, listen." Nyri looked around at her tribe, her family. "F-fighting the Woves will not save us. They are not—"

"What? Our enemy?" Daajir snapped. He turned, drawing the attention back to him, hands held out. "I told you she was crazy. She would let the Woves kill us all. You all know how she used to cling to that Forbidden half-breed as a child. Well, I say a *grishnaa* never changes her pelt. She was never one of us. She is a heretic. A thief. A traitor to Ninmah Herself! She should have no place among our People. Her very presence angers the great Ninmah and will bring further misfortune upon us. As did Rebaa. As did her own mother!"

"I—" Nyri was stunned into silence. *Never one of us.*

"Enough of this! It is time to perform the ritual. Call for Sefaan," Pelaan snarled. All his pain and anger for what had befallen Kyaati rolled out, raw in his voice. "She will know the pain she has caused and be cast to the elements for what she did to my daughter. Bring her forward."

"No!" Nyri protested as hands grabbed her arms and pulled her towards the centre of the circle. She caught Umaa's eye. The other woman was weeping, guilt scrawled upon her face as Nyri stumbled along towards her fate. She knew she should fight, but she could not think of a word to say in her own defence. She could never forgive herself for what she had let happen to Kyaati. Her friend would die because of her. She did not struggle as they forced her to her knees.

Nyri's cheeks were wet as she looked up into Aardn's impassive face, waiting for the words. But Aardn was silent.

"Aardn," Pelaan hissed, pulling Oraan forward with him. Oraan's deadened eyes were fixed upon Nyri as if she was the only thing that existed, the only thing that mattered. She bowed her head, balling her fists as her hands trembled uncontrollably. "Aardn!" Pelaan demanded. "It must be done. We must have justice. We must perform *zykiel* then cast her out."

Somehow, past everything, Nyri could taste the Elder's

uncertainty. She was reluctant to order death upon a member of the tribe, even with Daajir's damning accusations ringing in everyone's ears. A tribe that desperately needed all of its number.

"There is another solution," Aardn said slowly. Nyri held her breath. "*Zykiel* will indeed be performed as fitting to the crime but instead of casting her out, I suggest she be Joined."

Nyri's breath lodged in her throat.

"That way her mate will know her every thought and keep their attention on her night and day." Aardn met each one of their expectant gazes. "She could not spread her poison or betray our people without their knowing. And in this way, she will be serving the tribe and not wasted to death." The Elder faced Daajir. "Daajir, there is no one I would trust more with this task. Will you accept Nyriaana as your Joined One?"

The blood drained from Nyri's face at the same time she saw Daajir's skin flush with anger.

"No!" He baulked, disgust thick in his tone as he looked down on Nyri. "Such traitorous filth is not worthy of me! I do not have—"

One look from Aardn silenced his protest. "She will not be a traitor under your guard," she said. "She is a strong match for you, Daajir. Would you let your pride stand in the way of fulfilling Ninmah's most sacred plan?"

Daajir ground his teeth together. "No, respected Elder."

"Then you will accept this woman as your mate?"

He paused for a long time, his face twitching. "I accept her." He forced his agreement through tight lips. "I will make sure she causes no more harm. She will be a mother to strong children once the Wove curse has been lifted. *My* children whom I will raise to be *true* Ninkuraaja."

Revulsion swept through Nyri. She almost threw herself at Aardn's feet and begged for Pelaan's sentence. She could not be Joined to Daajir. She would rather die. A cold sweat started all over her body.

Aardn smiled. "Very well. After the ritual has been performed. She will become your Joined One, Daajir."

Nyri crumpled to the ground, her forehead in the earth. Aardn stepped forward. "I will perform the ritual. We will not wait for Sefaan."

Nyri gasped as she felt the Elder's hand come down on her head. She forced herself to look into Oraan's eyes and trembled. She knew what was within would tear her apart as certainly as being Joined to Daajir. She closed her eyes.

"Stop!" a voice rang out. The wave of energy that accompanied it had them all on their feet. Baarias was running towards them. Nyri's heart skipped a beat. Baarias would not interrupt an auscult unless…

No, Nyri swayed under Aardn's hand. *Kyaati.*

Pelaan's thoughts paralleled hers. "My daughter. Baarias… "

"Your daughter yet lives." Baarias gripped his arm. "It is Sefaan. She is dying."

A current of shock passed around the whole tribe.

Sefaan. Everything was unravelling so fast. Too fast. Sefaan was dying? Nyri hadn't seen her since….

"I must go to her." Aardn moved to step around Baarias.

"No," Baarias caught her arm. "She has asked for Nyri-aana."

"She cannot see her," Pelaan started. "She is sentenced. We were just about to pass—"

"Even so," Baarias cut him off. "She is asking for Nyri and Nyri alone. From this she will not be swayed. It is her last request. You can perform your punishment when she is gone if you wish, but not now. Nyri." He held out his hand. "Come with me."

Nyri did not trust her own legs. She took Baarias' hand and let him pull her to her feet. He led her through the crowd, back to his dwelling. She was conscious of the rest of the tribe following carefully. Their emotions were tremulous. The Last Kamaali was dying, and she had not fulfilled the promise of saving them. The tribe had never been without a Spirit guide before. There was still no sign of another child. Panic stood in all eyes. This was a terrible omen.

The *girru* moss glowed on the walls and danced in the air as they entered the great tree. The warmth caressed Nyri's cheeks. She had not known how cold she was until that moment.

Sefaan had been laid on a bower next to Kyaati. "Nyriaana." Her voice was a thin whisper. She reached out. "Girl."

Nyri caught the frail hand in hers, falling to her knees beside the Kamaali. The fleshless fingers were skin and bone. Cold as stone. "Sefaan," her voice broke. "What happened? Why are you...?" Nyri's free hand fluttered over the emaciated body.

Sefaan did not answer. Nyri turned to Baarias.

His face was grave. "Nobody guessed she was not feeding herself. Nobody thought to look. Her injuries." He trailed off and turned away. Nyri felt his rage and guilt as her own.

She looked down at the ancient woman lying before her, dying of starvation and unhealed wounds and knew she had failed yet another person who she cared about. She had been so caught up with Juaan; she had not given one thought to Sefaan's wellbeing. She had only thought about what the Kamaali could have done to save Juaan for her. Selfish to the core. She had not been here for her People.

"I'm so sorry, Sefaan." Nyri stroked the white hair back from her crinkled brow. "I'm sorry. I have failed in everything. I will answer for it all." Nyri hardly knew what she was saying. The words were tumbling out.

The Kamaali's eyes opened, and she glared at Nyri. "No. *You* must live." She jabbed a shaking finger at Kyaati. "*She* also must live. It is the only hope."

"Kyaati is dying, Sefaan," Nyri told her. "She threw herself from a tree and I was not there to save her. She is almost gone." Nyri could feel it. Kyaati would not last the night.

"No!" Sefaan thrust herself from the pile of moss. Baarias appeared, trying to make her lay back down, but she shook him off, fighting her way to Kyaati's side. She took a limp hand in her own. "You are not going anywhere, foolish girl. You are needed," she said, and her eyes closed. Nyri's skin prickled. "All my power I give to you so that you may live."

Nyri would never recall quite what happened next. The hairs on the back of her neck stood on end, as if a lightning storm had been summoned. The energy moved from Sefaan through the hand that clutched Kyaati's, and into the sleeping form. Bones healed, bruising disappeared, cuts vanished. Then it was done. The sense of immense power retreated and Sefaan collapsed to the floor. A husk.

Kyaati's chest rose and fell. Rose and fell. Deeply.

"She... will live now." Sefaan's voice was a fading croak. Nyri scooped her up in her arms and lifted the Kamaali back onto her bower. It was close. So close. Nyri was startled when Sefaan caught her face between her palms. Her eyes rolled, straining to keep Nyri in view. She pulled the sprouting *enu* seed from her throat and pressed it into Nyri's hand. "Give this to Ariyaana. Keep the boy with you. Remember what I said. She will save us... she is the Last. Find..."

"Ariyaana." Nyri finished, clutching the *enu* to her. Her tears fell on the old one's cheeks. "Sefaan..."

"Promise... me." Sefaan's eyes searched hers and Nyri knew instinctively that Sefaan would not rest, could not go until she had heard these two words from Nyri's lips.

"I promise," Nyri lied.

Sefaan smiled then. It lit her wise face for one last time as the remains of her life's energy went out of her. Nyri felt her leave. Her spirit rose on the air, visible only to those who knew how to see with the eyes of their soul, then disappeared. Sefaan had become one with the Great Spirit. Where she belonged. A wail went up from outside as the entire tribe felt it.

With trembling fingers, Nyri closed the eyes that still stared into hers, boring that last request into her soul. The old face, however, was oddly at peace, assured by Nyri's final lie.

"I'm so sorry."

Behind Nyri, Kyaati gasped and opened her eyes.

45

Betrayal

Baarias let her down from the stag. Nyriaana struggled in his arms, fighting to run back into the forest, back to her burning home.

"Don't," the healer's voice was frayed with sadness. "Don't, you'll hurt yourself. He is gone."

"No!" She fought harder. "Juaan!" she screamed into the forest behind. He would come back. He had promised he would never leave her. He never broke his promises. But as her shrill cry shivered into nothingness, this time there came no answering call. The empty space yawned behind, dark and desolate. Gone. The trees whispered. Gone. She screamed and wailed in Baarias' restraining arms. "Juaan!"

She was dimly aware of the tribe re-gathering around them. Some were weeping, most were beyond such tears. Pelaan came to Baarias' side. Kyaati was clinging to his legs, wide-eyed and terrified. The Elder stared back into the forest. "Our lives... gone."

Baarias nodded mutely.

Pelaan looked down at Nyri and his frozen features twisted. "The abomination did not escape?"

"Pelaan," Baarias growled in warning as Nyri's cries intensified. "The boy saved her life. Have a care."

The Elder ignored him. "He was dead anyway. Daajir told us about his attack. His true nature had finally surfaced. Forbidden filth." Pelaan spat.

Nyri saw red. She broke free of Baarias' firm grasp and flew at the Elder, flailing at him with her little fists. "You will not hurt my Juaan! You would not hurt him!" She pummelled any part of Pelaan she could reach. "I want him! You left him!"

Baarias dragged her off the stunned Elder.

"As bad as the mother," Pelaan straightened himself. "Who is going to take care of her now she is free?"

"I will. I need someone to pass my skills on to. She is very strong. I will teach her."

Pelaan's jaw flexed for a moment. "Very well." He looked back into the trees and the glow of destruction. "I hope you see now, Baarias. I hope you see what they are."

"I have always seen what they are, Pelaan. No more, no less."

Nyri was trying to escape into the trees again. He was dead anyway... Pelaan's cruel words rang through her mind. No. She had to go back to protect him. He had promised to protect her. She still needed him. He had promised!

"Come with me now, little one," Baarias' tone was gentle.

"No! Mama said I had to stay with him. She made him promise to look after me. I promised. He promised!"

"And he honoured that promise to the end. Let me look after you now. I will protect you as your Juaan did. I promise, too."

"No, I want Juaan!" But her strength had run out. She could not fight anymore. Tears streaming, she waited, but the forest remained silent and empty. He did not come for her. He was not coming back. Nyri crumbled to the ground and sobbed her grief *to the sky.*

Baarias gathered her to him. "You must let him go now. He could never stay with you. It is better this way. Let him go."

Nyri fought back against his hold. His were not the arms she wanted. They were gone. The Woves had taken them from her. Her family had left him to die. Baarias' words echoed in her head. It is better this way. You must let him go. He could never stay with you. You must let him go…

* * *

Kyaati's wail of dismay reverberated off the walls of the tree. "No! You brought me back! I did not want to come back!" she moaned, twisting in her bower.

Baarias rushed to her side, attempting to calm her. Her voice must have carried to the waiting crowd outside, for Pelaan appeared in an instant. His drawn face transformed into the expression of one who was witnessing the most miraculous of miracles. Nyri supposed he was. His daughter had been on the point of death, now here she was, crying lustily, very much alive and well.

"My daughter," he breathed. "How? Baarias?"

"She said she was needed," Nyri whispered, still holding Sefaan's hand, stroking her hair. "She gave the last of her energy to restore Kyaati. She said she was needed."

Pelaan threw himself to his knees beside his daughter. "Yes, she is." His eyes glowed.

"Get away from me!" Kyaati raged. "I wanted to be gone. Leave me."

492

"Kyaati." Her reaction took him aback. "It's me. It's your father."

"I know who you are," she spat. "You would give me over to Daajir. You would put me through it all again. You do not care about me, just your precious Ninmah. Now you will give me to someone just as cold. You selfish—"

"*I* am to be Joined to Daajir." Nyri began straightening Sefaan into the traditional death pose. It busied her hands. She could not think beyond this moment. Her thoughts were frozen. Sefaan had said she was needed. She had said Kyaati was needed; the Kamaali had given her strength for her, bringing her back from the brink of death.

But that wasn't enough. Kyaati was still unwell in her heart and mind. She needed more. She needed Nyri to look after her, and this time Nyri needed to give Kyaati her undivided attention. She could not lead the life she had been living. The thin branch had snapped beneath her. It had never meant to be walked. It was impossible and selfish. Nyri had to face the truth she had been denying from the very beginning. She had to face what she had never accepted all those years ago. She had to stop chasing visions and half hopes. She had to let go of it all.

She had to let Juaan go.

He could not help them as Sefaan had hoped, and if he was free, he would not need Nyri to stay alive. Kyaati did need her, and she was important.

So is he, Nyri's heart wailed, baulking at the thought of losing him for a second time. She squeezed her eyes shut against the pain.

You already lost him long ago. She thought back. *He cannot stay with you. Baarias told you that. He knew. You have known*

493

it from the start. He cannot stay in that Pit forever and he can never come here. They will kill him. That will never change. You must let him go. At least this time, you will know he is alive out there, somewhere. He survived this long.

It was a blessing that Nyri had no more tears left to cry as she turned to Pelaan. "I accept Daajir's offer. I will become his Joined One."

Pelaan's eyes were still cold as he regarded her, but the recovery of his daughter appeared to have softened his position on the death sentence. "That will need to be decided. Now my daughter has recovered…"

Of course he would want to put himself first. He would rather have his own grandchild born into the tribe now that it was once again a possibility.

Over my dead body, Nyri thought at him. Caring for Kyaati began now, even if it meant sacrificing herself to Daajir.

Kyaati turned her face away from her father. "I am tired. I want to sleep."

Pelaan kissed her brow. "Baarias, take care of her," he commanded. "I have much to discuss with my fellow Elders."

Baarias regarded him coolly. "Perhaps your plans can wait until we have cared for Sefaan."

Nyri loved that man.

Pelaan stared down at Sefaan's body, chagrined. "She will be treated with the greatest of honours," he vowed and disappeared to spread the word.

Nyri remained where she was for the rest of the night. Baarias left to attend to Omaal and did not return. Nyri was too exhausted to wonder at his whereabouts. She kept vigil over both Sefaan and Kyaati as she came to terms with what had happened and with the future she must soon face.

494

Once she had said farewell to Sefaan, she would let Juaan go. She needed to have prepared her heart by then. She did not sleep.

Kyaati awoke just before Ninmah.

"Nyri," she whispered to her.

Nyri lifted her heavy head. "Yes."

"Why did Sefaan bring me back?"

"She said you were needed," Nyri explained again tonelessly.

"I did not ask to be needed. Why am I needed?"

Nyri shook her head helplessly. "She did not say. Kyaati, why did you do it?" Beneath it all, Nyri realised she was angry at her. She needed to know why Kyaati had done what she had.

Her friend's eyes were wary. "I had to. I could not face it anymore. You know as well as I do our people are doomed."

Nyri was silent.

"Truth is, I knew you disappeared every night, but I did not tell Baarias because it suited my purposes. I had been thinking of doing what I did ever since I woke up after losing her. After Haana... it hardened my resolve. I envied her escape, but I did not find the courage to do it until the last."

Nyri shook her head. It seemed she had never been careful enough. "Your father wanted me cast out!" She blew out a breath, letting her anger go with it. "I'm so sorry, Kyaati. I failed you. It will not happen again."

"Where did you go every night?" her friend asked.

Nyri turned her face away. "I cannot tell you, and after tomorrow night, it will not matter anymore." A tear broke loose and leaked down her cold cheek.

To Nyri's dismay, Kyaati was not swayed. Her friend's

brow pinched together. "Before I woke the first time, I remember your voice. You were telling me you had found a Wove in the woods, trapped in the Pits. You told me afterward that I had been dreaming and so I said no more but… now I don't think I was. Is that where you have been going?"

Nyri could not look at her. She could not bring herself to deny it. There had been too many lies. Another tear tracked down her face.

Kyaati's breathing caught, Nyri's damning silence confirming her friend's worst fears. "W-why would you visit a Wove at night? What are you *thinking*?"

Nyri rose and paced away from Kyaati. Nyri could feel her friend's mind racing, trying to figure out what had possessed her to flaunt her safety with an enemy and how she came to be still alive.

"It's Juaan. Isn't it?" she said with dawning realisation. "There could be no other reason. They did not kill him. They raised him."

"Yes!" Nyri burst out. "It's Juaan down there."

Kyaati's face drained of what little colour it had. "Nyri-aana," she whispered.

"Do not judge me, Kyaati. I could not leave him to die. No matter what he is or what he has become. He was my saviour."

"He is a Forbidden, Nyri," Kyaati accused. "He could never be trusted. He looked after you to make himself look peaceful to the Elders. If he had given them even the slightest hint of his true nature, they would have expelled him. Promise to Sefaan be damned. He knew that."

"You're wrong!" Nyri argued. "Juaan was good. He is still

good, but he cannot remember. I want him to, but I have to let him go. Once I am Joined to Daajir, he will find out and he will test his poison on Juaan for sure. He promised when we were children. He promised he would kill Juaan one day. I cannot let that happen. I must protect him."

"Listen to yourself!" Kyaati hissed. "Listen to what you are saying. He is dangerous. He always was. You cannot go back. I will not—"

She cut herself off when Baarias entered the chamber. He looked upon Sefaan's body sadly.

"It is time," he said.

Nyri drew a deep breath and forced her hands to stop trembling. She nodded to him and caught Kyaati's wrist. *Please do not tell Baarias,* she pleaded. *You must trust me. Please. I* know *what I am doing.*

Kyaati shook her off. Her gaze was far from reassuring.

Pelaan and Imaani came in then and lifted Sefaan's body with the greatest of care. Nyri and Kyaati followed as they bore the old one in the direction of the river. Everyone was gathered on the banks as Ninmah rose above. Heads bowed as the body passed. Despair hung thick in the air. A few stunned glances turned towards Kyaati, however, with a renewed flicker of hope. A raft had been prepared and Sefaan was laid down upon it in a bed of *girru* moss.

"Where is the Kamaali's *enu?*" Aardn asked in sudden alarm, looking down at Sefaan's bare throat.

"I have it," Nyri murmured. "She gave it to me."

"Why?" Aardn demanded. "You are not the next Kamaali, traitor."

Nyri flinched. "I-I don't know. But I think she meant for me to keep it." She did not mention Ariyaana. It would raise

497

too many impossible questions.

"We will see." Aardn said flatly, but spoke no further. It was time to bid farewell. Nyri clutched the precious *enu* in her fist, determined to keep hold of it.

The ritual was a simple one. The entire tribe surrounded the raft and watched over the dead throughout the passing of the day, accompanying her for the last passing of Ninmah through Her Sky Path. All thoughts turned to Sefaan and how she had touched each of their lives and reflected on a family member lost. Nobody was to eat. The fast would only be broken once Ninmah had risen again to herald a new day.

When dusk fell, Aardn stirred from her vigil and touched Sefaan's still forehead with her own. "Go in peace and in the light of Ninmah," she said as the last rays fell upon the raft and its sole occupant. Aardn touched a piece of the *girru* moss as darkness fell, then stepped back. Pelaan took his turn. Then the next, then the next. Each touching and lighting a piece of the *girru* moss. Nyri tensed as Daajir approached, torn between the need to run and the desire to throw him from Sefaan's side. He had no right to touch her. Daajir met Nyri's eyes, but said nothing. Nyri was last of all to step forward.

"I'm sorry I cannot keep my promise to you, Sefaan," she whispered to an unhearing ear as she set the last of the moss aglow. "But I must keep our People safe." A lump rose in her throat as she caught sight of something tucked into Sefaan's hand. A toy hare with a red feather bound to its ear. Kyaati must have slipped it into her fingers. It would rest with the one who had made it. It was fitting.

Ninmah disappeared as the raft was pushed into the flow

of the river, but the light of the *girru* moss carried Sefaan on in a haze of beauty and light, enhanced by the darkness. Spores wafted into the air and danced over the water, casting eternal reflections, painting the wind.

When at last it was over; the tribe drifted away. They had to decide now how life would go on without their Kamaali. Such a challenge had never been faced. Nyri moved off quickly behind Kyaati and Baarias before Daajir could think to abuse her any more. Her own thoughts turned to the impossible task she would have to accomplish this night.

It was time to set Juaan free. Her heart begged for just a few more nights, but Nyri knew that was impossible. The risk was too high and worse, Kyaati had figured her out. To keep him with her any longer would spell his doom. Nyri could not let her selfishness cause her to fail him, too.

He would need food. She would have to get to her gathering baskets. They were no longer in Baarias' tree. They must have been moved to the stores. Nyri waited impatiently until Baarias had settled Kyaati into a deep sleep. Her body still needed rest if it was to recover fully.

She pretended to settle down herself in preparation to watch over Kyaati, awaiting her moment of opportunity. Nyri both wanted and dreaded it at the same time. She hadn't seen Juaan for two days now. She prayed he was safe.

He had been angry with her when she had last seen him, convinced she had used him. He had pushed her away. Now she would never be able to redeem herself. He would leave hating her, never knowing who she truly was. Nyri forced the tears away.

Finally, the opportunity she had waited for came. Baarias was asleep. Masking her presence, Nyri moved through the tree and crept out into the night, dashing for the nearest store. There would be no watcher. It was the night of Sefaan's Casting. No one should break their fast before Ninmah came again. It was a sacred law.

Her baskets were there, as predicted. Nyri took one and slung it over her shoulder. It was too late for her People. They had sealed their own doom. Juaan still had a chance, though. He could survive. Hefting her spoils, she leaped to the ground, intent on running into the forest. Time to say goodbye.

"Don't." A soft voice spilled from the dark. Nyri gave a low, strangled cry of dismay. "Do not do this, Nyriaana. I cannot let you."

Nyri turned to face Baarias as he stepped from the shadows. "Kyaati told you."

Kyaati appeared from behind Baarias. "Yes. You will not be reasoned with. You need saving from yourself."

Nyri glared at her, biting down on an incredulous laugh. How *dare* Kyaati lecture her. Kyaati had no place to speak after all she had put them through.

Baarias waved a hand. "Kyaati did not need to tell me anything, Nyri. I already knew. Omaal's dreams. They always involve the Pits. A Wove in the woods. He told me you are often with him. These were no ordinary dreams and when I pieced them together with your nightly disappearances... I realised that what he was seeing in his dreams must have some truth to them."

Nyri's mind worked. How could the boy have known? "Batai." The answer struck. The wolf had accompanied her on many of her visits to the Pits. How could she have been so blind? Nyri had underestimated the bond between the boy and that wolf for Omaal to be connected with him so far away from the tribe. She thought of the time Batai had attacked Juaan. Had Omaal been out in the woods with Batai? It would have explained his aggressive behaviour. He would defend the boy against any perceived threat. A sour taste saturated Nyri's mouth at the realisation of just how badly she had erred.

"Please Baarias. I have to let him go."

Baarias shook his head. "No."

"Baarias!" Nyri grew desperate. "He is Juaan. He is your *sister's* son. Let me help him!" She clutched for anything she might use to change his will. "You said yourself you wished you could right the wrongs you had done. The opportunity is here. Juaan is alive; but if they find him, they will kill him. Serve your sister's wish as you never did before. Help her son!"

Baarias' face was a carving of infinite sadness. "No. I lost my sister a long time ago, Nyri. The boy she brought to us has grown into everything I feared he would. Saving him would not right my wrongs. I will not let Rebaa's doom be yours. I *must* keep you safe. I do not care about anything else."

"No!" Nyri cried. "I won't lose him. Not again. You don't know anything! You have not seen him."

"I have seen him, Nyri."

"*What?*"

"Once I suspected Omaal's dreams, I went to the Pit last night, to see with my own eyes. Do not trust him. Do not go back."

"I trust him with my life!" Nyri turned to run. "Sefaan was right. You are a coward!"

501

"You are blinded!" his voice whipped out. "Nyri, don't you see? I cannot let you risk our People even if you would wilfully risk yourself. I cannot let you make the same mistake I did!"

Nyri turned as his words sent a chill through her. "What do you mean?"

Her teacher snapped his mouth closed and dropped his gaze.

"Baarias? What do you mean?"

He lifted his head. He looked like he was being devoured by the Woves' burning spirits. "I mean I trusted a Wove once and I very nearly paid for it with my life." He brushed the scar that ran along his jaw. "Fortunately for me, I was young and quick in those days. His blade missed my throat. I did not pay with my life that day, but I have been paying the price for that mistake every moment since. You cannot trust a Wove!"

Nyri began to shake. The pieces were falling into place faster than she could comprehend. She stared at the scar on Baarias' face as if seeing it for the first time. "It was you. You healed that Wove chief. You brought them down on our heads. *You.*"

Kyaati took a step back from him. "Baarias, what is she talking about?"

Baarias did not answer. He had eyes only for Nyri. "Yes." His voice was a mere whisper. "My darkest secret. My greatest pain. I found him. I could not believe what my eyes were showing me. For the first time, I saw the face of a Wove behind the mask. And when I healed him… I knew the truth. But in finding it…" he shuddered. "Sometimes I feel as if it would have been a kinder fate to have let that blade find its mark." He reached a trembling hand towards her. "Nyri, don't you see you are running recklessly down the same path? I cannot let you fall. You do not know the guilt you will have to bear."

"My mistakes are not yours!" Nyri spat mercilessly. She hated him so much at that moment. For all that he had done, for all that he was doing. She had to get away. The dreadful sense that time was running out gripped her heart. "This is all your fault, Baarias. You are responsible for what happened to your sister, you are responsible for Juaan's very existence. Help him!"

"No."

"Then I will."

He sighed. "I did not come here expecting I could change your mind. You have forced my hand. I am sorry. I hope you will forgive me in time."

Nyri froze. "Forgive you for what?"

He did not answer.

Nyri stumbled over to him and grabbed him by the woven leaf-leather on his chest. The sense of foreboding was now pounding on her skull. "Forgive you for *what*, Baarias? What have you done?"

"You are too late." His hands tried to steady her. "I already told Daajir where to find him. You will finally be free."

"*No!*" Nyri pushed away from Baarias and ran. She thought her heart would explode from the pain of betrayal. "You don't know what you have *done*!"

"You are too late, Nyri!" Baarias shouted after her. "You can't save him. I had to save you. I promised to look after you. Please forgive me!"

Nyri had stopped listening. She didn't care if they were

following or not. Nothing else mattered but reaching those Pits. If Juaan was already stabbed, pierced by that awful poison... Nyri could not imagine it. Not if she wanted to remain on her feet.

The forest ripped by. Nyri was heedless of the cuts and the whips. Twice she fell, but she rolled to her feet and ran on. *Please, please no.*

"Daajir! Don't do it! Daajir! Hear me!"

Silence.

Nyri continued screaming into the night.

At last she saw him there. She saw everything as if in slow motion, even as she rushed up to greet it.

Daajir stood poised on the edge of the Pit, the inscribed bone knife raised high. Nyri could see that it dripped with the bruised sheen of his terrible poison. He was preparing to throw.

"*Daajir!* No! Leave him alone!" She threw herself forward.

He did not heed her. He did not even look. He stared into the depths of the Pit. Nyri could picture Juaan glaring defiantly up at his death from the bottom. "I promised I would see you dead one day, Forbidden." Nyri heard Daajir speak. "Now I finally get the opportunity I thought stolen from me all those Furies ago." He drew back his arm with slow relish.

The rock was in Nyri's hand before she knew it.

"Nyri! Stop!" She heard Kyaati's warning distantly. They had followed her, but Nyri was as heedless to Kyaati's call as Daajir was to her. He didn't suspect. He would never suspect. The rock cracked into his skull before the knife left his fingers. Nyri hit him again. Limp, he dropped to her feet. She stood over him, gasping and sobbing. Juaan was staring up at her, just as she had imagined.

"I'm sorry," she whispered to him. "I am so sorry."

"Nyri." Baarias was suddenly there on his knees beside Daajir's crumpled form. "What have you *done*?"

There was stickiness on the hand that still clutched the rock. Nyri dropped it and wiped the blood hastily on her clothes. She could not think about what she had done, only about what she had come here to do. She had to save him. Nyri rushed to the Pit and threw the well-worn root into the dark depths.

"Come on," she rasped. She did not recognise her own voice. She was bodiless.

He did not need telling twice. Juaan grabbed the root and pulled himself up, up, and finally out. He stood before her. Free. In all the times she had imagined letting him out, she had never imagined this.

Throwing all caution to the wind, Nyri threw her arms around him and held him tight, trying to take in all that she could before he was lost to her forever. His scent, his warmth. Then she tore herself away. "Go!" She was sobbing. "Go, get away from here! Leave!"

He did not move. He stood still as a stone before her, towering above.

"What are you waiting for?" She shoved him. "Go!"

The only movement he made was to reach out and brush his fingers against Nyri's cheek. She closed her eyes and leaned into his touch.

"I can't," he whispered and withdrew his hand.

"Why not?" she demanded. "Leave me! They'll kill you! You need to go. I have given you your freedom!"

"You have." The green eyes bored down into hers. "But

505

I said nothing about being able to give you yours." For the barest of moments he looked sad, but then the eyes turned flat. "I told you you should have left me to die. It would have been better for the both of us."

"W-what," Nyri choked. "What do you mean? L-leave now, while you still can. I can't see you hurt."

"Nyri! Get away from him," Baarias cried.

"I am so very sorry." Then he pursed his lips and let out a low, thrilling whistle. Nyri recognised the sound in an instant. The bird call. Only, it had never come from any bird.

Nyri stared up into the green eyes she had so loved. She could look at nothing else even as the five dark skull-faced shapes detached themselves from the shadows to surround them. Nyri kept her eyes locked on those green points. She wished Daajir had stabbed her with that knife. It would have been a kinder blow to the killing betrayal she was now feeling.

When one of the dark shapes took a rough hold on her arm, she did not feel a thing.

"You!" Nyri heard Baarias snarl. He made to rush Juaan. "You will not take her!"

There was a shout, and something was thrown. A spear caught Baarias high in the chest. He went down in a heap.

A wordless scream ripped from Kyaati's throat, drowning out Juaan's sharp command. She threw herself to the healer's side, hands quickly growing bloody as she wrapped them around the spear.

The strength went out of Nyri. She dangled helplessly from the Wove's fist. *Baarias...*

One of the other Woves muttered to the man before her.

"Yes," he answered in Nyri's own tongue so she could understand. "Yes, they are all in the settlement. Nanna is fully awake. They will not venture far." He made a hand gesture towards Ninsiku's silver light.

The skull-headed beasts started forward, weapons in hand. The one holding Nyri dropped her arm to follow. She did not have the strength to hold herself up, and she collapsed to the ground.

"No." She crawled on her hands and knees to their leader. "No please. Take me. Just me. Leave my People. I'm a healer. I am everything your People want. Please. Grant me this one thing. Leave my family be. I-I'll do whatever you a-ask." Nyri clutched at his furs, beseeching, pleading with every fibre of her being.

The green eyes held hers. "You will die out there," he told her.

"Please. Please."

He closed his eyes and shook his head. "What *is* it about you?" he murmured, then louder for all to hear. "Leave her People."

The other Woves looked to their leader. One started towards the tall man, ripping off the skull mask to reveal the dark skin of his true face beneath. It was twisted with anger. The leader moved and suddenly the protester was on the ground, blood oozing from his nose. Nyri watched, detached.

"I said, *leave* her People." And they did. No one else dared to challenge him. "This one is valuable enough. Take her and the other girl. Leave the old man. He won't make it."

Two of the beasts grabbed a struggling Kyaati, dragging her from Baarias' side even as she tried to cling on.

"No!" Nyri rasped. "Please. Just me."

The leader with the green eyes leaned close. Now there was anger there. "I have done all I can for you. Be silent and ask no more. Accept if you are to live." He turned his back on her and walked away without another glance.

Rough arms caught Nyri from behind and bore her, unresisting, after Juaan. No. Not Juaan. The final knowledge of that sank in to Nyri's bones. Khalvir. There had only ever been Khalvir.

As she was borne into the darkness by her enemy, Nyri knew little of the terrible fate that awaited. She did not care. She knew only one thing. Juaan, the boy she had known and loved with all her heart, was truly dead. In his place stood a monster, a monster forbidden by the very fabric of nature, and she had unleashed him.

The night closed around Nyri's soul and did not let go.

* * *

THE END

Turn the page to continue your journey through time by reading The Prologue of *Enemy Tribe*, Book 3 of THE ANCESTORS SAGA.

You've read *Daughter of Ninmah*, now experience the Pit from Khalvir's own eyes.

***Captive: Daughter of Ninmah as told by Khalvir,* is available on Amazon: www.loriholmes.com/captive**

Enemy Tribe: Prologue - Loss

"Juaan, come here." His mother's voice was barely a whisper. The soft texture fading in the air chilled him to the centre of his being. He could not face her. He did not want to see. His breath plumed before him, the *girru* moss inside the tree doing little to fight back the bitter cold. It was dying, just like...

He choked back a sob as he stared out into the *eshaara* grove beyond. The only light emanated from a single tree in the hardening night. The rest of his mother's tribe were huddling together within its massive embrace, sharing warmth as they did on these harshest of nights.

He and his mother were not permitted to join them.

"Juaan."

He could not deny her plea. Drawing a deep breath, he turned and moved through the dim tree to where his mother lay. Agony threatened to overwhelm him as he saw her wasted form lying upon the meagre bower. He fought the urge to run. Here was his strength, and he did not want to watch as it slipped away. Nevertheless, he held his ground. His mother had taught him to be brave. He would not dishonour that teaching now.

The fading light in her eyes rekindled with tortured pride as she reached out with one stick-thin hand to brush his cheek. The skin of her fingers held no more warmth than a stone. It was close, so very close. Panic rippled through Juaan's chest. He didn't know what he was going to do. He could not live without his mother. She was the only one who didn't look upon him with hate. He couldn't survive without her love.

More than that; when she was gone, he knew what would happen. The Elders would kick him from their borders into the world beyond the forest, utterly alone, an easy meal for the fearsome predators waiting beyond. He could not use the power of the Ninkuraaja as they did. He would be defenceless.

His mother appeared to read his thoughts. Her hand moved from his cheek and groped into the leaves beneath her. After a moment, she pulled forth a long stick tipped with razor-sharp flint.

A spear.

Juaan flinched away. His mother had told him of such things. The tribe feared them; objects of evil, possessing the power of death.

Strangely, his mother did not flinch from the deadly object. Her fingers caressed the haft of smoothed wood as a sad smile touched her pale lips; her eyes shadowed by memory.

"Here." She held the weapon out to him.

Juaan stepped back in horror. A cold sweat broke over him as he was overcome by the feeling that if he took up that weapon, he would cease to be who he was. He would become something else entirely. The monster that everyone saw. A killer. Could his mother not see that? Could she not see *him*? A scarred and bitter warrior loomed before Juaan, the green eyes a frightening reflection of his own. Doom hung about the figure like the grisly furs he wore. Juaan shrank away.

"Do not worry." His mother's soothing voice shattered the vision, casting it back to the shadows. Juaan blinked, struggling to remember what he had just seen, but the ghostly figure was gone. There was only his mother within the familiar walls of their home, offering a gift. He could not understand why his heart was pounding so wildly, nor recall why he was so afraid. It was only a piece of wood and flint. Nothing to fear. The Ninkuraaja's superstitions were not his.

He was not one of them.

His mother's hand stretched further. "It won't hurt you. It is here to protect you."

Hesitantly, Juaan reached out to the weapon. His fingers brushed the worn wood and instead of fear this time, a feeling of *rightness* swept over him. His hands folded around the weapon as if they had been made to do so. Absorbed, he brushed his fingers along the haft until he reached the top. A band of curious carvings marred the otherwise smooth wood. "What are these?"

His mother's eyes drooped as though she no longer had the strength to keep them open; her breath rattled in her chest. Almost, Juaan dropped the spear, biting back a wail of helplessness behind his teeth. Before he could move, however, his mother pulled on the strength that had got them this far and spoke. "It-it was made by your *tarhe*. Those are her symbols of protection."

"*Tarhe?*" Juaan frowned over the strange word. He had never heard it before.

"Your protector mother, you will not remember her."

Juaan's breath caught, curiosity burning. "My protector

mother?"

A soft smile touched his mother's mouth, but her eyes were now unfocused. He did not think she had heard the question. "I was alone, so alone," she mumbled. "The world is not kind to one who travels alone. She loved you even before you were born and vowed to be your *tarhe,* to protect you with her own life."

Juaan's brows rose. *Nobody* loved him but her. He was Forbidden. A child of two Peoples. An abomination. The thought that anyone besides his mother had thought of him with any form of affection seemed an impossibility. "S-she loved me?"

His mother's eyes sharpened. The hatred her own people bore for him had been a constant wound to her heart. Even her own brother refused to look at him. "Yes, she loved you. She knew, even before she saw you, that you were going to be special. She lost her own baby, you see. He too was Forbidden. She did not want me to suffer the same fate." His mother's eyes drifted closed. "I can still remember the exact shade of her hair... red... so red..."

Her words were hard to follow, but the pain scrawled across her features was enough for Juaan to understand the hardship she had faced to keep him. Perhaps much more than he would ever know.

"Take the spear of your *tarhe,* Juaan. The weapon that was made by her hand will keep you safe."

Safe. The mysterious woman who had been his *tarhe* had wielded this spear. It called to him now. Juaan shifted his grip on the haft as some forgotten instinct stirred deep within his soul; a part of himself that remained as yet undiscovered. He swung it in an experimental arc, twisting the weapon around him before bracing his feet and thrusting the tip forward in challenge, imagining that he was facing down a ferocious enemy.

The glow in his mother's eyes was back, tinged with the sorrow that never left her. "So like your father..."

Embarrassed, Juaan relaxed his stance and ducked his head. His mother did not see the flush in his cheeks, however, she was reaching into the leaves of her bedding again, searching. Juaan watched, curious, as this time she drew out a small leaf-leather pouch tied with a long fibrous thong.

She spilled the single content on to a shaking palm. It looked like a large spearhead. Juaan stepped closer and saw, like the spear, this object was also marked with carvings, but this time, he recognised the etched shapes as those of a fierce black wolf. Overlaying it was a reddish brown smear, like dried blood.

"This was his," his mother said, offering the spearhead. "He wanted you to have it. The symbol of a Cro chief. Your father was a great and fair leader. He hoped you would grow to be the same. Like your *tarhe*, he also gave his life so that you might live." She dropped the spearhead back into the leather pouch. Then with a strength that surprised him, she pulled Juaan to her and tied the pouch firmly around his waist. "Keep it with you, and *remember*," she admonished. "Remember the people who have loved you and sacrificed themselves for you. *Live*, do you hear me? You must survive no matter what. For your father. For your *tarhe*. For me. Do you understand?"

Fear threatened to cripple him. She was preparing to leave him. Her eyes were drinking him in as if this might be the last time she would ever see him. He wasn't ready. He struggled to find the courage that she had taught him.

"Yes, mama." The tears slipped down his face. "I-I promise."

His mother's face crumpled at the sight of his tears. She pulled him to her and held him close. Juaan tried to draw strength from her warmth as his breath hitched into her shoulder. Her scent was fading.

"Rebaa." A familiar voice called from the bottom of their tree. His mother stiffened and pushed Juaan away, beckoning for the spear.

Struggling to control the wave of anger he felt at the intruder below, Juaan handed it to her and she thrust the weapon back into the leaves. "It must stay hidden until you need it," she hissed.

"Rebaa." The call came again, closer this time. Juaan glanced across to the entrance of their tree in time to see the creased face of the old Kamaali peering inside. He remained still as Sefaan entered. She was the only one of his mother's tribe that he even came close to trusting. If it wasn't for this woman, his mother would still be wandering the wilds alone.

Even so, Juaan tried not to flinch as the ancient eyes fixed upon him in a sober study. He always felt that those eyes could see right to the core of his soul and divine all of his innermost secrets. Perhaps they could.

"You have grown, boy," the Kamaali whispered. "But not enough, I fear. Not enough."

Juaan tasted the wave of despair emanating from his mother at the Kamaali's words. He frowned at Sefaan. His mother did not need to be distressed. *I am eight Furies old.*

514

He lifted his chin. *I am ready, mother, I will survive like you want. Don't cry.*

Sefaan had already turned away from him, however, and was calling to someone unseen. "Jaai," the cracked voice beckoned. "Come here. You do no good lurking outside."

Juaan took a step back as another Ninkuraa woman climbed inside the chamber. He scowled at this intrusion. His mother's closest childhood friend had made no secret of her disgust and fear of him. No different from the others. Her dark indigo gaze flickered apprehensively to him, as though he may turn into a raving beast at any moment. Juaan pressed his lips together to prevent himself from baring his teeth. Perhaps he should. It would serve them all right. It was their hatred that had made his mother sick. Their hatred that had-

He couldn't bear it. His heart burned, yearning to lash out in his pain. The air was suddenly too thin in the crowded chamber. He had to get out before he shamed his mother. He felt her try to hold on to him, but he broke loose from her grasp and swept past the intruders who had come to steal the last of his moments with her. Hate boiled in his veins as he climbed out of the tree and left them behind. He would come back only when they had left. He could not guess what it was they wanted, nor did he care.

The freezing ground bit at his feet as he touched down. He shivered, rubbing his arms as they bristled in protest against the cold. For a moment, he looked towards the giant tree at the centre of the ancient *eshaara* grove and the golden light glowing from inside. The tribe sheltering within the living walls was snug, warm, and safe. A sense of peace and belonging drifted from the tree. Juaan grimaced. It was a feeling that would be forever denied to him.

As if in answer to his bitter thought, a silhouette appeared in an entranceway. Juaan recognised the shape at once, and his feeling of resentment deepened. Baarias. His mother's brother. Baarias' shadowed face remained impassive as he regarded Juaan. He made no invite to the child shivering in the darkness, shunned from the light. The *akaab* healer's compassion did not extend to an abomination such as him. Juaan's lip curled as the *akaab* healer's attention turned from him up towards the tree above to where his mother lay dying. The controlled features cracked.

A hiss found its way between Juaan's bared teeth. *She doesn't need you! How dare you even* look *at her!*

Baarias seemed to hear his thoughts. The betrayal of emotion was quickly shuttered and with one hard stare in Juaan's direction, the *akaab* disappeared back into the tree with the rest of the hated tribe, where he belonged.

Juaan took a few deep breaths of the cold forest air to calm himself. The scent of the forest in mid-Fury filled his lungs; frost and decay. The song of the trees was muted, the creatures huddled down inside their homes to wait out the night.

Juaan dropped onto his haunches and rested his chin on his hands. Everything in the forest belonged. Where did he belong? The pouch that his mother had given him felt strange where it dangled against his hip. He lifted it, loosening the fibres tied around the top, and tipped his father's symbolic spearhead into his waiting palm.

His father.

It felt strange, holding this object that had belonged to the mysterious man who had sired him. A man whom he had never met but whose blood ran through his veins. A great Cro chief, his mother had told him. A good man and a powerful warrior. Juaan stroked the spearhead with his fingertips.

He could almost feel a shadowy figure standing unseen at his shoulder. A figure he had often fancied was there, watching over both him and his mother. Juaan wished he could have known him. He wished he could know what his father might think of him. He felt certain that he wouldn't have looked on him with hate. He might even have been proud.

Juaan turned the spearhead over and over in his fingers. Perhaps when he was banished from this forest, he could find his father's people. The Ninkuraaja named them as evil spirits, but his mother's people were mistaken about many things. His father had wanted him to have this symbol of his leadership in the hope that his son would follow in his footsteps. Could he become a great warrior and chief some day?

A tingle ran down his spine at the idea. He closed his fist around the carved piece of flint, feeling the bite of the sharp edges as they cut into the soft skin of his hand. As the blood dripped from his fist, mingling with the dried blood already smeared upon the spearhead, he made a vow. He would never forget those that had sacrificed themselves for him. He felt again the shadowy figures as they stood around and vowed that their sacrifice would not be in vain. He would survive. He would go on to become a great chief, as his father had once been. He would remember.

The sound of skin on bark above pulled him from his thoughts. His heart constricted when he saw that Sefaan and

Jaai were leaving his mother's tree. He slipped the spearhead back into the pouch. This pouch would keep his memories and the vows he made upon them safe. Hidden from all but his own heart.

Sefaan grunted as she alighted on the ground next to him. Jaai gave him one cursory glance, her red-rimmed eyes haunted, before disappearing into the darkness. Juaan spared her no mind.

"It is agreed." The Kamaali spoke. "I have done all I can for you now, boy. Keep your head down." She lifted her grizzled head, cocking it to one side as if listening to voices that no one else could hear. "Go to your mother now. Time is short. The Great Spirit is calling." She squeezed his arm, her pale lavender gaze filled with sorrow as she stared into his eyes. "Go."

Juaan's throat closed. He could barely feel his feet as he rose and turned for the tree. He was trembling. Numb, he forced himself to climb. One hand over the other until he was standing once more inside the only home he had ever known. He stumbled to the centre where the heart of it was beating its last. When she was gone, it would be his home no longer.

One weak hand reached out and pulled him closer. She smiled up at him. Her face was strangely at peace.

"Mama?"

"It is alright, my precious son," she whispered. "You are safe now… I have made you safe…"

Safe? How could he be safe? She was leaving him. "Mama, don't go." He heard the panic in his voice as he crumbled, all his bravery and vows forgotten.

"Do not be a-afraid. Remember… remember everything

I have told you… everything you p-promised. Y-you must live."

He could only nod, clutching at her as if he could hold her to life with his bare hands.

"Remember…"

"Mama?" He dropped his face on top of her head, gripping tighter.

But she slipped through his fingers, her spirit as insubstantial as the wind. It swirled around him for a moment, stirring the dark hair beneath his cheek. And then she was gone and he was alone. Nothingness stretched out endlessly before him.

"Mama."

Continue reading *Enemy Tribe*, Book 3 of the ANCESTORS SAGA:
www.loriholmes.com/enemytribe

About the Author

Growing up in England and having had a misspent youth devouring everything science fiction and fantasy, Lori enjoys reading and writing books that draw a reader into new and undiscovered worlds with characters that are hard to part with long after the journey comes to an end.

Lori's debut novel, The Forbidden, begins the epic journey into the Ancestors Saga, combining history, mystery and legend to retell a lost chapter in humanity's dark and distant past.

When not lost in the world of The Ancestors Saga, Lori enjoys spending time with her family (3 children, 2 whippets and her husband - it's a busy house!) usually outdoors walking and exploring the great British countryside.

Find out more at www.loriholmes.com

You can connect with me on:

- https://www.loriholmes.com
- https://www.facebook.com/loriholmesauthor
- https://www.amazon.com/-/e/B06XBFF5RR
- https://www.bookbub.com/profile/lori-holmes

Subscribe to my newsletter:

- https://loriholmes.com/forbidden-son

Also by Lori Holmes

The Ancestors Saga

Book 1, The Forbidden: **www.loriholmes.com/forbidden**
Book 2, Daughter of Ninmah: **www.loriholmes.com/ninmah**
Companion Novel To Book 2, Captive: **www.loriholmes.com/captive**
Book 3, Enemy Tribe: **www.loriholmes.com/enemytribe**
Book 4, The Last Kamaali: **www.loriholmes.com/kamaali**

The Raknari Trilogy

Book 1 | Echoes of The Forgotten: **www.loriholmes.com/echoes**
Book 2 | Call of The Warrior: *Launching Summer 2024*
Book 3 | Whispers of Fate: *Launching Summer 2025*

Made in the USA
Las Vegas, NV
11 October 2023

78949112R00308